ISAIAH'S DAUGHTER

Center Point
Large Print

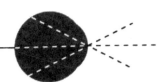

**This Large Print Book carries the
Seal of Approval of N.A.V.H.**

ISAIAH'S DAUGHTER

A NOVEL OF PROPHETS & KINGS

MESU ANDREWS

CENTER POINT LARGE PRINT
THORNDIKE, MAINE

ISBN: 978-1-64358-052-4

Library of Congress Cataloging-in-Publication Data

Names: Andrews, Mesu, 1963-author.
Title: Isaiah's daughter : a novel of prophets & kings / Mesu Andrews.
Description: Center Point Large Print edition. | Thorndike, Maine :
    Center Point Large Print, 2019.
Identifiers: LCCN 2018049018 | ISBN 9781643580524
    (hardcover : alk. paper)
Subjects: LCSH: Large type books.
Classification: LCC PS3601.N55274 I83 2019 | DDC 813/.6—dc23
LC record available at https://lccn.loc.gov/2018049018

To my husband, Roy.
Like Hezi and Zibah,
who knew each other since childhood . . .
There is only we.

CHARACTER LIST

Amram*: One of the king's Mighty Men; Queen Hephzibah's personal guard

Aya*: Isaiah's wife

Azariah: High priest during Hezekiah's reign

Dinah*: Servant girl in Isaiah's household

Eliakim: Royal official during Hezekiah's reign

Hephzibah: Hezekiah's wife; Queen of Judah

Hilkiah: Royal treasurer under both Ahaz and Hezekiah*

Isaiah: God's prophet in Judah

Ishma*: Orphan girl who becomes Hezekiah's friend

Jalon ben Enoch*: Commander of forced labor

Jashub (Shear-Jashub): Isaiah's firstborn son

Joah: Recorder during Hezekiah's reign

Jokim ben Hanan*: Commander of Judah's army

Joseph*: Shebna's abba

Kadmiel*: Isaiah's second son

King Ahaz: 11th King of Judah; Hezekiah's abba

King Hoshea: Paid Assyria to become 19th King of Israel

King Jotham: 10th King of Judah; Ahaz's abba

King Pekah: 8th King of Israel

King Sargon: King of Assyria (722–705 BCE); completed Samarian siege and Israel's exile during Ahaz's reign

King Sennacherib: King of Assyria (705–681 BCE); besieged Judean fortified cities, including Jerusalem, during Hezekiah's reign

King Shalmaneser: King of Assyria (727–722 BCE); began the siege on Samaria during Ahaz's reign

King Tiglath-Pileser: King of Assyria (747–727 BCE); destroyed Damascus and attacked Samaria when Ahaz paid tribute

Leah*: Servant girl in Isaiah's household

Maher (Maher-Shalal-Hash-Baz): Isaiah's third-born son (Scripture names only two sons)

Micah: God's prophet in Judah; Yaira's brother*

Oded: God's prophet in Samaria

Prince Bocheru*: Ahaz's firstborn son

Prince/King Hezekiah: Ahaz's son—second-born* (Bible doesn't order Ahaz's sons); 12th King of Judah

Prince Mattaniah*: Ahaz's third-born son

Queen Abijah: Ahaz's wife; daughter of Zechariah, the high priest

Rabshakeh: the Assyrian general during Sennacherib's reign

Rizpah*: Ahaz's second wife

Samuel*: One of the king's Mighty Men; Hezekiah's personal guard

Selah*: Ahaz's youngest widow

Shebna: Royal official during Hezekiah's reign
Tirhakah: General of Egypt's (Cush's) army
Uriah: Priest in Jerusalem Temple
Yaira*: Orphaned caregiver of Ishma; Micah's
    younger sister

BOLD names are mentioned in the Bible and/or historical documents

* Denotes fictional character or description

Songs are written of sons, but daughters are left to whispers.

So gather near, friend, to hear of a daughter beyond imagining. She had the heart of a lion. Braver than a soldier. Wiser than a king. She was queen in Judah long after King David's bones had turned to dust. Long after the arrogance of Solomon's son split Israel into two nations.

When the northern tribes seized the name Israel, the southern tribes called their new nation Judah and placed David's descendants on their throne. Judah's capital was the city of Jerusalem and its God was named Yahweh. But Israel bowed to pagan gods and even led some of Judah's kings astray.

Yahweh's prophets spewed warnings, and Judah's brave daughter, the lion-hearted queen, dared ask the prophets why? When? And how will Yahweh's judgment fall?

One incomparable prophet answered, foretelling Assyria's cruelty as Yahweh's weapon of wrath. Isaiah, a man born to royalty, shouted at kings and comforted beggars. The records proclaim him husband to a prophetess and father of two sons. This is recorded, detailed, written.

But what of his daughter?

Her story begins when the northern kingdom of Israel joins forces with Aram, a neighboring nation. They attack Judah in retribution for refusing to join their coalition against Assyria. Isaiah prophesies to Judah's King Ahaz—a promise and a warning. Ahaz ignores both. His decision forever changes the life of Isaiah's daughter.

ISAIAH'S
DAUGHTER

PART I

Now [Ahaz, King of Judah] was told, "Aram has allied itself with [Israel]"; so the hearts of Ahaz and his people were shaken . . .

Then the LORD said to Isaiah, "Go out, you and your son [Jashub], to meet Ahaz at the end of the aqueduct of the Upper Pool. . . . Say to him, . . . 'Don't be afraid . . . because of the fierce anger of . . . Aram and [Israel]. . . . This is what the Sovereign LORD says:

" 'It will not take place . . .
[but] if you do not stand firm in your
   faith, you will not stand at all.' "

Again the LORD spoke to Ahaz, "Ask the LORD your God for a sign, whether in the deepest depths or in the highest heights."

But Ahaz said, "I will not ask . . ."

Then Isaiah said, ". . . The LORD will bring on you and on your people and on the house of your father a time unlike any since [Israel] broke away from Judah—he will bring the king of Assyria."

—Isaiah 7:2–4, 7, 9–13, 17

1

The men of Israel took captive from their fellow Israelites who were from Judah two hundred thousand wives, sons and daughters. They also took a great deal of plunder, which they carried back to Samaria.

—2 Chronicles 28:8

732 BCE (Spring)
Judean Wilderness

My friend Yaira said to be brave—but why? Brave or scared, we kept marching. She told me to be a big girl, not to cry, but I'm only five, and I've seen big men crying. The raw brand on my arm throbbed and smelled like burning meat. I lost count of the days we'd been marching in the desert. Long enough that the sun baked blisters all over me.

These Israel-soldiers called us "captives." They whipped the ones who walked too slowly or cried too much. The woman in front of me kept crying for her dead children. I guess one of them looked like me because she grabbed me sometimes, as if I belonged to her. She didn't seem to care if we were whipped for slowing the march to wherever

17

we're going—somewhere in Israel. Yaira would help me push her away, but it wasn't always quick enough, and then we were all beaten. The woman was whipped until she couldn't fight anymore. She screamed for her children until she had no voice.

I haven't had a voice since the Israel-soldiers attacked us in Bethlehem. When soldiers came through the city gates, I screamed to my *abba,* but my words didn't save him. I ran into the house, crying, but my words didn't save Yaira from the soldiers who took her into the stable. They hurt her. More soldiers branded me even though I begged them to stop.

After all that, my words were gone.

"Ishma." Yaira nudged me from behind. "Eat this." My friend laid her hand on my shoulder, a small piece of bread hiding in her fist.

I shook my head. She needed it more than me.

"Take it," she whispered louder. "Before they see."

Yaira was twelve so I did what she said. I took the morsel and I ate it. The crumbs stuck in my mouth. We'd had no water since yesterday. *Please, Yahweh, give us water when we stop tonight.*

Sometimes my prayers worked. Sometimes they didn't. Mostly they didn't.

As if she knew what I was thinking, Yaira whispered again. "Every day I pray for Micah to rescue us." Her voice sounded dry like my throat. "He'll come, Ishma. I promise. He'll come. Yahweh will tell him and the other prophets where to find us."

I kept walking, glad I had no words. Yaira wouldn't like my questions. Why didn't Yahweh stop the soldiers before they killed my family? Who could ever find us among so many captives? Still, Yaira had as much faith in her brother, Micah, as she did in Yahweh. Micah was her only family because their parents died a long time ago. When he couldn't take care of her because he lived with the other prophets at their camp in Tekoa, Abba heard about Yaira and said she could live with us and serve as *Ima*'s maid. Yaira said Yahweh and Micah took care of her, but it seemed to me that my family did.

My face felt prickly when I thought too much about Ima and Abba. My tummy hurt too. I missed them. Who would make my favorite bread now that Ima was gone? Who would tickle me and make me giggle like Abba did?

Back in Bethlehem I held Ima's head in my lap and watched the light leave her eyes after the soldiers speared her through. I didn't see what they did to Abba. When the soldiers dragged me out of the house, Abba was lying by the stable with the same empty eyes as Ima. The soldiers wouldn't let me say good-bye.

"Ishma, look!" Yaira pointed toward a gleaming

19

white palace with black trimmings. It sat on a tall hill.

I'd never seen anything like it. Our house had been the nicest in Bethlehem because Abba was the chief elder, but it seemed tiny compared to the palace on the hill.

"That must be Samaria, Israel's capital," Yaira whispered. "Micah told me that he prophesied here with Hosea." Her breaths rumbled loud and fast as we climbed the steep hill. We kept walking, walking, walking toward the gates of the white city.

My legs ached and I stumbled, but Yaira tugged on my arms. "Don't stop, Ishma. We're almost there."

I was too tired. My legs felt like water.

"Think of something else, little one," she said. "What was Micah wearing the last time we saw him?"

That was a silly question. Micah always wore the same thing—a dirty brown robe. Abba said all prophets wore camel-hair robes, and I asked if all prophets were as serious as Micah. Abba laughed. Micah was kind but always frowning—especially on his last visit. He shouted at Abba that we must leave Bethlehem and go to Jerusalem where we would be safe behind its high walls. Ima took Yaira and me into the courtyard, but I could still hear them shouting. Abba was angry and told Micah to leave. Yaira started to cry. I hid against

Ima's legs and wrapped her cloak around me.

I wish Abba had taken us to Jerusalem.

Finally, the captive train slowed to a stop halfway up the hill, and I fell against Yaira. I covered my face with both arms, bracing for the soldier's whip. But they didn't beat me.

The crowd's spreading whispers made me curious, so I lowered my arms to get a better look at Samaria's palace on the hill. I couldn't see over the captives and soldiers, but they all asked the same question. "Why are they closing the city gates?" The sun hadn't set, and we needed food, water, and clothes.

One of the captives pointed to a tall tower casting a long shadow over us. A gray-haired man dressed like Micah stood at the top and looked over the edge. He began shouting at the Israel-soldiers, and they shouted back. The captives huddled together while the soldiers' faces got redder and they beat their fists against the air.

I curled into a ball, trying to make myself smaller. Yaira leaned over and covered me, like an ima bird covering her babies with its wings. Some of the soldiers began throwing stones at the watchtower. A sudden rumble of thunder boomed from a clear sky and shook the ground. Yaira and I trembled even after the rumbling stopped. I peeked up to the sky from beneath Yaira's arms and wondered, *Was that Yahweh's voice?*

Very slowly, she lowered her arms, knelt beside

me, and grinned a little. "Yahweh fought for us, Ishma."

All around us soldiers dropped their rocks. Some guards even fell to their knees. Others backed away from the captives as if touching us might hurt them.

I tapped Yaira's arm and pointed at the man in the watchtower, shrugging my shoulders.

"His name is Oded," she whispered. "He's a prophet of Yahweh in Israel. He said the soldiers treated us shamefully and must free us or face Yahweh's wrath. The city elders will lead us to Jericho where we'll reunite with our families." She kissed the top of my head. "We must pray the soldiers listen to Yahweh and that Micah finds us in Jericho."

Soldiers rose from their knees. Some still looked angry, but many stumbled like newborn calves on unsteady legs. They slashed ropes from the captives' waists and unlocked shackles from their necks and feet. When the soldiers freed Yaira and me, she pulled me to my feet and hugged me gently, careful not to break open our wounds or sun blisters.

"We're free," she said, glancing around us. "I think we're really going to be free."

All the captives moved away from the guards—slowly, like they were drinking a bowl of hot soup, testing each sip. Could we really be released at the word of a single prophet and a rumble of thunder?

The soldiers unpacked clothing, food, and bandages they'd stolen from Judean towns, and they began passing it out to all us captives. Even the sad woman who had lost her children smiled. Celebration spread, and one word floated on the evening breeze. "Free . . . free . . . free."

I'd heard that word many times before, but I understood it better now. A bird flew over, and I watched it circle and play in the sky. The bird was free—like us. No ropes or chains to bind it. No soldiers to burn or beat it. But when the bird settled into its peaceful nest at the fork of two branches, I knew we weren't the same at all. My peace died in Bethlehem, and my home had been burned.

"Ishma, what is it?" Yaira tilted my chin and dried my tears. "There's no need to cry, little one. I'm sure Micah will find us in Jericho."

I stared into her sparkly dark eyes. She was so happy about being free, but didn't she know? Freedom didn't matter if we had no nest to call home. She pulled me back into a hug.

I closed my eyes and pretended to be a bird.

2

So the soldiers gave up the prisoners
and plunder in the presence of the
officials. . . . All those who were weak
they put on donkeys. So they took them
back to their fellow Israelites at Jericho,
the City of Palms.
                    —2 Chronicles 28:14–15

I was tired of being brave, and I hated donkeys.
This was the third day I'd ridden on one of the
stinky, stubborn animals on our way to Jericho.
Yaira tugged on his lead rope, and the old woman
riding with me kicked his sides to make him keep
moving in the long line of returning captives. The
old woman breathed on the back of my neck and
smelled like yesterday's onions. She kept trying
to comb her fingers through my tangled hair. I
shoved her hand away, but it was like trying to
dig water out of a mud hole; she just kept coming
back. I'd rather walk with the woman who thought
I was her child. No. I'd rather walk with Yaira.

Again the old woman's fingers found my
tangles, and I couldn't stand it. "Aaahhh!" My
words were still lost, but I'd found my voice.

Yaira glanced over her shoulder. "Ishma, you're
too weak to walk." She winced as she returned

her eyes forward. Our wounds were still raw, and though the robes we wore from the burned-up villages were softer than our normal robes, they still felt like broken pottery scraping our wounds.

I looked down at my new robe and wondered what little girl had worn it before me. Was she still alive? Or did she die with her ima and abba? The old woman began combing my hair again. I needed to get off this donkey!

"Uh-uh!" Rocking and kicking, I nearly knocked myself and the old woman to the ground.

"Ishma, enough!" Yaira stopped, hands on her hips, eyes blazing.

I stared back, pressing my lips together. She looked angry. Yaira almost never got angry. I looked at the sky, refusing to cry.

"We're trying to protect you, little one." The onion-breathing woman squeezed me, breaking open my whipping wounds.

"Aah!" I cried out.

"Oh, I'm sorry, dear."

I shook my head and pooched out my bottom lip. Abba always said a bird might fly over and poop on it, but I didn't care.

Yaira stood beside us, her eyebrows drawn together. "Ishma, I won't speak to you until you put away your pouty lip." Yaira never lied. I knew she meant what she said. People were passing us on the road. Jericho might be full when we got there. I sucked in my lip.

Yaira and the old woman shared a smile, but I didn't see anything to smile about. The old woman pointed at a hill ahead. "Jericho is just over that ridge, little one. It's full of palm trees, and the streets are lined with all kinds of merchants' stalls: food, pottery, rugs, and . . . well, anything you can imagine. Perhaps you'll find your family waiting there."

Family. My only family was Yaira.

Yaira patted my leg. "Consider Yahweh's great mercy, Ishma. You have been saved twice over— once from death in Bethlehem and again from captivity in Samaria." She tugged at the donkey and started walking again, calling over her shoulder. "What big plans might Yahweh have for you that He has gone to such trouble to save you?"

The onion woman chuckled. "A good question for us all." She combed her fingers through my tangles again, and I pushed her hand away. Why couldn't she leave me alone?

Whatever plans Yahweh had for me, I wanted only Yaira included. We could live together, just the two of us. I crossed my arms and closed my eyes, thinking of the little sukkah we could build with palm branches when we arrived in Jericho. It was the only shelter we would need, and I never ate much. I yawned and leaned back against the old woman. Yaira and I could take good care of each other.

"Ishma? Ishma, wake up now." Yaira was standing beside the donkey—with Micah. Was I dreaming? Yaira smiled through her tears. "I told you Yahweh would send him to find us."

Micah lifted me off the donkey, and a man about my abba's age set another little girl in my place. *"Savta!"* The little girl hugged her tight.

The old woman began combing her crooked fingers through the girl's hair. "Oh, Savta, I've missed you." The girl leaned into her savta's chest. I looked away, feeling ashamed I hadn't been nicer to the woman.

The man took our donkey's lead rope. "Are you sure you don't need the donkey, Micah?"

"No, my friend. Your journey is farther than ours. We'll be in Jerusalem before nightfall."

Jerusalem? I didn't want to keep going. We'd gone from Bethlehem to Samaria to Jericho—and now Jerusalem?

Micah and Yaira waved good-bye. The old woman waved, but I couldn't wave back. Everyone looked so happy. The little girl. The abba. Like a family.

Yaira hugged Micah again. "I knew you'd be here."

My face felt prickly again, and my heart pounded hard in my chest. Micah and Yaira had each other. I had no family. Would they go to Jerusalem without me?

I lunged for Yaira, wrapped my arms around

her waist, and closed my eyes. *Please, don't leave me!* I shouldn't have made her angry on the road to Jericho. *I'll do whatever you say. I'll find Yahweh's plan for me if that's what you want.*

"Ishma, calm down. I'm right here," Yaira soothed. "Micah is here to take us both to Master Isaiah, another Yahweh prophet, who has agreed to let us serve in his household."

I didn't want to keep going, but I needed to be with Yaira. Why couldn't we be like the birds with a peaceful nest?

"Ishma." Micah's deep voice startled me. I opened my eyes and found him kneeling beside me, holding out his hand. "You don't have to walk. I can carry you on my shoulders."

I looked up at Yaira. She nodded, so I knew Micah was telling the truth. If she trusted him, maybe I could. I released Yaira and put my hand in Micah's. Abba used to carry me on his shoulders. I liked that. When Micah lifted me onto his shoulders, I bit my lip to keep from whimpering. My whole body hurt. Would it ever stop?

"Hold under my chin," he said, "so you won't fall." Micah laid one arm across my knees and offered his other hand to Yaira. "I know the sun is already at midday, but if we leave now and eat our evening meal while walking, we can make it to Jerusalem by sunset."

Yaira nodded and took his hand. She was trying to be brave like me. Couldn't Micah see how tired she was? How tired we both were? I looked at the other people—freed captives like Yaira and me—and they looked tired too. But everyone kept walking. We were people, not birds.

Micah led us through Jericho's market, and I remembered the old woman's description. Palm trees and market booths lined both sides of the busy street. Many hungry Judeans like us were in need of food and supplies for their journeys home. Animals ran from young shepherds, adding to the confusion. The smell of cooking meat and mounds of fresh fruit made my tummy growl as we passed the last of the shouting merchants.

More palm trees made swaying shadows all the way to the city gate where we joined a caravan of freed captives on their way to Jerusalem.

Once outside the city's walls, Yaira looked up at her brother, trying too hard to smile. "How did you know we would be in Jericho?"

He said something about the prophet we saw in Samaria sending a message to the camp where he lived in Tekoa. But Micah wasn't in the prophets' camp when the soldiers came. He was in Jerusalem—behind its high walls—when it was attacked last week.

Yaira stopped walking. "Why were you in Jerusalem?"

Of all the important things Yaira could have asked, why that? Why not ask if we would be safe there now?

"I was in Jerusalem because I have been appointed as a royal prophet." Yaira's eyes went wide, but Micah waved away her excitement. "King Ahaz selected me to join his royal counsel because I have no royal connections and little influence."

Yaira snapped off a small twig from a broom tree and began breaking it apart as she walked. "Why put someone with no influence on the counsel. Isn't the prophet Isaiah also on the counsel? He's got royal blood."

"He *was* on the counsel but is no more because he has too much influence. King Ahaz demoted Isaiah to royal tutor because he openly criticized the king's two newest advisors—a Philistine medium and a Judean witch."

I didn't like the sound of that. A witch and a medium? I squeezed Micah's chin, staring upside down into his eyes.

He chuckled. "Don't worry, little one. Although King Ahaz has fallen far from Yahweh's will in the past months, my place on his council meant I was safely hidden with the other advisors in the tunnels under the city when the Israel-Aram coalition attacked both Jerusalem and Bethlehem at the same time."

Yaira's hands stilled on the twig. "What did they do to Jerusalem?"

"The enemy troops destroyed most of southern Jerusalem, but Judean soldiers were able to stop their advance before they entered the Upper City." Micah shifted me on his shoulders. "Yahweh's Temple and the palace are safe, but many of the buildings in the Lower City—where the poorest people live—were nearly leveled. Our surrounding crops, orchards, and vineyards were also completely destroyed."

My body went rigid and began to shake. I didn't want to go to Jerusalem where there were mediums and witches and more soldiers attacking.

Micah lifted me from his shoulders, holding me against his chest, wrapping his strong arms around me. "It's all right, little Ishma. The Israelite soldiers are gone now. You'll be safe in Master Isaiah's household."

Yaira had crouched at the side of the road, retching. Micah hurried to her and tried to set me on my feet. I stumbled, my legs shaking too much to hold me. He scooped me up and guided Yaira farther down the road to rest. Sitting between us, he unwrapped a square of goat cheese and loaf of bread. We ate in silence, staring across the brown rolling wasteland. I wasn't hungry, but Yaira had given me a crust of bread with cheese on it. She nudged my hand toward my mouth. I knew she wouldn't eat until I did.

Micah didn't eat anything at all. "While we hid in the tunnels under the palace," he said, still staring at the desert hills, "with the king, his wives and children, the advisors, and their families, all I could think of was you, Yaira. I couldn't protect you." He bowed his head and pressed his thumbs against his eyes. "I'm so sorry."

Yaira set aside her food and laid her head on his shoulder. I realized Micah had been as scared as Yaira and I when the soldiers came. I patted Micah's arm and laid my head against him too. No wonder Yaira loved him.

"What happened to the people of the Lower City?" Yaira reached for her food again and took a bite. "Were they taken captive or . . . ?"

I didn't understand all of his answer, but his deep voice shook, telling of people dying, homes burning, and the poor getting poorer. What did that mean for Yaira and me? Nudging him, I pointed to Yaira and myself, lifting my eyebrows. Surely, a prophet who heard an invisible God speak could understand a girl who'd lost her words.

He looked at me and then back at Yaira. "She used to talk, didn't she?"

Yaira gave Micah that "mean sister" look she saved only for him. "She hasn't spoken since we were taken from Bethlehem. No child should witness what Ishma saw."

Micah wrapped his arm around Yaira. "You're a child too, sister."

Yaira shoved him away, her eyes filling with tears.

My chest felt like a big rock had fallen on it. Yaira never cried. Micah reached for her, but she stood and started walking again. Silent. Swiping tears.

Micah wrapped the food, shoved it into his shoulder bag, and then lifted me onto his shoulders again. We hurried to catch up with Yaira but didn't talk anymore. Sometimes bad things made everyone lose their words.

The sun beat down. I could hardly keep my eyes open when I heard Yaira whisper, "Let us stay with you, Micah. Don't leave me again."

"You know I can't, Yaira." He blew out a heavy breath. "I have no home to offer you. The prophets' camp in Tekoa was nearly destroyed, and I must help them rebuild. You and Ishma will be well cared for with Master Isaiah in Jerusalem."

Yaira's steps never slowed. Her eyes never left the path in front of us. "I understand." I knew her heart hurt like mine, maybe more. I didn't have a family. Yaira did. But he wouldn't keep her.

"I will visit you and Ishma as often as I can." Micah reached for her hand and patted my knee. "Ishma is our family now too—the little sister you always wanted."

Yaira looked at me, and I saw sadness in her eyes—but only for a moment. She patted my knee too. "Perhaps when Ishma and I get older, we can come to Tekoa and work the fields or—"

33

"No, Yaira." Micah kissed the back of her hand. "Serving in Master Isaiah's household is the best chance you both have for a good marriage and a normal life."

She looked at us both, sadness shoving away her smile. "I'll never marry, Micah, but perhaps Ishma can find a normal life in Jerusalem."

Yaira hurried her steps and blended into the caravan of freed captives. I looked to the sky and saw birds again, each flying alone. Did birds ever marry? Come to think of it, I'd only seen ima birds, never abba birds, with their babes in a nest. I squeezed my eyes shut and covered my head.

I didn't want to be a bird anymore. I didn't want to be alone.

3

Ahaz was twenty years old when he became king, and he reigned in Jerusalem sixteen years . . . He . . . sacrificed his son in the fire, engaging in the detestable practices of the nations the LORD had driven out before the Israelites.

—2 Kings 16:2–3

A deep sigh betrayed Isaiah's discouragement at the end of another day as royal tutor. His duties in the northwest corner of the palace were as bleak as this first-floor, windowless room. Trapped at the end of a hallway in one of the forgotten chambers of Solomon's overlarge harem complex, Isaiah attempted to instill wisdom and discipline in Judah's dawning generation.

"Prince Hezekiah, you will kindly return Eliakim's wax tablet." Isaiah spent most of his day redirecting the boundless energy of twenty boys, ages five to twelve. "Prince Bocheru, please name the capital cities of the armies that have breached Judah's borders in the past weeks: Aram, Israel, Edom, and Philistia."

King Ahaz's twelve-year-old firstborn stood; he was nearly the same height as his short, broad abba. "The capital of Israel is Damascus. Um . . ."

All color drained from Prince Bocheru's cheeks when Isaiah began shaking his head and rubbing his temples.

"No, Prince Bocheru." Isaiah pretended to search for another question on the scroll before him. Was he doomed to teach the king's and advisors' sons forever, or had impetuous King Ahaz removed him from the royal council for only a season?

"I know the answer, Master Isaiah." Eight-year-old Prince Hezekiah stood and sneered at his older brother. "The capital of Aram is Damascus, and the capital of Israel is Samaria. The cap—"

"He didn't ask you!" Crown Prince Bocheru balled his fist and slugged Hezekiah squarely in the nose.

Ten-year-old Eliakim—skinny as a broom-tree branch, quick as a cat—rushed to Hezekiah's aid, landing a solid punch to Prince Bocheru's gut. Eliakim and Hezekiah had been pairing up against Bocheru since Hezekiah learned to walk. Prince Mattaniah, King Ahaz's third-born of Queen Abijah, sat in the corner and cried. The queen had won her crown by bearing three sons to Ahaz: Bocheru, Hezekiah, and Mattaniah—all entirely different in temperament and character.

King Ahaz's five lesser wives had given him a total of six sons, all of whom sat on their cushions with little interest in what happened to the favored sons of Queen Abijah. The remaining students lined the outer walls. Some cheering. Some quaking. All waiting for Isaiah to end the fracas.

If this was the hope of Judah's next generation, perhaps Jerusalem should throw open the gates and invite its enemies to take the throne now. It would save considerable time and trouble.

"Enough!" Isaiah entered the fray, grabbing Crown Prince Bocheru's stout arm and pulling him off the royal treasurer's skinny son. "All of you be seated!"

Hezekiah got in one last shove at his older brother before retreating to his cushion with blood dripping from his nose. Bocheru had been trying to toughen up his little brother since the day Hezekiah was born.

Eliakim, Hezekiah's self-appointed messiah, rearranged his robe, ignoring his bloody lip. "I could have flattened him."

The sound of marching sandals in the hallway stilled them all.

"Now you've done it." Bocheru crossed his arms over his chest, glaring at Eliakim. "They're coming to arrest you for hitting the crown prince."

Sadly, the prince showed few signs of innate wisdom, and everyone except King Ahaz seemed to realize it. Too bad Hezekiah wasn't born first. He was as sharp as a Philistine sword. Isaiah assessed the disarray. If anyone would be arrested, it was the tutor standing beside two bloodied students.

Judah's commander appeared in the doorway, filling it with his broad shoulders and Goliathan height. He sneered at Isaiah before shoving several small white robes at his gut. "Your students are to wear these for tonight's ceremony. I'll wait while they put them on and then escort *all* of you."

"Ceremony? I've not been informed of a cere—"

"You're a tutor. You have no need to know in advance." He pressed the robes harder against Isaiah, emphasizing his singular responsibility.

Isaiah received the fine robes like salt in a wound. A few weeks ago, he would have ordered this pompous commander where to march and how fast. Now, he matched robes with the boys' sizes and pondered the possible reasons for tonight's ceremony. Perhaps tonight was a memorial for the mass burial of the thousands of soldiers killed in the attack. Or maybe a prayer vigil for the captives taken to Aram, Edom, and Samaria.

The faint sound of drums in the distance felt like the pounding of a stake into Isaiah's chest. He'd heard the sound before—in Ammon, after Ahaz's first military victory. When Isaiah served as foreign minister under Ahaz's abba, King Jotham, Isaiah had been sent to negotiate treaty conditions. While Judah's army celebrated, the Ammonites sacrificed their children to the god Molek. The beating drums, meant to drown out the cries of children thrown into the fire, mingled with piercing screams in a rhythmic death chant.

Isaiah charged at the commander. "What is that sound?" It was an accusation, not a question.

The big man spoke quietly through gritted teeth. "Only one will honor Molek with his life. Why tell them now and upset them all? We can carry them screaming through the streets or lead them quietly and with dignity."

Sickened, Isaiah turned away, watching his energetic students. Giggling and shoving, they acted like best friends anticipating a new adventure. Six-year-old Mattaniah showed his big brothers that their robes were identical to his, having no idea it could be his shroud. *Yahweh, show me how to stop this!*

Silence answered.

An invisible fist twisted Isaiah's insides. "Please, General, stop this before Judah commits the same abomination that caused Yahweh to drive out the Canaanites from this land."

The commander lifted a single brow in challenge. "I'll pretend I didn't hear your treasonous words—this time." With a nod to his captain, the commander began the night of terror. Utterly helpless, Isaiah watched his students march like condemned prisoners through two columns of

Judean soldiers that lined the hallway. Why had King Ahaz sent fifty men to collect less than half that number of boys?

Isaiah followed through the palace halls and entered the Middle Court—to the bone-chilling sound of a woman's scream.

"No!" Queen Abijah raced down the harem stairs toward her three sons, but guards intercepted her. The double line of soldiers collapsed around the boys, hiding the queen from young, worried eyes.

Isaiah stood paralyzed, torn between comforting the queen and following his students. *Yahweh, show me what to do!* The decision was made when guards carried Queen Abijah back up the stairs to the second level of the harem, where King Ahaz's six wives lived and only specified king's guards gained entry.

Isaiah hurried to catch up with the boys as they walked down the palace stairs onto the cobblestoned streets of Jerusalem's Upper City. Shoving his way through the ranks, he assumed a protective stance behind his students. Officially, they were in his care until released to their parents at the end of the day. He glanced over their heads at the homes lining the street, hoping a concerned advisor or ima might have heard the drums and come outside to investigate. He saw only neatly manicured courtyards. Not even a servant lingered in the waning daylight.

He looked behind him at his own home, standing alone in the northeast corner of the Upper City where palace property and Temple grounds converged. His courtyard was deserted as well. There was no time to tell his wife, Aya, what was happening. Were their sons safe? Jashub and Kadmiel were older than Isaiah's students. They were among Jerusalem's military trainees and would likely be forced to watch the ceremony.

Heart aching, he focused on his class and passed through the gate to the Lower City. Gone were the pristine streets and spacious homes. Human waste mingled with refuse flowing downhill in the middle of the street. Jerusalem's southern city had resembled a war-torn village even *before* Israel's troops attacked. Now many two-story stone buildings lay in rubble. The ones still standing housed multiple families and the poorest of the poor in Judah.

Only days ago Isaiah had worked alongside many of these families to rebuild their homes, the market, and the southern wall. Most of Isaiah's privileged students had never glimpsed the Lower City, and they stared wide-eyed and silent as the commander marched them through the Dung Gate, Jerusalem's southernmost entrance.

The drumbeats grew louder, and his stomach tightened as their destination became clear. In the Valley of Ben Hinnom stood Topheth, a pagan altar built in Solomon's days. As they approached the valley, Isaiah's knees turned to water. There, beside Topheth, stood a newly built bronze altar surrounded by an endless sea of people.

"Ooh!" The boys pointed and gawked at the altar fashioned in human form with the head of an ox. Seven compartments dotted its chest; six held an offering: a dove, grain, pieces of an ox, a ewe, a ram, and a calf. One compartment remained empty, prepared for the ultimate sacrifice. Molek's arms extended outward, forming a chute into the belly, an open furnace that glowed red hot. If Isaiah hadn't known its horrific purpose, he too might have marveled at its magnificence. The last rays of sunset reflected off the bronze beast, casting an eerie glow over the platform where King Ahaz stood among bald-headed, chanting priests. The new royal counsel lined the back of the platform—with the exception of Micah. He'd left for Jericho earlier in the day after hearing from Yahweh's prophets that Judah's captives might be returned there. By God's mercy Micah had been spared from standing on the platform with the king's other advisors.

The drums beat faster as Isaiah's royal offerings approached. Musicians accompanied the drums with flutes and lyres. Scantily clad dancers twisted and swayed among the gathered throng, tempting both men and women to the shoddy tents where ritual pleasures waited. Wine flowed freely, rousing the celebration to a frenzy.

Were these the same people who days ago had mourned their lost husbands and daughters? Had they forgotten the captives, the ruined fields and orchards? Why were they squandering supplies on a festival when many Judean families were sure to starve in months to come? Isaiah scanned the deep ravine of Hinnom extending toward the Kidron Valley along the city's eastern border. People as far as the eye could see. Yahweh had told him Judah still worshiped idols, but this was beyond anything he'd imagined.

The commander marched the line of boys straight to the platform, knocking aside any who hindered their progress. Isaiah finally understood the fifty-soldier escort. They were a mere drop in an ocean of chaos. Guarding little Mattaniah at the end of the line, Isaiah wished he could hide their eyes and close their ears as they ascended the platform. *Yahweh, if the stench of our unfaithfulness is this rancid, why haven't You destroyed us already?*

One of the priests bowed to Prince Bocheru, lifting the boy's hand to his forehead—a sign of fidelity and honor. The crowd cheered, and King Ahaz placed an approving hand on the boy's shoulder. Isaiah's mouth went dry. Had they made their choice?

The other royal students stood shoulder to

shoulder, eyes wide, taking in the priests' blood-stained white robes and bowls full of entrails. Had they guessed what was happening, or were they simply intrigued by the animals being sacrificed?

King Ahaz lifted his arms for silence. Priests and participants stilled. "Mighty Molek, greatest warrior of the fallen ones, receive our offerings. Hear our cries. By your favor I conquered your people in Ammon, and by your favor we will conquer the enemies that surround us now."

A mighty roar rose from the crowd, and Ahaz nodded to Molek's seven priests. Each carried a bowl full of blood and a branch of hyssop and stopped directly in front of one of Isaiah's students. After dipping the hyssop in the bowl, they moved down the line, spattering the boys' robes. More cheering erupted as the boys looked down at the stains on their beautiful robes, now ruined. Mattaniah began to whimper, but a stern stare from a priest quieted him immediately.

King Ahaz walked down the line of human offerings, listening to each priest whisper some deep secret. He stopped too long in front of Eliakim, and Isaiah's heart pounded in his ears.

He searched the sea of faces for Eliakim's abba—friend and royal treasurer, Hilkiah—but didn't see him. Of course, Hilkiah would never attend a pagan sacrifice. How could he know that the child he'd taught to know and love Yahweh might at any moment become a pagan sacrifice?

Even as the thoughts formed, King Ahaz placed his arm around Eliakim's shoulder and singled him out, whispering in his ear. Eliakim's knees gave way, and two bald priests grabbed his arms. Two more swept his legs out from under him. The boy fought. Kicked. Screamed.

The righteous rebellion stifled the celebration, quieting the crowd. The other boys huddled around Isaiah—all but one. "Wait!" Prince Hezekiah ran to his abba, pounding the king's back.

King Ahaz turned, fire in his eyes, and trapped the boy's arms at his side. Isaiah freed himself of his students and tried to reach Hezekiah. The commander and two soldiers held him back. The other boys tried to flee the platform. Guards surrounded them.

King Ahaz, seeming unnerved by the crowd's stillness, shouted at the chief priest. "Pray to Molek!" Then the king knelt beside Hezekiah, whispering.

Frantic, Isaiah strained to hear. He couldn't. *Yahweh, do something!*

With a stern look, King Ahaz shoved Hezekiah back to join the royal boys. "Line them up again!" The crowd murmured as the soldiers reconstructed the line. "Release that one." Ahaz pointed to Eliakim, and Isaiah sighed his relief. Had Hezekiah convinced his abba to forgo the human sacrifice? Perhaps fill the altar's seventh compartment with another animal portion? Isaiah assessed his students and noted exchanged glances, lifted brows, and smiles. They knew, as did all of Judah, that Hezekiah's words had spared his friend Eliakim.

King Ahaz spoke in low tones to the priests, who then took their places behind the seven oldest of Isaiah's students. They chanted a low guttural thrum. The musicians took up the dirge, a slow and hypnotic tune, building in intensity, while the drums beat loud and steady.

The king lifted his voice above the mounting tension. "Molek, the mighty warrior, has spoken through a child to save Judah from grave error this night." King Ahaz raised his arms, shouting, "We beseech you, great warrior among the gods, return to us those taken as captives and bind us to the greatest power on earth."

He let his arms fall to his sides—a signal to the priests.

With the speed of lightning, two bald-headed pagans slipped a rope around Prince Bocheru's arms. Two more swept him off his feet. The four of them carried Bocheru toward the glowing altar and hoisted him into the waiting arms of the blazing bronze altar.

Drums beat frantically, but nothing could drown out the prince's cries—or mask the smell of burning flesh. Some of the boys retched on the platform. Mattaniah buried his face in Eliakim's waist. Hezekiah stood like stone, silent, mouth slack. Isaiah shook him. No response. The king's second-born gazed at nothing in the distance, his limbs stiff. A stream of tears the only sign of life.

Drums kept beating, but the celebration died with Bocheru. King Ahaz panned the now-silent crowd. "If I, your king and sovereign, a descendent of David's eternal kingdom, have willingly offered my firstborn to Molek, can any among you withhold your sons?" A frantic murmur worked its way across the gathering like a wave rising over the sea, but King Ahaz spoke above the protests. "We will sacrifice a firstborn of Judah at each New Moon festival until our nation regains the cities we've lost to Israel, Aram, Edom, and Philistia. Molek will hear and answer our prayers if we give him our best. We must give our firstborns!"

King Ahaz wiped his face. Was it perspiration or tears he wiped away? Pointing to the tents surrounding the platform, King Ahaz raised his voice. "Rejoice, Jerusalem! Our sacrifice pleases Molek. He waits in those tents to offer you pleasure, wisdom, and victory! Partake, Judah! Partake!"

Isaiah lifted Hezekiah into his arms and marched three steps to the visibly shaken commander. "You led these children to Sheol. Now take them home."

The commander could only nod, his earlier bluster incinerated in the fires of Molek.

Isaiah looked into Hezekiah's distant stare and cradled the child close to his heart. *Please, Yahweh. Remove the sins of the abba from his sons. Protect this dear boy and restore him to Abijah.*

4

As a mother comforts her child,
so will I comfort you;
and you will be comforted over Jerusalem.
                                            —Isaiah 66:13

I couldn't keep my eyes open, so I laid my cheek on top of Micah's head. I woke, nearly tumbling backward. Micah took me off his shoulders because he said I was dozing. He held me close, his arms wrapped tight around me, while I hugged his neck and wrapped my legs around his waist. I liked that way better. I laid my head against his chest. Now I felt safe.

When he stopped, I opened my eyes, and it was dark. I turned in his arms and saw that we were at the top of a small hill. Yaira was bent over, bracing her hands against her knees, panting.

I patted Micah's cheek gently and pointed at her. Maybe he should put me down and carry her?

"I know, little one. She's tired, but see?" He nodded toward a glow above the hills ahead. "We're almost to Jerusalem."

"I'm all right," Yaira said. "Let's keep going." She started walking again.

At the top of the next hill, Yaira needed to rest

again. "What's causing such a bright light in Jerusalem?" she asked. I turned again to see one side of the city looked as bright as the sun but the other side only as bright as a candle.

Micah frowned like he was thinking hard. "Probably burning trash from the siege in the Valley of Ben Hinnom. They were cleaning up the damaged buildings in the Lower City when I left a couple of days ago."

I hid my face against Micah's chest. Would there be dead bodies staring at nothing like Ima and Abba? I could still see their faces when I closed my eyes.

Yaira rubbed my back, talking quietly. "We should avoid as much of the devastation as possible for Ishma's sake." Did she think I couldn't hear just because I'd lost my words?

"We shouldn't leave the caravan until we reach the city. Too much danger of bandits or jackals." Micah kissed the top of my head and whispered against my hair, "Ishma, keep your face against my chest until we reach Master Isaiah's house."

I gladly obeyed, snuggling into the bend of his neck and closing my eyes again.

Micah's gasp woke me. How far had we gone? I craned my neck and turned to see. We stood on another hill, this one across a narrow valley from Jerusalem. A huge glowing statue lit the night sky, and the smell of burning garbage made my stomach turn somersaults. Small tents dotted the hillside, and people lay beside them—some dressed only in tunics.

"Yahweh, forgive your people, Judah," Micah whispered while following the caravan into the valley.

We walked through the garbage until someone cried, "Molek has delivered the captives!" People lit torches and ran toward us. I tightened my arms and legs around Micah. My whole body began to shake. *Please don't let them take me.*

"Hide your face, Ishma. Close your eyes." Micah grabbed Yaira's arm after only a few steps. "We can't go any farther into the crowd. Ishma is terrified." He pointed toward the city. "We'll head north through the Kidron Valley and enter through the Horse Gate. It's closer to Isaiah's home, and we'll avoid the Lower City."

Even though I buried my head on his shoulder I could still smell the foul air. Micah and Yaira started running, downhill and then up again. I kept my eyes closed. They slowed, and their sandals slapped on a wooden plank. We stopped.

"I'm Micah, the king's prophet, to see Master Isaiah."

I peeked under my arm and saw a grumpy old guard open a big, heavy gate. We slipped through an opening barely the width of Ima's grain basket—into a different land. All was still. No one walked the streets, and not a single lamp

Dunn Public Library

shone in a window. Big stone houses surrounded us. A huge palace loomed ahead.

Micah released a deep breath. "We're safe now. Master Isaiah's home is at the end of the street."

I propped my chin on his shoulder to see where we'd been, not where we were going. Somehow the future scared me more. The shiny stone streets looked like Ima's polished bronze mirror in the moonlight. Every home had a garden and a gate. If I didn't know Jerusalem had been attacked, I wouldn't have thought people in these houses had any troubles at all.

Micah carried me down a wide street, the grand palace on one side, the perfect houses on the other. Finally, we came to a house separate from all the others, sitting at a corner, where two walls met. The palace was on the other side of one wall and a big, fancy building beyond the other.

I pointed at the golden top of the fancy building.

"That's Yahweh's Temple," Micah whispered, while nudging open the gate of the corner house. It squeaked. Yaira closed it behind us, and Micah led the way to the door.

A beautiful lady opened it before Micah knocked. "Yahweh, help us," she whispered and then shooed us into the entry. "Leah, put a pot of broth over the fire. Dinah, bring water and bandages for the girls' wounds. Isaiah, Micah has arrived!"

A tall man with a stern face appeared and

offered his hand to Yaira. "Welcome to our home. I'm sorry you've come to our beautiful city at such an ugly time." He looked at Micah. "Ahaz sacrificed the crown prince the night you left for Jericho. There's been feasting in the valley ever since."

Micah's arms tightened around me. "How could he—"

"We'll talk once the girls are settled." The man looked at me, his frown turning into a false smile. I hid my face against Micah's chest.

"Thank you, Master Isaiah, for taking us in as house servants," I heard Yaira say. "We'll work hard. We won't cause any trouble."

"Nonsense," said the pretty lady. "We have no servants here. Everyone works, everyone eats, and everyone serves Yahweh. We're a family, dear."

When I heard her say *family,* I turned to face her. The lady stepped closer to Micah and laid her hand on my cheek. "What's your name, little one?"

I pulled away.

"Shy, are we?"

Micah spoke for me. "She hasn't said a word since she was taken from Bethlehem. Perhaps you, Dinah, and Leah can coax her to talk again."

Two older boys entered the large room, one reading a scroll, the other carrying wood for the fire. Yaira's neck and cheeks turned bright red, and she slipped behind Micah.

"These are my sons, Jashub and Kadmiel." Master Isaiah fairly beamed with pride. Micah ruffled the oldest boy's hair. The two shoved playfully while I held tighter to Micah's neck.

He set me down on a soft cushion. Yaira sat beside me, drawing me close, while the women scurried around the cooking fire.

Master Isaiah, his sons, and Micah withdrew to a corner of the large room, their heads bowed together, whispering. I heard the master say something about a boy who died in a fire and another boy whose body lived though his spirit died. Deep concern wrinkled Micah's forehead. Or maybe he was confused, like me, by Master Isaiah's words.

The pretty lady brought two bowls of broth, one for me and one for Yaira. "My name is Aya," she said. "What are your names?"

"I'm Yaira, Micah's sister, and this is Ishma."

The lady frowned. "Ishma? Why would your parents name you *Desolation?*"

I pushed the broth away and hid my face against Yaira so I didn't have to look at the mean lady. Yaira stroked my hair and spoke for me. "Ishma was named as a reminder of blessing, Mistress. When my parents were killed in a Philistine attack, Micah found a couple in Bethlehem to care for me. I was despondent, but only days after I arrived, the woman gave birth to a precious daughter and named her Ishma—*desolation*—to show me that

54

new life can spring from despair." She nudged me, forcing me to sit up and face Mistress Aya. "It is a beautiful name for this beautiful girl, and I've told Ishma that Yahweh can also use our current desolation for a glorious purpose."

The woman's eyes were leaking. "I'm sorry, Ishma. It was rude of me to criticize your lovely name. Forgive me."

I held tight to Yaira and nodded. Maybe Mistress Aya wasn't so bad.

The two young women, Dinah and Leah, brought warm wet cloths, rolled bandages, and a basket of small pots and jars. Mistress Aya held up a warm cloth. "May I wash away your tear stains, little Ishma?"

I didn't know tears stained. Ima used to get cross if I stained my robe with stew or mud. But Mistress Aya didn't seem cross about the tears.

I nodded permission. The warm cloth felt good on my face. Even better was her gentle touch. She was even gentler than when Ima cleaned my scraped knees. *Ima* . . . More tears came, and I turned away, clinging to Yaira again. What good purpose could Yahweh have for taking away my ima's gentle touch?

Mistress Aya rinsed the cloths in a bowl of steaming water and handed one to Yaira. "I have prepared a room for you girls to share." She unrolled a bandage, smeared honey on it, and reached for my arm.

I pulled away, shaking my head frantically.

Yaira set aside her cloth and offered her arm to the mistress. "Honey doesn't hurt, Ishma. See?" The servant girls gasped when they saw Yaira's partly healed brand. I hid my arm behind my back. Yaira smiled and held out her hand. "Honey helps us heal faster. Let's compare our marks, Ishma. Is yours the same as mine?"

Dinah and Leah wiped away tears and put on false smiles for me. I didn't want smiles. I wanted Yaira.

"Look at me, Ishma." Yaira's voice was stern. Was she angry? When I looked at her, she smiled. "Show me your brand, love."

I didn't want to, but I had promised Yaira in Jericho that I would do as she said. So I showed her my brand. They were the same, of course, the image of a bull with lightning bolts as horns.

The mistress nodded to the younger women, who began dressing a bandage with honey. One of them held my hand as she wrapped the bandage around my arm. "My name is Dinah, and this is my sister Leah." They looked the same—like twins. "We came to work for Mistress Aya when we were about your age, Ishma." The honey soothed, and my lips curved into a smile without permission. Everyone clapped as if I'd brought in the first harvest by myself.

Mistress Aya turned her attention to Yaira. "Do you have wounds beneath your robe, dear?"

Yaira's cheeks bloomed crimson as she bowed her head. "Yes, Mistress."

"We'll dress them in your chamber. Dinah and Leah sleep in the room beside yours."

Yaira looked over her shoulder, and her cheeks faded to gray. "I'm sorry to be so bold, Mistress, but"—she swallowed hard—"if we've taken your sons' chamber, Ishma and I would be very comfortable sleeping in a corner of the courtyard or in a stable."

I'd never slept in a courtyard or stable, but we'd slept in the wilderness for nearly two weeks. I didn't think a courtyard or stable would be much different—but not nearly as comfortable as the chamber the mistress had prepared. Mistress must have thought the same thing. She reached for Yaira's hand and her voice became quieter. "My sons share a room on the opposite side of the house." Yaira relaxed under her touch, and Yaira and the big women talked and talked while I kept peeking over at the men.

They looked sad and angry. I hoped they wouldn't shout like Micah and Abba on Micah's last visit. When they bowed their heads and began whispering, I wondered if that was how prophets talked to Yahweh. I looked at the ceiling, waiting to see if God answered, but the only sound was the women's chatter. Was Yahweh even real? Did He hear our prayers?

"Ishma . . . Ishma." Mistress Aya's kind eyes

waited for my attention. "I think you and Yaira will feel better after a good night's rest." The way she rose from her cushion reminded me of an olive tree swaying in the breeze, gentle and appealing. I couldn't look away.

She paused, offering her hand.

Yaira kissed my head and whispered, "Go with the mistress. I'm right behind you."

My heart pounded in my ears as I let go of Yaira and reached for Mistress Aya. Maybe this house could be a peaceful nest for a lonely bird.

5

[Hezekiah's] mother's name was Abijah daughter of Zechariah.

—2 Kings 18:2

Isaiah closed the heavy oak door on his private wine cellar, smashing his thumb. *"Aah!"* He juggled two skins of Egyptian wine and stuck the throbbing appendage in his mouth. The mishap was another in the long list he'd suffered since Ishma and Hezekiah had been heavy on his mind. Why must children pay for adults' catastrophic decisions?

Aya appeared at his side. "May I take those wineskins before you stub your toe or run into a wall?" She hadn't always been feisty. Perhaps she'd become that way to survive as the wife of a Yahweh prophet—or perhaps as best friend of the queen.

Isaiah stood by the wine cellar door like a sentry. "We should have taken Ishma to meet Hezekiah at the palace. Why invite Queen Abijah here? What if she wants to tour our home?"

His wife handed the wineskins to the other women and continued preparing a tray of fruit. "Queen Abijah has been here dozens of times since we moved into your family's home. She's never asked for a tour."

59

Isaiah leaned against the door that hid their long-held secret, a secret revealed only to his household during Israel's recent attack. "Did she ask you how we arrived in the underground tunnels before the rest of the advisors?"

"No." Aya placed a few olives in a lovely arc over the dried figs.

"Did she mention any suspicion on King Ahaz's part?"

His wife looked up, breathing out her frustration. "No, and will you please go check on Ishma. She's supposed to be setting bowls and goblets on the table." Aya had decided to entertain their guests outside on this beautiful spring morning.

Isaiah wasn't sure he wanted to leave the cellar door. Perhaps he'd just stay here while the queen and her royal escort dined in the courtyard with Prince Hezekiah on his litter. In his worst nightmare, he imagined the queen excusing herself from their midday meal, sneaking into the wine cellar, lifting the loosened stone in the southeast corner, and discovering the network of tunnels below.

Over two hundred years ago, Solomon quarried much of the limestone for both Yahweh's Temple and his palace from the bedrock beneath Mount Zion. The quarry created a network of tunnels that secured safe passage from palace to Temple and out of the city—the purpose of which was to safeguard the Ark of God's presence. The secret escape was passed down through generations to the reigning king and high priest. During Israel's recent attack, however, Ahaz had chosen to reveal the tunnels, hiding there with his family and all his advisors' families. Isaiah had also hidden his household, entering one of the tunnels that extended under his home—positioned at the corner of the walls guarding the palace and Temple. Yahweh had somehow kept their private entrance hidden, and Isaiah was determined to keep it that way.

Little Ishma entered the kitchen, jostling him from his brooding. She headed straight for the lowest shelf to fetch bowls for the meal. Stacking four bowls up to her chin, she turned back toward the courtyard. With a resolute sigh, he walked across the kitchen, kissed his wife, and followed the adorable brown-eyed girl.

Both Ishma and Yaira were preparing the table. They'd healed nicely—body and soul—in the week since coming to Isaiah's house. Though Ishma still refused to speak or venture far from Yaira, Isaiah had coaxed a smile from her yesterday with a candied fig. Aya was certain Queen Abijah and Hezekiah's visit would mend the broken spirits of both children.

Isaiah wasn't so sure. He'd spent most of the morning in his study, waiting on direction from Yahweh that never came. At such times, he listened to his wife. She, too, had an ear for Yahweh's voice, and Isaiah trusted the one thing he would never have—a woman's instincts.

Ishma left the courtyard again and soon returned, hands and arms full of silver goblets. She frowned at the challenge of placing them upright on the long, rectangular table.

Isaiah bowed deeply. "May I be of service, Princess Ishma?"

Eyes wide and cheeks the color of roses, she nodded, and his heart turned over in his chest. As he reached for the goblets, he heard the telltale squeak of their courtyard gate. The queen's escort had arrived.

He'd barely taken a step toward the gate when he heard Ishma screech and saw goblets go flying. Aya, Dinah, and Leah raced from the kitchen to investigate. Ishma had run to Yaira's arms and was climbing and clawing up her in a panic unlike anything Isaiah had ever seen.

Yaira retreated from the approaching royal guards, stopping only when she'd backed up to the courtyard wall. "I'm sorry; it's the soldiers," she said over Ishma's inconsolable cries. "The queen's guards. They look like the men who beat us."

Before Isaiah could reply, Queen Abijah hovered over Prince Hezekiah, who lay silent and still on the litter carried by four guards. "Aya, why would you invite us to visit a traumatized girl whose screaming can only add to my son's trauma?"

Isaiah gathered Yaira and Ishma and hurried them into the house while Aya spoke quietly to her friend. "Abijah, please, listen . . ." It was all he heard over Ishma's whimpers as he guided both girls into his study. He pulled out two plush cushions and invited Yaira to sit.

She lowered the trembling Ishma to the ground, but Ishma refused to release Yaira's hand. The older girl folded her legs and lowered herself as gracefully as swaying willow-tree branches, all the while soothing and coaxing Ishma onto the cushion beside her. "Shh, little one. These are good soldiers. They help protect the queen and her son. They will protect us too." Yaira's hands were trembling as violently as Ishma's. Was it empathy for her charge, or was she equally affected by the guards' presence?

As Isaiah was contemplating what to say, Aya appeared in the doorway. "Abijah has agreed to stay. Samuel and the rest of her guards will wait outside the courtyard gate, out of sight."

Samuel had been one of King Ahaz's royal guards for over a decade. He was competent and kind, one of the king's best guards. Offering a favorite guard was likely King Ahaz's only form of comfort. Queen Abijah adored her son but had made no progress reviving him. Hezekiah's continued silence did little to encourage Isaiah's hope that the boy could get better. Aya needed to face the inevitable future of these two broken children.

"You and Abijah have supported each other through many hardships since you were girls," Isaiah said as gently as possible, "but your deep friendship can't be imparted to two children who have never met."

His wife answered through taut lips. "It's not *our* friendship that will heal these children, Isaiah ben Amoz. It is their unwinnowed innocence." She stepped inside and knelt beside the girls, speaking softly to Ishma. "Prince Hezekiah has experienced something awful—like you have—and it's stolen more than his voice. He can't walk or play or smile anymore. It's like his body is alive, but he's gone inside."

Ishma's trembling subsided some, but she kept her face hidden against Yaira's arm. Yaira began rocking her and asked, "What happened that caused the prince to become silent?"

Aya cast a prodding glance at Isaiah. He gave her a frown in return. He'd been a tutor for less than two months. Did she expect him to now be the expert on children? How does one explain to someone so young the atrocity that Hezekiah witnessed?

"King Ahaz, Hezekiah's abba, doesn't worship Yahweh," he began. "The night before you arrived, he worshiped a statue made of metal.

He chose one of Hezekiah's friends to give as a gift to the statue, and Prince Hezekiah offered himself to take his friend's place. King Ahaz chose instead to give Hezekiah's older brother, Prince Bocheru, to the statue. Bocheru died that night."

Aya wiped her tears and stuttered through emotions she couldn't control. "When Hezekiah saw his brother die such a terrible death, Prince Hezekiah died on the inside. I believe he blames both himself and the adults in his life for what happened to his brother, and he needs a child—one who understands his pain—to simply hold his hand, sit with him, and talk to him." She patted Ishma's knee. "Could you do that?"

The little girl nodded without lifting her head and then—surprising them all—crawled into Aya's lap. A smile lit Yaira's face at the first time Ishma left her side. Aya hugged the little one, then lifted Ishma into her arms and rose to her feet. She carried the girl back to the courtyard, while Isaiah and Yaira followed close behind.

Queen Abijah sat beside her son's litter and finished her wine as they entered the courtyard. Dinah hurried over to refill her goblet. Leah remained beside the table, a second amphora of spiced wine at the ready. The relief on their faces was palpable when the others returned.

The queen rolled her eyes. "Can the little girl walk, Aya, or must she be carried everywhere?"

Isaiah tamped down an angry response, letting his wife deal with her difficult friend.

"Did your son walk before his heart and mind were wounded, Abbi?" Only Aya called the queen Abbi and only when the royal guards were absent. The two women had shared more years and tears than most married couples.

Queen Abijah raised her goblet to Aya in surrender—a word battle well fought.

Isaiah's wife settled herself and Ishma on the opposite side of Hezekiah's litter in the shade of three palm trees. "Let's introduce the children."

Isaiah sat at the table less than two camel lengths away and patted a cushion to his left, guiding Yaira to the place of second-highest honor. The place at his right, of course, must be reserved for the queen.

Ishma's face remained buried in the bend of Aya's neck while Aya spoke to the boy on the litter. "Prince Hezekiah, I'd like to introduce Ishma. She lost her voice when her home in Bethlehem was burned and her parents died. I told her what happened to your brother Bocheru and that it wasn't your fault."

"Aya, stop!" Queen Abijah's eyes filled with tears. "He doesn't need to be reminded—"

Aya raised her chin. "Have you told him why Ahaz chose your firstborn son instead of Eliakim?"

The queen stroked her son's brow. "No. We need never speak of that night again."

"He needs to hear the truth," Isaiah said, unable to remain silent any longer. "You didn't see his face, Abijah. He thinks it was his fault."

She bowed her head on her son's arm and wept. Aya received it as permission to continue. "Prince Hezekiah was very brave," she said to Ishma.

The little girl raised her head, her brows knit together in a V. She squirmed from Aya's arms, standing like a soldier beside the litter. They waited, but she made no move to touch him or speak.

"Why isn't she *doing* something?" The queen's frustration had no effect on Ishma. The girl's eyes were trained on Hezekiah; she seemed oblivious to the world around them.

Isaiah clapped, startling everyone but the children. "Let's eat our meal," he said, rising from the table to approach the litter. "The women of my household have worked hard to prepare a sumptuous feast." He dared not say the meal had been prepared with the last portion of meat from their monthly allotment. Isaiah's wages had been reduced when he was demoted from the royal council. Even so, the allotment would have been more than enough—if they hadn't fed most of Jerusalem's southern city while helping people rebuild since the attack over two weeks ago.

Aya was first to come away from the litter. Isaiah offered his hand to Queen Abijah, hoping she'd allow the children time alone. He prayed his wife's instincts were right, that Ishma could do . . . whatever Aya thought she could do.

Queen Abijah was as unpredictable as an ima bear protecting a wounded cub. Aya said she was desperate to get Hezekiah back. But what would she do if Ishma couldn't help him? Would she mete out her frustration on Ishma? Or on Aya? King Ahaz had shown his wrath at Isaiah's prophecies by demoting him to royal tutor. If the queen turned against them as well, would Isaiah lose their family home? Would their sons pay the price?

Yahweh, I will trust You when I have more questions than answers.

6

A happy heart makes the face cheerful,
but heartache crushes the spirit.
—Proverbs 15:13

I almost ran back to Yaira when Mistress Aya set my feet on the ground, but Yaira's nod and smile told me it was safe to stay beside the prince. The big people kept staring at us even after they sat at the table. I still wasn't sure what Mistress Aya wanted me to do.

Afraid the soldiers might slip through the gate and snatch me from the courtyard, I stood by the litter, on the side closest to Yaira, and looked down at the prince. His face was the color of goat's milk. He lay on his back, staring at the palm trees above us, his eyes empty like Abba's and Ima's the last time I saw them. Was Mistress Aya sure his body lived? I leaned over his face and felt his soft breath on my cheek. Then I saw his chest rise and fall. He was definitely alive.

Why was he staring? Maybe he saw something up in the trees. I looked up and saw a nest with two birds. They were singing, and I hadn't even noticed. I was sure they weren't there yesterday. The birds looked like they'd been dipped in a rainbow—blue, pink, yellow, and orange. No wonder he was staring. Maybe his eyes weren't empty after all. I turned his face toward me.

"Be gentle with him!" the queen yelled.

I jerked my hand away, afraid she'd call for her soldiers to beat me. Mistress Aya shushed her, but I still huddled behind the litter.

My stomach growled. There was a lot of food on the table, more than we usually ate at a meal. The big people had begun eating, so I stood again and looked at the prince, wondering if he was hungry too. I wanted to ask him, but the words wouldn't come. I poked his tummy, and it growled. He *was* hungry!

I walked over to the table. Master Isaiah sat at the head, the queen at his place of honor. Mistress Aya let Yaira sit at second seat today. I nudged Yaira's shoulder, pointed at the bread, and rubbed my tummy. She broke off one piece of bread, so I pointed at the prince to explain that I needed two pieces.

"He can't eat bread." The queen talked extra loud as if my lost words meant I couldn't hear. "This is foolish, Aya. Don't let her shove bread into his mouth. He's only had broth since this happened."

Mistress Aya whispered something to her friend, but Yaira ignored them and gave me another piece of bread. "You eat some, Ishma, and if the prince wakes up, you can share."

I hesitated.

Master Isaiah gestured toward the prince. "Go on. It's all right."

I took a bite of bread on my way back to the litter. It stood on four legs, like a low table, with big gold rings on all four corners. Two long, sturdy poles fit through the gold rings. I saw the soldiers carrying the poles on their shoulders with the litter way up in the air. A wooden rim guarded all four sides, probably so the prince didn't slide off while he was up high. I wondered if the prince was scared, being lifted up like that.

I sat down on the litter's wooden rim and poked my fist into the puffy mattress beside the prince. It might have been stuffed with wool or straw or maybe feathers. I ran my hand over its curly, soft goat skin and wondered what the prince's life had been like before it was surrounded by this wooden rim. The rim seemed like a wall, separating him from everyone else in the whole world.

I looked up at the two pretty birds. *Two of them.* Even birds had someone. Why should the prince be alone in his nest? If I climbed over the rim and sat on the mattress with him, he wouldn't be alone.

I peeked over my shoulder at Yaira. The big people were all staring at me again. Master Isaiah whispered something, and they started eating. I bit off another piece of my bread and studied the prince some more. He was still staring into the tree. I decided the prince wanted to be like the two birds in one nest.

I glanced over my shoulder again and saw that everyone was eating and talking. Quietly, I slipped off my dusty sandals, scooted over the wooden rim, and knelt on the soft mattress. No one seemed to notice, so I huddled closer to the prince's face and tore off a small piece of bread.

I held it in front of his eyes.

He didn't even blink.

Rising on my knees, I hovered over his face, putting myself between him and the tree. His eyes were dark like Abba's. His nose was a little crooked and too big for his face. I waited a moment. Then I poofed a bit of air. His eyelids flickered. I poofed again. His eyes stayed distant, but he frowned like he was annoyed.

I looked up at the birds again. They were still singing—first one, then the other—like they were talking to each other. When I returned my attention to the prince, he was looking at me, straight into my eyes. His light was back! I leaned to one side, and his eyes followed me. To the other side. His eyes followed again.

I climbed over him and sat on the mattress between him and the rim of the litter. He turned his head, staring at me now instead of the tree. Blinking many times, he squinted and studied me. "Are you a dream?" His voice was so quiet it was almost like a breath.

I shook my head.

He looked at me, blinking some more. He lifted his hand and touched my face. "An angel then?"

"No, I'm Ishma." I covered my mouth as if a wild horse had rushed out. My words had come back at the same time someone lit the light in his eyes!

Everyone at the table gasped, and before I knew what was happening, someone scooped me off the litter and swung me around. Yaira held me tight, laughing and crying. "Ishma, you spoke! You spoke!" The master's deep voice joined the women's squeals, laughing and rejoicing. The queen sat on the edge of the litter, rocking the prince in her arms, while the mistress hugged them both.

Yaira paused her celebrating and set my feet on the ground. "What else have you to say, Ishma? You've saved up two weeks of words."

The clapping suddenly stopped, and fear replaced my joy. What if my words came only for the prince? I glanced in his direction but the queen was talking with him, her back to me, blocking my view of him. The others gathered around Yaira and me, everyone seeming anxious to hear what I had to say.

What could I say? I didn't want to talk about my nightmares. I could say the bread in my hand was tasty, but they already knew that because they'd eaten theirs. I could tell Master and

Mistress how grateful I was, but even the thought of it tightened my throat.

When I looked at Yaira, I knew exactly what to say to her. "I love you." The words came out on a whisper, but she heard them.

Grabbing me, she twirled me around until I was dizzy. "I love you too, sweet Ishma." She laughed through tears and then set my feet on the ground again.

That's when I heard it.

"Ishma." It was just a whisper with a voice as gravelly as mine. "Ishma." A little louder this time.

Yaira heard it too. She took my hand, and we walked toward Prince Hezekiah's litter together. The queen's face didn't look so scary. She nodded, which I think meant she liked me a little bit now. The prince patted a place on the mattress beside him. Yaira lifted me onto the litter, and he reached for my hand. His stomach growled again, and I giggled.

Master Isaiah sniffed and wiped his eyes. Putting his arm around Mistress, he said, "Aya, my love, remind me never to doubt you again."

She winked at him, then turned and hugged the queen so tight that the queen's head covering fell to her shoulders. Ugly bruises circled her neck.

Mistress Aya's smile disappeared. She grabbed the queen's shoulders and inspected the marks. "Where were your guards when Ahaz did this?"

The queen pushed her away, and it got very quiet. Queen Abijah glanced at Hezekiah and turned her back, arranging her veils to cover the area again. "You know my guards can't touch him—even when he does this."

I turned back to see Prince Hezekiah's eyes filling with tears. He turned his face away from the big people. I hurried to the other side of the litter so he could look at me. I didn't want his eyes to lose their light again. We stayed focused on each other.

"Why this time, Abijah?" Master Isaiah said. "The bruises are partially healed, so it must have happened several days ago."

There was a long silence before the queen answered. "When he returned from the sacrifice to tell me about Bocheru"—she paused—"let's just say his explanation of the sacrifice didn't appease this ima's heart, and I required more convincing than he anticipated."

Mistress Aya held the queen in her arms again, this time gently, speaking quietly. "Hold to the truth respectfully but firmly in the face of his idolatry, Abbi."

The queen pushed her away. "The truth isn't respectful, Aya. It's a ruse. The truth is, I will worship Molek publicly, as my husband requires, to save the lives of my other two sons."

"But Abbi, you're the daughter of Yahweh's high priest. You can't—"

"I am Queen Abijah, and I will do whatever I must to keep my children alive." Her lips trembled. "I will bed a husband I despise. I will bow and feast with vile and ridiculous men whom my husband wishes to impress with my beauty. And if Yahweh has any mercy, He will kill Ahaz—or give me the courage to do it myself."

Master Isaiah glanced at Hezekiah and me and cleared his throat. "Please, Abijah, let's rejoice in today's victories and deal with—"

She glared at him and pointed at me. "This girl will be transferred to the harem. She's the only effective medicine for Hezekiah. I will not lose my son again."

"I'm sorry, but that's impossible." Mistress Aya met the queen's mean stare. "Ishma saw everything when her parents were killed in the raid on Bethlehem, Abbi. She's as fragile as your son, and I won't allow you to separate her—"

"You won't *allow* me, Aya?" The queen stepped toward the mistress, and I thought she might hurt her.

I buried my face against Hezekiah's chest. He placed his hand on my head and spoke, softly but firmly. "Ishma stays here, Ima."

My head popped up in time to see the queen's face become kinder. She smiled at her son. "You will be a merciful king, my son, but I fear—"

Master Isaiah stepped between his wife and the queen. "Perhaps I could bring Ishma with me and tutor Hezekiah privately in the harem until he is well enough to join the others."

Queen Abijah examined the prince and me as if we were fruit in the market. Finally, she said, "Will the girl overcome her fear of soldiers enough to enter the palace for lessons?"

"There are soldiers in the harem?" Fear made my voice squeaky.

Master Isaiah knelt before me. "In the Upper City, you will be surrounded by Jerusalem's soldiers and the king's royal guards. They are here to protect us, Ishma. We'll help you learn to trust them by introducing you to some of them, so you can see they're good men."

I still wasn't sure any soldier could be a good man, but I wanted to learn about things with the prince. I faced the queen. "I'll be brave. I promise."

Master Isaiah chuckled. "We'll begin lessons tomorrow."

The queen almost smiled. "She seems to trust you, Isaiah, as my best friend has trusted you all these years." She flicked her wrist as if shooing a fly. "Bring Ishma to my chamber for private tutoring with Hezekiah. Your teaching duties for the other royals are suspended until Hezekiah is strong enough to rejoin the class. And Isaiah . . ."

The master bowed. "Yes, my queen?"

"Ishma will join the class with Hezekiah when he grows stronger. He needs an ally he can trust implicitly."

"Yes, my queen."

"Bring my escort!" Queen Abijah shouted the order.

Hezekiah squeezed my hand. "Go inside, Ishma. I'll introduce you to my guard, Samuel, tomorrow."

I raced to the doorway but hid just inside so I could watch as the queen's guards carried the prince away. They were gentle. The biggest guard even smiled and talked to Hezekiah. Maybe when I visited the harem tomorrow, I wouldn't be so afraid. Maybe.

7

[Isaiah had said to King Ahaz,] "The Lord himself will give you a sign: The virgin will conceive and give birth to a son, and will call him Immanuel. . . . Before the boy knows enough to reject the wrong and choose the right, the land of the two kings you dread will be laid waste."

—Isaiah 7:14, 16

"You're absolutely sure she's pregnant?" Micah stood before Isaiah, breathless. Isaiah wasn't sure if he'd run all the way from Tekoa or if the younger prophet was simply amazed at the Lord's miracle.

"Aya told me this morning, and I sent a messenger for you right away." He placed a hand on Micah's shoulder to steady him. "Yaira had all the signs of a pregnancy, so we called for a midwife who confirmed it before we sent the messenger."

Micah's eyes misted, his jaw muscle tense. "Are you sure she wasn't defiled during the raid on Bethlehem or during the captive march? Many of the women were."

"I know, but Aya asked Yaira, and the girl said she'd never been with a man." Isaiah felt both excitement and trepidation, joy and sorrow at what the fulfillment meant. "She's the one, Micah. Your sister's pregnancy fulfills Yahweh's prophecy to King Ahaz. Her child will be Immanuel—God With Us—and while he's yet a toddler, both Israel and Aram will be laid waste."

Micah scrubbed his face, leaving his chest-length beard skewed in every direction. With a deep sigh, he shook his head and closed his eyes. "I don't feel Yahweh's breath on this."

Isaiah's patience was waning. "Is it Yaira you don't trust, or is it me?"

Micah's eyes slid open. "My hesitation has nothing to do with you or Yaira. I am a prophet, like you, and I don't feel Yahweh's affirmation in my spirit about this fulfillment."

"And I'm telling you we should take Yaira and announce the fulfillment at the same place I uttered the original prophecy to King Ahaz." Years ago, King Ahaz had spurned Yahweh's message at the most crowded watering hole in Jerusalem—the Upper Pool on the road to Launderer's Field.

"Absolutely not!" Micah shouted. "I will not make my sister a spectacle as you've done with your family."

His words cut deep. "A spectacle? Was my first vision too much of a spectacle? When the six-winged seraphim sang, 'Holy, holy, holy' at Yahweh's throne and then touched my lips with a burning coal—should I have hidden in my house? Aya treated those burns for weeks afterward." Isaiah wiped the tears that came unbidden. "No, Micah. I will make a *spectacle* whenever He asks me to do so."

Micah clasped Isaiah's shoulder, releasing a deep sigh. "I know you've suffered for the calling—as have all Yahweh's prophets. But let me ask two simple questions. If your answer is yes, I'll do as you say."

Isaiah nodded, feeling a mounting sense of dread.

"Did Yahweh specifically instruct you to take Yaira to the Upper Pool?"

Isaiah's cheeks and neck warmed. He must answer truthfully. "No. I did not hear that specific instruction from Yahweh."

"Did you specifically hear from Yahweh that Yaira's pregnancy was the fulfillment?"

"No, but she told Aya she's never—"

Micah lifted his hand, stifling the argument. "Please, my friend. Simply wait until you hear from Yahweh. I ask because if you're wrong, the ramifications for my sister's future are irreparable. She is young and was so frightened when I found her in Jericho. She's not prone to deceit, but in this situation both the truth and the lie are equally frightening. Let's give her—and Yahweh—more time."

Isaiah felt disappointment akin to waving a

white flag in battle. Why would he feel defeated unless his selfish pride was involved? Was it selfish to prove King Ahaz's failure or that Yahweh had released the captives, not Molek? His inner voice shouted, *Yahweh can prove Himself and will judge King Ahaz,* and won the fight.

"You're right," he said finally. "There's no reason to rush." Isaiah wrapped his arm around Micah's shoulders, reminding himself of the trust on which their friendship was built. Isaiah's years of experience didn't exclude him from the need for wise counsel. "Thank you for saying hard things to your old teacher. Can you join us for tonight's meal and return to camp tomorrow? I'm sure Yaira would welcome an extended visit from her brother."

"Of course. My students can spare me for a night. Repairs are going well. We've restored the teaching hall, several homes, and the pottery shop. Hosea's wife and daughter have resumed their pottery sales, which will help pay for supplies."

"We can send some grain home with you." Isaiah yearned to give more, but his coffers were still empty from feeding the needy in Jerusalem. Next month's food allotment was only a few days away. "If you come back next week, I can share more."

Micah stopped and grasped his friend's wrist, eyes penetrating Isaiah's heart. "You're sharing your home with my sister and Ishma. It's more than enough."

8

> [King] Ahaz sent messengers to say to Tiglath-Pileser king of Assyria, "I am your servant and vassal. Come up and save me out of the hand of the king of Aram and of the king of Israel."
>
> —2 Kings 16:7

Two weeks had passed since Micah challenged Isaiah to wait for Yahweh's instruction concerning Yaira's role in the prophecy. Isaiah had heard nothing from on high, which fed his growing uncertainty. Not that he doubted Yahweh, but rather he doubted his own ministry and effectiveness. Had he grown too old? Too proud? Too jaded by political scheming at court?

"Why haven't you left for class?" Aya stood in the doorway of his study, Ishma at her side. Both looked perturbed. It was Ishma's first day to join the class of boys, and she'd been nervous for a week.

"We just finished the morning meal, woman. Give me a moment." Isaiah pretended to pack his shoulder bag. How could he teach the royal offspring about Yahweh's instruction to His people when Isaiah himself was struggling to hear?

As he turned to upbraid his wife for nagging, the heat of Yahweh's presence descended, driving Isaiah to his knees.

"I am the LORD your God who makes you holy. Make love to the prophetess. She will conceive and give birth to a son. You will name him Maher-Shalal-Hash-Baz. For before the boy knows how to say 'My father' or 'My mother,' the wealth of Damascus and the plunder of Samaria will be carried off by the king of Assyria."

The heat subsided, and as quickly as Yahweh had come, His presence lifted, leaving Isaiah sweaty and breathless. Aya stood over him, whispering in prayer, and little Ishma knelt beside him, watching him with grave concern. Isaiah kissed Ishma's head and then stood to meet Aya's gaze. How does a husband tell his wife God has ordered them to conceive a son?

"What is it?" Aya's cheeks lost their color. "Did Yahweh confirm Yaira's pregnancy?"

Isaiah's chest constricted at the realization. No, indeed He did not. Were Micah's fears warranted? Was Yaira afraid to admit she'd been defiled? "No, my love. Yahweh spoke of something else entirely." He kissed her forehead. "We'll discuss it tonight before bed, but as you said"—he grabbed his bag, herded Ishma toward the door, and called over his shoulder—"Ishma and I are already late for this morning's class."

He dared not look back, certain his wife's

stare was burning a hole in his back. Tonight's conversation would be difficult. Both Isaiah and Aya were middle-aged, almost thirty-six. Their youngest son, Kadmiel, was twelve. How would Aya feel about another baby this late in life? *Yahweh, I remember Your throne room, the live coal that touched my lips. Please remind my wife of her calling to prepare her for this news.*

"Master Isaiah?" He looked down and found Ishma's dark eyes glistening. "Does Yahweh hurt you when He speaks?" She wrapped his legs in a spontaneous hug, and he felt he might melt in a puddle on the cobblestone street.

He loosened her grip and knelt to meet her fears. "Yahweh wasn't hurting me, Ishma. He is so holy and good that our frail bodies can barely stand a shadow of His presence. When I hear His voice, it is the most glorious feeling in the world."

She brightened a bit. "Can you tell me what He said?"

He took her hand and started walking up the palace stairs. "I must tell Mistress Aya before anyone else, but He has great plans for our family."

"Yaira says Yahweh has great plans for me too. That's why He saved me from the soldiers and brought me to your house."

Isaiah chuckled. "Perhaps we should talk about prophecy in our class today. Would you like that?" His lingering doubts had been relieved by this morning's encounter.

"As long as prop-up-seas don't make Hezi sad." She frowned. "I don't want his light to go out again." Ishma walked confidently past six royal guards at the palace's only public entrance. One gave her a covert wink. She'd stolen his heart the first week of their visits to Queen Abijah's chamber. Ishma had marched up to him, tugged at his hand, and asked if he promised never to whip her. Stunned, he dropped to his knees and took her hands in pledge. Ishma had similarly disarmed most of King Ahaz's guards by the second week of their visits.

Even Queen Abijah had softened toward her, giving Ishma permission to use the nickname the queen used for her son. "Hezi" had responded to Ishma's wit and care, returning to the fun-loving boy he'd been before, with only an occasional shadow of Molek stealing his joy.

After passing through the Great Court, Isaiah turned left down a hallway rather than leading his charge on the familiar path upstairs to the queen's chambers. Ishma's grip tightened as they continued down a narrow corridor, turned right, and then right again. Windows lining one side of the hall overlooked the king's courtyard and allowed the spring sun to warm the limestone floors and walls. Isaiah's heart skipped a beat when their classroom came into view.

Would Hezekiah integrate into the class smoothly, or would seeing his friends bring back memories of Bocheru's death and cause him to retreat into silence? Would the other boys accept Ishma? Or would they complain to their abbas and cause King Ahaz to overrule Queen Abijah's command that Ishma be admitted to class? Dragging in a sustaining breath, Isaiah stopped in the doorway of the last room on the right.

The scene was bedlam. Twenty boys pounded each other with pillows, shouted good-natured threats, and laughed over the shouting. Hezekiah was at the center of the mischief with Eliakim as his captain. A satisfied grin settled across Isaiah's face despite his obligation to end the fun. One of his fears had vanished.

Ishma pulled him down to hear her whisper, "Boys are silly goats."

Unable to curb his laughter, Isaiah's deep rumble sent his students scurrying to arrange their cushions in the prescribed circle for instruction. When they all sat quietly, Isaiah entered with Ishma in tow.

The tutor and new student received sidelong glances from most in the class, but Hezekiah scooted away from his younger brother, Mattaniah, making room in the circle. "Ishma can sit by me, Master Isaiah."

"Choose a cushion, Ishma." Isaiah pointed

to the far corner where myriad lonely pillows waited for an owner.

She looked up at him with those large eyes, pleading. If he could spare her the awkwardness, he would do so gladly, but everyone must endure firsts in life. Ishma lifted her chin and straightened her shoulders, then marched courageously across the room. She chose the brightest red pillow in the pile.

Well done, little Ishma.

Placing her prize between Queen Abijah's two sons, she met curious stares with her brightest smile. Ishma had come a long way from the speechless little urchin at Isaiah's door a few weeks ago.

"Let me introduce our new student, Ish—"

"I'm sorry to interrupt your class." Joseph, Isaiah's friend and the Levitical choir master, stood at the doorway with an odd-looking boy who slumped and studied his sandals. "Might I speak with you privately, Isaiah?"

"Of course, Joseph." Isaiah turned to his class. "I'm stepping into the hallway, and I expect all of you to behave as if your abbas were standing right beside you." He cast a concerned glance at Ishma, but Hezekiah was introducing her to Eliakim and Mattaniah. She would be fine in their care.

Joseph nudged the boy into the hall and began talking the moment Isaiah reached the doorway.

"This is my youngest son, Shebna. He's sixteen, but smaller than other boys. Born early. Nearly killed his ima. He couldn't manage military training or physical tasks at the Temple, so I hoped you could teach him something useful for service in the palace."

The boy didn't speak or meet Isaiah's gaze. Who would with an introduction like that? Isaiah examined Shebna more closely. The boy was the same height and build as ten-year-old Eliakim but had scraggly hairs on his chin. A sixteen-year-old with Shebna's appearance would find life among his peers difficult.

"Do you want to attend my class, Shebna?"

The boy nodded but didn't speak.

"Answer the teacher," his abba growled.

"Yes, my lord." The three words seemed forced, a phrase he likely recited often.

"There. You see? He'll be a good student, Isaiah. I assure you. If he causes any trouble, simply tell me, and I'll make sure he obeys."

Isaiah felt less inclined to help his Levite friend the more he talked. "I'm sure Shebna would be a great addition to my class, but perhaps if you spent more time with him, Joseph. Perhaps he could compose psalms or play the flute or—"

"Please, Master Isaiah." Shebna's head snapped up, eyes pleading. "Please let me join your class."

The grief on the boy's features was more convincing than his abba's demands. Isaiah found his heart consenting though his mind warned of the consequences. The royal advisors would complain about a girl in the class, and now he was adding a student from the servant class of Temple workers. The noblemen would be livid that a boy like Shebna was given the same education as their royal sons. "We've been friends a long time, Joseph, so I'll admit Shebna to my class."

Joseph nodded once. "Shalom, Isaiah." He turned and left without a backward glance.

Shebna, head bowed, whispered, "Thank you, Master Isaiah."

Isaiah laid his arm across the boy's shoulders and jostled him. "Come. Let's meet the rest of the class." Inside, Isaiah was screaming, *What have I done?* His students would tell their abbas, and the advisors would tell King Ahaz that Isaiah had lowered the standards of royal education. The palace tutor would be demoted again. Where to now? Royal stable boy?

Isaiah nudged Shebna into the room and began introductions. "Class, we have two new students this morning, so I'll work my way around the circle, introducing everyone. This is Shebna. His abba is the director of music at Yahweh's Temple." Isaiah noted the sneers from several young royals whose veins already surged with arrogance. Next he introduced the student who had shown great promise in their private sessions.

"This is Prince Hezekiah, second-born of King Ahaz. To his right is Eliakim, son of Hilkiah, the royal treasurer." He continued around the circle, naming each child with his abba's position in court. "And finally, this is Ishma, a child who lives under my care."

"Why would you teach a girl?" asked a nine-year-old boy, the son of the forced-labor director. "Abba says women are useful only for cooking, cleaning, and procreating." His brow wrinkled. "What is *procreating,* Master Isaiah?"

Before Isaiah could answer the delicate question, Eliakim shouted the reply. "Giving birth, you Philistine. The real question is, why does Master Isaiah try to teach you?" The younger boy's cheeks bloomed red as a rose.

"That's enough, both of you." Isaiah used the quarrel to sidestep a procreation discussion. "Perhaps we should focus on gratitude rather than begrudging Yahweh's blessing on others." He turned to Shebna, who had slipped behind him. "Choose a cushion from the pile and join the circle."

"Yes, my lord." Shebna lumbered toward the cushions while Isaiah chose a scroll.

When he looked up, Shebna had placed his cushion outside the circle. "Oh no, Shebna. No one is excluded or sits at the front or back of this class. I stand in the middle of the circle to ensure everyone has equal opportunity to learn." He took his place and waited for Shebna to move.

None of the advisors' sons would scoot aside. If some tried, the stronger boys pressured the weaker to refuse Shebna space. Just before Isaiah enforced his authority, little Mattaniah scooted over, making a place between him and Ishma. Shebna looked as if he'd eaten a rotten fig but set his cushion between them. Yes, it would be a miracle on the order of dividing the Red Sea if Yahweh kept Isaiah from being demoted by morning.

Refusing to surrender to defeat, Isaiah studied the scroll in his hand. He remembered the sunny day years ago, when he spoke these words to King Ahaz. "Today we'll begin a discussion on prophecy. Years ago, I relayed to King Ahaz God's promise to protect Judah from the kings of Israel and Aram and a warning if our king did not trust in Yahweh alone. God prom—"

"But Yahweh didn't protect us, Master Isaiah." Hezekiah interrupted, which he often did.

"True, but we must look at the full prophecy. Yahweh's protection was conditional. He said, 'If you don't stand on your faith, you won't stand at all.' He then challenged King Ahaz to ask for a sign, an unprecedented gift—anything the king asked in the deepest depths or the highest heights. The king refused." Isaiah paused, letting the weight of the statement settle in. "Think of it, children. If God threw open the gates of heaven and said He would do anything to show you the vastness of His power, what would you ask Him to do?"

"I want a horse!" Mattaniah shouted. His round face beamed.

Isaiah chuckled. "Think bigger, young prince. What about you, Shebna? How would you ask Yahweh to display His power?"

"I would ask Him to change my lineage." Anger boiled just beneath the surface. "Why do only Aaron's descendants become priests, while Levites clean waste pots and pound on drums?"

Some students snickered, while others looked wide eyed at the outspoken new boy.

"Surely, Shebna, you realize your abba and the Levites do much more than that."

The boy bowed his head. "Yes, my lord."

Determined to continue, Isaiah probed his other new student. "Ishma, what would you ask of Yahweh?"

Her cheeks instantly flamed, and the light in her eyes faded. Perhaps he shouldn't have called on her the first day. He was about to call on Eliakim when he heard her small voice. "I would ask for my abba and ima to come back from paradise and live with us at your house."

Isaiah nearly choked on sudden emotion. He hid behind the scroll in his hands, trying to regain composure. Clearing his throat, he lowered the scroll and was encouraged to continue by the upturned faces. It seemed today's topic had sparked his students' interest. "Very good. All of you. Did you notice everyone asked for something personal? But because I prophesied to King Ahaz publicly, he didn't dare ask for something personal, so he asked for nothing at all. Therefore—"

"Maybe Abba didn't ask because he was afraid Yahweh wouldn't answer." Hezekiah's voice again. "Yahweh doesn't always answer, you know."

Other boys nodded, and Ishma's eyes grew wide, as they always did when she was gathering her courage. "Yahweh didn't answer when I prayed for the soldiers who killed my parents to go away. Why is that, Master Isaiah?"

Isaiah felt a stab of fear at the consequence of his undertaking. He wasn't simply teaching Israel's history or even prophetic interpretation. He was shaping the foundational truths that would grow these children into their adult faith. *Yahweh, give me wisdom!*

"Hezekiah, you've reminded me of an important fact. Only God knows the motives of a man's heart, so I can't know the reason your abba refused the sign from Yahweh. However, when God promises something, He most certainly will do it. Someday—it may not be today or tomorrow or even in our lifetimes—but someday all Yahweh's promises *will* come to pass."

Eliakim raised his hand. "What else did Yahweh promise?"

The question hit Isaiah like a stone. In the specific prophecy they were discussing, Yahweh promised that a virgin would conceive, but he'd promised Micah he wouldn't discuss Yaira's possible role in the fulfillment until Yahweh gave clear direction.

"In this particular prophecy, God's promise was twofold. First, He promised that a virgin would conceive and give birth to a child who would embody God's presence on earth."

The appropriate *ooh*s and *aah*s filled the room. "I received another prophecy this morning," he said, "in which Yahweh promised His people would see a time such as we've never seen before—when Assyria attacks us." The room fell so silent, a feather would have clattered on the floor.

Isaiah looked into terrified little faces and prayed for more wisdom. "We don't know how or when Yahweh's promises will be fulfilled, but the reason for His promises is always the same. Can anyone tell me the single reason Yahweh will send a child with the embodiment of His presence and why He will send Assyria to harm His chosen people?"

The silence lingered. Heads bowed. Only one hand lifted tentatively.

"Eliakim?"

"Could it be the same reason my abba swats me with a stick?"

"Explain."

"When I disobey, Abba swats me, and it hurts. But he hugs me after and says he disciplined me because he loves me. Maybe God will send His presence to comfort at a time when His discipline is most severe."

"Eliakim, I think you explained it even better than I could." Isaiah must tell his friend Hilkiah that his son was soaking up his wisdom.

"Why would the Assyrians attack us?" Shebna stroked the few hairs on his chin. "Just yesterday, King Ahaz ordered the Levites to strip all the gold and silver from Yahweh's Temple to purchase Assyria's protection. So Israel and Aram won't attack us again. Why would Assyria attack us when we've made such a friendly arrangement?"

Isaiah felt the blood drain from his face. "King Ahaz is voluntarily paying tribute—without a demand from the Assyrians?"

Shebna's growing confidence suddenly waned. "I don't know what prompted the gift, Master Isaiah, only that the Levites are stripping the gold and silver as we speak."

Isaiah's insides churned, this morning's prophecy replaying in his mind. Aya would conceive a son, and before he could speak, Assyria would plunder the capitals of Israel and Aram. Two years. Three, at most. Would they keep advancing south? Flow into Judah—regardless of the Temple treasure King Ahaz offered? *Yahweh, show me.*

"Master Isaiah!" Hezekiah stood beside him, shaking his arm. "Are you well?"

"No, I . . . uh . . ." Isaiah wiped the sweat from his brow. "We're finished for today. Return to your homes and say nothing of our discussion. We'll resume class tomorrow." He returned the scroll he'd been reading to the shelf and hurried toward Ishma. "Come, little one. We're going home."

"Master Isaiah." Shebna was on his feet, panicked. "I hope I didn't offend you. Please don't tell my abba. I'll be quiet from now on. I can't go back to Temple work. Abba brought me here because I couldn't keep up with the other Levites who were stripping the gold and silver. If I fail here, he'll take me to the servants' quarters." His voice squeaked on the last word, tears filling his eyes.

Isaiah laid a hand on his shoulder. "You're a smart boy, Shebna, and I'm pleased to have you in my class. I won't say a word to your abba, and I'm thankful you told me about what's happening in the Temple." He grabbed Ishma's hand and hurried out the door, leaving Shebna looking relieved and the rest of the boys confused.

"Why are we going home?" Ishma's little legs ran to keep up with his long strides.

He swung her into his arms and jogged, his heart galloping with him. "Yahweh is speaking today, Ishma, first this way, then that. When He speaks, I must listen." How could he explain to a five-year-old that he knew in his gut this morning's prophecy was only the beginning of a fuller revelation—a revelation that he would soon present to King Ahaz?

9

Bind up this testimony of warning
and seal up God's instruction among my
disciples.

—Isaiah 8:16

The warmest days of summer were upon us. Yaira
and I had been in Master Isaiah's household for
almost five months. We kept count with pebbles,
one for each New Moon festival when we heard
wailing in the southern city. Master Isaiah said
they mourned for another child thrown into the
big statue—like Hezi's brother had been. Each
day after Yaira added a new pebble, our whole
household filled baskets of food and delivered
them to the Lower City. I think they called it
"lower" because the stinky stuff in the streets all
runs downhill.

Our family gathered in the courtyard for meals
since it was cooler than the kitchen with the cook
fire. Dinah and Leah woke me before dawn so
I could help prepare food to break our fast. I'd
learned all sorts of important jobs—grinding
grain, setting the table, hanging herbs to dry—
but mostly I did what Dinah and Leah told me.

"Ishma, will you fill a pitcher of water, please?"
Dinah was making gruel this morning. I liked

her porridge better than Leah's or Mistress Aya's because she added a little honey.

I grabbed a pitcher from the lowest shelf, hurried out to the courtyard, and filled it from our water barrel. It was Jashub's job to fill the barrel. He was nice. He tried to talk to Yaira a lot, but her cheeks always got red and she walked away. Master Isaiah's younger son, Kadmiel, might have been nice too, but he was always busy—cutting wood, practicing with his sword, fixing something that was broken. He didn't talk to women much. Only to Master Isaiah.

"Ishma! Hurry with the water!" Dinah was always in a hurry. Maybe she burned the gruel again.

I passed Yaira in the hallway on her way to the table. She slept late now because the baby in her tummy made her tired. Her belly had grown round like a rising lump of bread dough, but when I pushed on it, it was hard, not soft.

Mistress Aya slept late now too. Yesterday, I heard the mistress retching in her chamber. I asked Leah if we should send for the physician. She giggled and said the mistress would feel better in a few months. Why would she giggle about Mistress Aya being sick so long?

Dinah took the pitcher from my hands. "You can go sit down, Ishma. The gruel is ready."

The master and mistress were coming out of their chamber. "Good morning, Ishma." Mistress Aya's face was a funny color.

"Good morning, Mistress. I hope you feel better soon."

"Thank you, little love."

I hurried to my place beside Yaira while Mistress Aya lowered herself on the other side, at Master Isaiah's right hand. Mistress pushed away the bowl of gruel. The boys took their places at the table, Jashub on my left and Kadmiel beside him.

When Dinah and Leah sat down across from us, Master Isaiah cleared his throat. "Aya and I have an announcement to make. She is with child—as Yahweh foretold—and will likely deliver in the month of Shevat."

The boys reached for their porridge as if Master had just recounted the day's weather, but Yaira, Dinah, and Leah clapped their hands. I did too.

Mistress Aya reached for the master's hand, her smile falling off her face too quickly. It scared me a little. "We have more news," she said. "Your abba will prophesy to the king this morning."

Jashub and Kadmiel looked up from their gruel. "May I go with you, Abba?" This from Jashub, the smart one. When he wasn't training for war, he had a scroll in his hand.

"No, Son. Yahweh didn't include you in this prophecy as He did before." Master Isaiah smiled but didn't look like he meant it. "He did tell me your ima will bear a son, and we are to name him Maher-Shalal-Hash-Baz."

I slapped my forehead. "I can't even say prop-up-sea. How will I say *that* name?"

The whole family laughed, and my cheeks felt warm. Jashub nudged me with his shoulder. "It's *pro-phe-cy,* and we'll find a nickname for the baby like my nickname. I'm just Jashub, not Shear-Jashub, right?" He pecked a kiss on my forehead—the first time he'd ever done that—and kept talking with the others. Was this how it felt to have a brother? I scooted a little closer to him, widening the gap between Yaira and me. She looked a little sad. Or was she just tired? She'd been tired a lot lately.

We spent the rest of the meal talking about a nickname for Mistress Aya's baby. When our gruel was gone, Master offered a prayer of thanks. "Holy One of Israel, You do not desire sacrifice or offerings but rather justice, mercy, and sharing with the poor. Multiply our provision that we might share it with others. Let it be so."

He rose from the low table and kissed each of us atop our head. "Jashub, Kadmiel, be safe during training, and don't forget to drop off our extra provisions at the Temple. Zechariah has agreed to disperse them to the poor who come for worship." He moved around the table. "Yaira, help Mistress Aya, but don't overtire yourself. Make sure you both get some rest." She tucked her chin, shy when anyone made a fuss. He kissed my head too. "There will be no class today, so perhaps you should teach the women in this house what we've been learning about prop-up-sea."

I rolled my eyes. "Jashub says it's prop-ufff-u-sea."

Master Isaiah chuckled and kissed my head again. "Closer." He finished with kisses and instructions for Dinah and Leah. Then lingered with a whisper over Mistress Aya. She watched him go, her eyes filling with tears.

No matter how I said prop-ufff-u-sea, it made my tummy hurt this morning. I hoped Yahweh was real. I hoped He was watching and listening and protecting Master Isaiah when he spoke to King Ahaz this morning.

I was carding wool in the courtyard when I heard the awful sound. Soldiers' sandals, many of them, marching in perfect rhythm. The gate squeaked open. I looked up and saw Master Isaiah surrounded by royal guards, his face pinched like a raisin. I dropped my wool and ran into the house to wake Mistress Aya. She'd been sleeping all morning.

I crashed into Yaira, making her cry out. She doubled over and grabbed her tiny round tummy. "Sorry!" I kept running. "Mistress Aya, you must get up. Soldiers are leading the master home."

She was on her feet and tying the belt of her robe as she walked out of her chamber. We hurried to the courtyard, but the soldiers were gone. Master Isaiah was bracing Yaira's shoulders with Leah and Dinah standing alongside.

"What's going on?" Mistress Aya still sounded sleepy. "Where are the soldiers?"

Master Isaiah released Yaira to Dinah's care and pulled the mistress into his arms. "They've gone to carry out Ahaz's execution order. When I spoke Yahweh's prophecy of a perfect vineyard that only bore bad fruit, he ordered the immediate execution of all Yahweh's prophets."

I felt a cry in my throat but didn't let it out. Mistress Aya tried to squirm from Master's arms, but he held her tighter. "I'm safe for now because I'm royal family, but I must go warn the prophets at Tekoa before the king's guards arrive." He released her and hurried out the gate.

Yaira crumpled to the ground, crying out in pain. Mistress rushed to her side, placed a hand on her belly, and pressed here and there. When the mistress looked up, I could see bad news on her face. "Dinah, fetch the midwife. Leah, put a kettle of water over the fire."

Yaira pressed her face against Mistress Aya's chest. "I'm losing my baby, and the king will kill Micah. It's all my fault. Yahweh is punishing me."

Mistress wiped the sweat from her brow with her sleeve. "Our God does not attack young girls, Yaira. He loves you and the babe in your womb."

"No, Mistress. I lied. I lied."

"Shh. Don't talk now." Mistress looked at me. "Come, Ishma. Hold Yaira's hand."

I fell to my knees beside my friend. She groaned, leaning back on one arm, and gritted her teeth. Clutching her robe in the other hand, she scrunched up her face and grunted. *Oh, Yahweh, no!* She must have lost her words. Tears leaked from her eyes.

"It's going to be all right, Yaira," Mistress said. "Let's get you into a nice, soft bed." She helped Yaira stand, and I held my friend's tummy so nothing fell out. We started toward our chamber, but Mistress Aya pulled Yaira toward her own private quarters. "You'll need a soft bed and our full attention. Isaiah and I can sleep with the boys tonight."

"Mistress, no, I don't deserve—" Yaira stopped and doubled over again.

Doubled over. Like she did when I bumped into her earlier. Then I saw blood running down her leg. I was so afraid; my hand shook when I pointed. "Yaira, you're bleeding."

Yaira groaned again, her face pale.

"I bumped you. This is my fault!"

Yaira didn't talk. Only bit her bottom lip. Mistress Aya cradled her shoulders. "Breathe, Yaira. You can't hold your breath or you'll faint."

I backed away. This was my fault. I shouldn't touch Yaira again.

My friend drew a deep breath and took her next step, holding her belly with both hands. Tears ran down her cheeks. "This is not your fault, Ishma. It's mine." She tried not to cry and turned her face away from us. "This is Yahweh's judgment because I lied about being defiled in Bethlehem. I was too ashamed to admit it."

Mistress turned her around and hugged her. "I suspected you'd been hurt, sweet girl, but if this is God's discipline for your deceit, He will honor your penitent heart."

Yaira pulled from her arms. "He'll save my baby?"

Bracing Yaira's shoulders, Mistress Aya looked sad. "Yahweh is both just and merciful. We will pray, dear. We will pray."

"*Aah!*" Yaira clutched at her middle and crumpled to the floor. "This feels like punishment." She rocked and cried, blood staining the tiles beneath her.

Mistress Aya cradled her, rocking and crying with her.

I didn't know what to do, what to say. Then I remembered Eliakim's explanation of discipline. I knelt beside my Yaira. "If this is Yahweh's discipline for your lie, He will come near to show His love."

Yaira kept rocking, but her wailing stopped. Mistress looked at me as though I'd startled her. "Ishma, that's right." She laid her head against

Yaira's. "Let's get you to my chamber. Yahweh has not abandoned you. We'll get through this together."

She helped Yaira stand and looked over her shoulder at me. "Ishma, please go help Leah prepare strips of cloth. I'll send Dinah to fetch you when you may enter the chamber. We'll take good care of Yaira."

I stood in the hallway, watching the mistress take away my Yaira, my life. I hadn't prayed since the soldiers attacked Bethlehem. If my prayers didn't help then, would they help now? *Yahweh, show Your love to Yaira—and bring her back to me.*

I awoke feeling Mistress Aya's warm breath on my ear. I was cradled in her arms, lying on a blanket-covered mat. The moon shone bright in the window, and lamplight filled the master's bedchamber. Everywhere I looked, something beautiful stared back. Tapestries, gold-rimmed vases, wooden chests with robes and jewelry. The queen's bedchamber, where I'd had private lessons with Hezi, had been grander, but not much.

"Ishma?" Mistress Aya brushed my cheek.

I must have been too noisy. "I'm sorry I woke you."

She pulled me closer, cuddling me, like my ima used to do. "It's all right. I carried you in from your mat while you slept so you could see Yaira if you woke in the night."

The memories rushed back. "Yaira!"

Mistress squeezed me tight when I tried to get up. "Shh, little one. Yaira is sleeping. See?" She pointed toward the elevated bed with its wool-stuffed mattress above us.

I sat up to see my friend, curled into a ball, and then relaxed into Mistress's arms again.

"Yaira's baby died today, Ishma. She's very sad, but she'll feel better in time."

Questions churned in my belly. "Was it Yahweh's discipline? Did He come near even though the baby is gone?"

"I think Yaira feels only sadness right now, but in time, she'll feel Yahweh's love again." She released a deep sigh. "I don't believe Yaira's miscarriage was discipline for her deception, and it had nothing to do with you bumping into her. She lost this baby because the soldiers in Bethlehem hurt her badly." She hugged me tighter. "The midwives said it was a miracle she carried the child this long, and she may never be able to have other children."

The soldiers. Would the horrible men wearing swords and spears always hurt us? Here, in Mistress Aya's arms, I felt safe, but . . . Panic shot through me. "Did the soldiers hurt the prophets? Where is Master Isaiah?"

"I'm here, Ishma." The master had been lying

on the other side of the mattress but now stood so I could see him. He looked older after his visit to King Ahaz.

I wriggled away from Mistress, ran around the bed, and jumped into his arms. "Please don't go see the king again. I don't like him." He buried his scratchy beard in my neck, but I didn't mind.

"I don't think any of Yahweh's prophets will speak to King Ahaz again, little one."

"Why? Did he kill them?" I covered my mouth, hoping Yaira hadn't heard.

Master Isaiah kissed my cheek. "No, Ishma. The prophets are safe. Jashub, Kadmiel, and I arrived in Tekoa to warn them before the king's soldiers could attack." Master looked over my shoulder to the mistress. "We've hidden all the prophets and every sacred scroll in a safe place, so now we must feed them and care for their needs."

Mistress Aya patted his arm. Tears filled her eyes.

"Where did you hide them?" I asked the master.

"Someplace where we trust Yahweh will keep them from King Ahaz's army."

"How will you keep them hidden?"

Mistress chuckled and rubbed my back while the master explained. "Yahweh will protect His Word and His prophets." He lifted an eyebrow at his wife. "But we must provide for them."

"That means we have a lot of mouths to feed,

Ishma," Mistress said. "Can you help me prepare enough bread and cheese for them?"

I nodded until my head felt like it might fall off, which made them both smile.

"I'd like to stay with Micah." Yaira's voice startled us all.

Master Isaiah whirled to face the bed. I wriggled from his arms and rushed to Yaira's side. "We get to live with the prophets?"

Yaira brushed my cheek but didn't smile.

Mistress Aya sat on the bed beside us. "Yaira, you don't need to leave our household. I've asked the midwife to keep quiet about your pregnancy. I think we can trust her."

Yaira wiped her tears. "I mean no disrespect, Mistress, but we know how word travels in Jerusalem. I don't want to shadow the house of Isaiah with the presence of a defiled woman."

Master Isaiah knelt by the bed. "The house of Isaiah will protect you, Yaira. You need never fear—"

"I want to be with Micah." Yaira wiped her face on the lamb's-wool pillow, then returned her gaze to the master and mistress. "I can serve the prophets wherever they're hiding. They'll need someone to tend to their needs while they copy the scrolls and continue to train for Yahweh's work."

Master Isaiah raised both eyebrows at the mistress.

Mistress nodded. "All right," she said. "As soon as you've regained your strength, Isaiah will move your things to the cave, but you're always welcome to return to the house."

A cave? I wasn't sure if I was happy or sad to live in a cave. I tapped Master Isaiah's shoulder. "Will it be dark in there? I'm scared of the dark."

He patted my knee. "You must stay here with Mistress Aya and me, little one. The cave is no place for a child."

My face felt prickly. My hands too. "No! I'm going with Yaira." I tried to climb up with her, but I bumped her tummy. She groaned and pushed me away. "I'm sorry," I cried. "I didn't mean to hurt you. Don't leave me, Yaira! Don't leave—"

"Shh, little Ishma." Strong hands lifted me, cradled me, stroked my hair. "Yaira isn't leaving you." Master Isaiah was carrying me out of the chamber. "Shh. You'll still see her. Calm down. Listen."

I tried to stop crying. I tried to hear his words, but I could only see my Yaira weeping, weak, curled into a ball as the door closed behind us. Master walked down the hallway, past other bedchambers, through the kitchen, and out to the courtyard. The cool night air slapped my face and stilled my crying.

He sat me on his favorite stool and placed a second stool for himself across from me. "If you live in the prophets' cave, Ishma, you couldn't attend class with me. You wouldn't see Hezi or Eliakim or Mattaniah. Mistress Aya would miss you terribly, and how could you help Dinah and Leah take care of the new baby when he comes?"

I listened, head bowed. Finally, words came. "Why can't Yaira stay here?"

He lifted my chin to look at him. "You're old enough to hear the truth. Yaira will likely never marry because of what the soldiers did to her. She has chosen to serve Yahweh by serving the prophets. It's an honorable life for a woman like Yaira. It gives her a family and purpose."

"But we're her family. I'm her purpose."

"And we will remain her family, but remember what Yaira told you? Yahweh saved you for a greater purpose. Perhaps this is Yaira's greater purpose—to serve the prophets."

I didn't like that purpose. "Did you say I'd still get to see her?"

He nodded. "We've hidden the prophets to save their lives from King Ahaz's wrath. We've hidden the scrolls to preserve Yahweh's words for generations to come. Yahweh will protect them, but we must do our part to keep them safe. We must keep the location secret and take meals to the prophets once a day. You may accompany whoever takes the meal if we can trust you to keep the secret."

I looked toward the house, where Yaira lay so

sad in the master's chamber. I'd never spent a night away from her. She was my sun and moon and stars. But I remembered our journey from Jericho to Jerusalem and how, even then, she wanted to be with Micah.

"All right," I said, even though I didn't like it. "I'm good at keeping secrets."

He offered his hand, and I placed mine in his. "I'm proud of you. You're a brave girl." He stood. "Let's go assure Yaira that you're all right."

"May I stay outside for a few moments longer?" I asked, needing to think about what I might say before seeing my Yaira again.

"Of course, but not too long. We must get some rest. Tomorrow must appear to be a normal day in our household so the king can't prove we had anything to do with the missing prophets."

The master disappeared into the house, but I stayed outside to look at the stars and listen to the night sounds. The same sounds that had frightened me during the captive march now made me feel peaceful. Familiar birdsong lifted my eyes to the nearby palm trees, and I spied the dove's nest I'd first seen the day I met Hezi.

Only one bird sat in the nest. My tears started again. In all the time I'd watched the nest, both birds were there. Why now, when I must let Yaira leave me, had one dove chosen to go?

"Ishma?" Mistress called from the doorway. "Are you all right?" Seeing my tears, she rushed to hold me. "Isaiah said you understood that Yaira must go."

I laid my head on her shoulder. "I do understand, Mistress, but one of my doves is gone."

She held me at arm's length. "What do you mean?" I pointed at the nest in the tree, and she squinted to see in the moonlight. "Oh, little Ishma. Palm doves are night feeders. If we were to stay here all night, you would see the second dove return to the nest and the other one leave to find food." She brushed my cheek. "They'll both be back in their nest to sing us their songs in the morning."

I'm not sure why, but the news made my heart lighter. Maybe because it gave me hope that Yaira would someday come back to our nest.

PART 2

So the king of Assyria attacked the Aramean capital of Damascus . . . King Ahaz then went to Damascus to meet with King Tiglath-Pileser of Assyria. While he was there, he took special note of the altar. Then he sent a model of the altar to Uriah the priest, along with its design in full detail. Uriah followed the king's instructions and built an altar just like it, and it was ready before the king returned from Damascus.

—**2 Kings 16:9–11** (NLT)

10

Can a mother forget the baby at her breast
   and have no compassion on the child
   she has borne?
Though she may forget,
I will not forget you!

—Isaiah 49:15

"Ishma, hurry!" Mistress Aya called from the courtyard. "I've just fed Maher, and I want to get to the queen's chamber before he falls asleep."

Dinah stuffed a loaf of date bread in the basket to accompany the other delicacies she'd included for our hospitality offering. I crossed my arms, fighting the urge to empty the basket and ask the queen to give us food—since we'd been feeding the prophets for the past two years while her husband tried to kill them.

"Go!" Dinah nudged my shoulder. "We must pretend we have plenty, or the king will grow suspicious."

I grudgingly hoisted the basket and paused at the doorway leading to the courtyard, watching Mistress and little Maher feed my doves a few crusts of leftover bread. Master Isaiah had allowed me to cut out small niches in the east courtyard wall, where four pairs of turtle doves now nested. We also had five families of palm doves that returned each spring to our palm trees. They'd become my joy and my friends after Yaira left. I tended them like an overprotective ima, and when I stood very still, one of the doves would even light on my arm.

"Ishma!" Mistress called again and then jumped when she saw me in the doorway. "Oh, there you are. Let's walk. He's bored with the birds."

Maher had been fussy all morning. "Here, let me take his hand. I'll walk with him and tire him out for a good morning nap."

"Good idea." Mistress Aya traded me basket for babe, and I skipped while the little one giggled and tried to keep up. Maher was the center of my heart, my doves filled the edges, but Yaira was the one that made my heart beat.

I saw my best friend each morning, as Master Isaiah had promised. And every time I accompanied either the master or Jashub to deliver the prophets' meals, Yaira seemed a little more content. I was hurt by it at first. How could she be happy without me? Then I remembered praying Yahweh would be near her. I also remembered Master Isaiah's words—that perhaps serving the prophets was Yaira's purpose. I was almost eight now, so I understood what Master Isaiah called the "eternal picture."

Still, I missed my friend.

I glanced down at little Maher. He was getting

tired, so I stopped skipping and walked a little slower. Someday he'd grow up and go to school. What purpose might Yahweh have for him? I considered asking Mistress Aya, but she already thought I was too old for my age.

"Why does Queen Abijah want us to visit?" I asked instead, as we rounded the corner onto palace grounds.

Mistress lowered her voice and drew me close. "Her messenger said she had a new couch to show me, but we should assume King Ahaz has put her up to it again. Remember to guard everything you say to Hezi even though he's your friend. For his safety and ours, it's best he not know of your involvement with the prophets."

I nodded but didn't understand. Why would Hezi be in danger if he knew I took meals to the prophets? I had never told him because the master and mistress asked me not to, but Hezi would keep my secrets. I trusted him almost as much as I trusted Yaira.

After passing through the Great and Middle Courts, we ascended the stairs to the royal residence chambers. The king's six wives and their children lived on the second level; his guests were housed on the third. After climbing the single flight of stairs, we turned right and approached Queen Abijah's door—the first and grandest chamber. Little Maher tugged on my arm, so I hoisted him onto my hip.

One of the queen's two chamber guards knocked on her door and then poked his head inside. "Lady Aya and the girl to see you, my queen." We'd been visiting Queen Abijah at least once a month but he'd never used my name. I was always "the girl."

The double doors swung open, and the queen greeted us, Hezi at her side. He immediately reached for Maher, who went willingly into his arms. "Hi, little one. Did you come to play with me?" Maher's eyes sparkled at the attention. Hezi nudged my shoulder. "Want to play tag in the courtyard?"

Before I could answer, the queen spoiled the fun. "Why don't you and Ishma stay with us today, Hezi."

His face registered the disappointment I felt, but he said, "We can play my new game while they talk."

I faced Mistress Aya, waiting for silent permission. She nodded, smiled, and took Maher from Prince Hezekiah's arms. Maher wailed louder than the New Moon mourners. I halted midstep, ready to take the toddler with us, but Mistress Aya grinned. "He's fine, little mama. Go play with your friend."

Hezi and I ran down the crimson carpet that split the queen's large chamber. There were now three couches in the sitting area arranged in the shape of a horseshoe. The newest addition was a deep shade of blue with matching pillows trimmed in gold braid and tassels. I admired it on my way to the marble-topped table where Hezi had laid two new games.

"Each one is a wooden triangle with fifteen holes and fourteen pegs." He flashed his crooked smile. "You jump one peg over another into an open hole and remove the peg you've jumped over. Whoever ends with the least number of pegs remaining wins."

I nudged his shoulder and reached for one of the boards. "I'll beat you every time."

"Only if I let you win."

"Don't you dare!"

I was vaguely aware of the mistress and Queen Abijah arriving at the couches. Maher still howled like a wounded jackal, and the queen was becoming more agitated by the moment. I checked Hezi's game progress and saw that he had four pegs left. I only had three, but they were spread too far apart.

"Ha!" Hezi raised his fist. "I did it!" He'd skipped over two more pegs and now had only two left.

"Let's play again." I started resetting the pegs before he agreed, but I knew he'd consent. Whether we were playing board games, memorizing the Law, or racing across the palace court, Hezi and I competed—and I even won sometimes.

"Can't you quiet him?" Queen Abijah was nearly as frantic as Maher.

"I can, but you never like my solution." Mistress Aya grinned at her friend as she turned her back to Hezi and me.

"Honestly, Aya. You're married to the king's cousin. We have nursemaids for that sort of thing."

The chamber grew quiet except for the sound of Maher's contented swallows. "He'll be asleep in a few minutes, Abbi. Then I'll put him down in your bed."

Hezi kept his eyes on his game, his cheeks pink. Maybe he was distracted enough that I could beat him. I worked out my strategy before moving any pegs.

The queen cleared her throat, breaking the silence. "You know King Ahaz has ordered me to ask, Aya. Do you know where Isaiah has hidden the prophets?"

"What makes you think Isaiah helped with the prophets' disappearance?" Mistress Aya was clever. She didn't exactly lie. Just replied with a veiled question.

"If you don't want to tell me, don't tell me. But don't treat me like a fool. I know Isaiah has hidden them and has undoubtedly involved you in the conspiracy." The queen's voice quavered. "I'm not sure I could save you if King Ahaz discovered you were complicit."

"Which is the very reason I would never involve you, Abbi." The mistress hesitated. "I've always trusted you, my friend, but how can I ask you to keep a secret that your husband would do anything—hurt anyone, say anything, go anywhere—to discover?"

Hezi reached for my hand. I hadn't realized it was trembling. He sat down and patted the marble floor beside him. I obeyed without thinking, and he moved my hand with the pegs until only one peg remained on the board.

"We always win when we work together." His smile made my heart a little lighter, but I now realized why I could never tell him about the prophets. Mistress Aya was right. It was for Hezi's safety as well as ours.

I'd never even met King Ahaz—only seen him across the courtyard a time or two—but I hated him. Hated him more than the soldiers who hurt Yaira. Even more than the soldiers who killed Ima and Abba. Because King Ahaz kept hurting the people I loved.

Yahweh, if You hear me, why don't you hurt King Ahaz instead of good people like Yaira and my parents? He didn't answer right away, but maybe He would in time, like He did for Yaira.

11

Then King Ahaz went to Damascus to meet Tiglath-Pileser king of Assyria.
—2 Kings 16:10

Dawn's lavender hues tinged the eastern sky. Isaiah waited in the dark corner of their wine cellar, praying. Jashub and Ishma were late returning from the prophets' cave.

For two years Ishma had accompanied either Jashub or Isaiah through the dark hole in the floor, into the passageways under Jerusalem's western city, to the secluded caves in the wilderness hills. They'd provided food, clothing, and parchment for Yahweh's prophets and always arrived home before dawn, even though they made the lengthy trek without torches. The complete darkness kept them hidden from the king's relentless troops, and a left hand on the tunnel wall guided them to the prophets' cave. Isaiah's family had learned to trust Yahweh for both sight and safety.

The faint sound of sandals scraping the rock below stole Isaiah's breath. It grew louder, and he strained to see beyond the darkness. Finally, two shadows emerged from the gloom.

Isaiah extended his arm and pulled Ishma up first. "What took so long?" His tone was harsher than intended. Fear had that effect on an abba.

Ishma wilted into the opposite corner as he reached for Jashub, who slapped away the proffered hand and hoisted himself through the opening. "I needed to speak with a prophet." He stood to full height, meeting Isaiah's gaze, shoulders stiff, chin raised. Everything was a fight with his eldest these days.

Ishma tugged on his robe. "I'm sorry, Master." She alternated concerned glances between the two men. "I talked longer with Yaira today while Jashub talked to Micah."

"Go, help Dinah." Jashub nudged the girl, but it was his tone that bruised her.

Before she walked away, Isaiah caught her hand. "You've done nothing wrong. I was worried about you. That's all." She nodded and cast a withering glance at Jashub before trudging to the kitchen and closing the door behind her.

Isaiah exhaled his frustration and tried to remember how he'd felt at sixteen. "Ishma is tender, Jashub. Please speak gently to her." The boy's shoulders sagged, hard features softening. The dim light of two oil lamps cast a hint of gold in his brown curls. Isaiah's chest constricted. *My little boy is becoming a man. I must loosen my grip.* "I understand if you needed to talk about Yahweh with a prophet other than your abba."

"I needed to talk with Micah about a betrothal." Jashub's voice was quiet, tentative. "I want to marry Yaira, but he said I must get your permission first."

To say Isaiah felt surprise was like comparing Mount Hermon to an anthill. Yaira was fourteen, of marriageable age, but Jashub was sixteen, too young to support a family. Women could marry at Yaira's age, but men often waited into their midtwenties, until they completed military service or established themselves in a trade.

"I've already resigned from military training, Abba, and the chief scribe has agreed to make me his apprentice."

Isaiah no longer saw gold curls; he no longer saw the child he knew. He saw a deceptive teenager. "Why haven't you talked with me about this?"

"Because I knew you wouldn't approve." Jashub held his gaze. "I love Yaira, and I want to take care of her for the rest of our lives."

His mind reeling, Isaiah tried to decide which question would be least hurtful. Had Yaira pressed Jashub for marriage? Had Jashub considered the stain on Yaira's reputation and on Jashub's should he marry her? Yaira had no parents, and Micah certainly couldn't pay a dowry. Dragging in a deep breath, Isaiah decided on a much safer question. "Does Yaira feel the same about you?"

Jashub's gaze fell to his sandals. "She refused marriage, but I know she loves me."

"Did she say why she wouldn't marry you?"

"Yes."

Isaiah waited, but Jashub remained silent. "Did she tell you she may never bear a child of her own?"

"Yes, but the midwives don't know for certain she can't bear children." His eyes sparked with passion. "She thinks because we're born of the line of David, she's beneath us. None of that matters, Abba. I love her, and I know she loves me."

Isaiah filled the silence with prayer. *Yahweh, I have spoken with kings of many nations and have never been this frightened. Please, give me Your words for my son.* "Children are a gift from the Lord, Jashub, but not essential to a union. The love between husband and wife was God's first gift in the garden. If Yaira is to be your wife, she must come to you with her whole heart. I will not bless the marriage until she is equally convinced of the match."

"You know how stubborn she can be. She may never believe I can truly love her." Isaiah's son was suddenly the pouty-lipped boy he remembered.

"If you hope to be her husband, Jashub, you will learn to respect her feelings. Give Yahweh time to work in both your hearts."

The morning meal had been awkwardly silent. Isaiah hated the tension between himself and

Jashub, but what was he to do? Packing his shoulder bag for class, he released a sigh and resigned himself to being the parent of an adolescent boy.

The courtyard gate squeaked, and within moments Aya appeared at the door of his study, reading a scroll with a royal seal. Her face matched the color of the parchment when she looked up. "Queen Abijah has sent word that Hezekiah won't be in class today—or for many days. He's to accompany King Ahaz on a journey."

A knot formed in Isaiah's stomach. As far as Isaiah knew, the king had barely spoken to Hezekiah since the Molek sacrifice more than two years ago. "Where is King Ahaz taking him?"

"The Assyrians have subdued Aram and destroyed the capital, Damascus. King Tiglath-Pileser has invited all vassal kings to a special celebration to witness the way he treats rebellious nations."

The name *Tiglath-Pileser* tightened the knot in Isaiah's stomach. Assyria's king was the most vicious ruler in recorded history. Whispers about his insanity were widely shared, but those who whispered too loudly found themselves impaled on six-cubit poles.

The thought of Hezekiah in that madman's presence propelled Isaiah toward the door, but

Aya blocked his way. "You can't march into the palace and detain a prince." She laid a calming hand on his arm. "Take Ishma with you. Say you've come to bid farewell. Try to reason with the queen. Maybe she'll keep Hezekiah in Jerusalem." She patted his arm and turned away, hiding her emotion.

Only a moment's pause convinced Isaiah of his wife's wisdom. "Ishma!" he shouted. "We will cancel today's class and visit Hezekiah in the queen's chamber instead."

When she arrived at the door of his study, her gaze alternated from Aya to Isaiah and back again. "What's wrong?"

Isaiah inhaled a sustaining breath and tried to smile. "King Ahaz is traveling to Damascus to meet Tiglath-Pileser and has asked Hezekiah to accompany him." Fear flashed across her features, but Isaiah rushed ahead before she could speak. "We will go to Queen Abijah's chamber to ask that the prince remain in Jerusalem to continue his education instead."

Relief visibly calmed her. "Yes. Yes, let's go, Master Isaiah." She was out the door before Isaiah could kiss his wife.

Ishma was silent on their way to the palace, while Isaiah's heart reeled with the gruesome possibilities Hezekiah might face in Damascus. Surely, King Ahaz wouldn't sacrifice another son. Did he realize the Assyrians believed their patron god, Rimmon, averse to human sacrifice? But would Judah's failure to pay their tribute last month place Hezekiah's life in jeopardy for other reasons? *Yahweh, protect Your people despite the foolish decisions made by this faithless king.*

Isaiah and Ishma hurried up the palace stairs, through the Great and Middle Courts, and halted in front of the guards stationed at the harem stairs. "The child and I desire to visit Queen Abijah in order to wish Prince Hezekiah a safe journey."

The harem guards exchanged a puzzled glance. "How did you know about the prince's journey?"

The question sent a new bolt of fear up his spine. Was King Ahaz trying to keep Hezekiah's accompaniment a secret? "I'm a prophet. Do you really need to ask how I knew?"

Grudgingly, they stepped aside, allowing Isaiah and Ishma to pass. They reached the queen's chamber and found an old friend, Samuel, at her door. But he focused forward, offering no recognition when Isaiah and Ishma stood before him.

Isaiah had served four kings in his lifetime and dealt with many stubborn guards. He addressed Samuel and the other guard at the queen's door loud enough for every soldier in the king's family hallway to hear. "It's obvious that Queen Abijah would wish to spend as much time as possible with Prince Hezekiah before he leaves for

Damascus with King Ahaz tomorrow, but she'll want to hear what I have to say. Do you think it's coincidence that I—a prophet of Yahweh—have come instead of my wife on the eve of the young prince's departure?"

The guard standing beside Samuel swallowed loud enough to be heard. "How did you know about Damascus?"

A slow grin softened Samuel's features, but his focus remained forward. "Isaiah, you sly fox."

Isaiah lifted a single brow—letting the guards draw their own conclusions—and hoped the bluff would gain him and Ishma entrance. Within two heartbeats, Samuel opened the door and led them into the room without asking permission. "The prophet Isaiah, my queen." He bowed and exited quickly.

Queen Abijah sat on the deep blue couch, her back to the door, while Hezekiah sat on a second couch to her right. The prince looked up, saw Isaiah approaching, and whispered something to his ima.

"What is it, Isaiah?" Queen Abijah asked, rising slowly from her couch. With her back still turned, she stared out beyond her balcony.

Must he talk to the back of her head? Bothered by her rudeness, Isaiah moved straight to the point. "How could you allow King Ahaz to take Hezekiah to Damascus when you know—"

"*Allow* Ahaz?" Queen Abijah turned, revealing

a swollen and battered face. "This is what happens when I try to stop Ahaz. He's the king of Judah. No one *allows* him to do anything."

Isaiah stepped closer, but the queen stepped back. "I don't need your pity. I've learned how to use his rage to my advantage." She removed her head covering and shawl, showing more cuts and bruises on her neck and arms. "It took a little patience, but Ahaz agreed to name Hezi crown prince on the journey to Damascus."

Righteous fury rose in Isaiah's chest. "What if he beats Hezi like that? We must stop him, my queen."

"Who is 'we'? You and me? Or perhaps you mean you and your god." She scoffed. "Yahweh has done nothing to help me, and my abba is no longer high priest. So, you see, no power on heaven or earth will intervene for me." Her eyes began to fill, but she looked up at the ceiling, blinking. "Isaiah, I appreciate your concern, but the king of Judah will do as he pleases, and I believe I've secured my son's safety—my own way."

What did she mean by her *own way?* She was desperate, but how desperate? "There are laws set in place, Queen Abijah. Ways to restrain a king's behavior. The king's counsel has the right to question him."

"He replaces anyone on his counsel who disagrees with him. You know it. Everyone knows it. They're all too worried about filling their stomachs and coffers to worry about justice."

She was right. Hadn't Yahweh spoken those very words to him in a prophecy just days ago? Isaiah held her gaze, saw the utter hopelessness, and offered the only way out. "Yahweh has not forgotten you, Abijah."

"Well, I have forgotten him."

"Queen Abijah . . ."

She turned away, hugging her bruised arms and wounded spirit.

Isaiah's eyes fell on her son, still seated on the couch. "Prince Hezekiah, how do you feel about traveling so far with your abba?"

The boy said nothing. Simply stared at his hands.

His silence drew the queen's attention. She nudged his shoulder, requiring him to stand. "Come, Hezi. Master Isaiah has addressed you. Answer your subject like the king you will be."

The prince straightened his shoulders. Isaiah noted his red-rimmed eyes and wished he hadn't asked. The boy's chin quivered as he spoke. "I look forward to winning Abba's favor with my intellect and wit. It is on this journey that I will win Judah's throne." The words were practiced and not Hezekiah's own, but Isaiah could hope they were accurate.

Isaiah walked around the couches and knelt

before his student. "You will undoubtedly win your abba's favor if you show him yourself." He pulled him into a ferocious hug, wishing his arms were shields to protect him. Finally, letting go, he turned to Ishma. "Do you have anything to say to Hezekiah before we leave?"

Confusion etched her features as she alternated glances between the queen and prince. "I don't know who makes me sadder," she said. "I'm sorry you're so unhappy, Queen Abijah, but I don't want Hezi to go." She raced around the couches and hugged her friend just as fiercely.

He laid his head atop hers. "I'll see you when I get back. You must keep Eliakim and Shebna on their toes. They think they're smarter than you, but they're not."

"Of course they're not," she said, "but you are. Master Isaiah says I need you in class to keep me from becoming proud."

Even Queen Abijah chuckled at that, but she nudged the children apart, signaling the time for Isaiah's departure.

He bowed to the boy he loved like his own. "When I see you next time, I will address you as *Crown Prince* Hezekiah." Isaiah could only hope the title provided more safety for Hezekiah than it had for Bocheru.

12

In the time of Pekah king of Israel,
Tiglath-Pileser king of Assyria came and
. . . deported the people to Assyria. Then
Hoshea . . . conspired against Pekah. . . .
He attacked and assassinated him, and
then succeeded him as king [of Israel].
—2 Kings 15:29–30

Hezi woke with the morning sun gleaming off
the polished white limestone of Israel's palace in
Samaria. How did anyone sleep past sunrise in
this city? But it had been easier to sleep here than
in Damascus.

He and Abba left Jerusalem six months ago,
endured an excruciatingly long camel ride, and
arrived outside Damascus to find conquered
Arameans impaled on poles. Hezi's aching
backside was immediately forgotten.

Screaming. That's what he would remember
about the banquets King Tiglath-Pileser forced
his vassal kings to attend in Damascus. The
Assyrians screamed while they tortured. The
Arameans screamed as they died. And Hezi
screamed from night terrors every time he slept.
He'd never been so relieved to flee city gates—
what was left of a city and its gates, that is.

Hezi examined Samaria's palace chamber. It had been both home and prison for two months now, though it was larger and grander than his chamber in Jerusalem. He missed Ima, Mattaniah, Eliakim—and Ishma. Hezi closed his eyes and remembered. Ima's gentle hugs. Mattaniah's chubby cheeks. Eliakim's red, curly hair. Most of all, he wanted to see Ishma, the girl who would understand what his eyes had seen and his heart felt. Today, he and Abba would begin their journey home.

Abba had planned a short sojourn in Samaria after leaving Damascus, but King Tiglath-Pileser *suggested* Abba should "train Israel's new king in Assyrian loyalty." Abba obeyed the two-month time frame Assyria's king suggested. Who wouldn't agree after what they'd witnessed in Damascus?

Hezi moped for the first week in Samaria. Then a secret gift arrived: two parchments from home. Hidden under three layers of goat skins that covered his wool-stuffed mattress, Ishma's most recent parchment beckoned. He reached for it and read:

To the honorable Hezekiah ben Ahaz,
Prince of Judah, Son of David.
From Ishma bat Abraham, servant of
Isaiah, Royal Tutor.

Grace and peace to you.
It is my greatest hope that you received my first letter and that you are well. I

pray for you daily, asking Yahweh to keep you and give you wisdom for the day and hour.

Eliakim has entered his thirteenth year and left our class to begin military training, which leaves only Shebna to keep me humble. Return soon, or I may become insufferable.

Your friend.

The edges of the letter were worn and thinning, but Hezi still smiled when he read it. Leave it to Ishma to find a way to communicate. She was smarter than him and definitely braver. He hadn't the courage to sneak a letter back to Jerusalem.

At the beginning of their second week in Samaria, a Judean messenger had delivered a pile of scrolls to Abba. He waited until Abba was busy reading before slipping Ishma's letters from behind his back and passing them to Hezi. One of Ima's purple ribbons decorated the scrolls that bore her seal. Though grateful for Ima's help, he was suspicious. She'd seemed hesitant about his friendship with Ishma. Why encourage it now? He would question her when he returned home.

A knock at the door forced Hezi to stash the parchment under the mattress. "Come!" he shouted.

His chamber steward entered, bowed, and offered him a clean towel. "It has been my honor to serve you, Prince Hezekiah of Judah."

The steward, Enoch, was midforties, short, balding, round—and very kind. He'd been balm to Hezi's wounded soul after the trauma of Damascus. Enoch had rushed into the chamber each night when nightmares tortured Hezi, and he remained at Hezi's bedside until sleep claimed him again.

"How can I repay your kindness, Enoch?" Hezi reached for the offered towel.

Enoch maintained his grip, causing Hezi to look up. "Be a better king than the two who rule Israel and Judah now." He winked and released the towel.

Startled by his candor, the young prince stuttered. "I-I will be." Hezi bowed, showing Enoch the respect his honesty deserved.

The surprise on Enoch's face matched his pleasure. "I believe it, my lord."

On this journey, Hezi had learned to study people. Really *see* them. Each one had a story, and each one could teach him something. He'd learned something very important while studying his abba. He was as tortured as those he tormented.

Ima had long warned Hezi, *"Molek loves royal blood,"* and the fear of sharing Bocheru's fate taunted Hezi in the early days of the journey. But no longer. When Abba had introduced him as Crown Prince Hezekiah to both the Assyrian king and Israel's King Hoshea, Abba essentially gave his word to the world community. To kill his crown prince now would display instability and uncertainty in decision making. Both foreign kings would deem him a disgrace and failure—something Abba feared more than Assyrian torture. For the first time since that horrible night, Hezi felt safe from Molek's fires.

He threw the towel over his shoulder and splashed his face with water from a copper basin. Home would feel safer as crown prince. If Abba was willing to ride camels, they could be in Jerusalem by nightfall. More likely, he'd prefer lounging in the bouncy royal carriage, and they'd spend three days sweaty and grouchy. Hezi muffled a frustrated growl in his towel.

Enoch helped him slip into a fresh robe. Next came the gold belt, jeweled collar, prince's crown, and sandals. He was ready to break his fast with King Hoshea as he'd done every morning since they'd arrived in Israel.

The steward led him to the king's private chamber, where King Hoshea had begun hosting their morning meal six weeks ago when it became clear Abba wouldn't rise before midday. From the whispers Hezi heard, Abba drank most of his meals long into the night with various women pouring the wine. King Hoshea said it seemed silly for him and Hezi to dine alone in the vast banquet hall.

When Hezi rounded the corner, he halted at the threshold of the king's chamber, astonished at the waiting bounty.

"Good morning, young prince." King Hoshea, reclining at a low-lying ebony table, swept his hand over the veritable feast. "I've had the cook prepare all your favorites for your last morning in Samaria. Let it never be said that Israel starves her guests."

"Did I hear something about starving Judeans?" Abba rounded the corner, placing his heavy hand on Hezi's shoulder. "Like the Judeans your soldiers killed or took captive because we refused to join the coalition against Assyria?" Abba's challenge sounded like a clanging cymbal amid the morning pleasantries.

King Hoshea's smile died, his face going crimson. "You mistake me for my predecessor, who joined with Aram in the coalition. It was King Pekah who attacked Judah—and I who killed him. Assyria's king personally chose me to sit on Israel's throne."

"Yet it was King Tiglath-Pileser who sent me to measure your loyalty." Abba squeezed Hezi's shoulder and pushed him toward the table. "I fear you may be loyal to yourself alone, King Hoshea. For weeks you entice my son with rich food and me with fine women. I must ask myself, 'What could Israel's king want in return?' "

Again, Israel's king spread his hands across the

bountiful table. "Friendship, King Ahaz. Only friendship."

Hezi's heart raced in the silence. Two of Abba's guards stood inside the chamber, but King Hoshea's royal guards waited outside the door. Had Abba forgotten Israel's army was within range of a ram's horn? The same army that sent troops to Bethlehem to kill Ishma's parents. Hezi had been safe during the raid on Jerusalem, hidden in secret tunnels beneath the city. He'd never faced an Israelite's sword. Now, King Hoshea could order an end to Judah's king and crown prince with the flick of his wrist. Why would Abba risk their lives?

But Israel's new king was too calm. Too friendly. "Let us eat together and talk plainly. No more veiled words or hidden agendas. If Israel and Judah are to survive, we must rely on integrity and courage to withstand Assyria's aggression."

King Ahaz pressed Hezi onto a cushion beside the table. "In the four new moons we spent together in Damascus, did any of the dying men cry out for more integrity or courage?" He choked out a laugh and loomed over King Hoshea. "No. They begged for mercy against Assyrian justice. We would serve our nations better to speak of loyalty and service to Tiglath-Pileser."

King Hoshea nodded his assent, and Abba sat across from him. Israel's king passed a bowl full of pomegranates. "Here, Prince Hezekiah. I know these are your favorites."

Hezi reached for a ripe fruit, but Abba nudged his hand away and reached instead for a bowl of dates. "Now that your nation has felt the sting of Assyria's invasion, you speak of friendship. Judah has only just begun to harvest crops and drink from new wells after your predecessor's attacks three years ago. Will you spread a banquet table like this for my people? Offer them fruit and bread as you've offered my son since we've been here?"

Only now did Hezi realize his abba had a plan. He was negotiating. The Assyrian king had honored Abba for his loyalty at the Damascus banquet by presenting him with gruesome gifts and gestures. Abba had received them without flinching, praising King Tiglath-Pileser's god. Surely, King Hoshea knew the Assyrian king sent Abba as his spy—which gave Abba the advantage of Assyrian favor.

King Hoshea popped a date in his mouth and leaned back on his elbow. "I thought you'd be in a better mood since you're leaving for home today, King Ahaz. Three of our temple priestesses are nursing broken ribs from your rages. What would it take to make the king of Judah forgive Israel for our trespasses?"

A slow smile brightened Abba's face. "I want a tenth of Israel's harvest."

King Hoshea laughed. "And I want to sire the goddess Asherah's next son, but both of these things are impossible." Sobering, he leaned across the table. "I'll share three percent of the temple tax from my treasury."

"Five," Abba said.

"Four."

"Done!" Abba slammed his hand on the table, and Hezi jumped like a maiden.

Both kings laughed. "King Ahaz, you have a fine son. His only fault is kindness." King Hoshea lifted his goblet of spiced wine, eyes fixed on Abba.

"Not to worry," Abba said. "I'll break him of that."

The two regents laughed again as if they were friends, while Hezi tried not to reveal his disdain. Had King Hoshea been truthful about anything during the past two months? He'd told Hezi he would restore worship of Yahweh to the people of Israel. Did he say it to win favor with Judah's crown prince or because he believed it was best for Israel? Hezi could only hope and pray that—whatever the motivation—King Hoshea would do as he said.

Abba guzzled to the last drop of wine in his glass. "Come, Hezekiah. We have time for one last training session before we leave for home."

"Yes, Abba!" Hezi stuffed more bread and goat cheese in his mouth and jumped to his feet.

"May I join you?" King Hoshea asked.

Abba's eyes narrowed. "Of course. We'll meet you in the courtyard after we retrieve battle gear from our chambers." The kings nodded in agreement, and Hezi moved to brace Abba's arm. He slapped away his son's help and rocked to his feet, marching ahead of him out the door.

The guest wing of Samaria's palace wasn't as large as the third floor of Solomon's palace in Jerusalem, but King Ahaz still needed the palace stewards to guide him. Hezi watched Judah's king weave as he walked, realizing he'd negotiated while wine still muddled his mind. How effective could his abba be if his mind was actually clear? How much more effective could he be if he turned to Yahweh? Before this journey together, Hezi hadn't realized his abba's frailty. He'd never seen King Ahaz, the man—his fear, his weakness, or his underlying drive to succeed. Master Isaiah's prophecy came screaming back: *If you do not stand firm in your faith, you will not stand at all.*

His abba was barely standing.

Leaving Abba in his chamber, Hezi walked farther down the hall, entered his chamber, and donned his training armor. He opened his travel trunk and strapped on the sword Abba had given him when they began their journey. Hurrying out the door, he found Abba waiting in full battle armor. Hezi's face must have registered surprise.

"When an enemy is eager to play with swords, we must make sure our swords are sharpest." Abba threw a silk scarf in the air and drew his sword, letting the scarf fall across its blade. The scarf fell to the floor in two pieces. Abba chuckled. "If she had wanted her scarf returned, she shouldn't have left it in my chamber." He started walking toward the courtyard but looked over his shoulder. "You mustn't tell your ima—I mean about your sword training. She'll say you're too young."

Hezekiah hurried to catch up. "I'm almost twelve. I start military training next year."

Abba looked at Hezekiah from beneath bushy red brows. "Yes, say it just like that if she ever finds out." Despite Abba's drinking, his carousing, his weight—he was still one of Judah's best swordsmen, and Hezi was honored by his personal instruction.

"Thank you, Abba." Hezi kept his eyes forward. Abba hated gushing.

Judah's king walked on as if he hadn't heard.

"And thank you for joining King Hoshea and me for a meal this morn—"

Abba turned abruptly, gathering Hezekiah's robe in his fist. "Joining King Hoshea and you for a meal? Don't think because you've become friendly with King Hoshea that you've secured my throne!"

Hezekiah shook his head violently. "I didn't. I don't. I only meant—"

145

"You are *my* son!" He pulled Hezekiah into a crushing hug. "The only good thing I've ever done."

Confused and terrified, Hezekiah wasn't sure whether he'd been reprimanded or shown affection. But he was certain of his abba's tortured soul, and for that Hezekiah returned the embrace. He whispered against his abba's ear, "I am and will always be Hezekiah ben Ahaz."

13

"The multitude of your sacrifices—what
    are they to me?" says the LORD.
"I have more than enough of burnt
    offerings, of rams and the fat of fattened
    animals. . . .
They have become a burden to me; I am
    weary of bearing them."
                                    —Isaiah 1:11, 14

Whispers of the king's return first came three
days ago with traveling merchants. Then the
royal heralds shouted in Jerusalem's streets late
last night, "The king returns tomorrow!"

Master Isaiah canceled class for today. The
market was closed. Military training ceased.
Everyone was expected to line the streets of
Jerusalem and welcome home a king they hated.

I didn't sleep a wink. Yaira noticed this
morning when Master and I delivered supplies
to the prophets. "What's wrong?" she asked.
"You look awful."

Master Isaiah whispered as he walked past,
"Hezi comes home today."

She muffled a squeal, and I joined her. "What
will you wear?" she asked. "Oh, I wish I could
braid your hair with a pretty red ribbon."

"Mistress Aya wants all of us to wear our best robes. We must appear well supplied on Master Isaiah's allowance as royal tutor."

"Did the queen send Hezi your letters as she promised?"

"I don't know." My stomach flip-flopped. "He never wrote back."

Too soon it was time to leave the caves. Master Isaiah and I crept through the darkness, keeping one hand on the wall to guide us. He hoisted me through the cellar floor into Jashub's waiting arms and then climbed onto the cool tiles. I hurried to help the women in the kitchen, hoping to stay busy and speed Hezi's return. We ate our morning meal; Dinah fixed my hair; I carded wool. The sun moved like a slug across the sky. Where was the king's procession?

After our midday meal, the trumpets blared, and I thought I might jump out of my skin. I raced to the courtyard gate, but Mistress called out, "We're walking like royalty to greet royalty, my girl, not running like a horse in a race." Sometimes it was hard to remember that we were a part of David's royal house. The master and mistress were so kind and generous compared to other royalty. However, certain customs were as absolute as the Law of Moses. An eight-year-old girl must *walk*.

We stood outside Master's courtyard to watch the royal procession enter the gate of the Upper

City. A contingent of soldiers came first, riding past the noblemen's houses on their right, guiding their battle-scarred horses straight toward us. I scooted closer to Master Isaiah, still unnerved by the clanging of soldiers' swords.

Next came six of the king's royal guard followed by the grand carriage with its golden wheels and purple sashes. I tried to peek inside when it halted at the palace stairs, but the curtains were drawn across the windows.

While looking down the street, I realized the other noblemen standing outside their courtyards weren't cheering the king's return. Shouldn't people celebrate when a king comes home?

When the door of the royal carriage swung open and King Ahaz emerged, I watched the waiting advisors and their families. All were dressed in fine robes, like we were, but their smiles and modest applause were as false as the floor in our wine cellar. Mistress tugged on my arm, and I bowed with the rest of the household. I lifted my eyes in time to see the king straighten his robe, lift his chin, and begin a lonely walk up the palace stairs.

The crowd quickly dispersed, but my focus remained on the golden coach. A little gasp escaped when Hezi stepped out. My friend was taller, his shoulders wider. He wore a golden band around his head. Suddenly, I felt as if I didn't know the boy—the prince—who stood at the palace steps. He waved at the crowd and cast a glance over his shoulder in our direction. My heart raced. I lifted my hand to wave, but he turned away and caught up with King Ahaz.

He disappeared into the palace, and I felt utterly defeated. Had he seen me and ignored my greeting? Or did he hope to see me but feel compelled to join his abba before our eyes met? Either way, Hezi had no time for the girl he once knew.

Baby Maher slid his chubby hand into mine. His smile warmed my heart and refocused my attention. "Come, little one. Let's feed the doves."

The rest of the household scattered to various projects and pastimes. Seldom did we get a day to do as we pleased. Jashub had promised to copy one of Master Isaiah's prophecies to a new scroll. Kadmiel planned to finish construction on Mistress Aya's new loom. Dinah, Leah, and the mistress hoped to dye all the thread we'd spun during the past week. Master Isaiah followed Maher and me to the dovecote. The master had helped me carve five new holes into the wall, each the size of a man's fist, since my doves were having babies and liked to nest in our garden. I helped Maher break a few dried crusts of bread to the proper size for our birds to eat.

Master Isaiah joined us, standing a camel length from the wall, tossing the crumbs to the packed earth and watching the birds descend on them. "Don't rush at the birds, Maher," he said. "Turtle doves are shy. We mustn't frighten them."

"Watch me, Maher." I settled him on a stool beside me. Then, holding a bread crumb in my hand, I lifted my forearm and began imitating the dove's song. Master and Maher were utterly still as my favorite palm dove descended to my arm. I whispered to her and fed her two more crumbs before Maher came bounding up and frightened her back to her nest.

He was so excited; I couldn't be angry with him. "Ishma, I want to do that!" He grabbed a bread crumb and started hooting, "Here bird! Come to me, bird!"

I heard laughter and found the whole household standing at the doorway. My cheeks burned at the thought of everyone seeing me call to my dove. Did they think my cooing was silly?

Mistress Aya stopped laughing and came to me. "You have a rare gift, Ishma. Doves don't trust everyone. Pigeons are easily trained and submit to anyone who feeds them, but doves . . ." She tilted my chin to look in my eyes. "Doves are tenderhearted, my girl. A rare breed." She hugged me. "Like you."

My throat was too tight to speak. I hugged her, hoping she knew I loved her, and kept my words simple. "Thank you."

Master Isaiah laid his hand on my shoulder, and

Mistress released me to face him. "How would you feel about helping me clean our classroom today? I don't suppose Prince Hezekiah realizes class was canceled. We wouldn't want him to arrive at an empty classroom."

I bowed my head, suddenly unnerved at the possibility of seeing Hezi. "I'm happy to serve, Master Isaiah."

"Go change your robe, dear." Mistress gave me a gentle nudge.

I trudged to the dressing chamber now shared by Dinah, Leah, and me. In it we kept all our clothes, linens, combs, and accessories. We slept in the adjoining second chamber. Choosing my worn school robe from the peg on the wall, I wondered for the first time if Hezi would think it plain. Would he think *me* plain? What if Hezi thought me boring? He'd met the horrible King Tiglath-Pileser. He'd lived within the walls of Samaria's palace—a city where I was denied entry even as a captive. Was there anything Hezi could like about me after all he'd seen and experienced?

"Ishma, let's go." Master Isaiah's deep voice echoed through the residence hallway.

"Coming!" I donned the plain robe, tied the belt, and stepped into the hall. If Hezi thought me plain, I must impress him with all I'd learned while he was gone.

Master Isaiah was waiting in the courtyard with his shoulder bag. We said good-bye to Mistress

Aya and Maher, whose backs were bent tending the garden.

I was deep in thought when Master's voice startled me. "You haven't said a word. What's bothering you?"

I felt silly for all my worrying, but perhaps the master would know. "Do you think this journey changed Hezi? Will he still like me?"

Master stopped and knelt beside me. "Of course he'll still like you, but I'm sure the things Hezekiah saw changed him. We must ask our friend good questions today, Ishma, and be good listeners."

Questions weren't so hard. "I can ask questions."

"Good girl." He stood and put his arm around my shoulders as we resumed our hurried pace to the classroom. Turning right, down the final hallway, we saw one lonely student waiting by the door.

Eliakim turned at the sound of our footsteps, but his excitement died when he saw us. "I had hoped to find Hezekiah here," he said. "All military training was canceled for the king's return. I have time to talk today but won't when training resumes tomorrow." Eliakim looked at me and then at the floor. I could tell he wanted to speak with the master privately.

"I can wait here in the hall if you two want to talk in the classroom."

Master Isaiah nodded and followed Eliakim across the threshold. I tried not to listen. I covered my ears, closed my eyes, and slid down the wall, sitting on the cool marble floor. I couldn't stand it. I uncovered one ear and heard just a little. Eliakim said something about his grueling training schedule, fear of his and Hezi's friendship changing because their worlds had changed. Eliakim was feeling some of my fears.

"What are you doing out here?" Hezekiah ben Ahaz stood over me, the sun casting a glow above his head that made him look like an angel.

I sprang to my feet and straightened my robe, my belt, my hair. If only I could straighten my words. "I was . . . I'm just . . . Eliakim is . . ."

He laughed. "I'd hoped to see you today and thank you for your letters." His neck and cheeks got splotchy red, and then we both stood awkwardly silent in the doorway.

"Hez!" Eliakim nearly tackled him with a hug. "You're here!"

Master Isaiah followed, eyes misty. "Welcome home, Hezekiah. We've missed you."

Eliakim pulled Hezi into the classroom. Master Isaiah joined them, but I hesitated a moment. I had the strange feeling I needed permission to join them. I didn't know why. I'd always felt comfortable with Eliakim and Hezi before.

"Tell us about Damascus, Hez." Eliakim sat on one of the four cushions the master had placed on the floor. "What were the Assyrians like? My commander says they're the most disciplined army in the world."

Hezi's face lost its color, and he turned to Master Isaiah, eyes pleading. "I was hoping you could first tell me about the class. What have you been teaching?" He looked at Eliakim and tugged on his leather breast piece. "I want to know about your training. Do you have to wear this all the time?"

"No. Our commander ordered us to wear partial armor to greet the procession." Eliakim waved away the question. "None of this is nearly as interesting as your journey. Come on, Hez."

I sat on my cushion but scooted close to Master Isaiah. Finally, Hezi looked at me. "And what about you, little Ishma?"

Little Ishma? He may have sprouted a few hairs on his chin, but he wasn't suddenly so old, and I was not *little Ishma*. "I believe your nose is larger than when you left," I said.

He grinned. "Well, at least I have a nose. Yours looks like Yahweh put a button there instead."

It felt good to tease. Normal. But his smile died too quickly. Master Isaiah noticed too. "Do you want to talk about your trip, Hezekiah? I've canceled class today. No one will interrupt us."

His cheeks and neck got pink, and his eyes found his sandals. "I can tell you some of it, but I don't want to tell all of it in front of Ishma."

Why not tell me? I started to fuss, but Master Isaiah lifted his hand. His eyebrows drew together, warning me to keep silent. I did. Even though I wanted to argue.

"Tell us only what you think is appropriate."

Hezi could decide what to tell as long as he included why he looked so sad. He began with the journey to Damascus, the Assyrians, the torture. Eliakim's excitement dwindled, and my stomach started to roll. Hezi stared into the distance as he told the stories, his eyes filling with tears. He would wipe them away, and new tears would come. I didn't know what to say. I didn't even have questions like Master Isaiah suggested. I could only listen, and even that was hard.

Hezi blinked a few times, as if waking from a dream, and then turned to Master Isaiah. "I learned a lot about Abba and why he worships other gods. He saw Assyria's brutality and decided their god, Rimmon, was greater than any other because Assyria's army has had greater success than any other. So he had plans drawn up to duplicate Rimmon's altar here in Jerusalem."

"An altar to Rimmon in Jerusalem?" Master Isaiah sounded both angry and surprised. "Will he fill the whole Valley of Hinnom with pagan altars?"

Hezi looked at him, equally confused. "The new altar was to be built in Yahweh's Temple.

How could you not have seen it when you attended sacrifices?"

Isaiah dragged his hands through his hair. "Hezekiah, I haven't attended the sacrifices for months."

"What? Why?" Hezi's voice rose. "If you'd attended the daily sacrifices, you could have talked to Uriah, maybe reasoned with him—"

"Yahweh spoke to me a few weeks after you left for Damascus and said, 'I've had more than enough of burnt offerings, of rams and the fat of fattened animals.' He even said, 'Stop bringing meaningless offerings! Your incense is detestable to me.' So I haven't stepped into the Temple courts since that day."

Hezi's shoulders lifted, his spine straight, chin held high. "If those with the light never walk the narrow path, how will the lost find their way?"

I stared at Prince Hezekiah and wasn't sure whether to be offended or proud that he would address Yahweh's prophet with such assurance. Where had he learned about lights and paths and the lost?

Master Isaiah's features softened, and he nodded. "You make a valid point, Prince Hezekiah, but a prophet must obey the word of the Lord no matter how foolish or harsh it appears. If you, however, believe you can speak to Uriah and make him understand . . ."

"You know I can't." Hezi picked at a loose

157

thread on his cushion. "Abba named me crown prince, but I've had no coronation as co-regent. I believe I'm safe from Molek's fires, but no one is safe from other ways Abba shows his wrath."

My stomach turned at the thought of Hezi living in constant fear, but at least there was hope for his future. "Now that you're crown prince," I said, "we know one day you'll lead Judah back to the light. Maybe even now you can find ways to help people return to Yahweh."

Eliakim sat straight as a measuring rod. "Maybe we can all help. I'm getting pretty good with my sword."

I looked at Master Isaiah, panicked. I didn't want Eliakim to fight. Seeing him in a soldier's breast piece was hard enough.

Hezi shoved Eliakim's shoulder, regaining some of his old spark. "The sword may not be the way to lead Judah to the light, but it's a good way to prove our worth to my abba."

"No!" I jumped to my feet. "You can't fight— either of you."

"Shh." Master Isaiah held out his hand, inviting me back to my cushion. "Ishma, sit down. Remember, today we listen."

His stern expression told me not to argue. I obeyed the master, keeping my head bowed so I didn't have to see the boys' faces. They were changing, and I didn't like it. Why did things have to change?

The master laid a gentle hand on my arm. "Every boy is trained to fight when he reaches the age of manhood. In another year Hezekiah will be thirteen and will leave our class to begin training like Eliakim, but they can still be your friends."

I tried to blink away my tears, but they wouldn't stop. I kept my head down so they'd drip into my lap.

"We'll always be friends, Ishma." Eliakim nudged my knee as he stood. "I need to get home. Hez, can you come over for archery practice? This is my only day off until the new moon."

The silence told me Hezi was undecided, but I didn't look up. "I need to tell Ishma something. Go ahead, Eli. I'm right behind you."

I covered my face with my hands. Why didn't he just go? This wasn't at all how I wanted our first meeting to be.

He gently pulled my hands away and tipped my chin, but I refused to look up. "Please, Ishma. Look at me."

Master Isaiah patted my shoulder. "I'll wait at the door and let you two talk."

I didn't want to talk, but Hezi waited . . . and waited. "Just go with Eliakim," I said.

"I need to thank you first."

My breath caught. Thank me? "Why?" I squeaked out the word.

He dangled a purple ribbon in front of my eyes,

forcing me to look up. I wiped my face and took it but must have shown my confusion.

"Ima wrapped it around your letters. Didn't you know she sent them?"

"She said she would, but I wasn't sure—" I gasped, realizing what my words implied. "I mean, of course she would if she said so."

His eyes were sad again, and he brushed my cheek. "No. Neither of my parents speaks truth, but she sent them, and I read them every day I was in Samaria."

"Samaria?" The word cut my heart like a dagger. "Why did your abba go to Israel—the same Israel that attacked Bethlehem and killed my parents?"

He straightened. "It wasn't my choice to go there, Ishma, but I'm glad we did. Abba negotiated an important treaty with King Hoshea while we were there."

"How long did you stay?"

"Two months."

I felt like the floor shifted beneath me. "Did they hold you prisoner?"

He laughed, seeming relieved. "No, no. King Hoshea was very hospitable."

"Hospitable?" I couldn't believe what I was hearing. "The army that killed my parents, burned Judean villages, and destroyed Jerusalem's southern city was hospitable?"

Master Isaiah was suddenly standing behind me. "Is everything all right?"

Hezi stood, and I stood to meet his challenge. "Ishma is upset, Master Isaiah, that the letters she wrote consoled me while I stayed in Israel for two months. She seems equally upset that I was not imprisoned or tortured by King Hoshea while there." He lifted his eyebrows, waiting for me to respond.

I turned to Master Isaiah, expecting him to expound on Israel's evils. Instead, he asked Hezi, "Was anything accomplished during your two-month visit in Israel?"

Why did it matter? Israel was our enemy.

Hezi nodded. "Abba secured a four percent tribute for Judah from Israel's treasury, and I received a promise from King Hoshea to reinstitute Yahweh worship among his people."

Money for Judah's treasury and a return of Israel's tribes to Yahweh. Everything I'd learned from Master Isaiah about foreign relations told me King Ahaz and Hezi had been successful in a difficult negotiation. But I felt like they'd discarded my stolen past when they made a treaty with Israel for the future.

Master Isaiah stared at Hezi, eyes narrowed, really studying him. Did he agree that Hezi had betrayed us, or would he side with Hezi?

Hezi's cheeks grew red. "Did I do something wrong, Master Isaiah?"

Our teacher shook his head, and his features brightened. "Hezekiah, I believe you will usher in a kingdom of peace in Judah such as God's chosen people have never seen before." His eyes grew misty again. "I believe you are the anointed Son of David Yahweh has spoken of in my prophecies."

Hezi looked as confused as I felt. "Master Isaiah," he said, "I've never heard you speak of an anointed Son of David."

"In the days since the prophets have been hidden, the Lord has spoken much, but His words have been hidden on parchment. The prophecies will one day be revealed, and I will teach them plainly, but for now"—he hesitated and placed a hand on Hezi's shoulder—"we need not discuss the anointed Deliverer today. Hezekiah, go practice archery with Eliakim. Ishma and I will see you in class tomorrow."

Hezi tucked my letters back into his belt and nudged my shoulder. "See you tomorrow, friend."

14

So Uriah the priest built an altar in accordance with all the plans that King Ahaz had sent from Damascus and finished it before King Ahaz returned. When the king came back from Damascus and saw the altar, he approached it and presented offerings on it.

—2 Kings 16:11–12

Hezekiah was glad to be home, but everything felt different. Because of his military training, Eliakim wouldn't be in class anymore. Master Isaiah suddenly thought Yahweh had chosen Hezekiah to bring peace to the whole world. And Ishma . . . He had thought that, of all those in his life, she might understand how the atrocities in Damascus had affected him. But her look of horror as he recounted the banquets made it clear he couldn't share more deeply.

"Hezi, you're moping." Ima set aside her embroidery. "The next king of Judah should not mope."

"The next king of Judah should do as he pleases." The words slipped out before he could restrain them. He looked at her, expecting a sharp reprimand. "Ima, I'm sorry!"

"My second-born isn't perfect after all," she said with a smile and then patted the seat beside her. "Tell me what's troubling you."

He left his game on the floor and flopped onto the couch. "I feel different."

"You are different. You're the crown prince."

Was that all she thought about? "But Eliakim and Ishma are different too."

"Hmm. Eliakim is training to be a soldier—as he should." She lifted a single brow. "Was Ishma upset that her letters were delivered to you in Samaria?"

Hezi tried not to react—tried not to accuse his ima of scheming before he gathered more facts. "I was surprised you sent her letters to me at all, Ima. You haven't encouraged our friendship recently."

She began to twirl his hair around her finger. "I sent the letters because I knew they would force you to tell Ishma you were in Samaria."

"I would have told her anyway," he said. "But I'm glad you sent them."

Ima stopped twirling his hair and laced her fingers together, knuckles white. "How did she react to the treaty you and your abba struck with King Hoshea?"

"I'm not going to talk about Ishma with you, Ima."

Ima smiled, sending dread up Hezi's spine. "What have you done now?" he asked.

"I've invited Isaiah and Ishma to my chamber this morning for a private tutoring session. Rather than throwing you back into the classroom on your first day back in Jerusalem—"

"Ima, no! I want to go—"

She turned with fire in her eyes. "Until you are crowned co-regent, you remain under my authority." A knock sounded on her door. "Come!" she shouted.

The door swung open, and Hezi wished he could crawl under the couch. Would his ima forever scheme?

Master Isaiah stood in the doorway, Ishma tucked under his protective arm. "Good morning, Queen Abijah. We're here as you requested."

Ima glided to her guests, arms open in greeting. "Come, Ishma. Let's all sit down and talk."

She nudged Isaiah aside and guided Hezi's friend to the deep blue couch. "Sit here beside me. You can play with Hezi's peg game while we three *grown-ups* talk."

Ishma kept her head bowed, but Hezi saw red creeping up her neck. "Thank you, my queen," she said in a clipped tone. Ishma sat where Ima instructed, hands in her lap.

Master Isaiah's jaw muscle tightened. "Why did you invite Ishma and me to your chamber, Queen Abijah, and force me to cancel class?"

Ima's expression lost all pretense. "Isaiah,

your wife has been my best friend for as long as I remember, and I wouldn't hurt her for all the gold in Assyria."

Isaiah nodded. "I realize that, Queen Abijah. What does that have to do with canceling my class?"

"For years, Aya and I have met regularly while the children played together. I still want to meet with my friend, but Hezi will no longer attend—nor should Ishma—because the girl cannot continue this friendship with my son now that he's been named crown prince."

Hezi's heart skipped a beat. "No, Ima, that's not fair!"

She lifted her hand to silence him. "You will listen before you speak, Hezi. I'll give you a chance to reply."

Isaiah sat calmly beside him. "I must agree with your son, my queen, and add a question. Why not tell Aya your decision?"

Hezi wondered the same, but when Ima's eyes began to fill, he knew.

"You must be the villain here, Isaiah, not me. This decision must appear to Aya as if it were yours."

Instead of the anger Hezi anticipated, Master Isaiah smiled. "And why would I lie to my wife for you, Abijah?"

Ima smiled too. "Because I'm your queen. I command it."

"Why separate the children now?"

"Hezi must be educated properly." She looked down at Ishma. "I'm sure Ishma is bright, but I don't believe she's the best influence on Hezi anymore."

Isaiah stroked his manicured beard, exaggerating his pondering. "Test her yourself, Queen Abijah. Ask Ishma whatever would assuage your fears. I'm sure she's up to the challenge."

Ishma's face lost its color, and Ima looked at her like a snake eyeing a mouse. "Tell me, dear. Should Hezi attend the dedication of Rimmon's altar at the Temple this afternoon?"

Ishma tried to look at Isaiah, but Ima grabbed her face, gripping her cheeks to focus her. "Don't look at him. Tell me *your* thoughts. The high priest, Uriah—who replaced my abba— placed the exact replica of Assyria's god on the spot where the Bronze Sea once sat. King Ahaz himself will present the sacrifice. Maybe Hezi should help?"

"Never."

Ima released her. "Tell me why."

Ishma rubbed her cheeks, where Ima's nails had left marks. "What kind of high priest would agree to build a pagan altar? Maybe that's why your abba was replaced. Maybe he said no to the requests of King Ahaz too many times."

Ima studied Hezi's friend before responding. "You're intuitive, Ishma. I'll give you that.

You're right. Abba was too stubborn to serve as King Ahaz's high priest."

Ishma looked up and said softly, "Isn't he supposed to be *Yahweh's* high priest?"

The queen looked at Hezi. "See? Unwise. Your abba would beat her if he heard that question."

"I have to go to the sacrifice, Ishma." Hezi spoke around a lump in his throat.

The disappointment in her eyes cut him like a knife. "No, Hezi. The Law says, 'You shall not make for yourself an image in the form of anything in heaven above or on the earth beneath or in the waters below.' You can't go."

Ima responded before he could. "I wish life was so simple, Ishma. Hot or cold, black or white, right or wrong."

"It is that simple, my queen," Ishma continued. "'Hear, O Israel: The LORD our God, the LORD is one.' 'You shall have no other gods before Me. You shall not—'"

Ima glanced at Hezi. "You see? She knows the Law of Moses but knows nothing of kings or the choices you must now make."

Hezi stood, pleading. "But she knows other things too, and the Law will still help me make good choices, Ima." He knelt before her. "Please." His voice broke, and he bowed his head on her knee, refusing to let Ishma see his tears.

"I will not lie to my wife." Isaiah's deep voice broke through Hezi's emotion. "And it is a mistake to remove Ishma from your son's training. Shebna will give Hezekiah the advice you seek. Not only is he older, he also is well educated in foreign policy and trade routes. Ishma knows most of the same facts, but her passion— that you fear might weaken Hezekiah—will actually make him the best king since Solomon."

Hezi sniffed, wiped his face, and sat on the floor with his back toward Ima and Ishma. Waiting.

"You must make her understand, Isaiah." Ima's voice was sharp as a blade.

Master Isaiah shifted on the couch. "Prince Hezekiah?" He spoke quietly and waited until he looked at him. "In Solomon's wisdom, he said, 'Iron sharpens iron.' If you want Ishma to remain as your classmate, *you* must logically defend your choices as crown prince against her logical rebuttal. It's the way a good king interacts with his advisors and will train you to rule."

Hezi couldn't move, didn't speak. Why must he explain it to Ishma? To anyone? Abba didn't explain himself. Even as the thought fluttered into his mind, he understood the need for the skill Isaiah proposed. With a calming breath, he turned to face Ishma. She looked so small sitting beside Ima.

He reached for the peg game and her hand. "Come, sit with me on the floor." She joined him, sitting across from him as she'd done dozens of times before, with the peg game between them. "When I move a peg, I'll explain the reasons I've decided to attend the dedication ceremony of the new altar. When you move a peg, you can tell me why you disagree."

She nodded and offered a tentative grin, and Hezi moved the first peg. "Many people in Judah believed it was Abba's sacrifice to Molek that saved the captives from Samaria three years ago."

"That's not true!" Ishma said.

Hezi pointed to the game. "Jump a peg."

She growled her frustration but moved a peg to jump another and removed one from the board. "I told you, Yaira and I saw the prophet Oded. We captives were released because Yahweh commanded it, not because your poor brother . . ." Her tone softened. "I'm sorry about Bocheru, Hezi. Your abba should never have—"

"You see, Isaiah?" Ima shouted. "Ishma is incapable of holding her tongue."

Before Isaiah answered, Hezi continued his explanation, jumping another peg. "The high priest, Uriah, agreed that by placing a new altar in Yahweh's Temple—even a pagan one—the nation of Judah might return to worship there and remember the God of our fathers."

Ishma slammed another peg from one hole to another, eyes blazing. "Yahweh's Temple is where the Holy One of Israel dwells. He'll remove His presence if the Temple is defiled by a pagan altar. And if His presence goes, why worship there at all?"

Hezi's fingers paused on the next peg. She was right. There were too many pegs left on the board, and he was running out of reasons to attend the dedication. He held her gaze. "My ima has been beaten and mistreated her whole life—to save mine. If I refuse Abba now, I fear it may not be only my life at stake."

Tears formed on her lashes, and she rested her hand on a peg for several heartbeats. Then she removed all the pegs except the last one Hezi had touched. "I will always tell you the truth, Prince Hezekiah, no matter how much it conflicts with your royal responsibilities. But because you will live with the consequences of your decisions, only you can make them."

The weight of her surrender nearly crushed him. He didn't want to make the decisions. He wanted to blame it on Ima's scheming or Abba's corruption. His only hope was in wise counselors. "She stays, Ima."

With a defeated sigh, his ima stood, stepping toward Isaiah to tower over him. "You and your students are shaping the next king of Judah. Make sure every word is measured and every lesson prepares my son for greatness."

Master Isaiah stood to meet her challenge. "I teach Yahweh's truth, and it is He who will make Hezekiah great."

Hezi stood quickly, hoping to prevent another clash. "Master Isaiah, can we convene class before the dedication ceremony?"

Ima spoke before his teacher could answer. "You may hold class today on one condition. Bring Aya to the ceremony and stand with me. I need others to surround me who know—" Ima ducked her head, tears forming. Were they real, or was she scheming again? "Though I must publicly support King Ahaz, I need others around me who know my true heart."

Isaiah didn't appear to be taken in. "Aya and I will not attend a celebration to place an abomination in Yahweh's Temple."

Hezi silently rejoiced, but Ima maintained her tears. "Please, Isaiah. Even Abba Zechariah, as retiring high priest, has agreed to stand with me. We all know placing this altar in the Temple was wrong, but Abba feels as helpless as I do. Shouldn't we stand together in the struggle?"

Isaiah invited Ishma to her feet and gathered her under his arm. "I will not struggle with you, Queen Abijah. I will stand firm and rest in Yahweh's right hand. For He has said, 'Do not fear, for I am with you; do not be dismayed, for I am your God. I will strengthen you and help you.'" He turned to Hezi. "We'll honor your ima's condition and not have class today. However, I'll see you in class tomorrow, young prince, anxious to hear more of your observations on balancing royal responsibility between your kingdom and family."

Hezi watched his teacher and friend walk down the long carpet toward the door and slip quietly from the chamber. Ima wiped her tears when the door clicked shut behind them. Taking up her embroidery, she resumed her place on the couch.

Silence. It was a weapon more painful than tears.

"I'm sorry Isaiah refused to attend the dedication, but I'm not sorry Ishma will remain my classmate. You must see that her perspective is essential, and she is willing, after all, to submit to my decisions."

"I see that Isaiah and that girl will cause trouble. I must find some way—"

"No!" Hezi shouted.

"Have you forgotten to whom you are speaking?"

He sat beside her and spoke gently. "I love you, Ima. I do. But you will leave this alone. As you keep reminding me, I am Judah's crown prince and have won Abba's favor. Ishma will remain with me in Isaiah's classroom. Do you understand?" He didn't look away until she nodded. "Enjoy your friendship with Mistress Aya, and let me enjoy mine with Ishma."

He didn't see full surrender in her eyes, but what he saw was enough that he could return to his peg game while he awaited the afternoon's ceremony.

15

Turn to me and be gracious to me,
for I am lonely and afflicted.
—Psalm 25:16

I walked four steps ahead of Master Isaiah, hoping—no, praying—my turtle doves would be nested in our courtyard niches when we reached home. They'd migrated for the winter, and Mistress assured me they'd return as they had for the past five years. But on this, Hezi's first day of military training and my first day in class without him, I needed to see my birds. The cold wind whipped my robe as the sun set on the first day of spring.

In my mind's eye, I saw Hezi laughing. He would think it ridiculous that two days without seeing him would send me into such a frenzy. Yesterday had been our Sabbath. Master and Mistress always observed Sabbath even though most of Jerusalem had forgotten Yahweh's commands. After two whole days without my best friend and months without my doves, I thought my chest might explode from the aching.

We reached our courtyard, and I flung open the gate. Rushing toward the dovecote on the eastern wall, I saw the niches and slowed halfway across the packed dirt.

Empty. The dovecote and my heart. Fighting back tears, I let my shoulder bag drop to the ground, and I dropped with it.

Master Isaiah crouched behind me and kissed the top of my head. "They'll return soon, my girl, and each day in class will get easier. We must be patient." His footsteps faded into the house.

Soon, I heard another set of sandals approach. The scent of cloves announced the mistress's presence. "It's only the first day of Aviv, Ishma. Your turtle doves can't read a calendar." She pulled my woolen cloak closer around my neck. "It's been a harsh winter. Perhaps the palm doves and turtle doves will come later this year. I didn't see a single rock dove in the city this winter. Did you?"

I knew she was trying to distract me. She knew more from Solomon's writings on birds than I did. I shook my head. "No, I didn't see any rock doves either." They sheltered among the rocks and cliffs year round but flew over Jerusalem's hills on nice days. "Why can't my little palms and turtles stay with me all year?"

Mistress tucked her robe beneath her legs on the cold ground and knelt beside me. "Is it the doves alone that caused your tears?" She offered me a cloth to dry my eyes.

I received it, needing it more now because she asked the question, and the answer tore at my heart. "When will I see Hezi now that he no longer attends class?" I fell into her arms, the full weight of my fear escaping in sobs.

Mistress held me until grief ebbed. Then she ventured a question that gathered my heart's broken pieces into a manageable pile. "Have you asked Yahweh to help?"

Startled by the question's simplicity, I was also intrigued by its possibilities. "No, Mistress, I haven't. Do you really believe Yahweh would care about a girl's lonely heart?"

She looked at me with glistening eyes. "Do you know why Master Isaiah calls me a prophetess?" I shook my head but was eager to hear. "It's not because I proclaimed Yahweh's words to kings or predicted future events that came to pass. Isaiah calls me prophetess because I speak with Yahweh as a friend—and He answers."

My mind began to spin with questions, but the most important came out first. "How do you hear Yahweh's voice?"

"How do you call a palm dove to light on your arm?"

Obedient but confused, I answered her question. "I become peaceful and then sing the dove's song." How could my call to the dove answer my interest in how Mistress heard Yahweh?

Her eyes sparkled as she helped me work it out. "If I became peaceful and tried to make dove noises, would your dove light on my arm?"

"Perhaps not." I thought more about what

made *my* dove come to me. "It's the trust and familiarity between me and my dove that creates the bond. Only after the second year would the dove light on a platform and take food from my hand. It was the third summer before it actually landed on my arm."

Mistress nodded. "Talk with Yahweh, Ishma. A bond will form, and He'll become familiar, Someone you can trust. You'll come to know His voice, and by that time He will likely have worked out how you can see Prince Hezekiah."

I found myself smiling on one of the hardest days I'd experienced since coming to Master Isaiah's household. My tears dried; my heart felt lighter. A memory came rushing in—Yaira and I standing at the gates of Samaria—set free. I'd envied a beautiful bird with its peaceful nest, despairing that I'd never feel peace or safety again in my life. "Thank you, Mistress." I'd found my nest.

She smiled, and I wrapped my arms around her neck. "I love you."

"And I love you, my little dove." She released me and wiped her own leaky eyes. "Come now. Our evening meal is ready, and the whole family is probably waiting at the table."

We brushed the dust from our robes and hurried into the kitchen. The cook fire warmed the air and made a comfortable place to gather. Dinah and Leah had just placed the last serving dishes on the table when we arrived. Mistress took her customary place at Master's right hand with little Maher next to her and me at the end. Jashub sat on his abba's left with Kadmiel beside him. Dinah and Leah completed the family on that side of the rectangular wood table. Master Isaiah always led in a prayer of thanks before a single crumb passed our lips.

"For this food we are grateful and for Your many blessings: shelter, health, family, friends, and more than all these, Your ever-abiding presence. May our lives reflect the truths You've spoken. Let it be so today and always."

The end of Master's prayer signaled permission to begin the meal. Jashub and Kadmiel were like chariot horses dashing from the start line. Jashub grabbed the plate of sliced oranges, dried fruit, and nuts, while Kadmiel began ladling his bowl full of lentil stew.

"How was the first day of class without Hezekiah?" Kadmiel threw out the question and then licked a drip of rich brown stew from the side of his bowl.

I shoved the cheese curds and nuts around my plate with a piece of bread and hoped Master Isaiah would answer for us. He told of the new children in class—all the noblemen's sons now, not just the advisors' heirs—and then about my new duties to teach the young ones David's psalms. The family congratulated me, but my heart and mind were fixed on Hezi.

How could life change so completely in two days? Hezi and I had spent so much time together—sometimes playing games under the watchful eye of his ima; other times in class as Master Isaiah plotted new topics for us to debate. When the queen allowed it, we walked in the palace's olive grove under the watchful eye of Samuel, Hezi's guard. Eliakim joined us occasionally, but I never let him bring his sword or bow. He and Hezi had other friends for that kind of thing. I didn't need other friends.

"We missed Hezi greatly, didn't we, Ishma?" Master Isaiah raised his voice, forcing me back to the family discussion.

"Yes," I said. "I missed him very much." I glanced at Mistress Aya, who offered a consoling smile.

Master Isaiah peeled an orange while he spoke. "I hadn't realized how much we'd come to rely on Hezekiah's experiences in Damascus and Samaria to enhance our lessons this past year."

I let the master's words play in the corners of my thoughts while I pondered what I missed most about Hezi today. What made his absence so difficult? Yes, Shebna was obnoxious, sounding like a know-it-all because Hezi wasn't there to stifle his overbearing comments. But it was more than that. Without Hezi, the class felt . . . it felt like straight lines rather than intersecting circles. Hezi had the ability to study other students as they spoke and perceive more than their words. Which meant more interesting discussions and deeper truths that drew students together no matter what their abba's occupation.

Kadmiel's comment broke through my thoughts. "Prince Hezekiah made quite an impression today during his sword drills as well."

Master Isaiah halted a spoonful of lentil stew before putting it in his mouth. "Good impression or bad?"

"Good impression. Evidently, King Ahaz had been working with the prince for a while on weapon skills. Hezekiah trained in the regiment next to mine, and I watched him best the third-year sword champion by midday."

I bowed my head to hide quick tears. The thought of Hezi with a sword in his hand had haunted me all day. I'd grown accustomed to Kadmiel being a gifted soldier. Our household was very proud that he'd risen through the ranks and now led his own division, but Master Isaiah always asked him to remove his battle gear before entering the courtyard. Though I routinely spoke to royal guards without reacting, the idea of someone I loved in battle armor sent me into sheer panic.

The conversation died. It was painfully apparent that all eyes were on me. I refused to look up and expose my fear.

Jashub rose from his cushion and knelt beside

me, taking my hands in his. "Ishma, come now. It's better to hear Hezekiah did well than that he did poorly."

I nodded but didn't lift my head. Dear, logical Jashub was trying to help. His special gift for sorting out an order or system or plan had earned him the role of assistant chief scribe. Now, his long hours distracted him from pressing Yaira further about marriage. Perhaps he knew better than anyone about a broken heart.

Keeping my head bowed, I wiped my eyes, my nose. "If you'll all excuse me," I said, "I'm extra tired tonight. May I go to my room now?"

"Of course." Master Isaiah rose from the table. "It's a shame you're tired. I had hoped you would accompany me to the study to help with my first private tutoring session."

I looked up, finding all eyes still on me. "Who is your student?" My heart leapt with hope at his smile.

"Perhaps you'd like to wash your face before Hezekiah arrives. I'm sure he missed you today too."

I bumped the table when I jumped to my feet. The laughter escorting me to my chamber said no one minded that I jostled their goblets of watered wine. Hurrying to my wash basin, I splashed my face with cool water, then searched blindly for the cloth I'd set out on the small table nearby. Someone pressed the cloth into my hand. I opened my eyes and found Dinah sorting through our robes hanging in a neat row on wall pegs.

I patted my face dry. "What are you doing?"

She lifted my finest robe from its peg and held it against my shoulders, measuring its length and width. "We haven't worn our fine robes since the king returned. Tonight may be your last chance to wear this before you grow out of it."

I looked down at the light blue linen, accented with bead work and fitted at the waist. "Why would I wear this to study with Hezi?"

Dinah's arms fell to her sides, and she rolled her eyes. "One day, you'll want to impress Prince Hezekiah. It's probably too small for you anyway." She rehung the robe on its peg and grabbed the ivory comb. "At least let me comb your hair and give you a fresh braid."

I lifted the polished bronze mirror to watch Dinah behind me—our daily routine. She combed in silence for several heartbeats, her features lined and serious. "Haven't you ever wondered who Prince Hezekiah will marry?"

The cool evening breeze sent a chill through me—or was it the thought of Hezi marrying? "I guess I haven't thought about it yet. Master Isaiah said Jashub was too young to marry at sixteen. Hezi is only thirteen."

"Yes, but Hezekiah is the crown prince. Royalty marries early to build the royal line of succession."

She started combing again, and I no longer felt the tangles. Hezi would have told me if his parents had talked of betrothal—wouldn't he? I scrubbed my face with the damp cloth, hoping to refocus my attention. "Dinah, why haven't you and Leah married?"

I watched in the mirror as her expression grew thoughtful. "Leah and I came to Master Isaiah's house almost twenty years ago when our abba died. He was a sandal maker in the southern city and was killed by bandits on his way home from Jericho. We had no other family to care for us, and Master and Mistress found us living on the streets, eating from garbage piles."

I put the mirror down and turned around, hugging Dinah's waist. "I'm sorry, Dinah. I didn't know."

She squeezed me and then held my cheeks between her hands. "Yahweh turns our mourning into dancing, Ishma." She kissed my forehead. "Now turn around so I can finish braiding your hair." I obeyed, and Dinah continued. "Leah and I both decided we'd rather serve Yahweh in Master Isaiah's household than serve a husband we didn't love for the rest of our lives." She paused, her brows pulled together as if thinking hard. "It was the best decision for us, though it's not right for everyone."

"Do you think Yaira will ever marry?" I wondered if Dinah had ever told Yaira her story, if maybe that was why Yaira had refused Jashub.

"I don't know, Ishma, but I understand why she chose a servant's life." She finished my braid with the purple ribbon and laid the braid over my shoulder. "In the few months that Yaira lived here, serving others seemed as woven into her character as the strands of hair in your braid."

She sat on a cushion across from me. "What about you, little Ishma? You will soon become a woman, faced with the decision to marry. Best ask Yahweh now to reveal His path for your future."

The thought of my future was nearly as terrifying as my past. Why must things keep changing?

Mistress Aya appeared at the doorway with a sly grin. "Are you two waiting for Ishma's hair to grow before she joins Isaiah in the study?"

"We've just finished," Dinah said, winking at me. "We were talking about the future."

Aya held out her hand to me. "Dreams are the fabric of a young girl's heart."

I walked with her down the hallway wondering if Yaira had any dreams. "When Yaira comes of age, who will pay her dowry?"

Mistress looked down, an amused grin on her face. "Didn't Yaira say she would never marry?"

"Yes, but she might change her mind."

"True." We walked a little farther before the mistress added, "Isaiah and I will pay Yaira's dowry whenever—and whomever—she decides to marry."

I wondered how that might work if Yaira someday agreed to marry Jashub, but we'd already arrived at the study. I hugged the mistress tight. "Thank you for loving us."

She hugged me back. "Thank you for being lovable."

I hurried into Master Isaiah's study and assumed my position on the red cushion, my favorite. He had laid out a scroll for me to read while we waited for Hezi. Master said Hezi would be here any moment. I began reading. And kept reading. I'd read nearly halfway through the scroll and still no prince. "Where is Hezi, Master Isaiah?"

The sun had disappeared over the western hills, and Master Isaiah paced like a prowling cat. He called out his window that overlooked the courtyard, "Any sign of a royal messenger?"

Mistress Aya was working late to dye some wool thread. "Be patient, my love."

Master Isaiah started pacing again, but I stood on a stool to look out the window. "Shouldn't he have been here by now?" I asked, resuming my place on the cushion.

"He'll come, Ishma, or he'll send a messenger with word." Master's tone wasn't very convincing.

The squeak of our courtyard gate sent us both running, Master Isaiah ahead of me.

"There you are!" Master Isaiah said, arriving in the courtyard first. "I was worried. My, my—you even came with an escort. Didn't Queen Abijah trust us to chaperone?"

I skidded to a stop as the moonlight shrouded two soldiers in our courtyard. One was taller than Master Isaiah, his shoulders as wide as the gate. The other soldier . . .

Hezi? Not *my* Hezi. This boy wore a leather breast piece, like my Israelite captors, and leather sandals that laced up to his knees. His right hand rested on his sword, and a spear was slung across his back. He stepped toward me.

"No!" I whimpered and stepped back.

The moonlight distorted Hezi's features. "Ishma. It's me."

One moment his face was Hezekiah's, the next it was the soldier who had whipped me.

"What's wrong?" The big soldier stepped closer. It was Samuel. I knew it. But the moonlight cast eerie shadows across his face. "Ishma, you know me."

I wanted to run, but my legs felt like water. Master Isaiah stood in front of me, blocking my view. "Look at me, Ishma." I tried to see around him, to make sure the soldiers didn't harm us. "Ishma, look at me!"

My head snapped to attention. He held my face gently, staring into my eyes. "You are safe, my girl. Safe. Samuel is our friend. He's here to protect Hezi, and Hezi loves you. Neither of them would ever harm you."

I heard a commotion behind us and tried to see what the soldiers were doing, but Master Isaiah held my face tight. "Do you hear me? Samuel and Hezi won't hurt you."

His words finally registered over the sound of my racing heart. "I hate swords. If I see swords, Master Isaiah, I see blood."

"I know, Ishma, but there is no blood here. Shalom, child." He pulled me into a ferocious hug and whispered a prayer, "Yahweh, let Your shalom destroy the chaos inside her."

I stayed there in his arms for a while, trying to remember what Abba's hugs felt like. When the master released me, Hezi stood beside us. His leather breast piece gone, he now wore only his tunic with his leather battle skirt.

"I'm sorry, Ishma. I don't have a robe, so I couldn't remove all my armor." His cheeks pinked as he said it.

I almost grinned. Almost. Instead, I bowed slightly. "Thank you, Hezi. You are kind."

He offered his hand. I hesitated but took it. Samuel stood in the shadows near an acacia bush by the gate. Hezi called him forward. "Ishma, I know you remember Samuel." The big man approached like one of my doves, timid and ready to fly if I reacted again.

He knelt beside Hezi. "You never need fear

me, little Ishma. I know I look scary, but I have three daughters and twin sons. My boys are four. I would never hurt a child. I'm here to protect the prince—and you whenever you're with him." He offered his hand too, and I gave mine, closing a circle of promises between Hezi, Samuel, and me. Samuel kissed my hand and rose to his feet. I felt my cheeks warm.

Hezi captured my gaze, waiting until I gave silent assurance that we were restored. Then he turned to Master Isaiah. "Samuel has been assigned as part of Abba's increased security for me. One of our spies delivered news this afternoon that King Tiglath-Pileser is dead and his son, Shalmaneser, will sit on Assyria's throne." The master looked startled, but Hezi continued. "It's only a precaution, but there will be added security on the city walls as well."

Fear stole my breath again. Would there be another attack on Jerusalem? Master Isaiah drew me close. "We'll begin our lessons tomorrow night. Go home and get some rest, Hezekiah."

Tomorrow night! Would Hezi come every night for lessons? I wanted to hug my friend, but it didn't feel right while he was wearing only his tunic.

Hezi hesitated too, but his attention was on Master Isaiah. "I'd like to review some of your prophecies for our lesson tomorrow. Do you think

King Tiglath-Pileser's death is the beginning of Yahweh's judgment on Assyria?"

A sad smile made Master Isaiah appear weary. "No, son. Yahweh has been very clear. Assyria will annihilate Israel—and possibly invade Judah—before the Lord's wrath is poured out on them."

I wondered if Hezi felt afraid like I did when Master Isaiah talked that way. I took the purple ribbon from my hair and offered it to him. "Be safe while you're training, Hezi."

He shoved it inside his leather wristband, then winked. "I'll see you tomorrow, Ishma."

My cheeks burned as I watched him go. Master Isaiah turned me to face him and spoke quietly. "Hezi will be king one day, Ishma. Guard your heart."

16

[King] Ahaz . . . removed the Sea from the bronze bulls that supported it and set it on a stone base. He took away the Sabbath canopy that had been built at the temple and removed the royal entryway outside the temple of the LORD, in deference to the king of Assyria.

—2 Kings 16:17–18

Isaiah studied one of his new prophecies while Ishma worked quietly beside him, copying the Shema onto a small parchment: "Hear, O Israel: The LORD our God, the LORD is one. Love the LORD your God with all your heart and with all your soul and with all your strength." Her handwritten parchments were hidden all over the southern city beneath small metal mezuzahs nailed to doorframes. Each time Aya and the girls delivered a basket of food, a ball of yarn, or a new robe to a family in need, they included one of Ishma's handwritten parchments to nourish the soul.

The girl dipped her reed into the pigment and paused from her work. "Did you notice increased tension in the palace when we walked home from class today?"

"Hmm, no. What do you mean?"

"I don't know. It seemed the guards were more watchful or something." She bent her head, resuming her task, but Isaiah stopped reading. Ishma was sensitive, perceptive. He would ask Hezekiah about her concerns when he arrived for tonight's tutoring session.

The courtyard gate squeaked, propelling Ishma to her feet and out the door before Isaiah could replace Micah's scroll on the shelf. A heavy sigh escaped. Ishma was twelve now. He'd need to begin thinking of a betrothal match. Who would she agree to marry? It had been obvious since she and Hezekiah were children that they shared a special bond, but King Ahaz would never betroth the crown prince to an orphan, even if her abba had been a nobleman from Bethlehem.

The children appeared in the doorway of his study—children no longer. Isaiah saw the blush of young love on Ishma's cheeks. Aya hadn't mentioned anything about her coming of age, but Ishma's figure had started to blossom, and she was no longer the little girl he'd rescued seven years ago.

Hezekiah looked at her with possessive tenderness. He was dark and handsome; his boyish features were fading into the good looks of his ima's family. His shoulders and chest were growing more muscular with military training, and he carried himself more like a king each day. Yes, it would be hard when both must choose another to marry.

"I was right, Master Isaiah." Ishma sounded worried, not proud.

Samuel joined them in the doorway. "Assyrian soldiers invaded Samaria overnight," the big guard explained. "They arrested King Hoshea and started a siege against the city. Our spies say Samaria can last for years within the high walls, so we're preparing for Assyrian frustrations to filter into northern Judean villages."

Hezekiah looked pale. "Because our royal treasuries are empty, Abba has taken more bronze from Yahweh's Temple—from the Sea and from the bulls on which it sat. He will send it to King Shalmaneser in Assyria, hoping to buy favor and protection for our northern people." Color returned to his cheeks and his jaw set. "I still say King Hoshea was brave to stop tribute payments and seek support from Pharaoh So in Egypt when King Tiglath-Pileser died two years ago. Maybe if Abba had refused to pay and joined their alliance, we could have stood stronger against the Assyrians and—"

"Samaria would still be under siege, Hezi." Ishma meandered toward her customary cushion, and the prince settled in beside her. Samuel stood in the doorway, ever alert. "King Hoshea would still have been arrested, and your abba might have been arrested with him—or worse."

Hezekiah refused to back down. "When Shalmaneser first ascended to Assyria's throne two years ago and others vied for that power, couldn't we then have thrown off their yoke while they scrambled for leadership?"

As Isaiah drew breath, Ishma again had the answer. "It's a good point, Hezi, but that was two years ago. Since we can't go backward, what can we do now to protect Judah's northern cities? They still haven't fully recovered from the Israel-Aram war seven years ago."

Isaiah returned to his writing stool, listening to this nightly ritual. Their debates sometimes lasted until past the moon's zenith, and he allowed it. No, truer yet, he enjoyed it. His task was simply to wait for the holy prompting and then find a scroll or speak a new word directly from Yahweh into the banter of his top two students.

"There must be something we can do to help King Hoshea." Hezekiah pinched his bottom lip, deep in thought.

Ishma crossed her arms over her chest. "I think you might be more concerned about Judah's citizens in the north than the king of a nation that attacked us less than a decade ago."

The whisper of Yahweh blew across Isaiah's spirit, and he retrieved a scroll he and Shebna had discussed with the older students today in class.

Hezekiah stilled when he saw Isaiah reach for

the scroll. "What is it, Isaiah? Something new from Yahweh?"

"Actually, no. It's Micah's first prophecy from nearly twenty years ago, when he began his training in Tekoa. Yahweh foretold Samaria's destruction as well as the destruction of Jerusalem. Listen:

'The Lord is coming from his dwelling
    place; he comes down and treads on the
    heights of the earth.
The mountains melt beneath him and the
    valleys split apart . . . because of the
    sins of the people of Israel.
What is Jacob's transgression? Is it not
    Samaria?
What is Judah's high place? Is it not
    Jerusalem?
Therefore I will make Samaria a heap of
    rubble.' "

Isaiah looked up from the scroll. "There's more, but Samaria's destruction is clear."

Hezekiah sat cross-legged, his arms resting on his knees, head bowed. "So there's no hope for Samaria now?"

Isaiah met his pleading with truth. "Israel has been given every chance to repent, Hezekiah."

"What about Judah?" Ishma's head shot up. "The prophecy mentions Jerusalem as the capital but doesn't specifically say it will be reduced to rubble." Her lips trembled. "Are they coming here, Master Isaiah?"

Hezekiah looked up then, eyes shot full of fear. "Are the Assyrians coming for Abba and his officials? For me?"

With all his heart, Isaiah wanted to say no, but he simply wasn't certain. "My concise answer is, I don't know."

Hezekiah dropped his head with a frustrated sigh.

"I'm frustrated too," Isaiah said. "I also want answers, but the rest of Micah's prophecy focused more on Israel and Samaria—not Judah." He paused, waiting for the prince to meet his gaze again. "At some point, Hezekiah, Yahweh will pour out His judgment on Judah and Jerusalem, exiling our people among many nations. We just don't know when. Micah's prophecy is being fulfilled in Israel and Samaria more than twenty years after it was spoken. The prophecy Yahweh gave me about the destruction of Damascus was fulfilled within three years. God's timing is his own. His thoughts are not our thoughts, and His ways are higher than our ways. But whether in rain or drought, He will accomplish His good purpose."

Hezekiah bowed his head again, hands shaking. "What benefit is prophecy when we can't understand it?" Ishma turned her eyes toward Isaiah, silently shouting the same question.

Isaiah remembered his early years at the

prophets' camp. Before his vision. Before that indisputable personal revelation of Yahweh's holy power and goodness. "Listen to me, children. Prophecy—even when we don't fully understand it—is given so we can watch God's sovereignty and power unfold. He offers clues to identify His activity in the world around us. For those who are alert to His activity, we find great reward in discovering His love and faithfulness. For those who ignore God's involvement in this world, there awaits disaster and regret when His meaning is revealed."

Hezekiah straightened. "So we will seek Him and find Him faithful."

Ishma nudged Hezekiah's shoulder. "And though both Micah and Master Isaiah warn of Assyria's attack, they also tell of a captive remnant that will return to Jerusalem." She lifted her sleeve to reveal the brand on her forearm. "Yaira and I returned to Jerusalem. Maybe the prophecies speak of us. Maybe not. But Yaira says Yahweh saved us for His purpose. We must trust in His plan for our future—no matter what the present is like."

"I'd rather know the exact time when the prophecy is supposed to happen." Hezekiah's grin chased his fears, and Ishma instinctively lightened his mood.

"I'd like to know when my doves' eggs will hatch, but that too is in God's hands." Ishma's eyes sparked with life. She became fully herself when Hezekiah was with her.

Isaiah put away his scrolls. They were so good for each other in so many ways. *Yahweh, how will You ever provide another for each of them to marry?*

17

In that day the Root of Jesse will stand as a banner for the peoples. . . . They will swoop down on the slopes of Philistia to the west; together they will plunder the people to the east. They will subdue Edom and Moab, and the Ammonites will be subject to them.

—Isaiah 11:10, 14

I dreaded this morning's visit with Yaira. For a year now, she'd pretended not to care about Jashub's betrothal to another. But I was there at the entrance to the caves on the morning he told her. I saw her spirit faint when her lips spoke blessing—all the while avoiding my eyes because she knew I would see into the windows of her soul. Perhaps today, I should avoid her eyes again so she wouldn't see my broken heart.

"Ishma, you must talk, or I won't know you're safe." Master Isaiah's reproof was gentle as we began our journey through the long, winding tunnels.

"I'm sorry. What shall we talk about?"

"We should talk about what's bothering you—Hezekiah's departure today with his regiment. King Ahaz wouldn't send his crown prince to regain Philistine territory if he didn't think Hezekiah was capable."

Our familiar dark trek suddenly felt like a heavy blanket over my face, making it hard to breathe or think. "King Ahaz is a madman."

I bumped into Master's open arms. He cradled me there. "Ishma, are you all right?"

I'd just spoken treason against Judah's king. "Forgive me, Master Isaiah. I spoke—"

"You spoke the truth, but you don't normally speak quite so bluntly about the king." He kissed the top of my head in the darkness. "Kadmiel has often said Hezekiah is one of the best swordsmen he's ever seen."

"Really, Master Isaiah. I'm fine."

He released me, and I heard the sound of his sandals on the rock beneath us. "Remember, left hand on the wall, and keep talking."

"I'm right behind you."

"Feel the rock beneath your left hand, Ishma. It is connected to the very foundations of the earth. Immovable. Unchangeable."

His words took root in my soul. "I like immovable and unchangeable."

He chuckled. "I know change is hard for you, my girl, but we can't fulfill God's plan and purpose for our lives without changing."

"What is God's plan and purpose for me, Master? He still hasn't shown me."

"His plan for you in this moment is to be

faithful where you are. That's a truth we all must embrace."

His answer sounded like a trap door for those who wanted to escape the hard work of seeking Yahweh. "I've been waiting for Yahweh to speak for years, like Mistress told me. I talk to Him every day, but I still can't say I've heard His voice clearly."

"Do you remember the first few months we made this journey through these tunnels to the caves?"

"Yes." I wondered what that had to do with hearing God's voice.

"Remember how many times we bumped our toes on rocks strewn across our path?"

"Yes."

"It took us years, Ishma, to clear the path so we could place our left hands on the unchanging rock wall and walk with certainty that we wouldn't stumble." He paused, and I let his words settle into my spirit. "Are you still with me?"

"Yes. Are you saying I have rocks in my life that are impeding my ability to hear God's voice clearly?"

I heard him sigh. "That could be one inter-pretation, but I think you're entirely too hard on yourself. What if our lives are simply full of rocks? Only as time passes do we discover the clear path on which Yahweh leads us."

My life had certainly been full of rocks. Now,

in the complete darkness of the tunnels and in the presence of the teacher who had loved me at my worst, I felt brave enough to face the boulder that perhaps blocked Yahweh's voice. "I don't want to walk a path that leads away from Hezi."

After a long pause, my master spoke in barely a whisper. "I know, my girl, but I feel certain Hezekiah is Yahweh's chosen king. And I'm not sure how Yahweh could include you on such a path."

It was the truth. Something I'd always valued from my teacher. But this time, it hurt. "I understand, Master Isaiah." Trying to breathe normally, I swallowed back tears and steadied my voice. "May I hold the back of your robe, rather than talk, to assure you I'm following? I'd like to be silent for a while." My voice cracked on the final word; I was unable to stem the tears any longer.

"Of course."

We walked the rest of the way in silence with our left hands skimming the smooth rock wall. Rounding a corner, we finally saw the distinct glow of torchlight that led us to the prophets' caves.

I released my hold on Master's robe and walked beside him, linking my arm in his for the rest of the way. "I hope Yaira isn't too upset about Jashub's wedding when we see her this morning."

As we approached the dimly lit archway leading to the network of connected caves, I saw that it was Micah, rather than Yaira, who waited to receive the food and supplies. "Good morning," he said, placing a scroll in Master Isaiah's hand. "The other prophets and I have written wedding blessings for Jashub and Hallel."

Master Isaiah accepted the scroll, careful not to damage the unique seal of Yahweh's prophets. He offered the basket of supplies in exchange.

Small baskets hung over both my arms, and I waited for Micah to answer my silent pleading. He shook his head. "I'm sorry, Ishma. You should leave the baskets with me. I could lead you to Yaira, but I fear it would be fruitless. She's been silent since yesterday."

I looked to Master for permission. He gave it with a nod. "I'd really like to see her, Micah."

He drew me close and kissed my forehead. "You're a good friend to her. Come." We entered the world of the prophets—Yaira's world. "Brothers, I bring guests!" At Micah's declaration, I sensed a stirring ahead. The light grew brighter and the tunnel more spacious as we walked.

Finally, we entered a large cavern—nearly the size of the palace's Middle Court. Tents dotted the rock surface, and a stream traveled through the center of the space. Ghostly white faces stared at us, but I didn't see Yaira.

Micah pointed to a small tent on an elevated plateau to our left. "She's there. Most of the time she lives among us, talking, serving, laughing, cooking. But she went to her tent yesterday after your visit and has not emerged since."

I started toward my friend's hideaway, but Master Isaiah touched my arm. "Ishma, I know this is important, but we can't risk exposing all the prophets by altering our daily routine. We must still return home by dawn."

Nodding my understanding, I prayed as I walked. *Yahweh, only You can mend what's broken on the inside of Yaira. I still fear swords and change and so many things, but You are mending my broken places. Mend Yaira's broken places too.*

Yaira's home was a simple structure: sticks connected with rope and covered by blankets. It kept her warm and gave her some privacy. I called to her from outside the flap, "Yaira, may I come in?"

No answer.

I poked my head inside. She sat, cross-legged, hands in her lap—face red, nose running, eyes swollen. Had she been like this since yesterday? "May I come in?"

She nodded.

Careful not to knock over the sticks, I lifted the flap and sat opposite my friend, saying the first thing that came to mind. "Why are you here, Yaira?"

"This is where I live, Ishma." She looked at me as though I were five years old again.

I didn't want to correct her, but I needed to clarify what I meant. "No. Why are you living with the prophets instead of with Master and Mistress?"

She rolled her eyes. "I'm defiled, Ishma. You're old enough to know what that means. A defiled woman in the house defiles the entire household."

"Do you think anyone would remember that about you, Yaira? It's been nine years." She said nothing. "Why are you really here, Yaira?"

"I'm serving the prophets. They need someone to help cook, to tend to their needs as they concentrate on hearing the word of Yahweh."

I held my tongue. If that was truly the purpose Yahweh had given Yaira, I didn't want to challenge it. Instead, I lifted my left sleeve, revealing the brand I'd received as a captive. I pointed to Yaira's left arm. "Let me see your brand."

"Why?" Yaira sounded perturbed.

"Let me see it."

She pulled up her sleeve, revealing the brand.

I grabbed Yaira's arm and placed our brands side by side. "You told me Yahweh saved my life in Bethlehem and freed me from slavery in Samaria because He had a purpose for me. Do you think God would give you the same brand but love you less?"

Yaira jerked her arm away and covered her

face, sobbing. "It is not Yahweh's love I doubt."

"Jashub's love then?" My voice carried, and Yaira shushed me. "He loves you still, Yaira, but because you hide in a cave with prophets, he's chosen to pursue a different purpose—one he believes is Yahweh's new direction for him."

Yaira buried her face in her hands. "Why can't I simply be happy for him? I know in my heart I'm not supposed to marry Jashub."

I reached for her hands, drawing them away from her face. "But do you know you've been called to serve the prophets? Or are you hiding from the world because you don't want to face Jashub?" Yaira stared at me with an unreadable expression. "What?" I asked. "Tell me what you're thinking."

"I'm so confused I don't know what to think. Until yesterday, I was certain Yahweh's purpose for me was to serve His prophets. Now, I'm not sure."

I cradled her hands in mine. "I'm about to say something, but I mean it in the most loving way, Yaira." I hesitated, hoping she wouldn't take offense. "If you are serving the prophets because it's Yahweh's purpose and calling, why are you sitting in this little tent crying because Jashub is marrying another?" Yaira looked as if I'd hit her in the stomach. "But if you're ready to consider that Yahweh may have a different purpose for you, perhaps it's time to come out of the caves and become a part of Master Isaiah's household again. Why not come home with me?"

She blinked. Blinked some more. "I can't just leave, Ishma. Who would care for the prophets?"

My heart skipped. Would she really consider coming home? "Perhaps we should begin to pray together for a solution."

Yaira nodded. "Yes, perhaps. Let me talk with Micah. I want him to understand." She studied her hands. "When does the wedding ceremony start?"

"At sunset." Now my tears invaded. "We needed to allow plenty of time for the streets to clear after Hezi's regiment leaves for Philistine territory."

"Oh, Ishma! How could I forget?" She pulled me into a ferocious hug. "I'm sorry. You must go. Hurry."

I wiped my cheeks. "Yes, but are you sure you're all right? Will you talk with Micah about leaving the caves?"

"I will. Yes. Today." She hugged me, and I hurried from the tent wiping tears.

Master Isaiah gathered me under his arm. "Is she all right? Are you all right?"

"I'm better," I said. Then looking at Micah, I added, "Yaira and I may both be better after she talks to you today."

Micah's brow furrowed, but there was no time to explain. He gave us instructions for departure and reminded us as we left, "Keep your hand on the rock. It will lead you to the light."

18

No longer will they call you Deserted, or
    name your land Desolate.
But you will be called Hephzibah, . . . for
    the LORD will take delight in you,
and your land will be married.

                        —Isaiah 62:4

Assyrian soldiers filled the valleys surrounding Jerusalem, and King Ahaz opened the Horse Gate, allowing King Shalmaneser's chariot to ride directly into Temple grounds. Assyrian soldiers held Hezi between them, tied and gagged, beside the beastly altar of Rimmon in the Temple court while King Ahaz laughed and danced with priestesses toward the altar. Drums pounded louder and louder.

I stood on the portico of the Temple, trying to scream, trying to free myself of the chains that held me. But I couldn't make a sound.

Suddenly, my chains fell off, and I ran. Down the stairs. Across the sacred court—but I couldn't reach Hezi in time. The guards lifted him off his feet, and King Ahaz drew back his spear to thrust it through his son. *"Nooo!"*

"Ishma!" Someone shook me. "Ishma wake up. You're dreaming."

I bolted upright, gasping for breath, and grabbed

Yaira in a strangling hug. "It was the same dream, Yaira." I couldn't stop shaking.

"It was just a dream, Ishma. It's not real. Hezi is safe."

"We don't know that!" I hugged her tighter. We both knew Yahweh spoke through dreams. My nightmares began soon after Master Isaiah received his first letter from Hezi. He'd been with the army less than a month, and King Ahaz had assigned Hezi's regiment to the front lines, fighting the Philistines on Judah's western border. Hezi wrote that his abba hoped to give him this battle experience to make him a more seasoned officer quickly. I feared it was King Ahaz's insecurity that placed his handsome, intelligent eldest son in the heaviest fighting.

I shared my suspicions with Yaira when she moved back to Master Isaiah's household shortly after my nightmares started. She tried to reason with me, but when my dreams continued she volunteered to sleep in a separate room with me so Dinah and Leah could rest. My screams need not keep everyone awake.

Tonight I looked at the dark circles under Yaira's eyes and realized the cost of her compassion. "Go rest in the extra bed in Dinah and Leah's room. I'll be fine."

She gave me that worried-ima look. "I'm never leaving you again. I told you that. Now what do you think the dream means?"

I didn't want to believe it and certainly dared not speak the words aloud, but I was convinced King Ahaz was willing to sacrifice his son to mollify Assyria. "I fear for Hezi's safety. Should I tell Master Isaiah?"

"Tell me what?" Startled, Yaira and I jumped as if we'd been bitten by a viper. Both the master and mistress stood in the moonlight, looking apologetic.

Mistress Aya knelt beside us. "We heard Ishma scream, but we were already awake." Master Isaiah knelt too, placing a hand on his wife's shoulder.

My stomach started to churn. Something was wrong. "Is it Hezi? Have you received word from the palace?"

"No, no. Nothing like that. I'm sure Hezekiah is well." A slow grin appeared on Master Isaiah's face. "In fact, I've never been more sure of anything."

I felt a little better when Mistress Aya sat down, relaxing against the wall. "Do you want to tell us about your nightmare? Was there anything different about it tonight?"

Recounting the horror in my mind, I halted when I remembered my chains. "I was freed." I glanced at Yaira. "Instead of remaining chained, as I had in every other dream, tonight the chains fell off, and I ran to Hezi."

Yaira turned to Master Isaiah. "Do you think the change is significant?"

He and Mistress Aya exchanged a glance, and they settled onto two cushions beside our sleeping mats. Mistress began first. "Master Isaiah and I had dreams tonight too—quite different from yours."

I looked at her, expectant.

"In my dream, I walked into the Throne Porch, and it was filled with people, dressed in their finest robes and jewels. When I looked at the throne, Prince Hezekiah was seated there, a grown man, handsome and regal looking."

My stomach did a flip at the thought. *Hezi, the king of Judah.* Of course, he was recognized as heir apparent throughout Judah, though there'd been no coronation ceremony to affirm him as official co-regent. Evidently, Yahweh would be the first to confirm King Hezekiah through His prophetess. The thought thrilled me, and I covered a smile.

"Keep smiling, my girl, because the rest of the vision concerns you." Mistress appraised me with a grin.

"Me?" I chuckled. "Was I scrubbing the palace floors?"

She leaned forward, all mischief gone. "You, Ishma, were seated beside Hezekiah on a smaller throne with a crown on your head."

I blinked a few times to be sure I wasn't still dreaming. Yaira's mouth gaped. Master and Mistress waited with hope-filled faces. I stared back, having no idea how to respond to such nonsense. "At least yours was a happy dream."

"Ishma!" she said, cupping my cheeks. "It wasn't a dream. It was a vision. Yahweh told me clearly—"

"No!" I pulled away, throat tightening with emotion. "You already explained that Hezi must marry a nobleman's daughter, and I've made my decision to remain single like Yaira, Dinah, and Leah." Tears threatened, but I sniffed them away. "Why would you tempt me with the thing I want more than breath?"

The master sat cross-legged and leaned over on his elbows. He closed his eyes and sighed. I could tell he was praying, and my frustration mounted. How was I supposed to argue while he spoke to the Creator of all things?

When he opened his eyes, he asked, "May I tell you about my vision?"

I swiped at stubborn tears, wishing I had the strength to refuse. I'd been asking Yahweh to reveal my purpose for years, and not once had He spoken clearly. Had He really spoken to Master and Mistress about my future? Was He speaking through my dream about Hezi? Feeling defeated, I nodded at Master Isaiah and bowed my head to listen.

"I saw Jerusalem and a jeweled crown descending from heaven upon it. The voice of Yahweh spoke and said, 'You will be called by a new name that the mouth of the Lord will bestow. You will no longer be called Desolate Ishma, but you will be called Hephzibah and your land Beulah, for the Lord takes delight in her and she will be married."

Something deep inside me shattered. The vision was too lovely to imagine, too beautiful to be true. I wept quietly in awed despair, grieving the impossibility of a prophet's fine words.

Master Isaiah tipped my chin, but I couldn't look up and let him glimpse my brokenness. I had worked so hard to discover Yahweh's purpose for me. Favored learning companion to the crown prince. Diligent servant in Isaiah's house. Even a member of this family as Master and Mistress included all those under their care. I'd spent long evenings with my doves to find the secret of grace and peace. But I could never be a queen. Never marry the boy I loved. How could Yahweh take delight in an orphan branded for life? How could He love a girl called "Desolation"?

"Hephzibah."

That name on my master's lips was more than I could bear.

"Did you hear me, *Hephzibah?* Yahweh also says, 'As a bridegroom rejoices over his bride, so will your God rejoice over you.' He has named you Hephzibah because He delights in you and rejoices over you as *His* bride."

I covered a sob at the unimaginable thought.

His delight is in me—as His bride. How could the master believe Yahweh deemed me His bride? The imagery of marriage blossomed in my mind—a husband's love and faithfulness, the security marriage offered. Even if Hezi never made me his queen, to be Yahweh's bride meant eternal blessing. *His delight is in me.* The words nestled into my heart and quieted my weeping, giving me strength to lift my eyes.

Master Isaiah was waiting. "We delight in you even as Yahweh delights in you, Hephzibah. King Ahaz will only agree to marry Hezekiah to a maiden with royal parents, so—"

"It's all right," I said and meant it. The news wasn't as devastating as it had been moments ago. "Hezekiah and I will always have a special bond. We'll remain friends—"

Mistress Aya pressed her finger against my lips. "We will legally adopt you."

Yaira stifled a squeal behind her hands.

"There's no legal precedent for adopting a girl," I said before thinking.

Mistress Aya covered a grin, and Master Isaiah had a ready answer. "You're right, as usual, but it's not *against* the law to adopt a girl. It's not done because there is no legal benefit for the family. It's the sons who inherit and pass down family wealth—not the daughters."

"What about your boys? Will an adoption affect your sons' inheritance?"

Mistress patted my hand. "Ish—I mean, Hephzibah, only you would want to discuss every legal detail before letting us call you Daughter."

My breath caught at the word. *Daughter.* I pressed my fingers against my lips to keep from quaking.

Master Isaiah tilted his head, his expression softening. "Yahweh will work it all out, my girl. Jashub can draw up the documents, and the royal recorder will approve the transaction in a stack of daily tasks without King Ahaz's knowledge." He snapped his fingers. "Just like that, you become our daughter! A royal maiden more than qualified to marry the next king of Judah."

Yaira's eyes filled with tears. "Yahweh has given you a new name as he did for Sarah and Abraham and Jacob. You are now Hephzibah." She hugged me so tight I could hardly breathe. "And you will marry the love of your life and have a dozen beautiful babies that I will help you raise. Perhaps this is God's grand purpose for us both."

I hugged her till my arms ached, grateful for such a friend, but I still struggled to take it all in. How could all this really come to pass? *Yahweh, I'm not sure which is more difficult to believe— that I could be Hezi's bride or Yours.*

I laid my head on Yaira's shoulder, amazed at

her gracious heart. How could she be so happy when she would never marry the man she loved? I pulled away, searching the windows of her soul. No envy. Only joy stared back at me. "No matter what happens," I said, "we'll always be together. I promise."

PART 3

[King] Ahaz gathered together the furnishings from the temple of God and cut them in pieces. He shut the doors of the LORD's temple and set up altars at every street corner in Jerusalem. In every town in Judah he built high places to burn sacrifices to other gods and aroused the anger of the LORD, the God of his ancestors.

—2 Chronicles 28:24–25

19

The king of Assyria invaded the entire land, marched against Samaria and laid siege to it for three years. In the ninth year of Hoshea, the king of Assyria captured Samaria and deported the Israelites to Assyria.

—2 Kings 17:5–6

Hezekiah wadded up the scroll and tossed it at the messenger who knelt before him. The nation of Israel was no more. Assyria had triumphed again.

"My lord, King Ahaz awaits your answer."

Hezekiah sat up on his mat, bone tired. "Tell Abba I will return to Jerusalem for the first time in a year just to attend his ridiculous banquet."

The messenger's eyes softened. "I'll tell the king his bravest captain will follow his command." The man was gone before Hezekiah could argue.

Bravest captain? What courage was required to obey his abba and fight Philistines? Perhaps true courage would have been to defy Abba and Assyria and rush to Israel's aid because they, like Judah, were God's chosen people. The twelve tribes had been one nation when

Yahweh ransomed Jacob's descendants from Egypt hundreds of years ago. Now, Assyria would exile most inhabitants of the northern ten tribes and import foreigners to work the land God had given them. Israelites sprinkled among many tribes and tongues would never be able to unite and rebel. Their nation was now only a memory and sad proof of the prophets' warnings.

With a defeated sigh, he began packing his meager belongings. He rolled his mat and collected his writing palette. His most valuable treasures hung around his neck—a small leather pouch containing his prince's seal and Ishma's purple ribbon.

He stepped outside his tent, looking out over the camp. *Ishma.* How he longed to see her. By the time they arrived in Jerusalem that evening and he washed a year's worth of Philistine blood and dust from his body, it would be too late to visit Isaiah's household.

Tomorrow. He strapped on his weapons. *Tomorrow I will see my Ishma.*

Hezekiah was awakened in his palace chamber barely past dawn by a persistent messenger who insisted Queen Abijah must see him right away. Hezi burst into her chamber, thinking her ill or injured, but instead found her bright and shining, welcoming her son to break his fast. Frustration, like a bad fig on moldy bread, roiled in his belly.

During and after the meal, Ima chattered on about noblemen's daughters and betrothals until Hezi thought his head would burst. Abba rescued him with a summons to his private chamber, where he demanded a full report of the Philistine conflict on Judah's southwestern border. He seemed pleased with Hezi's progress but complained about the amount of supplies the army used. Abba then recounted every gory detail of Assyria's victory over Samaria. Hezekiah would rather have endured Ima's betrothal chatter—almost.

When Abba unfurled a scroll with the banquet seating plan, Hezekiah could endure the inane banter no longer. "Excuse me, Abba, but I must send an invitation for tonight's banquet."

His eyes narrowed. "Who would you invite? I've commanded every nobleman's attendance."

Hezi hesitated but a moment. Abba deemed uncertainty weakness. "I'll invite Isaiah's best student—the one I've been competing against all these years."

"Make sure you return after you send the message," Abba said. "We still have much to prepare before tonight's banquet."

Hezi groaned inwardly, hurrying to the chief scribe's chambers. His first glimpse of Ishma would have to wait until tonight's banquet. He scribbled a handwritten message:

From Hezekiah ben Ahaz, Commander of Judah's 7th Regiment, Loyal Student of Master Isaiah, the Royal Tutor.

The teacher is invited to the celebration banquet of King Ahaz in the Throne Porch to be accompanied by his honorable wife and supreme student, Ishma.

Peace be with you until we meet this evening.

Hezi rolled the scroll, smeared on a dollop of wax, and pressed his seal into it. "Take this to Master Isaiah immediately, and return to me with his answer." The young messenger nodded and fled.

Knowing he would see Ishma would sustain him through the tasks of the day. He stared down the hall at Abba's chamber door. Perhaps he should be flattered that the king seemed pleased to see him, but he'd learned that there was always more to his abba than he revealed. His excitement was certainly genuine, but it likely had little to do with Hezekiah's return to Jerusalem.

20

From watchtower to fortified city they built themselves high places in all their towns. They set up sacred stones and Asherah poles on every high hill and under every spreading tree. At every high place they burned incense . . . They did wicked things that aroused the LORD's anger. They worshiped idols, though the LORD had said, "You shall not do this."

—2 Kings 17:9–12

Isaiah reclined at his lavishly stocked banquet table with four other noblemen—the recorder, two secretaries, and the royal treasurer, who was his dear friend and Eliakim's abba, Hilkiah—and Hephzibah. The secretaries offered curt bows to the lowly tutor, then began quiet conversation with the recorder. Isaiah was relieved to skip the polite banter. Hilkiah was far more intelligent and vastly more interesting.

Isaiah glanced at Hephzibah, who sat moping between him and Hilkiah. Isaiah nodded toward his daughter, signaling his friend to make an effort. "You look beautiful this evening, Hephzibah," Hilkiah said.

Lifting her head, she squared her shoulders.

"Thank you, Lord Hilkiah." Her smile faded, and she returned her attention to fidgeting hands.

"Tell me how we were so graced with your presence on the men's side of the hall?" Hilkiah's kind manner couched the question without a sting.

"The palace administrator assumed the invitation addressed to 'Isaiah's supreme student, Ishma,' was for a boy." Hephzibah looked up again, a spark in her eyes. "I must be a well-kept secret." Hilkiah's laughter joined with the celebration in the hall, where most of Judah's noble class had arrived from every town and village to celebrate Assyria's victory over Israel.

Isaiah peered at the recorder and secretaries, hoping they hadn't heard the name *Ishma*. The three men were self-sequestered, intent on their conversation. If Ahaz were to discover Hephzibah's story, the road to her prophecy's fulfillment might have a few more ruts. *How long, Lord, before You unite our Hephzibah with the new king of Judah?*

Hilkiah leaned across Hephzibah, keeping his voice low for Isaiah. "How long since her adoption papers were finalized?"

"Three weeks. Isn't Yahweh's timing remarkable? Only three weeks before Hezekiah returned home, our Hephzibah became eligible for a royal betrothal."

Isaiah noted his daughter's hands trembling

and furtively reached beneath the table to steady them. She grasped his hands with the strength of a soldier. The food on her plate had barely been touched. She'd eaten two bites of the lamb and one olive. She hadn't touched her goblet of wine. Probably wise. Seeing her so unsure of herself reminded him of her first day in class. He'd wanted to spare her then and wished he could spare her the current discomfort. Maybe a little reminder would help.

Leaning close, he whispered, "What if everyone here was sitting in a large circle, and it was the first day of a class. Then I told you to go to a large pile of cushions and choose your favorite. What color would it be?"

Her face brightened with a smile that lit her eyes. "You know what color, Abba."

"Red?"

She nodded with a little mist in her eyes. "Thank you, Abba." Hephzibah sat a little taller and picked up some bread to scoop another bite of lamb. She turned toward the man on her left. "So tell me, Lord Hilkiah, have you begun betrothal plans for my friend Eliakim?"

Isaiah released a sigh and searched the tables across the aisle to find his wife. Aya's beautiful face was etched with concern, but now he could offer a nod of assurance. Their girl was overcoming another obstacle with grace and courage.

The longer he scanned the crowd, however, the more he seethed. Didn't King Ahaz's celebration of Israel's demise cross some sort of divinely drawn line? King Ahaz and his six sons reclined at a table on an elevated dais. On their table, amid the trays and platters of food, sat cubit-tall statues of the various gods from surrounding nations. Molek. Chemosh. Asherah. Baal. And King Ahab's new obsession, Rimmon, Assyria's pagan deity.

To the right of those hideous idols sat Judah's elaborate throne. Overlaid with gold and inlaid with ivory, the throne's rounded back and cushioned seat and armrests bespoke comfort and confidence. But the roaring lions carved into the armrests displayed the power of Judah during Solomon's reign. Now King Solomon's lion-headed scepter leaned haphazardly against one of the armrests. And after King Ahaz had downed his second wineskin, his crown sat as haphazardly on his head.

Judah's king stood, and Hezekiah rose to steady him. The gathering stilled as the king lifted his goblet. "May the gods give us favor with Assyria's new king, Sargon." He stumbled back and added, "And grant the defeated Israelite king and his nobles swift deaths." He tossed back the full goblet of wine, then demanded a quick refill from a nearby serving maid. Hezekiah whispered something and tugged at his abba's arm, but King Ahaz shoved him away. "It's time I officially named Hezekiah my co-regent. Though he's entirellll . . ." He swallowed and tried again. "Entirelll . . ." A frown preceded a new attempt. "Though he's way too good to be my son, he'll make a fine king when the Assyrians stake me to the ground." He raised his goblet, oblivious to his son's reaction.

Was it surprise or fear on Hezekiah's face? Ahaz had always seemed so confident in the decision to align Judah with Assyria. If even he feared the new king, what must Hezekiah be thinking?

"Drink!" King Ahaz slapped Hezekiah's back. "Where are the dancers and musicians to celebrate my son's rise to power?" Musicians entered through the double doors at the rear of the hall playing a lively tune, while scantily clad women jumped and twirled trailing multicolored veils behind them.

One royal secretary leaned toward Isaiah and Hilkiah with lifted brow. "It's an unusually lighthearted coronation ceremony, isn't it? Don't these things usually happen in the Throne Hall with visiting dignitaries in a somber service?" He laughed and drained his goblet. "Why should we be surprised? King Ahaz has never done anything like other kings of Judah."

The treasurer grinned and rested the goblet on his ample belly. "Lady Hephzibah, I see you've eaten only a few bites of your meal. Shall I call over a serving maid to request something else? Duck? Venison? I believe I saw fish on one of the serving trays."

"Oh no, please don't. I—" Distracted, she looked toward the dais and then wilted into silence.

Isaiah followed her gaze and saw three dancing girls surrounding Hezekiah. Two draped him with veils and one draped herself across him.

Hephzibah's cheeks nearly matched the purple ribbon in her hair. "Abba, when can we leave?"

Isaiah shot a quick glance at Aya, who motioned for Hephzibah to cross the main aisle and sit with her. Isaiah nodded. "It would be rude to leave before the king retires, but I could escort you across the aisle to sit with—"

"Excuse me, Lord Isaiah." One of the stewards bowed, blocking his view of Aya.

"Yes, what is it?"

"Queen Abijah has asked the girl to join her on the dais."

Isaiah heard Hephzibah's breath catch. He looked toward the table at the right of the king's throne. Queen Abijah inclined her head slightly. Isaiah wasn't sure whether he should shout for joy or run for home, but he chose to match Queen Abijah's measured response. "As the queen wishes."

Hephzibah rose with grace and followed the

steward to the dais. As she ascended the six steps, Isaiah scanned the room and noticed nearly every head turned in his daughter's direction—including the king's. King Ahaz set down his goblet and shoved aside a dancer to point her out to Hezekiah. Isaiah read his lips. *Who is that girl?*

Panic lifted Isaiah to his feet and propelled him toward the dais before Hezekiah could reveal the whole truth. The prince would have no idea about Hephzibah's adoption. Three royal guards stopped Isaiah's progress at the foot of the dais, but he'd captured King Ahaz's attention. "My king, I'd like to introduce my daughter, Hephzibah."

The music died, and the hall grew quiet. Tension rose with King Ahaz. Hezekiah jumped to his feet and hurried toward Hephzibah. "Abba, I'd like to introduce you to Isaiah's prize student, Ishma."

The king appraised her head to toe, seeming suspicious at first and then approving. "By the gods, boy, must I give you lessons on beautiful women? Why would you call this one 'desolation'?" The tension snapped like a harp string, and laughter filtered through the hall.

Isaiah released the breath he'd been holding, but Hezekiah shot a piercing glance at his teacher before forcing a smile and raising his voice for the crowd. "I call her 'Ishma' because she was the only one of Isaiah's students whose quick mind cut me as ably as I use my sword. Her beauty is surpassed only by her intelligence. I am left desolate in her wake." Hezekiah offered Hephzibah an exaggerated bow, and the whole gathering erupted in applause.

Her face bloomed crimson, but she inclined her head like a queen. Hephzibah proceeded to her place beside Queen Abijah, seeming utterly relieved to relinquish focus to the musicians and dancers.

Hezekiah descended the dais, wrapping his arm around Isaiah's shoulder and squeezing as he spoke through gritted teeth. "Your *daughter?* Hephzibah? I go to fight Philistines for a year, and you parade Ishma in front of jackals like a pompous princess."

Halting before they reached his table, Isaiah kept his smile wide and his voice low. "We have much to discuss. When can we talk?"

"Now." Hezekiah guided him to a back corner, where serving maids filled fresh goblets from wineskins. "Leave us, please."

Isaiah noted the maids' furtive glances and giggles as they brushed past the new co-regent. Hezekiah offered an impish grin, seeming far too at ease with young maidens. Isaiah's stomach clenched like a fist. So many of Yahweh's prophecies during recent years had pointed to Hezekiah as the righteous ruler to restore Judah to faithfulness and prosperity. *Please, Yahweh! He must be the one.*

Hezekiah waited until the maids were a safe distance away before showing his displeasure. "Why did you lie to Abba about Ishma?"

"It wasn't a lie. Aya and I adopted her, and her legal name is Hephzibah, *God's delight is in her*. We've chosen to call her Zibah at home. It fits—she is a delight." Isaiah wanted to tell him about the dreams. He'd planned on it, in fact, but a nagging doubt gnawed at his belly. "What is it, Hezekiah? Why are you so upset?"

Sighing, the new ruler squeezed the back of his neck and looked away. He'd never struggled to meet Isaiah's gaze before. "I thought she was different." He choked on a cynical laugh.

Defenses rising, Isaiah grabbed his arm. "What are you implying?"

"It's obvious you've made her like all the other pampered and perfumed noblemen's daughters. You've probably arranged her betrothal, haven't you? Who is it, Isaiah? Who did you sell her to?"

Isaiah couldn't decide whether to slap him or hug him. Relief displaced his concerns and prompted a smile—which fueled Hezekiah's ire.

"I turned away priestesses in the temples of Dagon for her."

The frustration in his voice turned several heads at the back tables.

Isaiah shushed him and huddled closer. "If my daughter was the only reason you refused to sleep with temple prostitutes, then you aren't worthy of Hephzibah's love—or Yahweh's throne." He held the boy's gaze while his words hit their mark.

"You know that's not the only reason I refused the priestesses, Isaiah." He wiped both hands down his face and growled. "Abba sent orders to my captain that I was to spend the night with a priestess of Dagon before coming home. I took her into my tent, paid her a full shekel—which was more than she earned in a year—and taught her the Shema, the commandments, and three psalms of David." He raised his left eyebrow and grinned, and Isaiah couldn't remain cross.

Isaiah's laughter garnered disparaging looks from the musicians. He and Hezekiah were drawing more attention than the entertainment. He nudged the young co-regent's shoulder, and they both turned their backs to the tables. More certain than ever that Hezekiah was the prophesied king, Isaiah was ready to confide God's plan. "We adopted Hephzibah after Aya and I both heard from Yahweh that you would sit on the throne—with Ishma as your queen. But neither Ishma nor Judah would be characterized by desolation any longer. Yahweh changed her name, and He has shown me great and marvelous things about your reign as Judah's king."

Hezekiah blinked. No words.

"Did you hear me?" Isaiah braced the young man's shoulder.

Finally, as if waking from a dream, Hezekiah glanced around the room and back at Isaiah. "It's a lot to take in, Isaiah. Have you spoken to Abba about a betrothal?"

"No. I wanted to talk with you first." Isaiah hesitated. "I may not be the best person to propose the betrothal to your abba. Even if he considered it a good match, he'd likely refuse if he thought I wanted it or Yahweh decreed it."

Hezekiah didn't seem offended or even surprised. "You're right." Turning back toward the gathering, he gazed longingly at Hephzibah. "How will we convince Abba to make the match if you can't suggest it?"

While the lovesick co-regent stared at his heart's desire, Isaiah noted the king's sharp eyes assessing his son's gaze. Even after downing several wineskins, King Ahaz was as perceptive as any man Isaiah had met. Though loud, obnoxious, and contemptible, this king could read people like scribes read parchment. And it appeared he'd just recognized Hezekiah's greatest weakness.

King Ahaz rose and raised his goblet again, signaling the musicians to cease. "Isaiah, you can't have my new co-regent all to yourself. Hezekiah, my son, leave your teacher to his friends and come here so I may confer on you the blessings and responsibilities of your new office."

233

Hezekiah offered Isaiah an apologetic pat on the arm and made his way up the center aisle. King Ahaz welcomed him, reaching up to rest his arm around the shoulders of a son who was now two handbreadths taller than his abba.

King Ahaz signaled his high priest. "Uriah, come forward to anoint the new co-regent of Judah." Stepping back, he offered his hand as an invitation. "Queen Abijah will stand at her son's side as he is crowned." Surprised, yet pleased, Queen Abijah rose from her table and stood proudly beside Hezekiah.

Three servants emerged from a side chamber, each one carrying an element for the coronation. One held a flask of oil for the anointing. Another carried what appeared to be King Jotham's crown on a scarlet pillow. The third, a purple robe with a fox-fur collar—the style worn by Judah's king alone. Isaiah's sense of dread returned. Hezekiah's coronation wasn't a spontaneous decision made by a drunken king. King Ahaz had carefully planned it and worked hard to appear impulsive. Why?

The musicians began a lilting melody as King Ahaz instructed Hezekiah to kneel and then placed Solomon's golden scepter in his hand. Uriah invoked Yahweh's blessing on the new co-regent and poured the flask of oil on his head, letting it drip onto his cheeks and beard. The music swelled, and the audience cheered.

Hezekiah raised his arms, victorious, and King Ahaz urged him to his feet, embracing the son who was now equal in power and authority.

Isaiah, focused on Hezekiah's face, saw the moment a profound change happened. King Ahaz whispered something during the embrace, and the joy that had marked the occasion drained from Hezekiah's features like blood from a wound. Fear, anger, and confusion warred on the new co-regent's features.

King Ahaz released him and addressed the gathering like a proud abba. "My son has agreed that his first priority will be to travel throughout our nation, reinforcing damaged fortresses and rebuilding high places that have been too long neglected." Hezekiah's eyes were lifeless, his jaw set as King Ahaz gushed. "I've promised to approve his marriage to any maiden of his choice when he completes the task." The king patted Hezekiah's shoulder and chuckled. "By the time he learns the art of love from every priestess on Judah's high places, he'll be ready to settle down with a wife." Bawdy laughter erupted from the men, but the women sneered with the same disgust Isaiah felt.

Hephzibah's features were set like stone, her eyes fixed on Isaiah's face. Hezekiah returned to his place at the table without a word, without a glance at Isaiah's daughter.

21

May your fountain be blessed,
and may you rejoice in the wife of your
youth.

—Proverbs 5:18

I hadn't slept all night. Every time I closed my eyes, my mind replayed the memory of Hezi with dancing girls draped across his lap. So I took my mat to the courtyard and spent the night beside the dovecote. My birds' quiet cooing soothed my soul enough to think more clearly about the evening. Had Hezi touched the women? Smiled at them? Looked on them with desire? As hard as I tried, I remembered only his apparent discomfort, an awkwardness in his manner.

But neither had Hezi objected when King Ahaz assigned him the task of rebuilding high places and sleeping with temple prostitutes. Hezi was now co-regent and equal in authority to his abba in name, if not yet in practice. Without protest or debate he had bowed to his abba's will. Why? My doves cooed, but peace wouldn't come.

Before the eastern sky glowed with sunrise, Yaira appeared in the doorway with a few dried crusts of bread for my birds. "How long have you been with your doves?" She sat on the mat beside me, handing me a few crusts to crumble.

"All night," I said. "I didn't want to disturb you with my tossing and turning."

She laid a few crumbs in front of us so the tame doves would draw near enough to touch. Their iridescent feathers felt more delicate than Persian silk. "The master and mistress are awake," she said. "They sent me to check on you."

I didn't know what to say. How could I describe the void I felt? I'd maintained a stoic veil through last night's banquet but dissolved into tears the moment I returned home and saw Yaira. She'd poured out her compassion and wisdom before she slept, and I had no more words this morning.

Had I lost my words again as I did when I was five? No. I held tightly to Yahweh's promise, "As a bridegroom rejoices over his bride, so will your God rejoice over you." I was a bride whether I became Hezi's queen or not.

Yaira reached for my hand. "Master Isaiah said Hezekiah seemed troubled last night when King Ahaz announced he would restore the fortress cities and high places of Judah. The master is almost certain Hezekiah is being forced into it somehow."

Almost certain he's being forced. The thought brought bile to my throat. "He's being forced to sleep with temple prostitutes?"

"Zibah, you know he won't do that."

Stubborn tears burned my eyes. "The Hezi I

knew would never do that, it's true, but I'm not sure about the Hezi I saw at last night's banquet." The words tasted bitter on my tongue and sounded even worse to my ears. "I don't know what to think, Yaira. Before Abba and Ima's prophecy, I'd accepted that Hezi would marry someone else. But now, knowing that Yahweh chose me as Hezi's queen, the thought of another woman in Hezi's arms twists my stomach into knots."

Yaira straightened her shoulders and gave me that worried-ima look. "Hezi is now *King Hezekiah*. You know kings take many wives to build a legacy. Even King David had multiple wives—*and concubines*."

Her words came crashing into my already wounded heart. "I hadn't even considered Hezi marrying other women. He's always admired the marriage commitments of his great-*saba* Uzziah and *saba* Jotham. They remained faithful to one wife their whole lives."

The doves returned to their dovecote, and I felt their departure like the loss of a woolen blanket on a winter's night. I waited for Yaira to speak because I was tired of talking. Tired of thinking.

Keeping her focus on the dovecote, Yaira spoke into the breaking dawn. "If Hezi strays from Yahweh's righteous path and follows in Ahaz's footsteps, can you refuse to be his queen? Or must you fulfill the vision Yahweh showed Master and

Mistress regardless of Hezi's commitment to Yahweh?"

The questions stole my breath. Hezi following in King Ahaz's path? I couldn't imagine it. If he defiled himself with pagan priestesses, I couldn't marry him. On the other hand, how could I refuse him when Yahweh had decreed our union through the visions of both Abba and Ima? I dropped my head in my hands and groaned. "Maybe I'll go hide with the prophets for a while." Realizing how I might have sounded, I looked up and saw Yaira's eyes filling with tears. I wrapped her in a crushing hug. "Forgive me. I didn't mean—"

"I know," she said, releasing me and swiping at tears. "Sometimes I wish to return to Micah's quiet, hidden world, but out here I experience joy more deeply because I've known sadness. And I treasure the bonds of family because I've been lonely. The caves taught me to embrace the darkness so I could fully appreciate the light."

I hugged her again, remembering last month's Sabbath celebration when Jashub and Hallel announced the coming of their first child. Yaira had smiled and rejoiced with the rest of us, showing no sign of jealousy or regret. But how did she feel every time Jashub and Hallel joined the family for dinner? Each time Hallel accompanied the women to distribute supplies to the poor? "Do you regret coming back to live with Master and Mistress?"

I saw no change in her expression. No sign of regret or forced joy. "Not at all. Yahweh's purpose for me is to serve wherever I am. When you experienced the nightmares, I was here to serve you, and Yahweh allowed me to witness first-hand your name changing." Her eyes grew more distant. "When Master and Mistress spoke that prophecy over you, I received a portion of it for myself." She turned to me, suddenly concerned. "Can I do that—embrace the prophecy for myself when it was intended for you?"

Dear Yaira. I patted her knee. "Well, I don't know. How did you apply it?"

"Near the end of Master Isaiah's vision, he said something about Yahweh rejoicing over you as a bridegroom rejoices over a bride." She ducked her head and fiddled with her hands. "I know the prophecy was meant for you, Zibah, but it felt as if Yahweh was saying the same thing to me. That I could be His bride too."

My tears came again, this time from gratitude. *Thank You, Yahweh, for my friend, and thank You for answering my prayer from years ago—to love her and be near to her.* I hugged her like the lifeline she was and nodded. "I'm sure you can be Yahweh's bride too."

We wiped our faces, and she stood. "Shall I bring you a bowl of yogurt to break your fast?"

"No thank you," I said, rolling my mat. "I think I'll go back to our room and try to rest some."

The lack of sleep had begun to take its toll.

"I'll check on you later," she said over her shoulder.

I followed her into the house. Dinah, Leah, and Ima were already busy in the kitchen, preparing the morning meal.

"Zibah, you should eat something," Ima called as I passed through.

"I'll eat when I wake. I'm too tired now." I continued to my chamber, spread out my mat, and felt every muscle relax as I lay down. Though nothing had changed since the night before, I somehow felt more peaceful. My eyes eased shut with the image of Yaira and myself dressed in bridal robes, standing before a great white throne.

It seemed like only moments passed before I heard sandals slapping the tiled hallway outside our chamber. I squeezed my eyes shut and groaned. "Yaira, I don't want any yogurt."

"Hephzibah?" Ima called from the doorway.

I turned to face the wall. "Yes?"

"King Hezekiah is coming to see you this morning."

King Hezekiah. I would have rather had yogurt. "Tell him I've left Judah and will never return."

She stood over me now. "He will be a guest in our house, and you must receive him."

I threw off the linen sheet and shot past her into the courtyard, where I found Abba reading a scroll. "Why did you invite Hezi to come here?

I never want to see him again." My doves flew from the dovecote at the commotion.

Dark circles rimmed Abba's eyes, betraying his sleepless night. He set aside the scroll and stood. "I didn't invite him, Daughter. He is now the king of Judah and goes wherever he pleases. I received a message from the palace this morning." He appraised my disheveled appearance. "If you're going to be presentable, you'd best change your robe and ask Yaira to fix your hair."

"I refuse to be presentable for a king who will rebuild pagan high places and lie with temple priestesses."

The gate squeaked, and a familiar voice washed over me. "Would you be presentable for a king who chooses to keep his ima alive at great cost?"

Abba Isaiah bowed immediately. I squeezed my eyes shut and refused to turn around. I was a mess. Eyes undoubtedly swollen from a night's worth of crying, hair freshly out of bed. Footsteps drew near, and his presence loomed behind me. His breath on my neck smelled of cinnamon. *Hezekiah, no. Just leave me now.* A sob escaped before I could capture it.

He spun me around and held me tightly. "Isaiah, leave us alone please."

"I'm sorry, my king. I will not. She's my only daughter, and I won't leave her alone with you or any other man."

"Samuel!" Hezekiah shouted. I jumped but kept

my face buried against his chest. His heart was pounding like mine, and his voice was ragged. "Isaiah, my guard will remain in the courtyard as our chaperone. I need to speak with Hephzibah alone."

Silence. Curiosity overcame dignity, and I popped my head up. Abba waited. "Will you speak with the king alone? It is your choice, Hephzibah."

I would rather run to my room and hide under the mattress, but that's what little Ishma would do. I was Hephzibah now, married to Yahweh if never to Hezekiah. "I will speak with him."

Abba gently pulled me from Hezekiah's arms and sat me on his stool. He paused a handbreadth from the king's face. "She can speak with you from there."

I bowed my head, almost smiling, adoring his protectiveness.

Hezekiah waited until Abba disappeared into the house, and then he knelt before me. "Will you hear what I have to say, or have you already condemned me without knowing the truth?"

The question weakened my defenses.

"When Abba embraced me last night, he threatened Ima's life if I didn't agree to whatever undertaking he assigned. I was as surprised—and mortified—as you when he announced my 'top priority' to the banquet guests."

I kept my head bowed but considered his

explanation. It made sense from all I knew of King Ahaz's despicable character. He would threaten his queen and impose an equally vile task on his righteous son. And my best friend would protect his ima. But at what cost? "I'm not sure I know you anymore, *King Hezekiah*."

He tipped my chin and captured my gaze for the first time. "I'm your Hezi, and from what Isaiah tells me"—he wiped my tears with his thumbs—"you are Yahweh's delight, and mine, Hephzibah."

I looked away, mortified that he knew of the prophecy. How foolish I must have seemed to him last night, dressed in a fine silk robe, jewels braided into my hair. He couldn't know that Isaiah's household and the prophets we fed had skimped on meals for months to purchase those things. And for what? So I could impress a prince who became a king who will rebuild high places and—

"Zibah." Startled at his use of my new name, I found him smiling. "Isaiah said I could call you Zibah. I like it. It suits you." He scooted closer, leaning his elbow on one knee so our noses nearly touched. "For you are indeed my delight. You have given me life since the moment I saw your face hovering over mine in the stretcher. With Yahweh as my witness, I will remain faithful to you, Hephzibah—as my saba Jotham was faithful to his wife and great-saba Uzziah to his. I want you and only you."

Was he saying what I thought he was saying? One wife? Forever? My heart pounded so hard, I thought it might leap from my chest. I wanted to respond, but I didn't trust my voice.

He sobered and tucked a strand of hair behind my ear. "I must leave in a week, but I will see you every day while I'm in Jerusalem. When I'm traveling, I'll send messengers to assure you of my love and faithfulness." He kissed the tip of my nose, and Samuel cleared his throat. Hezekiah grinned. "I fear Samuel is a stricter chaperone than Master Isaiah."

Finally, heart lighter, I could grin with him. "The master wasn't as strict as my abba is now."

We laughed together, the sound summoning Abba Isaiah to the doorway. "It appears things are right again." Brow furrowed, he entered the courtyard without an invitation. "I'd like to hear how it can be so."

Hezekiah lifted my hand to his forehead, a sign of loyalty and honor. "If you'll excuse your abba and me, Zibah, we must come to terms on a somewhat unconventional betrothal."

22

Hope deferred makes the heart sick,
but a longing fulfilled is a tree of life.
—Proverbs 13:12

On most days, I loved teaching Abba's younger students while he and Shebna focused on the older ones. Today, however, was not one of those days.

"Samson, stop drawing on Jalon! Boys, back on your cushions." If my hair weren't under my head covering, I might pull it all out.

"Enough!" Under Abba's fiery stare my rowdy students melted like goat cheese in the summer sun. "Are you ready to listen to Lady Zibah, or must I bring out the rod of discipline?"

Samson was first to raise his hand. He was five. "Can we use the rod to play swords?"

"No," Abba said, admirably remaining stern. "You may play with sticks at home. In class you will play with words—using them to read and write."

Abba turned to me and removed a small scroll from his pocket. Keeping his voice low, he said, "Why don't you take a break and go home to read your letter." Hezekiah's seal gleamed in gold wax.

I hugged him, squealed, and rushed out the door. Ima had taught me long ago not to run. Perhaps that was why God granted me long legs—so I could move quickly. In no time, I was home, the squeaky gate announcing my arrival. Ima met me in the courtyard, wiping flour from her hands. "Hallel is here to help make bread for this afternoon's deliveries." She frowned a little. "You're home early. Are you well?" I waved the scroll in my hand, and her face lit up. "That boy is faithful. Do you want to share his news with Queen Abijah, or shall I go alone for my visit this morning?"

"Let me read the letter first, and then I'll tell you if there's anything I want to share."

Hezi had informed his ima of our betrothal before leaving for the construction tour of Judean fortress cities, but he didn't tell her that King Ahaz had threatened her life. The news of our betrothal had been difficult enough for her.

Since Hezi's departure, the queen occasionally invited me to visit with Ima and sometimes gave me gifts. I once received an embroidered belt, stitched by her own hands. It was lovely, and I treasured it. I also received a plate of moldy figs. Ima told me not to read too much into it. "Abijah has always run hot and cold, dear, but if you remain steady, she comes around."

King Ahaz kept news of military progress from Queen Abijah as part of her torture, so the news

I shared from Hezi's letters was like water in a desert to her. She seemed genuinely appreciative, and I kept our visits short. Perhaps someday we might actually enjoy each other's company. Someday.

I hurried to my chamber and sat on my mat, leaning against the wall. My fingers ran over the golden wax, imprinted with Hezi's seal. Then I broke it and devoured the words like a starving beggar:

> From Hezekiah ben Ahaz, Co-Regent of Judah, Commander of the 7th Regiment, Beloved of Hephzibah.
>
> I miss you every day, my love. The sun rises, and I survive only because you see the same sun. The stars I count on sleepless nights are the same stars that guard your sleep . . .

His letters both filled me and made my emptiness unbearable. I pressed the scroll to my chest; the ache so deep, I thought I might die. *How long, Oh Lord, how long must we wait?*

"Zibah?" Ima's voice made me jump, which startled her too. We both laughed. She looked at the scroll still clutched to my chest and sat down beside me. "Waiting is the hardest part of any betrothal, my dear." Hugging me tight, she laid her head on my shoulder. "I think it would be nice for you and Queen Abijah to spend some time alone together today."

My heart leapt into my throat. "I don't know. She really doesn't like—"

"You're about to marry her son, Zibah, and then you'll face Queen Abijah every day of your life." She searched my eyes and spoke gently. "You must learn to survive there, as Abbi has. She wields great power as King Ahaz's first wife because she bore him three sons." Her eyes grew softer. "Ahaz loved her once. My friend hasn't always been so hard to love."

I wondered then how much of Queen Abijah had been surrendered to survive the harem and how much had been broken by the king. The thought of living in a chamber on the second floor of the palace—the hall of the king's family—sent a shiver of terror through me. "Why can't I stay in Hezi's chamber?"

She offered a patient smile. "It simply isn't done, Zibah. A king must have privacy for meetings at any hour, day or night. His time is not his own."

I'd always assumed King Ahaz and Queen Abijah had separate chambers because they hated each other. "I can't live in the harem, Ima. Queen Abijah will destroy me."

Ima nodded. "If you let her."

Swallowing hard, I realized Ima was teaching

my first lesson on royal marriage. "How do I protect myself?"

"Take your letter from Hezi today and read the portions that his ima would appreciate."

My cheeks warmed. "I'm not sure there's much she'd appreciate. If she didn't approve of me as Hezi's learning companion, she most certainly won't approve of the love he shares in his letters."

"Then take the letter and tell her how much you love her son. Find something she can share about him that makes her the expert. Hallel lets me think I still know how to cook Jashub's favorite meals. Imas likes to think they're experts on their children."

"You *are* the expert on your children." I kissed her cheek and tucked the scroll into my belt. "Should I change into my nice robe before I go?"

Ima looked at me from beneath raised brows. "Zibah, have you ever seen Queen Abijah without pearls, braids, kohl on her eyes, and red ochre on her cheeks? Of course, while in the harem you must always look your best."

My stomach churned as I walked through the main room where the women were baking bread. I waved my greeting, passed through to our dressing chamber, and changed quickly, making sure Hezi's letter remained safely in my belt. My nerves grew more ragged with each step to the palace. I carefully considered which parts of the letter to read. Most of it was too personal. But I could ask Queen Abijah questions about Hezi. That would be easier. What were his fears as a child? What were his favorite foods? I already knew but I could pretend ignorance.

Too soon, I was standing at Queen Abijah's chamber door facing two guards I didn't recognize. "Please announce to Queen Abijah that Lady Hephzibah has come to visit with news of her son."

"The queen isn't accepting visitors today." The guard stared straight ahead without any recognition of my name.

I eyed his sword, his spear, his dagger, as well as his round belly and sagging jowls. The other guard looked equally slovenly, and my normal fear was replaced by revulsion. "I assure you the queen will be anxious to hear what I have to say." Stepping forward to pound on the door, I nearly succeeded, but the guard grabbed my arm. I let out a screech. "Don't touch me!"

The two guards looked at each other and laughed. "Be on your way, woman."

Fury overcame fear, and I refused to be cowed. I shouted, "Queen Abijah, I have news of your son!"

The guard grabbed me, clamped his hand over my mouth, and shoved me toward the stairway. Several doors on the hallway opened. Two of the king's younger wives peeked out. Not the way I would have wished to meet them, but this would surely give them something to talk about for weeks.

Queen Abijah's door opened, and I heard a servant say, "Let her in."

The guard released me, grumbling. I smiled sweetly at him and straightened my robe. "I'll make sure Queen Abijah knows how kindly I've been treated."

I stepped inside the darkened chamber and waited at the doorway, giving my eyes time to adjust. Servants scurried away from the queen, who sat on her favorite deep blue couch, clearing away wash basins and towels. She must have slept late and just finished washing.

"You have news of Hezi?" Queen Abijah's voice sounded gravelly.

Her question gave me permission to approach. "Not much news, but a letter at least. Ima sends her apologies, but sent me to visit instead. I hope you're not disappointed." I stepped off the crimson carpet and waited behind her.

No response. I almost turned and left, but I remembered Ima's words when I predicted Queen Abijah might destroy me. *"Don't let her."* Straightening my shoulders, I walked around the couches to the balcony and threw open the heavy tapestries. Sunlight streamed in, brightening the gloomy room and lifting my spirit.

I turned to find the queen working a small tapestry in her lap, but she didn't look up. This was even harder than I expected. Tamping down my annoyance, I made my way to the couch, sat down beside her, and stilled her hands. "Are you all right, my que—"

I gasped as she turned toward me. She'd been badly beaten again. Her left eye was swollen shut. There were cuts above her brow, across her nose, along her cheekbone, and splitting her lip.

She snorted and tried to smile. "This is what happens when you try to 'fix' the man you marry, Zibah." Speaking cost her. She gingerly touched the cut on her lip. "Ahaz was charming during the betrothal, even romantic, giving me gifts and sending me scrolls like Hezi sends you. He was a valiant warrior, all muscle and brawn."

She focused outside the balcony on a distant nothing. "The match was more than I could have dreamed—the high priest's daughter marries King Jotham's crown prince. In the early years, I thought I could love him, but each time he returned from battle, he drank wine more and liked me less." Tears streamed down her cheeks, dripping into the wounds, but she didn't try to wipe them. "I thought he'd love me when I gave him sons. I thought I could do more, be more, give more. I tried to be enough to chase away his demons." For the first time, her eyes met mine. "But now his demons chase me."

I didn't know what to say. "Why did he beat you this time?"

She choked out a laugh. "It started because he ran out of wine. After the servants brought more, he got drunker and grew angry about a report he received about Hezekiah—which he refused to read aloud. I assume my son has been successful, and it irritates his abba."

"Hezi has rebuilt three towns," I said.

She smiled and returned her gaze to the balcony. "Yes, well . . . that would throw Ahaz into a rage. Now I fight back with the only thing that hurts him—his failures and the success of others."

"Ima has told you many times not to taunt him." I covered my mouth, preparing for the queen's venomous reproof. Who was I to censure a queen?

Instead, she grinned. "You should have seen King Ahaz's face when I said he'd soon be forgotten in Hezi's shadow. I blacked out from his first blow. When I woke, he was ranting about his other wives and sons. I was conscious only long enough to remind him that he'd failed to find the Yahweh prophets. One more blow, and all went dark. I woke up here, on my favorite couch." She turned to look at me. "It was worth it to see him despairing."

I held Hezi's scroll and sat beside his ima, feeling an overwhelming darkness. How could I reach someone so lost? Then I remembered Abba's words to her on the day Ahaz dedicated the pagan altar. *As long as Yahweh was with us, we always had hope.* "Yahweh sees you, my queen. Your suffering is not hidden from His eyes."

Her cynical snort broke my heart. "It's easy to say when you're grasping a scroll declaring my son's love for you, little Ishma. You were a captive and will soon become queen. Why wouldn't you believe that Yahweh loves you?" She resumed work on her tapestry. "I needed Yahweh's help years ago, when I thought my husband might still love me. When my firstborn stood before Molek's fire. Now, Hezi is co-regent and has the wits to wage his own war with King Ahaz. Mattaniah, on the other hand, hasn't the wits for Ahaz to feel threatened, but my youngest will at least command his own regiment." She turned, tilted her head, and cupped my cheek. "Both my sons are old enough to defend themselves and hate their abba freely."

I felt as if I'd swallowed a rock. Her quiet resignation was more terrifying than the fear that had plagued her all these years. I kissed Queen Abijah's cheek. "I'll come back tomorrow to read the scroll when you're feeling better."

Queen Abijah's chamber doors burst open and slammed against the walls. "I see you have a visitor, Abbi. I heard the voice of an angel from the hallway." King Ahaz weaved across the crimson carpet, his robe disheveled, his hair a tangled mess. "Yes, Isaiah's daughter. It's been over a year since I saw you at the banquet, but I have dreamed of your beauty every night since."

I shot off the couch like a stone from a sling. The queen struggled to stand as well, but it was obvious her ribs had been broken. I reached for her to lend support as the king sidled up beside me.

He smelled of sour wine and stale sweat. "I see you have a scroll in your hand." He grabbed it before I could stop him. "Ah, my son's seal." He began reading aloud: "I miss you every day, my love. The sun rises, and I survive only because we see the same sun. The stars I count on sleepless nights are the same stars that guard your sleep."

The king threw the scroll to the floor and stepped to within a handbreadth from me. "My son writes with flowery words like a prophet when he speaks of you, Isaiah's daughter. Perhaps if I taste of your forbidden fruit, I would speak like a prophet too." He grabbed my waist and pulled me against him.

"No! *Noooo!*" I screamed, struggling and beating his chest. But he was too strong.

He dragged me under one arm toward the queen's bedchamber as I thrashed. "That's right, little Zibah. You can tell my son it was all my fault, and he'll probably believe you."

"Ahh! No!"

He threw me on the bed, and I tried to crawl

away, but he grabbed my leg and dragged me back.

I heard my robe tear and felt the cold air on my body. "No!"

And then *thud!*

I lay curled in a ball on the bed, eyes closed, weeping. And alone. *This is a dream. Just another bad dream.*

"Get up, my king." A man's husky voice shattered my illusion.

I opened my eyes and covered myself. One of the queen's regular chamber guards—a man I recognized—stood over King Ahaz, holding a bloody knife.

The king stood, gripping his right shoulder. "You're a dead man," he said to the guard.

The man stepped forward, forcing the king back a step. "And you could have been had I not been loyal enough to spare you."

"You have eaten your last meal." King Ahaz stormed out of the chamber and screamed for the two guards at the door. "Execute that traitor, and send the physician to my chamber."

Queen Abijah covered me with her fine sheets and turned to the man who'd saved me. "Where have you been and how did you know to come now?"

The guard's eyes lingered on the queen's face, her form. "Heber and I tried to help you this morning. The king's guards held us at the tips of their swords while King Ahaz beat you and then . . ." He touched her bruised cheek. "I'm sorry. He reassigned us to the throne room, but I came as soon as I could. Then I heard screaming." He dropped his hand and stared at his sandals. "I thought he was killing you."

She glanced at me, shame coloring her cheeks, and then back at the man who saved me. "You've been a loyal friend, Gedor."

He pressed the hilt of his dagger into her hand and whispered, "Keep it. Use it."

Six royal guards rushed into the chamber and separated them. The queen hid the dagger behind her back as the guards appraised the room before leading their comrade to execution. Would they really kill Gedor for stopping pure evil?

Queen Abijah sat beside me, silent. Her glare said she blamed me for what happened to her guard. "You must never return to the palace. Not with Aya. Not with Hezi. Never again—until King Ahaz is dead."

My mind whirring, I could barely comprehend her words. "Do you mean to punish me, or do you think King Ahaz would try this again?" I could still smell his fetid breath on my skin.

The queen scoffed and looked away. "How can you be so naive? King Ahaz's pride has been damaged, even more than his shoulder. He is like a wounded animal, unpredictable and more dangerous than ever."

I would stay as far away from the palace as possible. Queen Abijah trembled alongside me, shaking the bed. "What about you?" I asked.

"King Ahaz will kill my guard because he knows it will hurt me more than another beating. And those beasts out there?" She gestured toward the door with a flutter of her hand. "They are the new guards reassigned to my chamber because mine had become too protective." She turned her face away. "Did Yahweh see what just happened to us, Zibah? Does He love you more than my loyal guard? Is that why he'll die and you'll live?"

I thought she was angry with me, but she reached for me and wept, deep racking sobs. "Gedor showed me kindness. He showed you kindness. Why must good people suffer for the sins of the wicked?"

We clung to each other in this chamber of questions. My trembling eased as I prayed; hers didn't. "I don't understand everything either, my queen. All I know is the peace I feel when I remember Yahweh is near and He is constant."

I felt her stiffen. She sniffed and pulled away. The pretend smile reappeared as she stood, still wincing at her broken ribs. "It's settled then, Zibah. You believe Yahweh loves you, and I will keep sewing my tapestry until I can stand it no longer."

Frightened by her facade, I placed a hand on

her arm. "What will you do when you can't bear your life any longer?"

Her smile disappeared. "Then I will finish what my guard was too cowardly to do."

23

Honor your father and your mother, so that you may live long in the land the LORD your God is giving you.

—Exodus 20:12

Hezi rolled his scroll neatly and tied it with a strip of leather. He held the gold-dusted slab of wax over the lamp's flame and let a few drops fall onto the seam of the scroll, quickly pressing the stone emblem he wore around his neck into the soft wax.

Too tired to call for a messenger tonight, he decided he would send one of his trusted men to Zibah with the newest missive tomorrow. His regiment accompanied him to every Judean fortress town and helped rebuild walls and reinforce garrisons. Hezi's goal was always to encourage and improve, so he and his men never took food or supplies from the town they'd come to serve. He and his soldiers camped outside the city walls, hunted game for food, and sourced water from springs in the surrounding hills or desert. So far, they'd been well received by every city—though Hezi refused to worship in their pagan temples. But even their overwhelming success couldn't fill the void in his heart.

He set the scroll aside, missing Zibah so much his chest ached.

The shuffle of sandals outside his tent set the hairs on the back of his neck at attention. Hezi doused the flame with his fingers, reached for his dagger, and pressed his back against the tent beside the flap. Waiting. Something fell in the dirt at his threshold, and retreating footsteps signaled a coward's retreat.

Dagger still in hand, Hezi cautiously peered out the flap. The camp was sleeping. Whoever dropped the package was likely a skilled soldier able to slip past his guards on the perimeter.

He bent to retrieve a sackcloth bundle tied with a purple ribbon like the one Zibah had given him. His heart skipped a beat, and he looked around the camp again. Who could have delivered a package from Zibah? He untied the ribbon and tucked it in his belt. The sackcloth fell open, revealing the familiar cloth of Zibah's finest robe. A satisfied smile crept across his lips. He grasped the garment at the shoulders and shook it out in the moonlight. A scrap of parchment fell at his feet, but it was the robe that stole his breath.

Torn from neck to waist.

A groan lodged in his throat. He picked up the parchment and read the message scrawled on it: *Return to Jerusalem before King Ahaz defiles your bride.*

He stared at the writing for several heartbeats until a guttural moan escaped. He covered his mouth with his fist to stop the sound, biting down on his knuckles until the taste of blood brought him to his senses.

"Hezi?" Eliakim laid a hand on his shoulder, and Hezi whirled on him.

"Get me a dromedary. I'm leaving for Jerusalem—now."

"You can't ride a camel through the mountains in the dark, Hez. Tell me what's happened." He looked at the robe and reached for it. "Is that Zibah's?"

Hezi yanked it away and stuffed the piece of parchment into his belt. "I leave at first light. Tell the men to continue our work here at Azekah. I'll return as soon as possible."

Eliakim studied him. "You're not going to tell me what's going on?"

The boulder in Hezi's throat kept him from speaking. He shook his head and retreated into his tent. Darkness nearly suffocated him. His mind wandered to places his heart couldn't bear. When he finally heard the plodding of camel's hooves, he leapt from his mat and met Eliakim outside. The eastern sky showed the first gray hints of a new day.

His best friend hoisted him into the saddle. "I don't know what's wrong, but I do know Yahweh has a good plan for you, Hez. Remember Whom you serve. Remember Judah's future rests on your shoulders." He slapped the camel's hindquarters and waved good-bye.

The sun rose quickly over the horizon, and the camel's long legs flew over the rugged terrain. He should make Jerusalem just after midday—in time to discover who sent the robe and parchment and confront Abba.

The cool morning air helped clear his head. If Abba actually attacked her, how many people knew? And of those who knew, who actually had access to Zibah's torn robe? The list grew smaller with each question. When he reached Jerusalem's Horse Gate, he dismounted and ran straight to Isaiah's house.

Mistress Aya sat huddled in the courtyard with her two serving maids. She looked up, startled, when he pushed open the squeaky gate.

"King Hezekiah?" She stood and bowed deeply. "Isaiah is in class. Zibah and Yaira are making their deliveries in the southern city."

He clenched his fists, not knowing what to do next. If he interrupted Isaiah's class, it might draw too much attention and alert Abba to his return.

"You must be thirsty," she said, walking toward the house. "Won't you join me for a goblet of spiced wine?"

He followed, not wishing to offend.

Mistress Aya continued past the study down

a short hallway and led him into a large open space. She pointed to a worn pillow beside a large low-lying table—the only furniture in the room. "Please, sit down, King Hezekiah, and I'll tell you why my son Jashub delivered Zibah's robe to your tent last night."

He stopped where he stood. "You sent it? Why? How could your son make it past my sentries? Who else knows my abba attacked Zibah?"

Her face lost all expression. "Sit down, Hezekiah."

He obeyed, mind spinning, and watched her pour the wine.

"When Yahweh protects, He can blind the eyes of even the finest soldiers." She returned to face him. "How do you think our family has successfully hidden Yahweh's prophets and provided for their needs all these years? Yahweh is faithful—and my son Jashub is quite good at being silent and unseen."

When she placed the goblets on the table, he could stand it no longer. "Who else knows Abba attacked Zibah?"

Eyes ablaze, she leaned in. "I would think you might ask, How is Zibah?"

He felt blood drain from his face. "The note said Abba had not defiled her."

Mistress Aya changed from sweet mistress to ima bear. "Must a woman be defiled or have broken bones to be wounded and scarred? Have no fear, King Hezekiah, your queen will stain the white sheet on your wedding night, but what of her spirit? Can its innocence be restored? Your ima's guard, who stopped King Ahaz before he could ruin my daughter, was executed at dawn." Tears escaped down her cheeks. "Zibah carries shame and blame that are not hers to own."

Hezi bowed his head, letting the full horror of what Zibah experienced pierce him. The helplessness. The terror and revulsion. Sobs erupted from the center of his being with a new realization. "Does she hate me for leaving her here unprotected?"

Aya cupped his chin, forcing him to look her in the eye. "I'm the one who sent Zibah to visit Abijah's chamber unescorted. That responsibility is mine to bear. You have no share in the blame, Hezekiah. The evil is in King Ahaz. God will judge him alone for this crime."

Hezi seethed. "Perhaps I will be God's wrath on my abba."

"No, son," she said, brushing his cheek. "That would be a mistake."

He pulled away, firm in his decision. "My next visit will be to Abba's chamber to mete out justice long overdue."

"Don't you realize that's what he wants?"

Hezi stared at her, confused. "You think Abba planned to attack Zibah so I'd kill him? That's absurd."

"Yes, it's absurd, and it's politics. Ahaz is terrified of your success, Hezekiah. As long as he maintains power over the larger army in Jerusalem, he is the stronger co-regent. If you charge into his chamber to defend your betrothed, he'll call it insurrection, and Jerusalem's standing army will kill you as well as anyone who tries to defend you. I don't believe he planned to attack Zibah, but he will certainly use your rage to destroy you—if you let him."

Hezi could only stare in disbelief. Her political acumen was spot on. Abba had stirred Hezi's anger to the point of murder—whether calculated or impulsive, it didn't matter. King Ahaz would, without hesitation, kill his son for treason. That was the level of depravity on Judah's throne. "Yahweh, save us."

She lifted her brows. "My husband says He's called *you* to do that."

The thought terrified him. He reached for his goblet and his first sip of wine. It was mostly water. His heart softened toward this woman who would someday become his ima by marriage. "What can I do to help Zibah?"

Aya exhaled a deep breath and reached for his hand. "She is confused and broken, Hezekiah. I fear only you can reach her. Be here tonight for the evening meal."

"I will. I promise."

. . .

Four new chamber guards bowed but blocked Hezi from Ima's doorway. "I'm sorry, my king, but Queen Abijah cannot be disturbed."

Anger flared, but Hezi remembered that he was no longer a prince. He was co-regent and king. "Has King Ahaz ordered my ima sequestered in her chamber?"

The guards exchanged a nervous glance, and the one on the left ventured the truth. "Yes, my lord."

"I see your dilemma. Let me make it simple. I am also your king. If you don't obey me and step aside, I'll have all four of you arrested for treason."

The one wearing captain's leather knocked on the door and announced as he opened it, "Your son, King Hezekiah, my queen." All four guards bowed as Hezi entered.

The chamber was dimly lit, with heavy tapestries pulled over the tall windows and balcony. Ima emerged from her bedchamber, head lowered. "Hezi, what a lovely surprise."

"Is it really?" He grabbed her shoulders. She cried out, and he released her. "What—" Then he saw her face, swollen and bruised. Worse than he'd ever seen it.

Gasping made her wounds more pronounced. "How did you find out?"

Rage roiled in his belly. "Did he do this before or after he attacked my bride?"

"Zibah should never have told you." She turned her back, walking toward the window and parting the tapestries.

"You wouldn't have told me, would you, Ima?" The realization infuriated him.

"Zibah doesn't understand nobility, Hezi. She can't be the queen you need her to be. Marry another first. Let Zibah become a second or third wife."

"Zibah will be my only wife, and she is everything I need in a queen. Intelligent. Honest." Stepping closer, he repeated, "Honest."

Ima whirled to face him. "What about reckless and opinionated, Hezi? Don't forget those."

Her level of disapproval birthed a thought too horrific to consider. She was capable of deception, but surely, she couldn't . . . she wouldn't . . . Hezi closed the distance between them and gently cradled her elbow, leading her to the couch they'd shared for serious talks since he was a boy. "Sit with me, Ima. I need to ask you a difficult question."

Suspicion laced her features, but she obliged, her graceful movements impeded only by the way she protected her sides. No doubt, her ribs were broken.

With a deep sigh, he asked the hardest question of his life. "Did you arrange Abba's attack on Zibah?"

A slow, menacing grin graced her swollen lips.

"I did not arrange it, but I wouldn't mind if you killed him for it."

A chill ran through Hezi's veins.

Her smile died, and a shadow of real grief darkened her features. "The only man brave enough to lift a sword against Ahaz was executed this morning." She gazed into the distance. "It wasn't supposed to happen that way. Gedor wasn't supposed to die."

"How was it *supposed* to happen, Ima?" Had she just confessed? He stood and backed away.

"I didn't plan it, Hezi." She stood and stepped toward him, pleading. "Ahaz has been entranced by Zibah from the moment he saw her. He could talk of little else. The other wives have been jealous, but I . . ." Ima tilted her head and spoke as if he were eight years old. "Hezi, I simply stoked the fire. I knew someday your abba would act on his impulses, but I thought you would be here to protect her. I thought you—my brave boy—would take the throne that is rightfully yours."

She moved closer, but Hezi stepped back again, feeling ill. "You encouraged Abba's obsession with my betrothed? You are as depraved as he."

"Hezekiah ben Ahaz! Don't speak to me in that tone—"

"Don't ever call me by Abba's name again, Ima." *Yahweh, how can I obey Your command to honor parents like these?* "Your deception makes you dangerous to yourself and others. I can't talk to you right now." He would spend time praying in his chamber before going to confront Abba in the king's private chamber.

With his first step toward the door, Ima blocked his departure. "Please, Hezi. Everything I do is for you, for your throne."

He gripped her arms and stared into her weepy eyes. "If you believe that, Ima, you have deceived yourself most of all."

24

Wisdom makes one wise person more powerful than ten rulers in a city.
—Ecclesiastes 7:19

Hezi woke on the floor of his chamber to the sound of panicked voices. He must have dozed off while praying. Hurried footsteps outside his door hurled him from slumber to the hallway. Abba's wives and other children peeked out their doorways on the family wing while at least two dozen royal guards poured into Ima's chamber. Her screams filled the air, but what frightened him most were his abba's angry shouts. Why had Abba returned to Ima's chamber after all that had happened?

Hezi shoved his way past the crowd of guards and found the queen shackled, a bloody dagger in her hand.

"Ima, where did you get that?"

She lifted her head, swollen eyes wet with tears. "Gedor dropped it after he stabbed Ahaz. I hid it, knowing your abba would come back to gloat over Gedor's death." Her features twisted into a face he didn't recognize. "Ahaz just won't die, Hezi. No matter how hard I try."

"Get her out of here!" King Ahaz shouted from

behind the bedchamber curtain. "Where is my physician?"

The guards started to march Ima out of the chamber, but Hezi stopped them with a command. "Close the chamber doors!" The men halted, most looking uncertain, but one obeyed.

Hezi stood in the middle of the soldiers, turning to face those who had witnessed the ugly relationship of Judah's royal couple. He spoke in barely a whisper. "You will not tell anyone of my ima's actions here today. If you are asked—even by the other royals on this floor—you will not lie but will answer with a generality. Say, 'The king and queen experienced a marital skirmish—as they often do.' Am I clear?"

The men exchanged questioning glances, but Hezi had no time for indecision. "I am your king. You will do as I say or face the executioner. I have no patience with soldiers who can't follow my commands." He received general affirmations, but Hezi couldn't wager his ima's life on a general consensus. "Form two lines to pledge your allegiance." Hezi made his way down both lines of soldiers as every man saluted him, fist to chest.

Ima stood in the corner, chin held high—shaking. "Take Ima to my chamber. Get her maids to clean her up, and keep her there."

"Yes, my king." Two guards grabbed her, nearly lifting her off her feet.

"Gently! She is your queen!" Hezi shouted.

Two other guards opened the chamber door and found the physician waiting with his basket of herbs and potions. "Come in." Hezi welcomed him at the threshold and spoke loudly enough for those down the hall to hear. "Abba has taken ill and will recover in Ima's chamber." He draped his arm around the physician's shoulder and guided him into Ima's chamber. The guards bowed to their king as they filed out of the room. The last man closed the chamber doors behind them.

The physician looked up, wary. "I take it the king isn't simply ill."

Hezi shook his head at the absurdity of his life. "I'm afraid not. If you'd like to stuff something in your ears, now is the time. If you repeat anything you hear in this chamber"—he patted the man's back—"it will cost you your life."

"I think you'll discover I'm quite good at keeping secrets." The man walked alongside Hezi down his ima's crimson carpet.

The young king threw back the dividing curtain, exposing the disheveled bed in his ima's chamber. His abba lay on his side, hugging a cushion. Four guards surrounded him, his personal guard pressing a blood-soaked cloth against his back.

Ahaz looked over his shoulder and scoffed, "Your ima is as mad as a rabid dog!"

274

Everything within Hezi wanted to finish what his ima started. *Yahweh, I can't forgive him. I can't even look at him without Your help.* He took a step closer to the bed, and every guard placed a hand on his sword. They were good men, protecting their king. They need not die for doing their jobs.

Hezi lifted his hands in the air. "I am no danger to my abba, I assure you." Slowly, he unbuckled his sword belt and placed it on a nearby table. Then he removed the dagger he had tucked behind his back in his belt and laid it on the table as well. "I have no other weapons." Again, he held his hands aloft.

The guards relaxed somewhat, so the physician nudged aside the one nearest the king to check the wound. "This will require several stitches. You're still breathing, my king, so the blade missed your heart."

Ahaz grunted. "Many will be disappointed with that news." He looked over his shoulder again. "Including my son. Right, Hezekiah? Did you suggest your ima's attempt on my life, or did she muster the courage to do it herself?"

The royal guards stared at Hezi, equally interested. "I had nothing to do with this attempt on his life, men." He met the gaze of each one and waited to receive a nod before moving to the next man. "I must now speak with King Ahaz alone. Take my weapons with you if you like, but

I assure you, my abba is safe with me. Now, go." He grabbed a stool from the corner and pulled it close to the mattress on the side the king was facing. The guards exchanged uneasy glances but finally took his weapons and filed out.

His abba lay with his eyes closed. Good. Maybe Hezi could talk to the man he'd feared his whole life if Abba's eyes remained closed. "Why did you come to Ima's chamber? Didn't you beat her enough yesterday?"

Abba's eyes shot open. "Your ima is the only one who tells me the truth. Don't act like you know anything about marriage, boy."

Hezi saw rage in those deep-set eyes, and his insides quaked. Tamping down his own rage, he said, "I know only a coward hits a woman—and attacks his son's betrothed."

Ahaz closed his eyes again. "Abbi told me you knew I tasted a little honey from your betrothed." A slow grin replaced his anger and sent a shiver up Hezi's spine.

He clenched his fists. *Yahweh, control the anger his taunts arouse.* "Are you surprised Ima wants you dead? You've mistreated her for years."

Abba laughed, wincing at the physician's first stitch. "Many people want me dead. Why do you think I keep my guards close and pay them so well?"

The summation of Abba's life. No account-ability. Problems fixed with force and bribery. "I don't want you dead, Abba. I want you to be a better man."

"It would be easier to die." A long pause while the physician sewed.

"You don't mean that, Abba."

"The physician says I'll be dead in five years if I keep drinking. I considered letting your ima do the job quickly but decided it would be more fun to watch her die for the attempted assassination." He choked out a laugh. "Abbi should have waited five years. She could have danced at my burial. Now I'll look at her cold, dead face."

"No." Hezi's single word opened his abba's eyes. "You will stop drinking and forgive Ima for tonight's *mishap*."

Abba laughed this time, a full belly laugh—and then groaned with pain. "You're mistaken, boy. I will enjoy both my wine and your ima's execution."

Hezi's hands were around his abba's neck before he realized it. The physician dropped his needle and backed against the wall, eyes as round as shields. Hezi pressed against his abba's throat, cutting off his ability to cry out—or breathe. "You have mocked me and bullied Ima for the last time. Zibah is not a toy for your amusement. Do we understand each other?"

King Ahaz nodded, his face growing crimson. Hezi released him, and Ahaz seethed. "You will regret that."

"No, Abba. We're about to negotiate a treaty, you and I. It's what kings do." Hezi nodded to the physician, who resumed his work on Ahaz's back.

"Aah!" King Ahaz roared. "Hurry up with those stitches." He turned a heated look at his son. "Why should I negotiate with a cowardly weakling who can't even protect his betrothed?"

Hezi looked into the bloodshot eyes and yellowing face of a dying man and pity suddenly replaced his anger. He need not take his abba's life when it was already crumbling around him. "Why should you negotiate, Abba? Because I have the loyalty of the Judean army and the hearts of our people. The palace guards obey you but hate you. You're behind on tribute payments to Assyria, and you've squandered your relationships with foreign allies. You are in no condition to fight a civil war. Do not cross swords with me."

Real fear flashed in Ahaz's eyes, and Hezi knew he'd won before negotiations began.

"What do you want, Hezekiah?"

"You will never again see or speak to Ima. When the physician finishes sewing you up, you will return to your chamber on the first level, and Ima will occupy this chamber. Guards of my choosing will ensure she remains here or visits the private gardens when you aren't present, for her own safety and yours."

Relief lightened Ahaz's features. "Agreed."

"You will never see or speak to Zibah again." Hezi leaned close. "Never."

The king whispered through gritted teeth. "Agreed."

"And I will continue rebuilding the fortresses and city walls of Judean cities until you summon me back to Jerusalem."

Ahaz curled his knees to his chest. "Wrong. You will leave Jerusalem immediately and return only for my burial."

Hezi's heart ached. He must see Zibah tonight, to make sure she was all right. "I will return to Jerusalem occasionally to see Zibah."

Another pause, and Hezi searched his abba's expression. Would this sticking point sink all negotiations?

Finally, Ahaz squeezed his eyes shut as if the words he was about to say pained him. "To be crowned sole king, the high priest must place the crown on your head and anoint you with oil *in Jerusalem*. If you stay away, the people here— who see me die more each day—may not crown you until I'm gone."

There it was. The insecurity that made King Ahaz the ineffective leader he was. "I have business in Jerusalem tonight, but I will leave at dawn. And won't return . . . until your burial."

King Ahaz nodded once. His only response.

"Good-bye, Abba."

Nothing.

Hezi stood, walked toward the dividing curtain, and looked back at the physician. "When you're finished tending Abba's wound, I'll send new guards to help move his chamber downstairs. But please stay here. Queen Abijah will return, and she has wounds that have too long been neglected."

"Yes, my king." The physician bowed his head but continued working.

King Hezekiah drew the curtain and paused on the other side, listening, as his abba cursed the man trying to help him. It would be his last memory of Ahaz ben Jotham.

25

Those who hope in the LORD
will renew their strength.
They will soar on wings like eagles;
they will run and not grow weary,
they will walk and not be faint.
—Isaiah 40:31

I set the plates around the table as usual but noticed Ima had added one too many to the stack.

Starting toward the shelves to return it, I halted at her voice. "Go ahead and set that extra plate, dear. We've invited a guest tonight."

I turned and heaved a weary sigh. I couldn't face a guest tonight. We'd only just returned from delivering baskets to the southern city. Ima was trying to keep me distracted, but I still felt King Ahaz's hands on me, smelled his breath, saw his face. I closed my eyes and pressed a hand to my forehead, wishing I could erase the memories.

A deep voice shot through me. "I had hoped we could talk after the meal."

I opened my eyes, and Hezi stood before me. Was I dreaming? He'd never been invited this far into the house.

He knows!

I saw it on his face—the pity, the sorrow. The

plate slipped from my hand, shattering into a thousand pieces, and I ran.

My eyes blurred by tears, I ran down the long hallway to my bedchamber and closed the door behind me. I crawled under my cover, crying, shaking, trying not to scream. I couldn't face him. Never again. How could he ever love me, knowing I'd been pawed like meat in the market, and not by just anyone but by his abba. I was dirty, shamed. I couldn't be a queen. I could never belong to the anointed Son of David.

"Zibah?" Yaira's voice was as soft as her knock on our door. "We're coming in."

"No!" I sat in the corner, rocking, trembling, hiding my face. I heard the door open. *"Noo! I can't face Hezi."* Sandals shuffled, and a hand touched my shoulder. I flinched and cried out.

"It's all right, Zibah." Yaira's voice. "Hezi's gone now."

I lifted my head. She sat beside me. My trembling turned to convulsive shakes, and my breaths came in gulps. "I'm stained, Yaira. Groped by evil. God's anointed king can't marry me now."

She gathered me into her arms. Rocked me. Stroked my hair. "Go to sleep, Zibah. You need rest."

I closed my eyes, but panic rose. "When I sleep, I see King Ahaz."

"Shh, Zibah." Yaira held me tighter. "You're

safe here. I'll stay with you while you sleep."

She loosened my braid, and I tried to relax as she combed her fingers through my hair. Would I ever feel safe again?

Slowly, I became aware of the darkened chamber and my waking. Why was I still dressed and lying next to someone leaning against the wall? Memories came flooding back, and I jerked upright, startling Hezi, who sat next to me.

Yaira sat beside him.

"Am I dreaming?" I asked them.

"No." Hezi smiled tenderly. "But I have been dreaming of our lives together as I watched you sleep."

"Stop, Hezi. You don't know."

"I do know," he said, tears twisting his handsome face. "I'm sorry I wasn't here to protect you. I'm sorry my abba is pure evil and my ima is so broken." He hung his head, sobbing.

My hands lay in my lap, unable to console him. Here we were again, deeply wounded, but this time we were not children who would laugh and play tomorrow. *Yahweh, how can You heal what's broken between us now?* I turned my face away, unable to watch Hezi suffer on my account.

Yaira began to whisper prayers like a song lifted on our behalf, when we had no prayers of our own. There, in the silence, our healing began.

Hezi sat near but didn't try to touch me. Finally

he said softly, "I love you, Hephzibah bat Isaiah."
He lifted his hand to my cheek, hesitating before
touching, asking silent permission.

I intercepted his hand, pressing mine against
his, and studied the way they fit together. Our
hands had played games, written on scrolls, and
even tenderly laced together during our betrothal
week. I could trust his touch. "My love for you
hasn't changed, but I can never call you son of
Ahaz again. To me, you will now be Hezekiah
ben David—son of David—King of Judah."

He nodded his approval. "I promise you, Zibah.
I will be as great a king as my ancestor David."
He paused, the returning peace quickly draining
from his features. "I don't want any secrets
between us, Zibah. Something happened with my
parents this afternoon at the palace, but what I
say must not leave this room." He looked at Yaira
and waited for her assent before he continued.
"Ima tried to take Abba's life."

Yaira gasped, but I lowered my eyes. I wasn't
surprised. It seemed Queen Abijah had tired of
her needlework more quickly than I imagined.

"Thankfully, I was there to intervene. Abba has
agreed to stay Ima's execution. She will remain
under house arrest in her chamber and gardens."
He brushed my cheek. "Abba has promised he
will never attempt to contact you again, but I'd
like you to stay away from the palace."

"I don't want you to leave." The words were

out before I could stop them, and fear loosed all restraint. "How can you be sure King Ahaz won't try to hurt me again? Your ima said he would be even more determined now—"

Hezi pulled me into his arms, whispering against my ear. "Abba is dying, Zibah. I made a vow to him that secured both Ima's safety and yours. I must leave Jerusalem by dawn and will not return until his burial."

"How long?" I could barely squeak out the words.

"The royal physician has given him only five years to live."

"Five years? You will leave me alone for five years to honor the wish of a man who beats your ima and attacks your bride?"

"It is obedience to the Lord, Zibah. I will honor my abba and ima so that I may live long in the land Yahweh gives me to rule. It is a choice I made to obey Yahweh, not because my abba is honorable, but because I am."

He lifted my hands to his lips, and my eyes followed. "I tell you again," he said. "I will be faithful to you, Zibah. You are my *one* wife, forever. I will use our time apart to win the hearts of the people Yahweh has called me to rule and to draw Judah back to Him."

I jerked my hands away. "What am I supposed to do for five years while you win the hearts of Judah?"

He smiled with that crooked grin. "Perhaps you should win the hearts of Jerusalem so when I return to sit on the throne, they'll welcome the king because they already love their new queen."

The thought of it overwhelmed me. "I'm not like your ima, Hezi. I haven't the strength. I can't flit from house to house, chasing gossip and putting out political fires."

"Ima is a canary, all chirping and brightly colored." He drew me close, and I let him, resting against his muscled chest. Yaira gave us a chaperone's stern look, but I ignored it for the moment. "Unlike her, you must be an eagle, Hephzibah."

"Why an eagle?" I closed my eyes and concentrated on his voice, replacing the horrible images of King Ahaz with the reality of my Hezi.

"When the regiment is on a long hike through the mountains, I watch for eagles. They're fascinating." His finger traced a flight pattern on my arm. "The eagle waits in its high nest on a cliff for an updraft, and then it merely spreads its wings, catching the draft beneath and soaring with hardly any effort at all." He kissed the top of my head. "We must both find strength in the waiting, Zibah. Trust that it's from Yahweh—for our good—and then soar like the eagles when He breathes wind under our wings."

"So you have your eagles, and I have my doves." The thought pleased me.

"Yes, my love, but the difference is a dove must be coaxed from its nest to make human connections. You'll have to leave your nest willingly to make friends with noblemen's daughters and rely on Yahweh's strength to overcome their sharp edges."

He had no idea how very sharp noblewomen's edges could be. I sat up and faced him. "I'd rather go with you and build city walls."

He traced my jawline. "The next time we see each other, you will become my wife. We must let that truth strengthen us in these difficult days." He leaned forward and brushed a gentle kiss over my lips. "You are now and will always be my delight, Hephzibah bat Isaiah."

26

People of Zion, who live in Jerusalem, you will weep no more. How gracious he will be when you cry for help! As soon as he hears, he will answer you. Although the Lord gives you the bread of adversity and the water of affliction, your teachers will be hidden no more; with your own eyes you will see them.

—Isaiah 30:19–20

"Please, Abba, don't go." Zibah blocked his path at the courtyard gate, refusing to budge. "The last time you prophesied to King Ahaz, he threatened to kill Yahweh's prophets. What if he's done threatening and takes action—beginning with you?"

"The king summoned me this time. I'm not going to prophesy."

"Even worse! It's almost certainly a trap."

He grabbed her shoulders and kissed her forehead. "I am going, Daughter. Out of my way." Scooting her aside, he opened the squeaky gate and set off for the palace.

During the three years since King Ahaz attacked Zibah, their household had been relatively settled. Zibah had stayed away from the palace, working with the other women of Isaiah's household to prepare and deliver meals for the family, the poor, and the prophets. Zibah also began mingling in the Upper City market with young women from royal families. Relationships among royals were slow to develop since family alliances and suspicion ran deep. Political grappling among the men meant social intrigue among the women. But Zibah was gentle, wise, and persistent. Most importantly, she trusted Yahweh to guide her. His favor opened doors for Zibah to attend many sewing circles and social events in noblewomen's homes. She wasn't idle while she waited, but her waiting had grown long.

When Hezekiah's correspondence arrived regularly, she seemed content. Lately his messages had become less frequent, and Zibah had grown anxious. Aya's contact with Queen Abijah had been cut off when the queen was placed under house arrest. No one in the palace commented openly, but rumors circulated that Aya's banishment had something to do with King Ahaz's temper.

Isaiah hurried through the Great Court, through the Middle Court, and down the private hall to the king's chamber. Isaiah showed his summons to the royal guards at King Ahaz's door and was ushered in immediately. No grudging looks or sneers. He was welcomed as he had been while serving kings Jotham and Uzziah.

King Ahaz's antechamber was empty and dark.

Only three small lamps offered a flickering glow.

"Isaiah?" King Ahaz's voice, gravelly and weak, called to him from behind a floor-to-ceiling purple curtain.

"Yes, my king. How may I serve?"

A guard nudged him forward, keeping his voice low. "Go in. He isn't strong enough to shout."

Caught between disbelief and concern, Isaiah hurried into the king's bedchamber and barely recognized the man propped on pillows. His stomach was swollen, his cheeks gaunt, and sores covered his arms and cheeks. When King Ahaz saw Isaiah, his eyes opened wide—the white portions a sickly yellow. "Did you bring the treaty? We must sign the treaty."

Three physicians and two maids scurried around his chamber, rolling bandages, crushing herbs, and avoiding Isaiah's questioning looks.

The guard spoke softly. "He moves in and out of reason. The physicians say not to upset him. Just agree and keep him calm."

"The treaty!" King Ahaz scratched his arms, digging at already raw wounds. A maid stroked his brow and spoke soothingly. He calmed and focused on Isaiah again. "What are you doing here, Prophet?"

Mercy stirred in Isaiah's belly. He showed him the scroll with the king's seal. "I received your summons this morning." Isaiah approached the bed, pulling a stool close to speak face to face.

"I had no idea you were ill, King Ahaz. What can the physicians do to heal you?"

The king choked on a laugh with no humor. "They told me years ago to give up wine, but I thought Abijah paid them to nag me." His smile died. "I summoned her last night for comfort. It's the first time I've broken my agreement with Hezekiah and called Abbi from her chamber since she tried to kill me."

"King Ahaz! Abijah would never try to—"

"Yes, Isaiah, she would, and she almost succeeded." He glanced at Isaiah. "I thought my son would have told you. Perhaps you're losing your control over him after all these years."

"I've never controlled your son, Ahaz. Only loved him. You should try it." Isaiah glared at the king until he looked away. "Tell me more about what happened between you and Abijah." King Ahaz coughed, leaving specks of blood on the back of his hand. Pity softened Isaiah's anger as the king began the recounting. "After the unfortunate incident with your daughter, I executed the guard who intervened. He was Abbi's favorite, so she stabbed me. Hezekiah sequestered her to her chamber and the gardens— for both her safety and mine. I didn't see her again until I invited her to my chamber last night so I could apologize for the way I've treated her. I'm trying to make amends before the end."

Isaiah shook his head, stomach roiling. "Abijah

has been imprisoned in her chamber for three years?"

He turned and held Isaiah's gaze. "Don't ever pity Queen Abijah. She laughed when she saw me and then spit in my face. She said I was already dead to her—the night I burned our son Bocheru in the fire." A cynical smile lifted the corners of his lips. "She's had her vengeance."

Isaiah dropped his face into his hands. *Yahweh, what do I say to a man whose heart is twisted beyond recognition?*

Mercy. Forgiveness. Atonement. The words came as if on a breeze, and Isaiah presented to King Ahaz the only true consolation. "Have you asked Uriah to present a sin offering for you on Yahweh's altar?"

"Now you sound like the one who's drunk too much wine." King Ahaz turned his face toward the wall. "I'm sure my illness is Yahweh's judgment. Why poke an angry lion after he's mauled you and walked away?"

God's holy fire washed over Isaiah. "Yahweh has said, 'In repentance and rest is your salvation, in quietness and trust is your strength, but you would have none of it. You said, "No, we will ride off on swift horses." Therefore, your pursuers will be swift!' "

King Ahaz's yellow eyes stared back, blank. "I never understand your word pictures. Why can't you speak plainly?"

Isaiah sighed. At least he was willing to listen. "Here is the meaning, King Ahaz. Yahweh offered you peace, forgiveness, and love your whole life, but every time He offered it, you slapped away His hand and chose to do things your own way. So He finally allowed your life choices to catch up with you." Isaiah leaned to within a handbreadth. "Is that plain enough?"

"Was that an attempt to make me feel better?"

Isaiah sat back and produced the king's summons. "Did you command my presence to make you feel better or speak truth? Because the truth is, Yahweh longs to be gracious to you, Ahaz. He will rise up to show you compassion because He is a God of justice."

"If He was a God of justice, He would have killed me years ago."

Hope surged through Isaiah. That sounded gloriously close to a confession on its way to repentance. "If He was only a God of justice, perhaps. But He is also a God of mercy. As soon as He hears your cry for help, He will be gracious. Though He has given you the bread of adversity and the water of affliction, He has also given you teachers and prophets who can lead you back to Him."

At the mention of the prophets, King Ahaz snapped to attention, his eyes narrowing. "You know where they are, don't you?"

"They will be hidden no more if only you

will throw away your idols, my king. Trust in Yahweh, and then—whatever decisions you make, whether you turn right or left—your ears will hear a voice behind you, saying, 'This is the way; walk in it.' "

Isaiah fell silent, realizing he'd likely over-whelmed his king. Ahaz's blank stare disclosed nothing of the thoughts behind his yellowed eyes.

"I'll stop the New Moon sacrifices to Molek," he finally said. "Though you must admit we've regained many of our cities from the Edomites and Philistines since the sacrifices began."

"I'll admit nothing. You've regained those cities because of soldiers like Hezekiah and Mattaniah—your *living* sons, King Ahaz. It had nothing to do with a bronze statue and children's deaths."

"Ah, yes. Hezekiah." Bitterness laced the king's tone. "The whole nation will rejoice when I die and my handsome, brilliant son takes my throne."

"He is an honorable man, King Ahaz. You should be proud."

"He is a leech and has sucked life from me ever since I threw his brother into the fire." King Ahaz suddenly arched his back, his head tossing back and forth. His eyes searched the room and then focused on something in the distance. "Abijah, where is Bocheru? He must dress for the ceremony."

One of the physicians laid his hand on Isaiah's shoulder. "The king should rest now." Two maids now took their places beside the king, pressing his hands down when he tried to scratch his wounds again.

Isaiah approached the three huddled physicians. "Is there truly nothing you can do to help him?"

"We are treating him with milk-thistle tea and adding turmeric to his food. He's shown some improvement since yesterday." Isaiah raised his brows, and the physician acknowledged his disbelief. "King Ahaz wouldn't have been able to carry on a conversation earlier this morning. We're seeing good results."

"So he could recover?"

The physician's grave expression answered before he spoke. "Unfortunately, no, but we can perhaps give him more time." He added from lowered brows, "*If* he stops drinking wine."

Isaiah looked over his shoulder at the wasting flesh of a human life. "Has anyone sent word to King Hezekiah? He should be prepared if—"

"King Hezekiah has known of his abba's failing health for years, but King Ahaz has forbidden his son to return to Jerusalem until after his death."

Isaiah's head snapped back to the physician. "Forbidden? King Ahaz doesn't want to see him?"

"Nor will he see the queen again after last night's . . . encounter." The man's eyes softened.

"I suspect you are the only family he had left to summon."

"What about his other sons?" At least two of the princes served on the royal counsel.

"They've refused his summons, offering excuses of travel and illness. Now, if you'll excuse me"—the physician bowed—"I must return to my patient."

Isaiah stood at the foot of the king's bed, a terrible mixture of emotions warring within. He had watched Ahaz grow up from a boy with curly red hair into this sad mound of wasting flesh. Caregivers worked frantically to save his life from reckless living. Was it heartless to pray for his repentance and wish him dead? *Yahweh, how do I pray for my cousin Ahaz?*

God's answer blew over his spirit: *Let one who walks in darkness, one who has no light, trust in the name of the* LORD.

Isaiah squeezed his eyes shut and whispered, "Holy One of Israel, work in King Ahaz to give up control to the God who is King of all."

27

You who live in Lachish . . .
You are where the sin of Daughter Zion
    began,
for the transgressions of Israel were found
    in you.

                           —Micah 1:13

Hezekiah wiped his brow with the tail of his headband. Spring had arrived in Lachish with a vengeance, and sweat dripped from the ringlets around his face as he worked. "Ready, teams one and two?" he shouted to the men on the far side of the retaining wall, dropping his hammer and bracing his feet.

Every man on both teams nodded. "Yes, my lord."

Leaning down, Hezi grabbed his rope and looked over at team four standing across from him. "Ready to steady it after we lift?" Their foreman nodded, his team lightly grasping the rope for now.

Glancing over his shoulder, Hezi made sure the six men behind him on team three grabbed the rope and were ready to pull. "Put your backs into it men. Now—pull!"

Like teams of oxen, his group and team one

on the far side tugged in unison, digging their heels into the dusty soil, hoisting the wall off the ground. The two steadying teams now held their ropes taut, lending support until the wall was perfectly erect. "Gently! Pull it back gently, now," Hezi shouted.

Eliakim stood at the end, yellow flag extended, and closed one eye to measure plumb with his thumb. "A little to my left. A little more. Good! Hold it!" he shouted, thrusting his red flag into the air. "Carpenters, get in there and shore it up!"

All four teams held the giant wall steady while the carpenters built an ingenious bracing system. Eliakim, with his magnificent brain, had been inventing and building things since he and Hezi were children. He'd started with twigs and rocks but had proven himself in the past six years by rebuilding Judah's fortress cities and reinforcing their walls.

Hezi's muscles burned with the now-familiar thrill that hard labor brought. "Hurry up, women! I can't be late for Sabbath."

A carpenter shouted back, "I can't hear you with that golden spoon in your mouth." All the crews laughed.

Hezi dished it right back. "I'll shove my golden spoon in your ear if you don't get this wall up by sundown." These men had become friends, colaborers, and loyal Judeans. In this city, where Judean idolatry began, the citizens had shown respect for the co-regent by keeping the Sabbath since he and Eliakim had arrived.

After a bit more heckling and insults, the wall was secured, and Eliakim waved his green flag. "Well done, men. Well done." The hoisters dropped their ropes, shaking out tired muscles and offering congratulatory slaps on the back.

Hezi bent over and braced his hands on his knees to catch his breath when he noticed a little boy of about five or six, watching the men with awe. Like a dagger to Hezi's chest, the dark-haired little boy reminded him so much of his brother Mattaniah when he was that age. Mattaniah now governed Judah's fortress in Philistine territory. Word had reached Hezi that he'd reopened the temple of Dagon that Hezi had closed. Another life damaged by Abba's wickedness. Struggling for composure, Hezi turned to go and glimpsed a lone camel rider bearing the royal flag of Judah.

It was a messenger from Jerusalem—and he knew. He'd waited for word of Abba's death since Isaiah sent word three years ago that King Ahaz's life was nearly over. Something in his spirit said this messenger brought the news.

"Eliakim, follow me to the palace. Now!" Both of them ran, trying to beat the messenger to the palace of Lachish.

"What are we doing, Hez?" Eliakim kept looking over his shoulder. "It's the third palace messenger today. Why are we running from him?"

"Because we seldom get three messengers."

Eliakim looked at him like he'd lost his mind, but somehow Hezi knew he was about to become the sole reigning king of Judah, and he needed a moment alone with Yahweh before his life changed forever. "Stall the messenger when he gets here. Give me a few minutes in my chamber before he hands me the scroll he's carrying. Promise me, Eli."

They reached the stairway leading to the entrance hall, and Eliakim waved him on. "I'll meet him here. You go."

Hezekiah took the stairs two at a time, ran through the throne room, past the curtained doorway, and into his private chamber. He stripped off his robe as if it were chains and fell to the floor on his knees. But he wasn't low enough. He lay flat on his belly, face down on the marble, hands extended over his head.

"Yahweh. El Shaddai—God Almighty. El Roi—the God who sees. I knew this day would come, but I am not ready. Am I this Immanuel of whom the prophets speak?" The familiar fear choked off his words, and he pressed his forehead against the cold marble, willing himself to be stronger.

"Thank You for these years of rest from Jerusalem's constant conniving and deception.

In Judah's towns and villages, You've shown me the transparency of true love and hate. Those who hated me offered a chance to win their trust, and because of Your mercy, O Righteous One of Israel, I found favor in their eyes and Yours. Make me Your humble servant, O God, and give me wisdom as You gave my great father Solomon to rule Your people well."

A fleeting thought of Zibah lit a spark like flint stones. "She will be mine!" Hezi's eyes popped open, and an overwhelming joy washed over him. The coming days would be difficult, yes, but after mourning his abba, Hezekiah would finally marry his best friend.

"If she'll still have me." The whisper escaped on a thread of doubt. Her messages had been sterile for the past year, information only, devoid of feeling or the usual fire that was so genuinely his delight. "I have trusted You, Yahweh, to tend her love for me as the Master Gardener would tend His prize vineyard. Please, let the harvest come."

When Yahweh placed Judah in his hands, he would need Zibah's strong heart and mind to fulfill those prophecies.

From the corner of his eye, he spied a bug crawling across the marble. He'd never lain prone on the floor before, and the world appeared very different from this vantage point. Two bugs, in fact, crawled very near his waste pot. Deciding

Yahweh wouldn't mind the brief interruption, he grabbed a soiled cloth from his nightstand, ready to smash the creepy visitors, but halted with hand poised in midattack. They were dung beetles—little insects placed on this earth for a singular purpose: to eliminate dung. Devour it. Destroy it. Dispatch it. Hezekiah chuckled. Then laughed. Then rolled on his side and dissolved into hilarity.

Eliakim opened the door. "King Hezeki—" He closed it immediately, locking the messenger outside. "Hez, what are you doing?" Concern etched his features. "The messenger brings important news."

Hezi picked up one of the bugs and stood. "I've decided on a new royal seal that will embody the essence of my reign. The dung beetle, Eli." He lifted the creepy crawler aloft, watching its legs squirm. "Because my reign will destroy the pagan dung my abba built all over Judah."

"Your abba is dead, Hez." Eliakim was appropriately sober.

"I know. We'll leave for Jerusalem after Sabbath."

Verging on alarm, Eliakim stepped closer, lowering his voice. "After Sabbath? The messenger said the advisors are waiting for you now. If we ride dromedaries, like he did, we can reach Jerusalem by the moon's zenith."

Hezekiah considered what his friend said. The

advisors were waiting. "Call in the messenger, please."

Eliakim nodded and opened the door. "The king will see you."

The dusty messenger boy hurried in and immediately fell to his knees, face on the floor, hands extended. "Long live King Hezekiah. Please show me mercy as the bearer of such tragic news. Your abba was a great man, my lord."

"Rise, boy."

The messenger stood but kept his eyes averted.

"What's your name?"

"Eshtemoa, my lord."

"Eshtemoa, my abba was not a great man, but we will leave further comment to the record of kings. You have nothing to fear from your new king." The boy's eyes grew wide. "We will lead Judah out of idolatry, and we're going to start tonight—right now."

The boy looked at Eliakim as if he might save him from whatever Hezekiah was about to do. Even Eliakim looked a little nervous. "Hez— sorry—my king, what do you mean? We need to—"

"We need to celebrate Sabbath, friends, and that's what we'll do. Tonight." He pointed out the window at the setting sun. "We obey Yahweh first. My advisors in Jerusalem will wait, and next Sabbath they too will celebrate—or they won't be my advisors."

Eliakim's face brightened with a slow, knowing smile. "I'll alert the cooks that we'll have another guest for Shabbat this evening."

If the boy's eyes got any bigger, they might burst. Hezekiah tossed him a cushion. "Sit down, son. You look a little flushed."

28

As a bridegroom rejoices over his bride,
so will your God rejoice over you.

—Isaiah 62:5

King Hezekiah entered the city this morning,
leading a procession of Yahweh's prophets with
Kadmiel's seventh regiment as their guard. The
streets of Jerusalem were crowded with people,
silent but waving brightly colored scarves. An
unusually subdued welcome for their coming
king but appropriate in light of mourning
traditions for King Ahaz.

Not long after the processional, a palace
messenger arrived, and my heart fluttered like a
bird's wings. He bowed to Abba. "King Hezekiah
requests the presence of Master Isaiah. You are
needed at the palace immediately." Without a
backward glance, Abba followed the messenger
from our courtyard.

Evidently, the new king didn't need Hephzibah.

I'd suspected it for some time. Hezi wrote only
occasionally. His scrolls were always dated on
a Sabbath, and the scroll arrived the next day.
He still vowed his faithfulness and love, but his
words were an amendment at the end of a military
report—an obligation—rather than an outpouring

of his heart. Perhaps he was too honorable to break our betrothal. I would talk with Abba when he returned from the palace about how to rescind it without casting a shadow on the beginning of Hezi's reign.

I spent the morning with my doves, while the rest of my family chattered endlessly about how life would change because of our new king. I'd never seen them so happy. Yaira sat with her brother, Micah, and Dinah under the shade of our palm trees. Leah tended Jashub's oldest daughter, while Hallel nursed their new son. Jashub wore a proud smile as did Ima and Kadmiel, who talked of Maher's induction to the new king's royal guard.

I sat with my doves. They were restless today. Perhaps they sensed my turmoil, or maybe they were troubled by the whole family's presence in the courtyard. They, like me, thrived on quiet. *Is that why I'll never be queen, Yahweh? Are You sparing me from the constant havoc of palace life?* I tried to prepare myself for any good reason Yahweh might have to rip my heart from my chest.

I moved closer to the dovecote, cooing, lifting my arm and offering crumbs in my outstretched hand. My favorite turtle dove left its nest and landed on my arm. I offered the crumbs from my pocket and then stroked its soft feathers for comfort—the bird's and mine.

I heard Yaira's lilting laughter and glanced over my shoulder. How quickly our lives had changed since Hezi's return this morning. Micah and the other prophets had been restored under the king's protection. Yaira had her brother back—the brother she loved more than breath. And I would now be alone in my old age. Now that I was twenty-two, suitors would not line up to offer Abba a bride price. Nor would I accept. I hadn't met a man—noble or common—who compared to Hezi.

Oh, how embarrassing to take the name Hephzibah and seize the hope that went with it. *Yahweh, were those dreams of coincidence and chance? Or perhaps meant solely for Jerusalem with no personal significance?*

How could I have believed the dreams were meant for me? I would never again try to apply God's imagery to an immediate circumstance. But such a stringent restriction didn't seem right either. Yahweh had proven true to His words in becoming Yaira's Bridegroom. She seemed utterly content to be single. Perhaps, in time, I could be too.

"Zibah. Zibah!" Abba stood at the courtyard gate, an impish grin on his face.

Startled from my thoughts, I felt my cheeks warm. "You're back from the palace so soon?" How many times had he called my name?

"You're too young to have lost your hearing." Everyone laughed, and my throat tightened.

No teasing. Not today. "No. Of course. What is it?" My soberness stilled the others.

His tender expression almost broke me. "I've been asked to escort you back to the palace."

"Why?" It was more of a squeak than a word, more plea than question. I stood, my tension so profound, my dove flew away and several others with it.

"The king needs you, Hephzibah. You are his delight."

My legs turned to water. I reached behind me for a nearby stool, but the women of my household rushed me inside. Their excited chatter was lost in my swirl of emotion. Abba seemed convinced Hezi still wanted me, but I'd spent the whole morning convincing myself he didn't. Which was true? Would I know by the look on Hezi's face whether he summoned me from obligation or desire? *Yahweh, give me wisdom.*

Dinah and Leah pressed me onto a stool in the bedchamber Yaira and I shared. Ima disappeared into her room while my three dearest friends stripped off my old woolen robe. What would I wear to see a boy—a man—I had only glimpsed in this morning's royal processional? I picked up the bronze mirror and poked at my cheeks. They were fuller than the last time he saw me, my hair longer. Would he notice? Would he care?

Ima appeared in the doorway with a new linen

gown—with all its accessories—that stole my breath.

"Ima, no. We can't afford—"

"We have been saving for quite some time for this moment, my dear." Tears shimmered on her lashes, and a smile lit her face. It required all four of them to dress me. Ima slipped the robe over my head, while Yaira stood ready with the wide embroidered belt for my waist. Dinah and Leah concentrated on the jeweled collar and matching wristbands, while Ima tied the shawl around my shoulders—sheer as a butterfly's wings.

Yaira brushed my hair while the others worked lotion and scented oils into my feet and work-callused hands. I set aside the mirror and closed my eyes. How could a king love these hands, these feet, this face?

Yaira leaned down and whispered, "You are going to see your Hezi. Remember. *Your* Hezi." I tried to remember, but my Hezi felt like a dream of so long ago.

When I opened my eyes, Ima had disappeared again and returned with a box I recognized from her chamber. She pulled out a strand of precious stones. "Weave these into her braid, Yaira. I wore them on my wedding day."

"Ima, I'm not getting married. Hezi simply asked me to appear at the palace."

She patted my cheek. "We'll see, dear." She

winked at Yaira and picked up a jar of lotion to begin more work on my callused hands.

Again, Yaira paused her braiding and furtively leaned around to capture my attention. Without words, her eyes questioned me. I poured out my doubts, my hopes, my fears—all in a look. She knew me so well. There was no need for words. I knew she'd hidden all my cares in her heart. She kissed my cheek, and in that moment, my heart felt lighter.

When all their pampering was finished, Ima held out her hand and helped me to my feet. "Let us look at you." Her eyes grew misty again.

"He just wants to talk, Ima." I pretended calm, but my heart raced like war chariots.

"All right, all right. Go then." She waved me out amid giggles and squeals.

Abba waited impatiently in the kitchen, snacking on our midday leftovers. He looked up once, and again, then smiled. "You look like the queen you'll soon be."

I couldn't bear the hope in his voice. "Please, Abba. I'm not a queen—and I never will be."

He gripped my shoulders like a vise. "But you will. Yahweh has spoken, and He does not lie."

His certainty bludgeoned me, and I immediately bowed my head. "Forgive me, Abba. I know I should believe without question, but . . ." How could I say it without offending him? "If we've misinterpreted the personal meaning of the prophecy, I'm afraid my heart may never recover."

Abba reached for my trembling hand and kissed it gently. "No longer will you be called Desolate, but you will be Hephzibah, for the Lord will take great delight in you. As a bridegroom rejoices over his bride, so does our God rejoice over you." He tipped my chin to look me in the eye. "No matter what happens today in the king's chamber, you are loved. You are married. You are a delight. There can be no misinterpretation of that."

Abba turned toward the door and offered his arm. I laid my hand on it, and we walked like royalty toward the palace, a thousand thoughts racing through my mind. Our home was a mere thirty camel-lengths from the palace, and for the first time, I wished we lived on the west side of the Upper City. I would have had more time to prepare what to say.

I'd gotten only a quick look at our new king as he rode into the city on his stallion. I hadn't noticed if Hezi's nose still looked too big for his face. Had he grown taller? Fatter? Thinner? I suppose I'd changed drastically from the girl of sixteen to a woman of twenty-two. Would he still think me lovely at all? The more I wondered, the more nervous I became.

"Breathe, my girl. Breathe." Abba patted my hand. "He's still your Hezekiah."

The same words Yaira spoke—which both

consoled and angered me. If he was still my Hezi, why had his letters changed so drastically?

We crossed the threshold of the Great Court and too soon entered the Middle Court. I veered left toward the stairs, but Abba pulled right. "This way, Daughter. Hezi no longer lives on the family's second level. He awaits your presence in the king's private chamber."

My feet felt rooted to the floor. "Abba, what if . . ." Panic set in. "Did he ask to see me, or did you force him? Because if you forced him—"

"He is the king, Hephzibah. No one may force Hezekiah anymore." He smiled, but I could tell his patience was waning.

I am Hephzibah, not Ishma. Hephzibah, a daughter. Not a captive, not an orphan. I took a deep breath. And another. Then I nodded. Resting my hand on his arm again, I followed him into a hallway I'd never entered before. When we walked on tiny mosaic tiles that formed the portrait of a lion, the reality of Hezi's lineage hit me like a hammer. The blood of King David flowed in his veins. The same King David who wrote the psalms I taught to children all those years. The same King David whose heir would forever reign on Judah's throne. The same King David I'd studied all my life—he was my Hezi's relative. *My Hezi.*

Would he still be *my* Hezi?

A giant double door loomed ahead with two

royal guards. Both soldiers looked as if they'd eaten pottery shards at midday. Abba Isaiah walked between them without comment and knocked on the door.

"Come!" A deep voice shouted from within.

I grabbed Abba's arm as the doors opened, and he gingerly loosened my grip. I glimpsed the marks my fingernails had made on his arm. At the same moment, a very tanned and handsome Eliakim rushed to greet us.

"Ish—I mean Zibah!" He kissed my hand, and I bowed, which felt unbearably awkward. "King Hezekiah stepped out to speak with his brothers, but he'll return soon."

He and Abba exchanged a knowing look.

I fidgeted, feeling like an outsider, memories of the day Hezi returned from Damascus flitting across my mind. I felt awkward during that reunion too. We'd both changed so much in six months. How awkward would this reunion be after six years? *Yahweh, please. Give me wisdom to reunite well with my friend, my beloved.*

Glancing at Eliakim, I wondered if my old friend would soon marry. "Surely, as counsel to the king, you'll soon settle down, Eli—"

I heard a low chuckle from the corner. Annoyed, I turned to see who had the gall to eavesdrop on our conversation. "Already arranging a betrothal for my chief engineer?" Hezi leaned against the doorframe, devastatingly handsome. His lazy grin and come-to-me eyes made my chest ache.

Sheer instinct sent me to my knees. The only alternative was running into his arms like a complete fool. "Greetings, my king," I said, head bowed. All was silent but the sound of my breathing. *Please, please, Hezi. Leave now if you don't love me.*

The click of his sandals crossed the floor, and I feared my heart would stop when he paused in front of me. He stood there, waiting, but I couldn't look up. He was a son of David. I was an orphan. He was king. I, a servant.

Then serve him.

Words so clear, they could have been spoken aloud. They were spoken to my spirit by my eternal Husband, and I understood. My tears had wet both my cheeks and Hezi's feet. Slowly, I reached for the end of my braid and removed the purple ribbon. Loosening my hair, I dried Hezi's feet—washing them, anointing them with my love. I would serve this man without demands because I was God's delight.

Tender hands lifted me as jewels from my braid tumbled to the floor. Hezi held me at a distance, searching the windows of my soul. "I have loved you my whole life, and I will love you forever." He brushed my lips with his gentle kiss. "And I will marry you today."

I held my breath, overwhelmed at the moment. I'd dreamed of my wedding day a thousand times yet feared it would never come. I saw the truth of his love in his eyes, but I had to know why my seeds of doubt had grown. "Why did your letters change?"

"You didn't know?" he asked, seeming surprised. "Someone in the palace intercepted every messenger and read our letters."

His words hit me like a splash of cold water. "Who read them?"

"I'm not sure, but I think it was Abba." He released me and stepped back, sudden concern darkening his countenance. "I thought you knew because your responses became as cool as mine. Apparently, your letters became aloof for another reason." He swallowed hard. "Have your feelings for me changed, Zibah?"

"Yes," I said, framing his face with my hands. "I love you more than I did six years ago. Will you marry me?"

He grabbed my waist and twirled me around, while I buried my face in his neck, breathing in the scent of him. Ima would have said we were acting completely un-royal, and it felt wonderful. *Thank You, Yahweh, for keeping Your promise to a captive orphan who is about to become a queen.*

29

So Zadok the priest, Nathan the prophet,
Benaiah son of Jehoiada . . . went down and
had Solomon mount King David's mule,
and they escorted him to Gihon [spring].
—1 Kings 1:38

Isaiah watched the reunion of Hezekiah and
Hephzibah with more than a prophet's satis-
faction. These were the children of his heart. But
when the scene grew uncomfortably intimate, he
and Eliakim shared an uneasy glance. Hephzibah
should never have loosened her hair—but the
moment felt almost holy, too precious to
interrupt. Isaiah swallowed his reprimand and
averted his eyes.

He and Eliakim stood by the doors to give the
young couple a modicum of privacy. Isaiah heard
Hezekiah say something about ". . . love you . . .
forever . . . marry you today," and the panicked
abba nearly ran across the room. Then he heard
Zibah's cool-headed logic, exactly what he'd
expect of his prize student. Tension stretched
between them when Hezekiah revealed their
correspondence had been intercepted by someone
at the palace. The king assumed it was his abba.
Isaiah wasn't so sure, but it didn't matter now.

The next thing Isaiah heard sent him charging across the king's tiled chamber. "Zibah, wait!" he shouted. "You cannot propose marriage to the king of Judah!"

Hezekiah stopped twirling Hephzibah and set her feet on the floor. "Technically, I asked her first. And I believe we've waited long enough, don't you?"

Hephzibah nodded, the look of dreams in her eyes.

Isaiah pressed his palms against his head, forestalling an impending headache. Every decision this boy made was crucial if he was meant to successfully usher in Yahweh's new Jerusalem. "Hezekiah, please consider what impact a hurried wedding might have on your long-term reign. The customary mourning period for a king is thirty days. The nation must mourn King Ahaz."

Hezi's anger flared. "It's also customary to bury the king of Judah in the Tombs of the Kings, but Abba was dishonored by his wives and my brothers when they instead buried him in the family tomb in the southern city." He walked to his chamber window and pointed to the street below. "Do you see those people down there, Isaiah? Not one is wearing sackcloth. Their robes aren't torn. The mourning customs you're so worried about observing are not a priority for my family or the people of Judah, who obviously held no fondness for King Ahaz. I seem to be the only one who desired to show respect by moving his body to the Tombs of the Kings. However, after further consideration, I've decided against it." He dragged his hand through his hair and spoke quietly, perhaps to himself. "Moving Abba's body would bring more dishonor than leaving it at rest."

Isaiah bowed, relieved the boy wasn't going to cause a scene by moving Ahaz's body. "You're wise to leave your abba at rest, my king." Hesitantly, he straightened but kept his head lowered. "There is still the issue of your coronation. If you marry Zibah before you are crowned king, she will not be considered your queen. Only a woman taken to wife while the regent is actively reigning will be deemed queen."

Hephzibah found her place at Hezekiah's side again. "I don't care about being queen. I care only about marrying Hezi." Then, turning her attention to him, she added, "But part of our lives will always include considering what is best for Judah."

Hezekiah pulled her into a crushing hug, and they whispered things Isaiah and Eliakim couldn't hear. Eliakim stood awkwardly, picking at a stray thread on his new royal robe. Isaiah nudged him toward the double-door entry to give the couple more privacy. Keeping his voice low, he asked, "Has Hezekiah chosen his other council members yet? They could help him with decisions like these."

"Abba will remain his treasurer. He'll keep Jalon as director of forced labor. And he's made Azariah the chief priest."

"Azariah?" Isaiah's heart beat fast. "Azariah, from the family of Zadok?"

Eliakim nodded. "I can see in your eyes that you've got a plan."

Isaiah kept his voice low despite his excitement. "If Hezekiah insists on a wedding today, his coronation must precede it."

"We can't organize a coronation in only a few hours."

"We can, and we will." He became Eliakim's teacher again. "Tell me whose coronation in Israel's history was planned and executed within so short a time."

Eliakim pulled his brows together, deep in thought. Suddenly his eyes brightened. "Solomon!"

His shout wrested the lovebirds' attention away from each other, and Hezekiah looked perturbed. "What about King Solomon?"

Isaiah grabbed Eliakim's arm and pulled him toward the couple. "My king, if you wish to marry my daughter today—"

"I *will* marry her today."

Isaiah nodded, holding his annoyance in check.

"Then we must harken back to a historical coronation so significant that Jerusalem feels you cherish the foundations of the throne you've inherited."

"You mentioned Solomon?" Hezi said. "He rode King David's white mule to the Gihon spring in a rushed ceremony because one of David's other sons was trying to steal the throne. In those days, they didn't invite foreign dignitaries and noblemen from every Judean city." Hezekiah grimaced. "How can my coronation be in any way similar?"

"We will duplicate Solomon's process—using a priest from Zadok's family, a prophet, and the king's personal guard—to lead you on a white mule to crown you king at Gihon. The gathered crowd will resound with celebration so deafening, it will echo from Gihon to En Rogel and beyond."

The king looked at Eliakim and back to Isaiah. "What about the wedding? When would it take place?"

"We'll add the wedding at the end of the coronation," Isaiah said. "Combining the two will make it an event no one will ever forget."

Hezekiah still looked skeptical but didn't refuse immediately. He wrapped his arms around his bride-to-be and searched her eyes. "Every Judean maiden dreams of her wedding day. The months of preparation. The bridegroom's march and week-long banquet. Will you be disappointed to forgo those beloved traditions?"

She covered his hands with her own, her gaze unwavering. "I've had years to prepare my heart for the man I've loved all my life. You will never disappoint me, Hezekiah, son of David, King of Judah."

Isaiah stepped closer to the pair. "We have little time to accomplish much. Hezekiah, which three men would you like to lead your white mule to the Gihon spring: the high priest, a prophet, and the captain of your bodyguard?" Isaiah waited, hoping Hezi would designate him the prophet.

"My new high priest, Azariah, is a descendant of David's priest Zadok," Hezi said. "So it appears Yahweh has already gone before us. I've named Samuel as captain of my royal guard, and I suppose Micah would be the logical choice for prophet since you're the bride's abba, Isaiah."

Isaiah tried to mask his disappointment, but the look on Zibah's face told him he'd failed.

"Why don't we postpone the wedding," she said with forced joy. "Let's focus on the coronation today."

"No!" Isaiah and Hezekiah said in unison.

Feeling as low as a snake by the Dead Sea, Isaiah took his daughter's hand and held it against his forehead in a sign of loyalty and service. "I was caught up in the excitement, Daughter. Please forgive me. It would be my greatest honor to lead my only daughter to her wedding canopy." He glanced at the king and then winked at Zibah. "You were my delight before you were his." Zibah hugged him, and Isaiah knew he'd been forgiven.

Eliakim made a strange sound and captured Isaiah's attention. Brows knit together, he appeared deep in thought.

"What is it, Eli?" Hezekiah chuckled. "You only make that sound when you're calculating a new project."

"The road leading to the Gihon spring is narrow, but we need to fill the valley leading to it with as many people as we can find. The angle of the valley, the height of the city wall . . . We'll need something more than voices if we hope to be heard beyond En Rogel."

"How about musical instruments?" Isaiah asked. "Tambourines? Drums? I'll ask Shebna to gather tambourines and drums from the storage closets in the Temple. Our students can disperse the instruments throughout the city so when both ceremonies have concluded, the shouting and noise will echo far and wide."

"Perfect." Eliakim turned on his heel. "I'm going home to eat, and I'll build the wedding canopy soon after." He called over his shoulder before closing the door, "We'll have a new king and queen by nightfall."

30

Let my beloved come into his garden
and taste its choice fruits.

—Song of Songs 4:16

Abba remained at the palace to marshal Jerusalem's
heralds and send them out with word of Hezekiah's
coronation and our wedding. I returned home, the
reality of *home* becoming more precious with each
step. Which of my belongings would I take to the
palace? When would I do that? Tonight? Later?

I pushed open the squeaky gate, alerting
the courtyard full of people that I'd returned.
Though I tried to maintain a sober expression, an
uncontrollable smile betrayed me. Yaira, Dinah,
and Leah began squealing as they nearly tackled
me with hugs.

"Tell us," Dinah said. "How long before you
marry?"

I hesitated, suddenly nervous about our haste.
"Tonight—at dusk." The timing sounded so
logical in Hezi's chamber, but the shock on my
family's faces made me shy.

Ima strolled up, a mischievous grin firmly
in place. "I knew we were preparing for your
wedding while we were dressing you earlier.
Yahweh and I have our secrets."

Everyone laughed, breaking the tension, and my misgivings fled. "I wish Yahweh included me on some of those secrets." I hugged her and thanked Yahweh for such a woman in my life.

Yaira seemed genuinely happy, but tears filled her eyes. "May I serve as your maid at the palace?"

"My maid? Absolutely not!" The thought was appalling. "But you may come as my friend."

Ima gently placed her hand on my arm. "A queen doesn't bring friends to live with her in the harem, dear. Yaira came to your abba and me this morning and offered to become your bond servant. We've included her as a part of your *shiluhim*—the gifts parents give as the bride's inheritance."

Stricken, I looked first at Ima and then back at Yaira, unable to stop my tears. "No, I won't make my friend a slave."

Yaira tilted her head and brushed my cheek. "I'm not a slave, beloved. A slave acts out of duty. I serve you out of love. Don't rob *me* of the gift I want to give."

I fell into her arms. Gratitude, relief, trepidation all warring within me. "I'm so thankful you're coming. You'll always be my friend first." Though happiness had gained the upper hand, I was still overwhelmed with unanswered questions. I needed time with my doves. "My doves!" I pulled away from Yaira. "What will I do without my doves?"

Ima looked uncomfortable. "There are many adjustments when a bride leaves her abba's household, my girl. It's been a while since you've faced changes as drastic as these." She reached for my hand and squeezed it. "You have a solid foundation now—Yahweh and your family. Stand firm and embrace your new life."

I worked at a smile but looked longingly at my birds. They'd been trained to flock to this courtyard. They roosted in this dovecote. I could come back and visit, but would they stay without me to care for them? "Of course, Ima. I know you're right."

She squeezed my hand again, drawing my attention back to her. "We need to prepare you for the ceremony. Come." Taking her first step toward the house, she said over her shoulder, "I'll call you other girls to help in a few moments. I wish to speak with my daughter alone."

I glanced back and saw Dinah, Leah, and Yaira grinning and whispering. My stomach rolled. Ima was about to have *that* conversation with me. I would spend tonight in the king's chamber—with my husband. I had a vague idea of what would happen. I'd seen sheep mating in the pastures, lambs born in the spring, and I knew the curse of Eve's pain at childbirth from witnessing Hallel's two births. Ima had explained my red moon when the way of women came upon me, but the one-flesh act of marriage was still a mystery.

Ima led me to her chamber, sat on her bed, and patted the place beside her. I sat, head bowed, fidgeting with my hands. She stilled them with her gentle touch. "I have no speech prepared, my girl. I'm here to answer your questions and nothing more."

My head shot up, surprised, terrified. "I don't know what questions to ask."

Her cheeks pinked as did mine. "Then I suspect you and Hezekiah will learn together."

The reminder that Hezi might be as nervous as I made me feel better. "What if Hezi doesn't know any more than I do? We might be at a serious disadvantage at a rather important event." She laughed so hard, she cried, and my cheeks flamed. "Ima! I'm serious!"

She wiped her eyes, letting her laughter wind down like a child's spinning top. "Oh, Zibah, you worry too much. The king will likely have some idea of how this night will progress. Men seem to talk about it among themselves more than women, in general if not the specifics." She gathered my hands into hers. "You and Hezekiah share an advantage that most couples don't. You know each other's hearts. Your bodies will respond."

The rest of the day was spent watching everyone else rush around me. Abba returned to say I need not take any of my belongings to the palace before the wedding, so I sat idly while Dinah,

Leah, Yaira, and Ima primped and pampered me to perfection.

Then came the waiting. I sat in our kitchen—alone and veiled—while the rest of my family waited in the courtyard for Hezi and his companions to arrive for the traditional ceremony of Jacob. Since the days of our patriarch's deceived marriage, when Jacob married the veiled Leah instead of his beloved Rachel, a groom had the right and privilege to peek under his bride's opaque veil before the wedding ceremony began.

The sound of tambourines and lyres piqued my senses, and then I heard men singing. My heart raced with an unsteady beat as the music drew nearer. Through the street, into the courtyard, and then one lone voice sang in the room where I waited.

His singing stopped, and I tried to stop trembling. Familiar hands grasped the edges of my veil. Slowly—oh, so slowly—he lifted the tightly woven white cloth. *Hurry! I must see your face!* The lifting revealed his purple robe trimmed in gold braids. A golden belt studded with every kind and color of precious gems guarded his waist. No sword or dagger today.

Finally, I saw Hezi's smile, brighter than all the jewels in the world, and the face I'd loved for as long as I could remember. "You are mine today," he said. "You are mine every day for the rest of our lives."

He leaned in to kiss me, and I heard a harsh clearing of a man's throat. Hezi stopped, chuckled, and lifted my veil farther to reveal Samuel standing behind him. "It appears my bodyguard is determined to protect you." He released the veil with one hand to brush my cheek. "We'll save that kiss for later."

He dropped the veil and took my hand, leading me out of the house. I stumbled through the courtyard, and then he hoisted me onto my royal mule. I could see nothing through my veil, only my hands gripping the reins as someone led my pure white mount to the Gihon spring.

The procession through the city seemed endless, the noise of the crowd a steady roar as we passed from the Upper City to Lower and then out the gate to the valley below. I only heard the coronation and imagined my Hezi with Judah's crown on his head.

It was Azariah, the newly appointed high priest, who announced the official beginning of Hezi's sole reign. "I present to you, people of Judah and guests of Jerusalem, your new king, the son of David—King Hezekiah!"

The noise was overwhelming. I hated the thick veil that hid me from Judah and Judah from me. The celebration continued longer than our march from the palace, and even with my veil, I could tell dusk was fading to darkness. Would our wedding be postponed?

Even as the thought entered my mind, the crowd settled, and I heard Azariah's voice again. "Let the house of Isaiah bring forward the bride."

My little mule lurched forward, and my breath caught. Abba placed his hand on my knees to steady me while my mule plodded down a steep incline. I held onto the reins with a grip of iron.

We reached level ground, and Abba helped me slide off. I stood unsteadily after so long on my mount. Abba supported me with his strong arm around my waist. Someone took the mule away, and Ima appeared on my left, lacing her fingers with mine.

The high priest spoke only a few words, and the ceremony began: the reading of our betrothal contract and the seven blessings. Then I circled my husband seven times—led by my parents. I would remember each moment, treasure every one more than the jewels dangling from my headpiece.

"I present to you, people of Judah and guests of Jerusalem," Azariah's voice intruded, "the wife of our king, Queen Hephzibah!"

My heart leapt into my throat as my parents' hands fell away, and Hezi's gentle touch led me to my mount again. The rejoicing was deafening but I dared not cover my ears.

Hezi leaned close, pressing his lips against my veil. "Almost done, my love." He lifted me onto the mule as though I weighed nothing at all. I'm not sure when the celebration stopped for I heard nothing but the noise of my own insecurities. Would I please him tonight or disappoint? Would he love me less or more in the morning? My cheeks burned like fire, and now I thanked Yahweh for my veil.

The procession stopped, and I stiffened. My mule danced nervously on the smooth stones of the palace court. Strong hands gripped my waist and I startled.

"Shh, my love." Hezi lifted me off and held me close, pressing his lips against my ear. "Only a little longer, and then it's just you and me." Was that supposed to calm me?

He sheltered me under his arm and began walking. Pressed against the contours of his side, I followed left and right, climbed stairs, and halted abruptly.

Someone reached for my hands. A soft, gentle grasp that I recognized right away. "Welcome home, little Ishma." The queen's voice.

Hezi's muscles tensed. "Her name is Hephzibah, Ima. We've talked about this."

"I knew her first as Ishma." Her lilting voice sounded like a song. "It's what came to mind. I meant no harm."

"No, Ima. There will be no deceit in my palace. No games or hidden agendas." He moved me behind him, breaking Abijah's grip. "You will address my queen as Hephzibah or Zibah, or you will not speak to her at all."

I pressed my forehead against his back. *Please, Hezi. Don't make her my enemy. The harem is her world.*

"As you wish, my king." I heard her retreating footsteps and Hezi's deep sigh.

He gathered me to his side again, and we moved through the courtyards. I could see only my feet and their progress. The marble floors of the Middle and Great Courts, across the lion-tiled mosaic, and then toward the black-and-white-inlaid entryway to his chamber. "Good evening, my king." Two voices greeted him. We crossed the threshold, doors slammed, and Hezi released me—gasping as if he, too, had been holding his breath.

I stood like a statue, waiting, trembling. The room was dark except for the glow of a few lamps. I saw only the shadow of my bridegroom moving around the room. What was he doing? He sat down near an elevated table and reached into a basket of some kind. I could see only the outline of it through the ridiculous veil. Why wasn't he taking off the veil?

"Hezi?"

"Mm-hmm?"

"What are you doing?"

"Come and see."

"Aren't you supposed to take off my veil?" My voice quaked and revealed my fear. I shouldn't talk.

"Do you want me to?"

My heart nearly stopped. If I said yes, he'd think I was bold. If I said no, he'd think me a prude. With a huff, I tugged off my veil and saw Hezi seated by a loosely woven basket with two birds in it. Birds. I hurried over, leaving my veil on the floor, and found a gold-chested, brown-winged pair of petite birds in the cage. "What are they?" I knelt beside him, laid my hand against the cage, and made the cooing sound to see if they would come near.

"They're called 'stonechats,' and they pair up for winters in Israel." He opened a small door in the cage and caught the more brightly colored of the two. "One of my guards told me about stonechats while we were recovering our villages from the Philistines. He said stonechats pair for the winter because they're more effective at fighting off other birds than single stonechats that try to fight alone."

Hezi knew that doves had been my comfort when Yaira lived in the caves and during the time he'd been away. He likely suspected I'd need a distraction tonight as well. "How long have you planned this?"

"I've planned this night a thousand times, Zibah." He restored the stonechat to its mate and slid off the couch to join me on the floor. "You consume my thoughts, my dreams, my heart. Your abba has often told us that my reign

332

will fulfill many prophecies." I grinned. He had no idea how often I'd heard it during our years of separation. "No one man could accomplish everything your abba predicts in his prophecies, but I think Yahweh paired us together to restore Judah—as we have restored each other."

I nodded, finding it impossible to speak. How could I love him more now than this morning?

He brushed my lips with a kiss that tasted of cinnamon and honey. My body responded as our passion deepened. I felt no fear, only the overwhelming desire to be his in every way. The pain was fleeting. The sheet was stained. And our hearts were full. Let my beloved come into his garden and taste its choice fruits. Again. And again.

31

Hezekiah was twenty-five years old when he became king, and . . . he did what was right in the eyes of the LORD, just as his father David had done.

—2 Chronicles 29:1–2

Our wedding week had passed too quickly. My newly assigned personal guard was kind but stubborn from our first meeting. "But, my queen, I was ordered to escort you to your harem chamber immediately."

I wasn't trying to be difficult. Really. "I have a few personal belongings that need to be moved from my abba's home to the harem. Why not go to Abba's house first?"

The man dragged his huge hand down his face before answering. I'm sure he was counting to ten. That's what Ima taught me to do when I was frustrated by something— or someone. I would have rather had Samuel guard me, but he would remain with Hezi now since he was captain of the king's guard. I had been assigned Amram, a new guard, who was every bit as big as Samuel and equally hairy. Did all royal guards look like they wore bear rugs?

"Listen, Amram, we'll go quickly and return before midday."

He affixed a smile and bowed. "I am here to serve, my queen."

I hoped he would come to that conclusion with less persuading in the future.

On the way to Abba's house, I tried to walk beside him, but Amram insisted on walking behind me. "I must provide rear guard," he explained.

We exited the palace, and before descending the stairs to the street, I looked toward abba's home. Yaira waited at our courtyard gate. "Yaira!" I shouted and waved, then hurried down the stairs.

Amram lumbered behind me all the way, shouting to clear a wide path through the crowded street. Yaira's eyes were as round as a camel's hoof when she saw us coming. I reached for our courtyard gate, but Amram stayed my hand. "I need to go before you, my queen, to be certain it's safe."

"It's my family's house."

My annoyance evident, the guard lowered his hand and inspected the ground at his feet. "Yes, my queen. Forgive me."

I felt like I'd wounded a faithful ox. "Thank you, Amram, but really, I'm safe here. You can wait at the gate while Yaira and I visit and collect my things."

He bowed and established his outpost at the acacia bush.

I opened the squeaky gate, alerting the entire house of my arrival. Yaira attacked me with a hug.

"Zibah!" Ima set aside her sewing and nudged Yaira aside. "You must share her with the rest of us!" Dinah and Leah weren't far behind.

Yaira caught my eye with her silent question. *Are you well, Queen Hephzibah?* I assured her, with a wink and a grin, I was more than well.

The twins smothered me with questions about the wedding week. My cheeks warmed. I looked over my shoulder and found the guard beyond hearing, but how could I describe the light that now shone in corners of my heart I hadn't even realized were dark?

"Our week was wonderful. The king is still my Hezi."

"Aww," they cooed, eyes dreamy.

"Enough nonsense." Ima waved them away. "He has loved you well. I can see it in your countenance. I'm proud of him." She patted my arm, and we walked toward the house.

Our visit was lovely. We enjoyed mint tea. I fed my doves, drinking in their peaceful cooing. But before the sun rose to midday, my chest ached with missing Hezi. How long before he called for me? Tonight? Tomorrow? I needed to return to the palace to be ready for his summons.

"We should start packing my belongings," I said, gathering our dishes.

"I've got all your things packed with mine," Yaira said.

Dinah and Leah began stacking the cups and clearing the table. "Leave all this." Leah swatted my hand. "Go gather your things. You're a guest now."

A guest. My chest tightened as I followed Ima and Yaira down the hallway and entered the stark chamber. Dinah and Leah weren't far behind and stood in the doorway, eyes glistening. Yaira's and my sleeping mats were rolled up in the corner, the floor swept clean. I turned to hug Dinah. "We'll visit as often as we can." She nodded and reached for Yaira while I grabbed Leah and held her tight. When the hugs ended, I wiped my face with my head covering. "Why can't my husband move into our house?" They all laughed and grabbed a basket, then carried them to the gate.

Ima offered to accompany us for our first day in the harem. Relief washed over me like a cool rain. Ima, Yaira, and I each carried one small basket, and we piled the rest into Amram's arms, stopping only when he could no longer see the street in front of him. We began our short trek to the palace—Ima, Yaira, and I making a quick purchase from a fruit vendor on the way—while poor Amram balanced our baskets like a juggler in the king's court. I'm not sure what he would have done had an attack been made on his queen. Perhaps toss the baskets at them?

We entered the palace complex and crossed the Great Court. Yaira's eyes rounded as we advanced into the Middle Court, and I realized she'd never visited this part of the palace before. Her eyes devoured the grand columns, the tapestries, the vines overflowing their huge hanging pots. She looked like an owl, her head turning this way and that to take it all in.

I looked longingly at the king's private hall but veered toward the harem stairway instead. We arrived on the second floor. Abijah—now called *Gevirah,* the queen mother—ruled the wives, the royal children, and their guards. Not officially with any law written on parchment, but in everyday life with the rules taught by hurt and heartache. Her chamber loomed ahead.

Suddenly nervous, I stopped abruptly, and my guard nearly tumbled over me. "What is it, my queen?"

My mouth was as dry as the eastern desert. "Which chamber is mine?"

Kindness softened his features. "You will occupy the chamber next to the Gevirah's." He gestured to the left. "This way, my queen."

"But that's Rizpah's chamber."

He shifted the baskets to meet my gaze. "Yes, my queen."

Ima spoke, keeping her voice low. "You are

the queen now, Zibah. First lady of Judah. Your chamber must reflect that honor and status. It must equal the Gevirah's in size and location. Rizpah is no longer second wife to the king."

My guard lowered his eyes, waiting.

I'd visited Rizpah in her chamber—once. When I'd attempted friendship with Selah, Ahaz's youngest wife, she'd introduced me to Rizpah. Selah had shoved past the guards, entering the older woman's chamber uninvited. I was mortified. Rizpah stared at me without comment while Selah chatted like a canary. I studied the chamber's floor-to-ceiling purple tapestry, avoiding Rizpah's burning gaze. It was my grandest failure at royal friendship. Perhaps if I returned to Rizpah the only home she'd known in this palace, she would someday speak a civil word to me.

"I'm not taking Rizpah's chamber from her, Amram."

"But you must. It—"

"Amram!" We both seemed startled by my shout. I inhaled and blew out a calming breath. "I will not displace Rizpah from the only home she's known while in this palace. However, I'd like to thank whoever assigned this lovely chamber to me. Did Abijah assign it?"

He kept his head bowed. "I've been commanded not to say."

Surprise quickly bloomed to anger, and I shot

a glance at Ima. She lifted her brows and shook her head. "The guards are a part of the game, Zibah. When Abbi married Ahaz, she had to learn the harem rules. Now she plays the game with utmost skill." Ima turned to my guard. "You must help my daughter learn to survive, soldier. You are on her side now."

"No, Ima!" Indignant, I turned to Amram and recited the words Hezi spoke to Queen Abijah on our wedding night. "King Hezekiah will have no deceit or games in this palace, nor will I. Amram, you will tell me who assigned the chamber, or you will explain yourself to the captain of the guard."

Amram looked away, sighed, and rolled his eyes to the ceiling. "The Gevirah."

I was encouraged by his display of frustration. "Are you weary of the games of the harem?" I asked him.

His face was a mixture of fear and hope. "I apologize, my queen, for revealing my emotions. I . . ."

"Answer my question, please."

He squared his shoulders and raised his chin. "Yes, my queen. Weary to the bone."

I could work with that. "You will restore Rizpah and her possessions to her chamber. Today."

Ima grabbed my arm, turning me to face her. I pulled away. "I won't let the Gevirah rule me and wound Rizpah in the process."

She stared at me for a long moment, and I wondered if I was about to feel her wrath. Instead, she bowed. The woman I trusted more than any other stepped back and bowed. "You, Queen Hephzibah, are a woman I can respect." Ima rose with eyes glistening. "Yahweh will honor your candor and kindness."

I wanted to fall into her arms or run back home, but my guard cleared his throat, demanding my attention. "My queen, where will you live?" He shifted the baskets in his arms.

"Are there any empty chambers in this harem?"

"Of course. We're in Solomon's palace. He had hundreds of wives."

His answer was so forthright, it broke the tension, and I grinned. "Imagine the games of women in *his* harem, Amram."

He ducked his head, hiding a chuckle, and suddenly I was simply speaking with a friend.

"I intend to live in my husband's chamber," I said, causing all three in my company to look appropriately shocked. I was undaunted. "I'll ask for my husband's decision on the matter. If he asks me to stay in the harem, Yaira and I will share one of the smaller, empty chambers."

Amram attempted a restricted bow and toppled one of the baskets to the floor. Yaira picked it up and stacked it on top. "Thank you," he said. "I'll issue orders for Lady Rizpah's belongings to be replaced immediately. I'm sure you've made a friend today, my queen."

Ima pointed toward Abijah's door. "And I'm sure you've made an enemy, my girl. Assigning Rizpah's chamber was Abijah's first show of power as Gevirah, and by refusing you've crossed swords with her. She wields great influence among the royal wives and guards, Zibah. I can't protect you here."

"Only the king can protect you against the Gevirah, my queen." Amram started walking down the hallway, past the other family chambers.

Ima grabbed my hand. "I'll go to Abijah, thank her for her thoughtfulness, and explain that yours and Hezi's is a unique relationship that will look different than any other king and queen of Judah. She'll be angry, but I'll try to forestall any wrath until you can talk with your husband." She kissed my cheek.

Amram paused until Yaira and I could catch up with him. "I'm stepping into the stoning pit with you, my queen, by obeying you over the Gevirah. But if you secure the king's permission to live in his chamber, we can more easily avoid harem politics." I exchanged a hopeful glance with Yaira and reached for her hand as Amram led us through the king's private gardens and a hall lined with servants' chambers.

Finally, we emerged on the king's hallway, a few cubits from Hezi's chamber. I smoothed my robe, and Yaira straightened my crown. With a deep breath and hurried prayer, I followed Amram regally toward Hezi's double doors.

"Shalom, my queen." One of the guards bowed and opened the door. No knock. No announcement.

My heart leapt for joy on the inside, but on the outside I simply inclined my head in a serene bow. "And shalom to you." Amram waited outside. Yaira followed me.

"There you are!" Hezi opened his arms when he saw me. "I came back from my meeting and you were gone."

I rushed into his arms, consoled by his love, empowered by his strength. "I missed you this morning too."

Over my shoulder, he greeted Yaira. "I'm glad you've come, Yaira. You're like her right arm. She's lost without you." He released me, and I stood gazing into his wide, hopeful eyes. "How's your harem chamber? Did Ima choose one suitable for my bride?"

The question nearly waylaid my plan. Hezi knew his ima would choose a nice chamber? "Your ima gave me Rizpah's chamber, second largest and next to hers. It was a very kind gesture."

He backed onto a couch and pulled me to his lap. "You don't sound happy about Rizpah's chamber. We can have it redecorated."

The absurdity of the moment rammed me like a war machine. Hezi had spent all morning speaking with advisors about Judah's future, and I was complaining about harem assignments? I refused to be one of those royal ninnies who talked of nothing with substance.

"I want to sleep with you."

His cheeks pinked. Snatching a discreet glance at Yaira, he lowered his voice and leaned close. "I've been thinking about nothing else all morning, but why did you bring Yaira with you?"

I swatted him. "No, I mean . . ." Looking toward the servants' quarters, I noticed Yaira had already slipped out of the room. I rested my arms around my husband's neck. "I want to sleep in your chamber and have Yaira attend us."

Hezi pushed my head covering behind my shoulder, exposing my neck—and placed a gentle kiss there. "Tell me why you asked to stay in my chamber. Did something happen in the harem?"

We'd been apart for six years. Before that we had been learning partners and best friends. A single wedding week wasn't enough for me to lay myself bare to a man who understood so little of a woman's heart.

"Hephzibah, my delight," he whispered. "I can't know your heart if you don't tell me what's on your mind."

"I want to live in your chamber. Sleep with you. Eat with you. *Live* with you. Forever."

He paused, his focus on something beyond me, clearly thinking. I waited, heart pounding. He looked toward the servants' quarters, where the door was ajar. "The servants who attended us last week have moved out," he said, more to himself than to me. "My chamber attendant was to move in this afternoon."

I suddenly felt like another burden in his new list of duties. I was being ridiculous. Queens lived in the harem. I fairly leapt to my feet. "Yaira! We must go!"

"No, Yaira!" His shout jolted me to a halt. "Give us a moment longer."

I stood facing the servant's chamber, cheeks flaming. His presence loomed behind me, but I couldn't look at him. I'd been impulsive, strong willed. Change had always been hard, and I must—

His arms encircled me, and he leaned over my shoulder, his breath warm on my neck. "I will have your personal things moved into my chamber in time for this evening's meal," he said with clear delight. "Yaira may stay in the adjoining servant's chamber—if she agrees."

Without warning, he spun me around to face him. I stared at the most handsome man I'd ever seen. And he was mine. He kissed my cheek and left a trail of kisses down my neck. "Is there anything else we should discuss before I return to court?"

I shook my head and swallowed hard. With one final kiss, he left me in the chamber—*our* chamber now.

Yaira must have heard the double doors shut because she peeked out the moment he was gone. "Well? What did he say?"

Still reeling from his presence, I whispered, "We're home, Yaira. Both of us. This is our new home."

32

In the first month of the first year of Hezekiah's reign, he opened the doors of the temple of the LORD and repaired them.

—2 Chronicles 29:3

Hezi stood on the balcony of his private chamber at dawn, awakened on the sixteenth day of his reign by the smell of smoke and a sense of awe. He looked out over the Valley of Kidron at the smoldering piles of rubble that were testimony to the purifying of Yahweh's Temple and of Jerusalem.

His royal council said the Temple couldn't be repaired and consecrated in so short a time. "It would require a miracle akin to crossing the Red Sea," they said. The city had sheltered covert idol worship for nearly two hundred years, and the Temple itself lay in ruin after Ahaz closed its doors years ago.

"We must attempt more than is humanly possible to witness what only God can do," Hezi had told them. Now the streets and high places were being purged of incense altars and Asherah poles. The nightmarish statue of Molek had been disassembled and, along with every unclean thing that had defiled Yahweh's Temple, was discarded in the Kidron on the city's eastern side. The fires had burned hot and long but were a sweet aroma to Judah's Holy God.

Familiar arms slid around his waist, sending fire through his veins. He closed his eyes and let the feel of Zibah's nearness soothe his concerns about the day. Why would any king wish to relegate his wife to a separate chamber?

She pressed a kiss against his back. "You're up earlier than usual. Excited about the consecration ceremony?"

"Yes, and trying to make a decision." Glancing to his left, he gestured toward his abba's prized sundial. "It was a gift from a Babylonian king, but surprisingly, I can find no engravings depicting their gods. Do we keep it, or shall I toss it into the Kidron?"

His wife ran her hand over the two-cubit-tall monstrosity. "It's been rather helpful to keep time, hasn't it?" He nodded. "I like it. It stays."

He pulled her back into his arms, grinning. "If only my advisors could make decisions so easily."

She frowned. "Most of your advisors are new. How can they cause trouble already?"

"Have you forgotten that my newest advisor is Shebna?" They laughed together about their brash and opinionated classmate from the past. "He's meticulous and not afraid to disagree. He's the perfect palace administrator—and the center of every conflict."

"Hmm," she said, resting her head against his chest. "Who else is giving you trouble?"

That was a question he must step around carefully. "I've named Jokim ben Hanan as the new commander of our troops. Jalon ben Enoch is in charge of forced labor. Jekuthiel isn't a new advisor, so he adds experience—"

"Why aren't you answering my question?" She pulled away, meeting his gaze.

"What do you mean?"

"Who is causing trou—" Her eyes lit with understanding. "What has Abba done?"

He chuckled and tried to pull her back into his arms. "What makes you think Isaiah has done anything?"

"You're only vague when you're afraid we'll argue."

He waved off her observation and walked into their chamber. Perhaps changing the subject would work. "Be sure your whole family knows they can stand on the Temple's eastern portico with you. Dinah and Leah too."

She stood in the balcony doorway, arms folded. "Why won't you tell me what Abba did?"

She was too smart for evasion. He sat on the couch and let his head drop into his hands. "Your abba asked if I was willing to destroy *all the high places* in Judah." He looked up, frustration rising.

349

"He went on to remind the whole council that I'd actually rebuilt them during my six years away. Then he asked if I would destroy even the high places where Yahweh was worshiped alongside the pagan gods."

His wife sat down beside him. "Why do you think Abba asked?"

Raising an eyebrow, he paused. "Why don't you ask what I answered?"

"I know what your answer was. The Law clearly states we must worship only at Yahweh's Temple." She looked at him as if he were a first-year student in her abba's class. "Now, why did Abba ask it?"

"It was clear why he asked it when my advisors began to argue over whether we should destroy the high places or not. Poor Joah, my newly appointed recorder, scribbled his reed across parchment to document their debate for the archives of kings, but he finally shrugged and set the reed aside." Hezi felt the reality like a millstone across his shoulders. "My advisors will need careful guidance to adhere to the Law completely."

Zibah placed her hand inside his. "What does the Law require of *you*, King Hezekiah?"

That insufferable set of her jaw didn't require an answer, but he gave it, grinning. "We will worship in Yahweh's Temple only—starting this morning at the consecration ceremony."

● ● ●

King Hezekiah stepped through the Guard's Gate—the dividing threshold between the palace complex and Temple grounds—the separation between common and consecrated. He removed his sandals and gawked like a beggar at a baker's booth. The transformation of the Temple was nothing short of miraculous.

The abominable statue of Rimmon was gone, crushed to pieces in the Valley of Kidron. Yahweh's bronze altar had been restored to its rightful place, the holy Sea returned to the backs of the four bronze bulls, and the priests—descendants of Aaron—were preparing animals for sacrifice. Hezekiah and his officials had dedicated seven bulls, seven rams, seven male lambs, and seven male goats as a sin offering that would atone for the entire nation of Judah. Azariah, the high priest, looked exhausted enough to fall over, but he soldiered on, slaughtering beast after beast according to every requirement of the Law.

The king and his invited guests were allowed into the inner court—where the priests ministered—to stand on a platform called the upper pavement. Today, Hezi had invited his advisors to accompany him, and they stood in reverent awe. Even the prophets were silent. Isaiah and Micah had arrived in sackcloth, the typical prophets' garb, but so far seemed as overwhelmed as the rest.

When Hezi lifted his gaze to the eastern portico, a balcony overlooking the area on which he and his guests stood, he saw Zibah with her ima, Yaira, Dinah, and Leah. Someday soon all the porticos and public outer courts would be teeming with people. Jerusalem would once again resound with the worship of the one true God.

Hezi's thoughts were interrupted by the bleating and bawling of skittish animals. The priests led seven goats to wait at his feet. The poor beasts looked up with soulful eyes when Hezi and his officials laid their hands on them. Azariah lifted his voice above the noise. "Hear our prayers, Yahweh, God of our fathers. May our sins and the sins of all Judah pass through our hands to these innocent animals so that their atoning blood would give us life in Your holy presence."

Without warning or hesitation, the high priest made the death cut while another priest caught the blood in a bowl. Hezi watched the spark of life leave the animal's eyes, and his elder brother's screams suddenly replayed in his mind. Hezi held the limp body in his arms—no longer a goat, but now his brother Bocheru. Hezi blinked, but the image remained. He began to tremble, then sob. "Take him! Take him away!"

Nervous hands removed the body, and Hezi scrambled to his feet, straightening his blood-spattered robe, regaining his bearings.

"Hez?" Eliakim grabbed his shoulders. "Hez, look at me. Are you all right?"

Hezekiah tried desperately to clear his mind, blinking, breathing deeply.

Isaiah nudged others aside and grasped Hezi's head, his hands like a vise, then looked into his eyes. "This is a sacrifice for Judah's sin, Hezekiah, not a pagan bribe to an imagined god made by human hands. Yahweh never requires human blood." He pulled Hezi into a fierce hug.

"Why must any god have blood?" Hezi whispered, careful not to spread his doubt.

Isaiah held him, never wavering. "I don't know why. But this truth we do know: Life is in the blood. And Yahweh—the gracious God—accepts an animal's blood to pay for human sin." Isaiah pressed his forehead against Hezi's. "Bocheru's death wasn't your fault, Hezekiah. No one could have stopped your abba."

Hezi squeezed his eyes closed and nodded against his teacher's head. "We will end pagan worship in Judah, Isaiah. I swear, we will end it."

His teacher patted his shoulders, eyes misty. "Yes, we will, my king. Yes, we will."

The Levites began their worship of the Holy God with cymbals, harps, and lyres—instruments prescribed by David and prophets of old. Priests grabbed their trumpets, and the assembly bowed before the Lord, swept away by the overwhelming sound and aroma of Yahweh's Temple.

Hezi paid no attention to time or changing guards as the sun moved across the sky. The bleating of sheep and lowing of cattle, however, grew distracting. Rising from his knees, Hezi turned toward the eastern gate and found Temple guards barring it to keep a throng of people from invading the priests' inner court.

With equal parts laughter and tears, Azariah explained, "The Levites told me that people began bringing sacrifices and offerings when they heard the worship. But we don't have enough priests to present the offerings. Only two hundred have been consecrated."

Hezi noted the priests at the slaughter tables, wearing the sacred blue tunics, sashes, and caps. "Has Aaron's line diminished so much?"

Azariah studied his bare feet on the Temple pavement. "I'm sorry to report that the priests haven't been as conscientious about their consecration rites as the Levites since we've begun renovation of the Temple. There would have been enough if they'd all reported for duty when you sent out the summons."

Hezekiah clenched his jaw to keep from shouting and squeezed his eyes shut. *Yahweh, why should Your people's offerings be refused because Your priests have shirked their duty?* Since great-saba Uzziah's days, Judeans had abandoned Yahweh's Temple, worshiping instead on pagan high places. Hezi had taken away those high places to follow God's Law completely. Should he now turn the people away from God's Temple?

Hezi looked again toward the eastern gate at the crowd of people pleading to worship. They were like drowning men in a stormy sea. He returned his attention to the high priest. "You will receive their offerings, Azariah. These people have obeyed Yahweh's commands, and they will not be turned away. Do you hear me?"

"My lord, we haven't enough priests to—"

"You will allow the Levites to present the burnt offerings until enough of your lazy relatives are consecrated."

"The Law requires that only priests sacrifice the burnt—"

"The Law requires that priests fulfill their duties to Yahweh, but that hasn't moved them into service, now has it, Azariah?"

"No . . . I mean . . . I'll assign some of the Levites to present the sacrifices, my lord." Azariah hurried to obey, shouting at Levites, priests, and Temple guards to receive the offerings of all who came.

Isaiah stood like a boulder, silent and immovable. "You've just ordered Yahweh's high priest to break the Law of Moses. You know Levites are to *assist* in sacrifices only. They are never to touch the sacred utensils or approach the altar."

The condemnation sizzled like a branding iron in Hezi's gut. "You haven't stepped onto Temple grounds for years because you said Yahweh was weary of meaningless sacrifices. Now look, Isaiah." He pointed at the waiting crowd. "These people yearn to offer Yahweh gifts—meaningful sacrifices—and we will not turn them away."

"I'm not the enemy, Hezekiah." Isaiah's tone never changed. "I'm here to remind you that Yahweh gave us His Law to protect and guide us. There will be unforeseen consequences if you break His commands. As with the atoning blood, we may not fully understand, but we must trust and obey Him." Isaiah walked away, his sackcloth robe billowing in the wake of his judgment.

Hezi wanted to follow him and continue the debate, but he need not prove himself to his teacher any longer. Hezekiah was king. The thought did little to comfort. If Isaiah was right, and Yahweh was displeased with the Levites' hands on the offerings, consequences could be severe. *Please, Yahweh, know our hearts. See the yearning of Your people to honor You.*

He looked for Zibah in the crowd. She would have an opinion and perhaps offer insights neither he nor her abba had considered. The eastern portico bulged with people, but he didn't see his wife or her family. They must have returned home, making room for more worshipers. A disturbing realization struck. His ima hadn't attended the consecration ceremony even though he'd ordered a guard to escort her.

Troubled, he began walking toward the Guard's Gate and signaled Samuel. "We're returning to the palace," he said as the big man fell into step with him. "Did you send a guard to the Gevirah's chamber this morning to collect her for the consecration ceremony?"

"I did, my king."

"And did he report why she didn't come?"

"He said she refused him entry." Samuel's voice held no judgment or hint at more of the story.

They finished their walk to the palace in silence, and Hezi bid his guard farewell at the door of his chamber. Yaira was inside, preparing the table for their evening meal.

"Where's Zibah?" She rarely went anywhere without Yaira.

"She went to check on your ima. She was concerned when we didn't see her at the Temple." Yaira placed a vase of buttercups and tiger tulips on the table. "I thought she would have returned by now."

A chill raced up Hezi's spine. "How long has she been with Ima?"

Yaira's face dawned a sickly gray. "Too long."

He ran out the door, through the Middle

Court, and up the harem stairs. Isaiah's warning rang in his mind. *"There will be unforeseen consequences if you break His commands."* Was Zibah's life in danger because Hezi had broken Yahweh's Law?

33

You shall not bow down to them or worship them; for I, the LORD your God, am a jealous God, punishing the children for the sin of the parents to the third and the fourth generation of those who hate me, but showing love to a thousand generations of those who love me and keep my commandments.

—Exodus 20:5–6

My intentions were purely innocent. I was concerned that Abijah might be ill when I didn't see her at the Temple consecration. Amram escorted me to her chamber, and we found only one guard at the door. *Odd.* He took a wide stance as we approached.

"I've come to check on the Gevirah's health. Is she well?"

"Yes, my queen." The guard bowed but kept his eyes fixed on Amram. "Extremely well. I'll inform her you inquired."

Had I just been dismissed by a chamber guard? "Announce me."

"I'm sorry, my queen. I can't do that."

"Ridiculous." I tried to step past him and reached for the door, but he blocked my way, bumping me inadvertently. My feet tangled, and I landed on the floor. The next moments were a blur, but drawn swords clanged, and somehow Amram stood over the guard with the tip of his sword poised at the man's throat.

"You may go in now, my queen."

On wobbly legs, I stumbled past the two men and opened the door slowly. Amram released the guard and shooed him away. He followed me inside, sword at the ready. Tapestries were drawn over the windows, and the cloying smell of incense made my head swim. Low droning chants came from the bedchamber, and I heard the voices of both a man and woman. I stepped toward the dividing curtain, but Amram grabbed my arm and shook his head *no*. After pulling me aside, he entered the bedchamber, leaving me to hear the ugly truth.

Abijah screamed, and her guard cursed.

"Get your clothes on, both of you." Amram's voice dripped with disdain.

"Get out!" Abijah's indignation was as sharp as Amram's sword. "Leave while I dress."

"After the Asherah ritual I just witnessed, you have no right to feign modesty." Amram stood at the curtain while giving me instruction. "Light some lamps, my queen. I'll escort them to the audience chamber, and you can decide how to proceed." He tossed me a figurine, a multibreasted woman with six arms and a tree budding from her head. *Asherah.* I'd never before held an idol in my hands.

I set it aside and found two flint stones and a basket of twigs to light the lamps. *Decide how to proceed? This is the Gevirah. Hezi's beloved ima. Master Isaiah never taught a class on this. Yahweh, give me wisdom.*

Amram directed the Gevirah and her guard to the couches. "Sit down, both of you."

I gawked at them like a stupid camel until the twig in my hand burned down to my fingers. I dropped it and had to step out the sparks on her crimson carpet.

No one moved. No one spoke. It was my turn, I supposed. "Why, Abijah?"

She tilted her head and affixed her smile. "Hephzibah, dear, give me a chance to explain."

I shot a glance at Amram, but he'd retreated into the role of silent protector. Abijah's guard, too, sat like a lump on a log.

"Of course. Explain."

Her smile dipped only for a moment before using the singsong voice that signaled deceit. "I began worshiping Asherah after Ahaz killed Bocheru. She was the mother goddess who understood my pain. She is sympathetic to a woman's tears, Zibah."

I retrieved the statue and shook it in front of her. "She is a piece of rock, Abijah! Trampled underfoot for centuries before a merchant chiseled her into something he could sell for profit."

"You don't understand." The Gevirah's condescending smile was infuriating. "To enjoy the companionship of a female goddess is beyond any comfort I received from the stiff rules and rituals of Yahweh. Yahweh demands blood. Asherah offers pleasure."

"Who taught you Asherah's pleasures, Abijah?" I nodded to her silent guard. "Was it him?"

She measured me before answering. "King Ahaz taught me and then forced me to . . ." Her eyes darted to Amram and her guard, then back to me. "I learned the priestess rituals from my husband. I suspect he taught them to every woman in the harem." There was challenge in her voice. She wanted me to think idolatry flourished in King Hezekiah's palace. Did it?

"Do the other wives in the harem perform these rituals with their guards?"

A slow, sinister smile curved her lips. "I suppose you must ask them. I'm sure you'll be fast friends after that conversation."

A shudder worked its way through me. All along I'd imagined Abijah the victim. I thought she'd gained power over the guards because of their pity. How long had she purchased loyalty with her body and beauty? Would Hezi even believe me? His love for his ima sometimes blinded him.

As if the thought summoned him, he opened

the door and looked as stunned as I felt. "Zibah?" He ran and grabbed me, lifting me off the floor, burying his face in my neck. "You're all right. I was afraid . . ."

Emotion choked me. I wasn't all right. Nothing was right. "What were you afraid of?"

He set me down and only then seemed to notice the Asherah in my hand. He snatched it away. "What's going on here?"

Abijah jumped off the couch. "I'm so glad you came, Hezi. Zibah and her guard barged into my chamber—"

Hezi lifted his hand to silence her and turned to me. "Tell me what happened."

I swallowed the lump in my throat and pulled him toward the bedchamber. "I'd rather show you." The remains of the pagan rituals spoke for me. He couldn't argue with what he saw. The bed askew. Another Asherah on the bed. Incense smoldering on leaf-shaped brass plates.

My husband staggered and fell against the wall. "Yahweh, no."

"I'm sorry, Hezi." Bowing my head, I began the hardest explanation of my life. "I came to check on your ima because she didn't come to the Temple this morning. When Amram and I arrived, one of her guards refused me entrance, so Amram forced our way inside. He shielded me from seeing what happened here and kept them under guard while I questioned your ima."

Hezi turned slowly, an eyebrow lifted in challenge. "*You* questioned my ima?"

I kept my voice steady, keeping in mind how upset he was. "She said she began her worship after Bocheru's death. That your abba taught her. She insinuated that some of your abba's other wives also perform Asherah's rituals with their guards." I bowed at the waist, keeping my eyes on the floor. "I questioned your ima only to discover the truth. You said on the night of our wedding that there would be no more deceit in your palace, no more games or hidden agendas. I am living by your rules, my husband—my king."

He held my head between his hands, kissed it, and returned to the audience chamber. I sighed my relief, but relief was short lived.

Hezi halted barely a handbreadth from his ima. "How could you do this?" Trembling with rage, he waited in silence.

Abijah resumed her seat on the couch, pale as goat's milk. "Everything I've done was to survive."

"No, Ima. No!" Hezi leaned close, trapping her between his hands on the couch. "Abba has been gone for weeks. There is no threat to your life. You have everything you could want or need."

"I want love, Hezi! I need love!" she shouted into his face, and tears finally came. "I've never been loved."

He wilted then, gathering her into his arms,

letting his own tears fall. "I love you, Ima. Mattaniah loves you." He paused, squeezed his eyes closed as if in pain. "And I remember a time when Abba loved us all."

I turned away, respecting their private grief. Only they knew what their lives were like before Ahaz's battle fury and pagan gods stained his soul. Was Abijah a loving ima before she'd been beaten and tossed aside by her husband? Mistress Aya once said that as a child, Abijah was carefree, growing up on Temple grounds with her abba, the high priest.

The Gevirah sniffed and pulled from her son's embrace. "Please, Hezi, listen to me. Asherah speaks to me. She comforts me, and I feel loved while worshiping her. I won't tell anyone. I'll—"

Hezi bolted to his feet, horror on his features. "You have seen what Abba's idolatry did to Judah. To you! To Bocheru! How could you even ask me to turn aside?"

She scooted off the couch and knelt at his feet, hands pressed together, pleading. "All right, all right. Just let my guards remain. I trust them. They are loyal to me, and—"

Hezi reached for her arm and lifted her gently to her feet. "I give you this one chance, Ima, to go into your chamber now and gather whatever idols and pagan images you own." He hugged her and spoke softly. "One chance, Ima, as I've given every person under my care. Yahweh has promised us incredible blessing if we obey and cursing if we continue on Abba's path. Please, Ima. Be obedient to Yahweh and return to His love and presence."

I watched her walk woodenly to her chamber. Hezi caught my eye and motioned for me to follow her.

Before I ducked behind her dividing tapestry, Hezi's voice echoed in the chamber. "Samuel!" His personal guard entered. "Ima's chamber guard is under arrest. Take him to the dungeon until I pass sentence."

Abijah was quiet when I entered, her tears dried. "You've won," she said, tossing incense and idols onto her bed.

"Nobody won, Abijah, and Hezi lost most of all." I pulled one of her veils off a peg and laid it on the bed, transferring the trappings to its center to make a pouch in which to carry them.

"You've taken my son, my guards, and my gods. What more could you possibly do to me?"

"Someday, I hope to love you, Abijah." Startled, she looked up, and I cocked my head. "Not today, but someday."

34

Wounds from a friend can be trusted,
but an enemy multiplies kisses.

—Proverbs 27:6

Hezi flopped across his bed after another exhausting afternoon with Ima. For a week, he had canceled his court sessions after his midday meal in order to spend time with her.

Not that it helped. Ima still refused to speak to him because he'd sent her guard to Moab. Hezi had merely "cut him off from his people," even though the strictest interpretation of the Law required stoning.

Isaiah would undoubtedly accuse him of shunning the Law again, something the anointed King of his prophecies would never do. But Zibah had reminded Hezi that no one in Judah had been stoned for idolatry during the purification after Abba's reign. In the end, Hezi felt the whisper of Yahweh's mercy and listened to his wife.

The other idolaters in the harem—both Abba's wives and their guards—were given the same chance he'd given Ima. One more opportunity to discard any idols, incense, or other items with pagan engravings. Their lives would be forfeit if any were discovered in their chambers or on their persons in the future. The bad news was that the pile of collected items filled two storage chests. The good news was perhaps Ahaz's wives and guards had truly relinquished all their idols. Hezi reassigned the guards to surround the Temple, and placed the royal guards he trusted to guard the angry, hurting women. It felt like a victory among impending wars.

Spring breezes carried the scent of almond blossoms, and war among nations was as certain as the season. Surely Yahweh would prosper Judah as the people proved their faithfulness to Him.

Lord, how will You fill our treasuries when Assyria keeps raising our tribute payments? He turned over with a groan and heard the stonechats squawking. He glanced toward their woven cage and saw a flutter of feathers. Hurrying to his feet, he went to the cage and cooed as Zibah had taught him, trying to soothe them. The male clung to the lattice at the top, but the female huddled in a corner at the bottom. His friend told him this might happen. Stonechats paired only for the winter. The guard had seen only single stonechats flying from spring to fall. The realization of war in springtime had dawned in his own chamber. He must separate the birds. But how would he tell Zibah?

"Hezi?" The door opened. Zibah and Yaira tiptoed into the chamber, lifting the muddy hems of their robes off the marble floors. It was the sight he needed to lift his heart.

"I see you've been distributing food in the southern city again." He ran at them both, grabbed their waists, and swung them in a circle till their feet flew. They squealed like children, threatening him with his life if he didn't put them down.

He obeyed and was immediately rewarded with a kiss from his bride. Yaira laughed all the way to her chamber, lifting her robe to her ankles to keep mud off the tiles. Zibah cradled his face when their kiss was over. "You seem in better spirits this afternoon. Did Abijah talk with you today?"

He kissed her nose and led her to the couch, caring little about the mud trailing behind her. "No. She worked on her embroidery, and I read a scroll. But we were together. I hope in time that will mean something."

Zibah forfeited the couch and chose his lap instead. "You're a great king and an even better son."

"How was your day in the city?" He was stalling on the stonechat issue.

"Good. We delivered twelve baskets of food, three robes, and a blanket. It seems Abba's allowance has increased with his new position on the king's—" Her brows knit together. "What are you not telling me?"

Hezi saw the concern in her eyes and didn't

want to scare her. "It's not awful, but it's disappointing."

She settled on the couch beside him. "What is it?"

Pointing to the birds' cage, he explained, "My friend told me we might have to separate the birds come springtime. I think it would be best to do it today."

She sprang off the couch and knelt by the cage to inspect them. "Is she hurt?"

"I don't think so. Not yet. But I fear she might be if we leave them together in the cage."

Placing her hand flat against the lattice, Zibah was silent.

"Tell me what you're thinking," Hezi said.

"Will *we* need to be separated someday?"

He lifted her by the shoulders and turned her to face him. "Stonechats were meant to be free, Zibah. Frankly, they were simply my attempt to calm you on our wedding night. I wasn't even sure they'd last in a cage this long."

She hid her face against his chest. "I'll miss them. They've helped me transition from my doves."

His heart constricted as his mind whirred. Surely there was a place on palace grounds where he could build a dovecote for her. The thought of working with his hands again pleased him. He kissed the top of her head. "Let's take the stonechats to the balcony and release them together."

She pulled away, stricken. "Now?"

"It must be soon, Zibah."

She nodded, sighed, and Hezi carried the cage to the balcony. "Why don't you open the door when you're ready," he said, "and we'll see if they fly out by themselves."

She leaned down to coo, but the birds began flapping at each other again. "No, no! Don't!" Zibah shouted, and opened the door. Both birds flew out, one turning right, the other going left.

Hezi watched them go but watched his wife more closely. Was she terribly disappointed?

Zibah wiped a tear. "If we start flapping at each other—"

"I forbid any flapping." He rushed to hold her.

She chuckled and put her arms around his neck. "How was your day—before your visit with Abijah?"

The weight of increasing Temple worship, the royal treasury, and their military defenses pressed him down. "My day was heavy."

Keeping her eyes focused on the valley below, Zibah asked simply, "Do you want to share the load?"

Good question. How much should he share with his wife? A woman. Tradition said she should live in a harem, removed from the political pressures and decisions of her husband. "Do you want to bear the weight?"

Zibah thought for a long moment. No quick

answer. "I want to try. If it proves too much, I'd rather step back than start flapping and have to fly away."

He led her back inside, and they resumed their places on the couch. "We must find a way to increase Temple worship since we've destroyed all high places and committed to obey the Law wholeheartedly. Unfortunately, the next scheduled festival is the Festival of Weeks, two months away."

Zibah listened intently, chin in hand, but made no comment.

"If more people come to Jerusalem to worship, it will naturally fatten our treasury without raising taxes. More people means more trade, and more trade means more foreign merchants who will spend money on Judean soil."

She grinned. "I sat beside you in class when you learned that. Go on."

"Right." What a relief not to have to defend his position the way he must with his advisors. "The final burden is spring."

"King Hezekiah, I didn't realize you were responsible for the change of seasons too." If she kept interrupting, he would have to kiss her, and they'd never decide anything.

"Spring is the season for war." She sobered immediately, but he continued. "Because Assyria is now focused on internal bickering, we're left to defend ourselves against greedy neighbors who may seek to move boundary stones and steal our harvest."

"I thought our army had recovered to an adequate force since . . ."

Hezi cradled her shaking hands. "It has, my love. We are safe. A king must think years ahead to preempt future attacks." He realized this was not a weight she could bear. "So, my chief advisor, what is your counsel on increasing Temple worship and revenue for the treasury?"

Zibah laid her hand against his cheek, acknowledging his distraction, and then thought for a moment. "If only we had restored the Temple in time for Passover. It would have been the perfect feast to welcome Judah back into Yahweh's arms."

Hezi's heart quickened, his spirit lightening. "That's it, Zibah. There's still time to celebrate late Passover in the second month."

"Judah hasn't celebrated a Passover since before your great-saba Uzziah was struck with leprosy. Do any of the priests even know how?"

"They'll learn!"

"Do we even qualify for the second-month celebration?" She began recounting the Law, "If any are unclean because of a dead body—"

"Which many of us were because of Abba's death and mourning."

"Or are away on a journey, they are still to celebrate the Lord's Passover, but they are to do it on the fourteenth day of the second month at twilight."

"You see? Our whole nation has been on a journey, Zibah. Away from the Lord. Now we've returned and are ready to celebrate the most sacred of all celebrations."

"But, Hezi, it's already the third day of Ziv. How can we spread the news to the whole nation that they must choose a lamb by the tenth, care for it as they travel to Jerusalem, and then slaughter it at twilight? The idea may be good but the details are impossible."

"Is it more impossible than freeing a nation of slaves from Egypt?"

"Hezi." She groused, giving him that "don't be a dreamer" look.

"Zibah, I don't think the second-month celebration requires the care of lambs from the tenth to the fourteenth day, so the people's travel to Jerusalem will be quicker. We'll sell the Passover lambs from nearby flocks, which will increase trade. And—" Hezi stopped suddenly.

"And what? Don't stop explaining now." Zibah's eyes lit up. "I'm finally starting to imagine this could work."

She wouldn't like what he was about to say. "I have a plan to avert political tensions and decrease hostile incursions on our northern villages."

Zibah grew still. "Why mention military invasions? We were talking about Passover."

374

Hezi held her gaze. "Come into my arms, Zibah." He opened them wide.

"Hezi, you're scaring me."

"I'm going to show you there's no reason to fear. Now, come into my arms." She obeyed, turning to recline against his chest. He wrapped her tight and laid his lips against her hair. "We're going to invite our remaining brothers in Israel to our Passover."

"No!" She broke away from him. "No, Hezi."

Calmly, quietly, he opened his arms again. "Come into my arms, Zibah."

She stared at him, defiant. The trembling began in her shoulders, then spread to her chin. Her eyes filled with accusation, and he nearly relented. She turned and lay against him again. Silent. Terrified.

Hezi squeezed his eyes shut, certain of his decision. Wishing he wasn't. He wrapped his arms around her, his legs too. "I will keep you safe. Do you hear me? You will be safe. You and Yaira." He let his words penetrate her fear and felt her heart breaking beneath his arms. "Israel has been repopulated with people from many foreign nations. Those from Jacob's tribes need to remember their one true God, Zibah. I feel Yahweh pulling me in this direction. He will keep us safe and reward our faithfulness."

She released a sigh and seemed to gather some composure. "I thought you were inviting them to decrease the likelihood of invasions on Judah's northern cities."

He kissed the top of her head. "Perhaps if we extend peace in the name of our Father Jacob, they won't raid our northern villages, the land of their brethren."

"Perhaps." Zibah curled into a ball, and Hezi carried her like a child to their bed.

They lay on their sides, facing each other, fingers touching. "What are you thinking?" he asked again.

A sad smile curved her lips. "I don't want to be like the stonechats, flapping and then forced to fly away."

"I would never—"

She pressed her finger against his lips, silencing his quick promise. "A king should consider carefully before he says *never*."

35

The man said, "This is now bone of my
bones and flesh of my flesh . . ."
That is why a man leaves his father and
mother and is united to his wife, and
they become one flesh.

—Genesis 2:23–24

After my warning to consider his words carefully,
Hezi scooted off our bed and immediately called
a special council meeting to start the Passover
plans rolling. So much for careful deliberation.
While I remained in our chamber, pacing the
floor, my husband sat on his throne and invited
Israel to Judah's Passover. This time they
wouldn't bring their swords and spears—so Hezi
promised—but would come with money in their
pockets and a desire to worship Yahweh.

When Hezi returned to our chamber after the
meeting, I was quiet but not unpleasant. We
enjoyed amiable conversation over our evening
meal. I donned my winter cloak to stroll with
him in the olive groves. We inspected the
budding leaves and played tag in the orchards.
There was no more talk of war. No mention of
Israel's invasion of my peace and our Passover
plan. When the stars shone bright, we lay in

each other's arms until I heard the steady, deep breaths of my husband's slumber. I watched the stations of the moon progress, wondering if any of his council members voiced the same concerns I held.

In the morning, I asked Yaira to bring my meal to the balcony so we could speak privately while Hezi finished his ministrations. I told her of the invitation extended to the people who had marched us to Samaria as captives when we were children. Her reaction was considerably calmer than mine.

"When he returned from the council meeting, did he mention how the advisors reacted to the plan?" Calm and inquisitive, Yaira's voice betrayed no emotion.

"No." I glanced over my shoulder and lowered my voice. "When Hezi leaves for court, we'll visit Ima and see if Abba said anything after last night's meeting."

Yaira joined me to break our fast. I watched her for fidgeting hands or a tapping foot, but she showed no sign of nervousness. I listened to spring birdsong and let the morning sun wash my face. I wished Hezi would hurry and leave.

Finally, he stepped onto the balcony and bent over for our good-bye kiss. Hovering, he searched my eyes. "Are you sure you're all right?"

I held his cheeks and loved him for his concern. "I'm getting all right." He kissed my forehead and left. I suppose it was the kiss I deserved after such an answer.

Yaira and I washed, quick as birds in a puddle. We emerged, lotioned and dressed, before Amram had strapped on his sword. "My queen? I didn't realize you were going into the city today."

"We're going to visit Ima." Yaira and I left the palace, arm in arm, my heart pounding. Why did I feel as though I was betraying my husband?

We entered through the squeaky gate, leaving Amram to wait outside, and Abba looked up from a scroll he was reading. Surprised, I ran into his arms. "Abba, what are you doing home? Why aren't you in court with Hezi today? I thought I could rely on the royal council to temper my husband." I was only partially teasing.

"Your husband canceled this morning's court session, didn't he tell you?" He reached around me to hug Yaira, while I considered the question.

Why wouldn't Hezi have told me he didn't have court today? "Has Maher left for training yet?" I asked, avoiding his question.

"Yes, and the women are in the house."

Heat began to rise from my neck to my cheeks. "I wonder if I might speak with you and Ima alone?"

Yaira squeezed my hand and started toward the house. "I'll send the mistress out."

Abba braced my shoulders. "What is it, my girl?"

Why does a little sympathy unleash emotion? I hugged him to hide what my face would surely reveal. "I love you, Abba."

"And you are my delight, Hephzibah, my long-awaited daughter." He held me tight.

I basked in the security of his arms until Ima arrived in the courtyard. "What's wrong?" Panicked, she rushed over.

"I'm fine, Ima." I donned a smile and released Abba, waving away her concern. "I need wisdom from you both."

Ima gathered stools for all of us and placed them in a circle. "What's troubling you, dear?"

I looked at their worried faces and suddenly felt silly. "There are two things that Hezi and I seem to be incapable of talking about: Abijah and Israel. He becomes defensive about one, and I'm terrified about the other."

Ima exchanged a glance with Abba, a mingling of emotions on their faces. "Why don't you tell her about our family, my love," Abba said. "I can never share the stories without weeping."

Ima began the recounting. Parents, brothers, and sisters tragically killed or taken by illness. Those who remained in her family had rejected Ima and turned from Yahweh. Abba's story was bittersweet—an abba who had worshiped idols was brought to faith in Yahweh by Ima's persistent care. Gone now many years, Abba had sweet memories of their final years together.

I watched and listened as these two people told of the difficulties they bore while forging their own family. The love they shared. The God they served. It bound them together in ways Hezi and I had yet to experience.

Ima turned her attention to me. "Abijah is deeply wounded from years of pain and disappointment. She may require years of love and loyalty to trust again. Only Yahweh can know for certain."

Years. How many years had Ima loved Abijah even when she was so difficult? I thought back to the many times I watched the two friends together. Ima was never unkind, but she never allowed Abijah's unkindness to go unchecked.

Abba broke into my thoughts. "And as for Israel—I told Hezekiah at last night's meeting what I think about his plan to invite Israel to our Passover." He raised his eyebrow in that *Master Isaiah* frown of disapproval.

"So, you agree with me." My heart felt a bit lighter. "Though Israel is no longer the nation it was when they attacked Judah, they are still a threat. It's unwise to allow—"

"No, no, no, Daughter." He waved away my argument as if my head were full of wool. "It's about consecration and Hezekiah's position as anointed King. He broke the Law at the first Temple sacrifice when he allowed Levites instead of priests to present offerings. Will he now invite

Israelites to the Passover table who know nothing about what our God requires? They must wash their clothes, abstain from sexual relations, eat their meals standing with their cloaks tucked in their belts as the Israelites did in Egypt. The Law must be kept, Zibah. Hezekiah can't continue to do as he pleases and expect Yahweh to bless disobedience."

My defenses rose, but I didn't want to argue—with Abba or Hezi. At least Abba agreed that the Israelites shouldn't come, even if his reasoning was flawed. Hezi's decision to involve the Levites at the Temple consecration was the right one. Attendance at the Temple's daily worship since then had soared, and more Judeans were making their first visit to the Temple from outlying villages because they'd heard of that day's worship. Yahweh continued to bless. Why couldn't Abba see that?

Ima pressed her hand against Abba's knee and nodded in my direction. Before I was married, I might have missed the signal. Now I recognized it.

Abba cleared his throat. "I'm sorry, Zibah. What were you saying about Israel at Passover?"

I exchanged a knowing look with Ima. It was the glance of a friend, not just a daughter. "I think you summed it up well, Abba."

We sat in a moment of awkward silence, and I realized this was no longer my home. No longer the peaceful nest I craved. I would always be loved and welcomed here, but Hezi was now my home, my nest. I glanced at my dovecote, empty from the winter's migration. Would my birds come back later this spring? The thought pricked my heart, but I knew somehow that I would be only a visitor, not a caretaker, if they did. Perhaps a queen must learn from eagles, not doves.

"Thank you," I said, standing. "I should get back to the palace and find out what my husband is doing this morning."

I called for Yaira, we said our good-byes, and Amram opened the courtyard gate, then provided rear guard on our short walk back to the palace. My thoughts tumbled over the conversation with Ima and Abba as we passed familiar homes, and I waved at now-friendly neighbors. The topics of family and Israel still troubled me, though perhaps a relationship with Abijah wasn't impossible.

But there was little in Abba's comments about Israel that I could embrace. Perhaps Israel would always be a strained subject for Hezi and me. I realized, however, that if Hezi endured Abba's uncensored criticism—and possibly criticism from others—while in court, I must be gentle with my words. He still needed my counsel—even he acknowledged that—but I must remember that our chamber is a place of respite for my husband. Not an extension of the courtroom.

As we approached the king's chamber, I noticed Samuel slip inside without his normal greeting to me. Within a few moments, he returned to the hallway with a beaming smile. "Good morning, my queen."

A furry bear looks odd when it smiles that brightly. "What are you hiding, Samuel?"

"Nothing, my queen."

His lips twitched, and I knew he was lying. "Is Hezi in there?"

"Why do you ask?"

My heart began to beat wildly. Why would Samuel avoid my question? I tried to step past him, but he blocked me. I felt like I was at Abijah's door again. "Is this my chamber, Samuel? Or have I somehow forgotten where the king sleeps?"

"If you'll wait a few moments, my queen, I'll be happy to open the door."

Wait? Why would a few moments . . . ? Sickening dread stole the blood from my face. Hezi was hiding something—or someone—in our chamber and sneaking them out Yaira's chamber through the servant's entrance. I turned to my friend. "Yaira, go now and see who emerges from your room at the servant's entrance. Hurry!"

She ran even as my words died in my throat.

Samuel's eyes slid shut. "You shouldn't have done that."

I held my chin high, swallowing back tears,

refusing to let my anger turn to despair. Hezi couldn't have another woman in our chamber. He wouldn't. He'd been faithful too long. I would know if his promises had been false. I would know if his words tasted of honey but swallowed like vinegar. I would know. Surely, I would know.

Moments later, I heard sandals clicking on the tiles of an adjoining hallway, and Yaira rounded the corner—with Eliakim.

Confused. Angry. Elated. I wasn't sure whether to hug him or slug him. "Eliakim, what were you doing in our chamber, and why couldn't I come in?"

He walked as if strolling through a garden, smiling, hands tucked behind his back. His expression was that of a child caught raiding the candied figs.

"What are you hiding behind your back?"

The chamber door suddenly opened, and Hezi poked his head out the door. Seeing Eliakim, he groaned. "Eli, you got caught? You'd make a terrible spy."

Feeling slightly better at the playfulness in my husband's voice, I shoved my fists at my hips. "What were you two doing in there?"

Eliakim lifted both brows at Hezi, asking silent permission. Hezi nodded. "Show her."

In Eliakim's hands were a toolbox and a scroll. Hardly items worthy of kingdom secrets.

Hezi opened the door wide and swept his hand

inside. "You might as well come in now. Yaira, you and Eliakim too. We can all talk about the plans Eli has drawn up for the palace dovecote with which I'd hoped to surprise my wife after our Passover celebra—"

I jumped into his arms and smothered him with kisses, completely unqueenlike. He carried me into the chamber, laughing. Yaira and Eliakim didn't follow us. The guards closed the door. We'd talk about the dovecote later.

36

A very large crowd of people assembled in Jerusalem to celebrate the Festival of Unleavened Bread. . . .

They slaughtered the Passover lamb on the fourteenth day of the second month. . . .

When all this had ended, the Israelites who were there went out to the towns of Judah, smashed the sacred stones and cut down the Asherah poles.

—2 Chronicles 30:13, 15; 31:1

Hezekiah became vaguely aware of a rooster's crow in the distance. Dawn's glow split the tapestries, demanding he rise, but he was king, was he not? On this cool morning, the warmth of his wife molded to his back both soothed and saddened him. Even in her sleep, she clung to him. He turned and slid his arm beneath her, pulling her closer to nuzzle her neck. The scent of nard and saffron. This was his wife. These, his favorite moments of each day.

Her eyelids fluttered but stayed closed. "A few more moments before we have to begin another day," she whispered.

"Look at me, my delight."

Slowly, almost painfully, she opened her eyes,

and he looked deeply into them. He saw longing, pleading, but for more than he could give. Insatiable fear now tortured her. Her lion's heart had become a lamb's.

"Tell me what I can do to make you feel safe again."

She turned away, shutting him out.

He tamped down his anger. Took a deep breath. *I must try to understand.* A few weeks ago, he'd imagined seeing his brother Bocheru as the sacrificial lamb at the Temple consecration. Were his fears rational? It had been seventeen years since Bocheru's death and since Zibah lost her parents. How long would both he and his bride be marred by their past?

Forgiveness wasn't easy. Forgetting was impossible. But they were trying.

Zibah had made a valiant effort to overcome her lingering bitterness and dread during the traditional seven days of Passover. She'd even been supportive when Hezi extended the celebration another seven days. His queen stood shoulder to shoulder with men and women from Israel, the nation whose troops killed thousands of Judeans and marched her and Yaira to Samaria as captives. He loved her strength.

Hezi pressed his lips against her ear. "You roared like a lion at your fear during the feast."

"And now I've become a mewing kitten."

He kept her sheltered under his arm. "I know

you're frightened because the Israelites acted violently when they left Jerusalem after Passover, but they didn't harm people. Nor did they attempt to. They smashed pagan altars and destroyed high places in our northern villages. They were fueled by their renewed commitment to Yahweh. It was a good thing, my love."

She began to tremble but remained silent.

Hezi buried his head in the pile of dark brown curls, feeling helpless. *Yahweh, how can I comfort my wife?*

Pray. The answer was like a trumpet though the word came silently in his spirit. He rested his head on his arm and obeyed.

Dawn stretched into morning, and Zibah's trembling ceased. Hezi peered over her shoulder again to see if she slept. She was awake, quiet. He lay back down beside her and continued his prayer vigil.

Yaira knocked on the door, opened it, and closed it hurriedly when she saw them still in bed. Zibah didn't move.

Finally, when a sliver of light peeked through their balcony tapestry, she said, "You're late for court."

Hezi leaned up on his elbow. "I'm not going to court. My wife needs me."

She covered her face. He resumed his place, willing to wait as long as needed for her to open her heart.

Releasing a frustrated sigh, she said, "You can't stay here all day."

"Why not?"

"Because you're the king of Judah."

He didn't speak. More prayer was needed.

"Hezi." She turned toward him, their faces less than a handbreadth away. "You can't be nursemaid to your wife and tend a whole nation too."

"Then tell me how to help you."

Fresh tears came, but this time she reached out and stroked his cheek. "Why are you so wonderful?"

He captured her hand and kissed her palm. "Talk to me, Zibah, my delight." She tried to turn away, but he captured her again. "If angry tears were red, and sad tears were blue, and frightened tears were green, what color would your tears be?"

She lay still for a long moment, staring at him. He'd almost resigned himself to more prayer when she answered in barely a whisper. "What color would confused tears be?"

It was a start. "Perhaps they would be brown," he offered, "mixing anger, sadness, and fear together."

She scooted closer and nodded against his chest.

"Can you describe the colors one at a time for me, or are the emotions too murky?"

She paused, and he waited. "I think it's all too murky. The emotions, the arguments, even Abba's prophecies. Everything is jumbled up in my head and making me feel more afraid because I can't sort it out."

"It's easy to feel afraid in the confusion, isn't it?"

She nodded again.

"Let's see if we can sort it out together." He began gently with the event that happened Passover night. "When your abba rebuked me publicly for allowing unconsecrated Israelites to eat the Passover meal, his proclamation sounded like a message from Yahweh, even though it was merely his opinion."

Zibah was quiet for several heartbeats. "I'm not sure it was simply his opinion, Hezi. The Law is plain. The unconsecrated must not eat the Passover meal."

Hezi tried not to bristle. "I prayed before the meal that all those who set their hearts on truly seeking Yahweh would be pardoned. Yahweh blessed this situation much as He did the Temple consecration ceremony when the Levites stepped in—against the Law—to help with sacrifices because the priests had not consecrated themselves for service." He stroked her hair, hoping his words penetrated her already turbulent emotions. "I believe Yahweh forgives our imperfect attempts at obedience when we act in sincere faith to live out His commands."

"You should never have invited the Israelites to the Passover in the first place." Her tone was harsh, commanding. He'd never heard her so defiant.

He uttered a silent prayer before saying the hard truth. "If I hadn't invited the Israelites, a portion of God's chosen people wouldn't have heard the Levites' teaching. They wouldn't have experienced fourteen days of worship in Yahweh's holy Temple. And they wouldn't have enjoyed the restored fellowship of their Judean brethren. Would you deny Yahweh's people—"

"Yes!" she cried. "I would deny them as they denied me my family, my home, my peace." She curled into a ball and wept, this time deep, racking sobs that shook her.

Startled, Hezi lay beside her, staring at the ceiling, utterly defeated. *Yahweh, I don't know what else to do. Only You can help my Zibah.* Perhaps it would be best for him to give her time alone—or with Yaira. He drew close to tell her he was going.

"Go," she shrugged him off, her tone lifeless. "Please go."

Hezi left their bed, splashed his face, and dressed quickly, without opening the balcony tapestries or lighting a lamp. He entered his courtroom with a heavy heart, carrying with him the darkness of his chamber.

37

See, I lay a stone in Zion, a tested stone,
a precious cornerstone for a sure foundation.
—Isaiah 28:16

The same anger and fear Zibah expressed in
tears was vented with shouting by Hezi's royal
council. The Israelites' inglorious departure from
Jerusalem had provoked enough debate fodder
for weeks. His advisors had been yelling at each
other—and him—all afternoon. He rested his
elbow on the armrest of his throne and cradled
his chin. Was Zibah all right?

When Shebna called one of the royal secretaries
a reckless Philistine, Hezi had heard enough. He
signaled Samuel, who slammed his spear to the
marble floor with a thunderous *slap!* The noise
startled the council into silence.

Hezi rose from his throne and descended the
dais, approaching the gallery of advisors. "We
will not second-guess our decision to invite the
Israelites to the Passover feast. God honored the
celebration, and He used our northern brothers to
eradicate even more idolatry from Judah. Let that
be the end of it."

Commander Jokim's anger had rendered his
face the shade of ripe grapes. "They raided and

destroyed Judean property on their way back to Israel. We cannot let that go unpunished."

"No, Jokim," Hezi said. "They destroyed Judah's high places, the job you and your troops were supposed to do two months ago." Commander Jokim offered no reply, and the near-empty courtroom throbbed with silence. "We spent fourteen days worshiping Yahweh in His Temple—a celebration unlike any since the days of Solomon—and you will rejoice, brothers, or I will find new advisors who will!"

Fifteen men avoided his gaze, but Hezi continued. "The question is, What now? For three months, my reign has been about smashing idols and refurbishing the Temple. We've successfully restored Yahweh worship in Judah. Now we must maintain it, and that means caring for the Temple's servants—the priests and Levites." Nervous glances said the advisors had not yet considered these economics. "For now, I will continue to contribute from my own possessions the morning and evening burnt offerings and the burnt offerings on Sabbaths, new moons, and the appointed feasts. The priests and their families will take their appropriate portions from each sacrifice as described in the Law."

Joah, the recorder, interrupted. "My lord, you already provided a thousand bulls and seven thousand sheep for the second week of Passover. Are you sure—"

Hezi waved off his concern. "My personal wealth will be replenished when I return to the battlefield and take my share of soldiers' plunder."

"Your generosity supplies the priests' needs, but who will provide for the Levites?" Shebna was quick to defend his ancestral tribe. "They aren't allowed a portion from the sacrifices."

Leveling a warning stare at his old classmate, Hezi said, "You know the Law, Shebna. You've taught it to your students for years. Why don't you enlighten the rest of the council?"

Frustration tinged his tone. "The Law requires every family in Judah to bring the *best* one-tenth of every harvest—both grain and vine—to the Temple as a tithe. That is to be the Levites' portion."

"Thank you, Sheb—"

"Then the Levites must offer a tenth of what they receive to the priests. And how many Judeans will actually bring a tithe?"

Hezi scanned the gallery of advisors. "If the people of Judah see us, the leaders of this nation, following God's laws with a spirit of generosity, I believe they will care well for the Levites and priests." Hezi raised both brows, impressing his will on the men under his authority.

Surprisingly, every man answered with an affirming nod. Shebna, seeing no one else joining his cause, said, "I hope you're right, my king."

Perhaps the next item of business would encourage them all. "Eliakim, what are the building updates on our fortified cities?"

Eliakim gave a quick report, including the good news that their troops had recaptured more cities from the Philistines.

"Thank you, Eli," Hezi said, pleased with the report. "Commander Jokim, where should we place our efforts to regain ground lost during Abba's reign? What territory is most susceptible to attack?"

A little spark lit in the commander's eye. "We should continue the campaign in Philistine territory, my king. I believe we can regain our towns and villages all the way to Gaza if we strike now."

Anxious faces looked to Hezi for a response. Was Judah ready to go on the offensive to grow the nation? Hezi had led on the field of battle but never managed a kingdom while battles raged all around.

His eyes lingered on Isaiah, who had appeared wearing a sackcloth robe instead of his fine linen. He wore sackcloth only when he planned to deliver a prophecy. Hezi's stomach clenched like a fist. Micah wore linen. Only Isaiah was dressed to prophesy.

Hezi's sudden unease made further deliberation impossible. "We are adjourned for now. Please pray for Yahweh's clear direction on the

Philistine campaign, and we'll make the decision tomorrow. Isaiah, please remain. The rest of you may go."

The advisors filed out, and Isaiah's eyes locked onto Hezi. When the last counselor had gone and the heavy cedar door slammed shut, Isaiah's words echoed in the grand hall. "So this is what the Sovereign LORD says: 'See, I lay a stone in Zion, a tested stone, a precious cornerstone for a sure foundation; the one who relies on it will never be stricken with panic. I will make justice the measuring line and righteousness the plumb line; hail will sweep away your refuge, the lie, and water will overflow your hiding place.'"

Hezi wasn't sure whether he should run away or fall to his knees in worship. "I have no idea what that means."

"Nor do I," said Isaiah. "But I can assure you the words are the Lord's."

"Not your opinion like the Passover criticism?"

Isaiah's eyes narrowed. "The anointed King will fulfill every letter of the Law."

"Will the anointed King feel utterly terrified at the daunting task of ruling Judah?"

Surprise softened Isaiah's features, and the beginnings of a smile touched his lips. "I think every good king fears and then trusts in Yahweh for answers. King Solomon said, 'The fear of the LORD is the beginning of wisdom.'"

Hezi sobered. "Why did the Lord send you to speak a prophecy to me that neither of us understands?"

"I believe you asked me a similar question when you were a prince of fifteen on the night Assyria began its siege on Samaria. I told you then, 'Prophecy—even when we don't fully understand it—is given so we can recognize God's sovereignty and power when it unfolds.' "

Hezi didn't like his vague answer now any better than he did when he was fifteen.

He studied his teacher, and his teacher studied him in return. "You were distracted today during the council meeting."

Instantly uneasy, Hezi didn't want Isaiah to know about Zibah. Isaiah's marriage seemed so perfect. "Distracted? How so?" The king leaned against the gallery rail, hoping to appear relaxed.

Isaiah lifted a brow. "Is my daughter all right?"

Hezi straightened and clasped his hands behind his back. "Why do you ask?"

"Because asking about my daughter has suddenly made you nervous."

"She's a little upset since hearing of the Israelites' violence in the north." Hezi shrugged. "That's all."

"That's not all, or your neck wouldn't be splotching with red patches."

Hezi dropped his head, sighing his defeat. "When I left her in our chamber this morning, she was inconsolable, Isaiah. I don't know what to do. She won't eat. She cries uncontrollably." He dragged his hand through his hair and lifted his eyes.

Instead of the judgment Hezi expected, he saw compassion in Isaiah's face. "Change has always been difficult for Zibah. Even though your marriage and Judah's cleansing has been exciting, it's also displaced her from her family, from her home."

"She said as much, right before I left the chamber this morning—that the Israelites had taken her family and home and peace." Now that Hezi knew the problem was Zibah's aversion to change, he could work toward fixing it. "Eliakim and I will begin building a new dovecote in the royal courtyard tomorrow. Perhaps her own flock here at the palace will give her more of a sense of home and—"

Isaiah had already begun shaking his head.

"What?" Hezi said, annoyed.

"Today's prophecy wasn't for you, Hezekiah." His eye misted. An abba's tender smile graced his lips. "Yahweh's words, of course, are meant for Judah and will be recorded on a scroll, but I believe they also have meaning for my Zibah. Listen again. This time, as if you're a woman searching for security and safety.

So this is what the Sovereign LORD says: "See, I lay a stone in Zion, a tested stone, a precious cornerstone for a sure foundation; the one who relies on it will never be stricken with panic. I will make justice the measuring line and righteousness the plumb line; hail will sweep away your refuge, the lie, and water will overflow your hiding place."

Hezi was startled by the sudden and gentle revelation. Awed, he interpreted for his teacher, "Whatever refuge, lie, or hiding place Zibah has believed to be her security will be taken from her, and Yahweh will prove Himself the only sure foundation—a tested stone, a precious cornerstone. And she will never be panic-stricken again."

"Yes." Isaiah gripped the king's shoulder. "My daughter believes home and family—even her doves—give her peace, Hezekiah, but Yahweh is about to prove that He is her only sure foundation." He paused, seeming hesitant to continue.

"What, Isaiah? Is there more to the prophecy?"

His hand dropped from Hezi's shoulder and he stepped back. "No, what I was about to say is simply my *opinion.*"

The stab hit its mark. "This time I'd like to hear it."

Isaiah inhaled a labored breath and forced it out. "Why would Yahweh speak to you a message that was meant for Zibah? Unless whatever he pries from Zibah's hands will also be pulled from your grasp."

38

In the year that the supreme commander, sent by Sargon king of Assyria, came to Ashdod and attacked and captured it—at that time the LORD spoke through Isaiah son of Amoz.

—Isaiah 20:1–2

The royal messenger arrived yesterday with news that King Hezekiah and his troops would return today from their year-long campaign against the Philistines. I felt the same rush of emotion surge through me that I experienced more than two years ago, when I waited for Hezi's processional to enter the city after King Ahaz's death. Except this time my arms ached to hold the husband who was part of me.

Yaira stood with me and other anxious noblemen's wives on the top palace step. As the highest platform in the city, it was our best chance to capture a glimpse of the troops as they entered the Upper City.

"Do you see him yet?" she asked.

"Not yet." I shouted over the blaring trumpets and cheering crowd. "They must be entering the western gate if the trumpets are sounding."

I'd battled fear after last year's Passover—and

had nearly overcome it—until Hezi's departure with the troops sent me reeling. He'd honored the law in Deuteronomy which stated that newly-wed husbands must remain with their wives for the first year of marriage. Hezi's sense of duty, however, called him to war only days after our first-year anniversary. I couldn't forbid him to leave, but I tried mightily to reason him out of it.

"Why not wait until I conceive your heir before running away to fight Philistines?" I pretended a playful calm as we walked in the orchards on a cool winter night.

He lifted my hand to his lips, kissed it, and seemed truly at peace. "We'll have a son when Yahweh wills it."

The Gevirah was not so patient. Abijah stoked my fear of barrenness every time I visited the harem. "If I hadn't born Bocheru in our first year of marriage, King Ahaz would have set me aside."

One more of a thousand reasons I thanked Yahweh Hezi was not like his abba.

When my husband left to fight Philistines, I cried for a month in our chamber. Immune to Yaira's consolations, my self-pity was ultimately defeated when Ima brought noblemen's wives to my chamber for a visit—women whose husbands fought alongside mine. Her plan worked. I joined the sisterhood of those who waited, yearning for and yet dreading news from the battlefield.

Finally, something I could share with noblemen's wives. I now had friends waiting just as anxiously as I on these palace steps.

"There!" Yaira pointed to the single street leading to the Upper Gate. "See him?"

I lifted my hand over my eyes to shade the sun's glare. Yes. The glint of gold from my husband's crown captured my attention. I could barely see him, but the sounds of tambourines and lyres grew louder as the procession drew nearer.

Led by dancing young maidens and Yahweh's rejoicing Levites and priests, Judah's king returned a conquering hero. All praise to Yahweh, Judah had seen victory in every battle and gained territory stretching to Solomon's ancient borders.

Hezi's white stallion passed under the archway separating the Upper and Lower City. There, on his magnificent steed, was Judah's king—my husband and beloved. His gold crown rested at a slight angle across his brow, and he cradled Solomon's scepter in the bend of his right arm. The chill in the air demanded he wear his fox-collared purple cape. But when I saw his left thigh was bandaged, a slight bloodstain showing through, I thought my heart might fail.

I ran down the palace steps and into the street, fighting any guard who at first thought me a crazed spectator. Hezi saw the commotion and slid off his horse, limping as he ran to meet me. "I'm all right. I'm all right." I fell into his arms weeping. He pressed his lips against my ear. "It's nothing, really. You can kiss it and make it better."

I laughed and cried, clutching his robe in both hands. "Why didn't you send a messenger with news that you'd been injured?"

"It's a small cut by a Philistine blade." He kissed me, and the crowd roared its approval. I'd nearly forgotten they were watching. We ducked our heads, and he tossed his horse's reins to the stable boy. "See that he's fed and groomed, will you?" The boy nodded, and we began our walk toward the palace, Hezi leaning heavily on my shoulder as we climbed the stairs to the palace entrance. We turned and waved to the crowd, smiling. Hezi spoke without moving his lips. "I hope you realize you're not leaving my bed for the next week."

I spoke with the same feigned smile. "I hope you realize you're not leaving Jerusalem again—ever."

The applause ebbed, and we escaped into our semiprivate world. Guards, servants, and noblemen scurried around us with a barrage of greetings and questions. Hezi treated each one with a measure of grace and kindness beyond my patience.

Finally, we arrived at our private chamber. The guards broke protocol and offered their king a smile. "Welcome home, my king."

"Thank you, men." Hezi winced.

I'd seen him injured a dozen times while training, and he never acknowledged pain. "Call for the physicians immediately." My tone brooked no argument. One guard obeyed immediately, and the other guard opened the door. Yaira waited with a basin of warm water, towels, and scented oils.

She was as worried as I about his leg. "What happened?"

"Philistine sword," I said. "Physician is on the way." Yaira supported his other arm, and we walked him to the bed.

Hezi rolled his eyes. "Truly, ladies, I'm fine."

After settling him with cushions behind his back, Yaira grinned. "I'll be in the other room if you need me." She was gone before we could thank her.

Hezi lunged, pulled me into his arms, and pushed off my head covering. "Tell me about your dovecote. Only two pairs of turtle doves had nested when I left last spring. Did more come?"

I loved that he cared. "Every niche was filled by the end of mating season. We had fourteen pairs, and the courtyard palm trees were full of palm doves. One of them even lit on my arm—the first summer!" He threw back his head and laughed, sending his deep, resonant voice through me. I nestled into his chest and breathed in his scent, musky cinnamon with a hint of aloe. "My world is right when you are in it."

He laid his cheek on my head. "Your world must be right with or without me here, Zibah."

I sat up, startled by his foreboding tone. "What do you mean?" His brow knitted with concern, and I could tell something weighed heavily. "Tell me."

"Lie down and let's talk about your doves."

"No, Hezi, please. I'd rather be prepared if something is wrong. Tell me."

Hezi pulled me to his chest. I could hear his heart beating like chariot horses in a race. "We returned to Jerusalem because our scouts warned that Assyria was on the move against the Philistines. Anytime Assyria moves this far south, Judah is in danger." He fell silent, no doubt waiting for my response.

"I know," I said. "Abba told me."

His breathing quickened. His chest muscles tightened. I could tell he was angry.

I sat up, measuring the severity in his eyes. "Abba knows that I don't respond well to surprises. So he told me Assyria would no doubt see we've taken back Philistine territory and demand higher tribute."

"Did your abba also put on his sackcloth and then offer his opinion about paying that higher tribute?"

His sarcasm stirred my ire. "He need not give an opinion when the answer is plain. You must meet Assyria's demands."

His silence said *no*.

"Give it to them, Hezi."

"I have sent Shebna to talk with Egypt and Cush about forming a coalition."

"No! No one can stop Assyria."

"Zibah, even your abba's prophecies say that someday Assyria will fall. What if I am the anointed King who will unite the nations and bring about Assyria's annihilation?" His eyes sparked with excitement. Excitement!

"You aren't thinking clearly. You've let blood-lust cloud your judgment. Send messengers to call Shebna back." Suddenly, the contradiction in that statement dawned. "Abba is your foreign minister. Why did you send Shebna to negotiate?"

He looked away, his jaw muscle dancing to an impatient tune. "Please don't tell your abba, Zibah. Shebna's mission to Egypt must remain a secret between you and me alone. I haven't even told Eliakim."

What had happened during his time away that had made Abba an enemy, Shebna a friend, and Eliakim an outsider? I gently cupped his chin and pulled his attention back to me. "You didn't answer my question. Why did you send Shebna to Egypt instead of Abba?"

He closed his eyes and released a weary sigh. "Your abba has sent me multiple scrolls filled with prophecy while I've been away. According to him, every nation on earth will perish—

including Judah—and somehow Jerusalem will rise like a glittering jewel." When he opened his eyes, the lines on his face became hard, all tenderness evaporated. "I think your abba has lost his faculties, Zibah. His correspondence has become increasingly nonsensical. One sentence portends doom. The next assures redemption."

My emotions reeled, and my mind scattered in a thousand directions. Why hadn't Abba mentioned these new prophecies? "Abba's prophecies have always been difficult to understand, Hezi. Perhaps we need to sit down with him and talk through them. Like we used to."

"This is different, Zibah. Every prophecy talks about the anointed King . . ." He pinched the bridge of his nose and squinted his eyes. "And makes it very clear that if I fall short, Assyria is waiting to pounce."

Would Assyria attack Jerusalem? Was Hezi leaving to fight again? How could I give him an heir if he was never home? Paralyzed by questions, I could do nothing but stare.

In the stillness, Hezi opened his eyes, and his expression softened. "Zibah." He scrubbed his face and growled. "I'm sorry, my love. I've been talking to soldiers for a year. Please, please"—he opened his arms and beckoned me close—"let's talk about something else. Do I need to build another dovecote? We could fill the courtyard with them."

His feigned smile couldn't erase what I'd just heard. A new dovecote couldn't heal the wound on his thigh or stop an Assyrian invasion or reverse my abba's demotion. I placed my hand on his chest. "I love my doves, and, yes, another dovecote would be nice, but that's not enough. I—"

Tears threatened, and Hezi's instant concern nearly broke me. But I couldn't ask what I was about to request through a shade of tears. I exhaled a steadying breath, then started again. "When Yaira and I were freed from captivity, she said Yahweh surely had a special purpose for my life, and I believed her."

Hezi brushed my arm. "And here you are. Queen of Judah."

"Yes, but what do I do as queen, Hezi? With the knowledge I gained as Abba's student, as his fellow teacher, and now as a friend to noblemen's wives—what do I do where Yahweh has placed me?" I shook my head and dashed away tears. "I think I must do more than coo at doves."

My husband stopped looking at me as if I were a wounded sparrow. "So, what is it you wish to do?"

I swiped at a few more tears and chuckled. "I'm still not sure, but I know it involves arguing with you." He laughed with me. "Like stonechats, I think you'll be stronger if we pair up, my love. If we're to face an Assyrian invasion—"

Hezi suddenly covered my mouth, looking over my shoulder. "Come in. Come in."

I turned and found the palace physician, mouth gaping. "Uh, I . . . uh, please forgive me. Your guards told me it was urgent and sent me in. I can . . . uh . . . did you say *invasion?*"

I hurried off the bed, wiping my face, and stopped the physician on his way to the patient. "Thank you for coming so promptly. Let me assure you, there is no impending invasion." He appeared relieved. "But let me also remind you, anything you hear in the king's chamber is private, and it would be an act of treason to repeat it." He nodded politely and followed me to my husband.

Hezi chuckled as did the physician. The elderly man greeted the king. "I see your wife is already a fine queen, my lord." He unwrapped the bandages on my husband's thigh to inspect the wound, and I had to look away. The smell alone nearly made me retch.

"The infection is severe, my queen, but I believe we can manage it. I brought henna, turmeric, and honey. He'll be fine."

Hezi's color waned when the doctor began cleaning the wound, so I called for Yaira to bring cool cloths for his head. When the doctor finished his ministrations, he left poppy-seed tea to help Hezi rest. I sang to my patient until his deep, steady breaths proved he slept soundly, and then I retreated to our balcony, my sanctuary under the stars.

After a year apart, Hezi was still gentle and tender with me; however, he had no patience for Abba and seemed suspicious of my relationship with him. My husband's personal confidence had been honed by his recent successes. Was it wise to replace Abba as foreign minister? Had his prophecies truly become unreliable?

My heart ached at the thought. I heard Hezi groan, toss and turn on our bed, and wondered if my tumultuous thoughts somehow unsettled him. Dare I question him about replacing Abba? Had my husband considered how our teacher might respond to another royal demotion? Isaiah, servant of Yahweh, was faithful to a fault—but his pride might be bruised. *Yahweh, prepare Abba's heart for the news. Assure him of his worth in Your eyes regardless of an earthly title.*

An earthly title. What did *my* earthly title mean—Queen of Judah? I'd valiantly declared I was ready to help in every aspect of kingdom rule. Did the husband who knew me realize how terrified I was? Did he know that talk of tribute and Egypt and Assyria made my skin crawl? Yet something deep inside heightened my desire to be more involved in the coming decisions. *How can it be, Yahweh, when I am such a frightened lamb?*

"Not the reunion you'd hoped for, I suspect."

Hezi planted gentle kisses in the curve of my neck.

I drank in the feel of his arms around me. "Nor you, I suspect." We swayed together to a silent tune—until I remembered. "Oh! Your leg!" I whirled and held out my arms to steady him.

He shook his head. "Zibah, relax. Didn't you hear the physician? I'll be fine." He drew me into a tight hug. "If you are to rule beside me, you can't project the worst possible outcome. We must believe in Yahweh's best and let His good plan unfold."

I closed my eyes. "You must teach me that talent."

"We are stonechats, my love. We may flap at each other from time to time, but we learn from each other."

I didn't respond, hoping the silence would become my assent.

"I'll send word to cancel tomorrow's court sessions," he whispered against my hair. "We'll spend the whole day together. How does that sound?"

I looked up in the moonlight and saw the face I'd loved for nearly all my life. "It sounds like the best day I've had all year. You may get an heir after all."

39

[Yahweh said to Isaiah], "Take off the sackcloth from your body and the sandals from your feet." And he did so, going around stripped and barefoot.

—Isaiah 20:2

Isaiah spent the morning in the prophets' caves. It felt like holy ground as he peered through torchlight at abandoned tents and the ashes of cook fires. Yahweh had hidden his friends here for almost twenty years. Isaiah needed the assurance of that miracle-working God after the message Yahweh delivered during the night.

Yahweh revealed that Hezekiah had sent Shebna instead of Isaiah as Judah's foreign minister to Egypt and Cush. Of course, Isaiah's pride was stung, but beyond his hurt pride, the prophet's heart was broken. Hezekiah had pursued an alliance with Egypt's Cushite pharaoh to fight Judah's enemy—just as King Ahaz had turned to Assyria—rather than trust in God to save their nation.

"Yahweh, forgive him." Isaiah rubbed tears from his eyes as the whisper passed his lips. The remainder of last night's message had been just as disturbing. Isaiah must be sure he'd heard God's voice and wasn't responding out of personal angst or wounded pride. Isaiah had questioned his calling more than once since Hezekiah began regularly accusing him of speaking his opinion. Of last night's unusual message, Isaiah must be certain.

Isaiah ran his hand along the walls of the cave, reminding himself of Yahweh's faithfulness to his family. The Lord had protected them the whole time as they delivered food and supplies to God's faithful prophets. Judean troops never detected them, and provisions never ran out. "If you can protect thirty prophets for almost twenty years, surely you can protect one naked prophet for three years." Even saying it out loud made Isaiah's cheeks flush.

He cried out in the depths of the cave, "How will you provide for my family this time, Yahweh?" Racking sobs shook him, and he fell to his knees. Was it pride that made the coming task so frightening? "Please, send someone else to do this." But the heaviness remained. He was the one Yahweh chose to walk barefoot and naked through Jerusalem's streets for three years—Isaiah ben Amoz, cousin to kings.

He'd been humbled when King Ahaz demoted him from foreign minister to royal tutor. Yet teaching young minds had become his richest blessing. "Will I ever look back on my three-year nakedness and call it a blessing?" He laughed through tears, aching at the shame Aya would endure. How could she bear it?

Tekoa. He would send her to the prophets' camp. They would care for her tenderly while Isaiah destroyed their life in Jerusalem. At least she wouldn't see his shame.

Surely, people in Jerusalem would get used to his wandering. At first, imas would hide their children's eyes, and women would turn away. Eventually, they'd ignore him. Wouldn't they?

Everyone would think him mad. Perhaps he was mad. *Yahweh, am I?* The gentle flutter in his spirit assured Isaiah his mind was meant for heavenly matters, so yes, indeed. He was a little mad—and had been ever since he saw the Lord seated on a throne.

The train of Yahweh's robe filled the heavenly Temple, and Isaiah saw the indescribable creatures with six wings flying around God's throne, calling, "Holy, holy, holy is the LORD Almighty." How did he know they were called *seraphim?* Had anyone ever described them to him? No. Yet he knew what they were called as surely as he heard God's voice saying, "Whom shall I send?"

Isaiah dropped his face into his hands. Weeping, he repeated his answer—as true now as it was then. "Send me, Lord. Send me. I will go wherever You lead and say whatever You speak." The tears washed him, soothed him. Though he didn't bear the blisters on his lips, as he had after the original vision, the fire in his soul burned as bright as the torch in his hand. "I trust You, Yahweh, to accomplish that which You have promised." He began his journey home—clothed, for the final time in three years.

He noticed the birds. A snake slithered across his path. The breeze lifted his beard, and he pondered just how chilly his next three years would be.

Too soon, he pushed open his squeaky court-yard gate and found his beautiful wife bent over her embroidery. She looked up and immediately grew pale. "What is it this time?"

He couldn't help but grin. She knew her husband and their God too well. "I want you to take Leah and Dinah to Tekoa for a while. Maher can choose whether he stays or goes after he hears the Lord's command."

"How long will we be gone?"

"Three years."

She looked as if she'd swallowed an egg sideways. How would she react to the real news? "I'm not leaving you," she said.

"Yes, Aya. You are."

She set aside her embroidery and stood, hands on hips. "Tell me why."

That stopped him. His cheeks warmed, and the words stuck in his throat. He must be able to tell his wife before he could obey the command. With a deep sigh, he closed his eyes. "I am to walk barefoot and naked for three years proclaiming both Lower and Upper Egypt's eventual captivity to Assyria." He swallowed hard and opened his eyes. The horror on Aya's face was worse than he'd expected. He closed his eyes again. *Lord, please send someone else.*

He waited to hear her footsteps retreating. Surely, she'd run as fast and far from Isaiah as possible. Instead, she embraced him, resting her head against his chest. "I'm not leaving you. We'll send Leah and Dinah to Tekoa right away."

Emotion washed over him like a flood, and he enfolded this woman, this part of his heart. "I can't let you see my shame." They wept together, grieving the losses that were sure to come.

Finally, she dried her eyes against his robe and stepped back. "You said from the beginning that God called you to proclaim His message to a people ever hearing but never understanding, ever seeing but never perceiving. As long as you're obedient to Yahweh, my love, there is no shame." She swallowed more tears. "I'll prepare Leah and Dinah for the journey. Can you find someone to escort them to Tekoa?"

Isaiah nodded. "I'm sure Jashub would be willing." She turned toward the house, but he caught her arm. "As soon as they leave, I must obey the call."

She pressed her lips and tried to smile. "I'd better stoke the fire then. You'll get chilly."

40

Woe to those who go down to Egypt for
  help . . .
but do not look to the Holy One of Israel,
  or seek help from the LORD.

—Isaiah 31:1

I was up early with Hezi to help him dress before his first day back in the Throne Hall. Yesterday, we played our favorite childhood game—the two wooden triangles with pegs—and I beat him seven out of thirteen times. He slept some, and I lay beside him, watching the love of my life breathe in and breathe out.

When he woke, we talked of my life in Judah while he was gone. "I visit your ima in the harem each day. She still hates me." I smiled, but I knew he believed me. "Rizpah also hates me."

"She hates everyone."

I agreed. "Selah, the youngest wife, has been very kind. We've gone to the market together a few times, and she's even helped make sure the other wives and children go to all the Temple services."

"That's an improvement." Hezi rubbed a circle on the back of my hand, thinking before he spoke. "Does Ima attend Temple services with you?"

"Not yet." My heart broke for him. "I continue to tell her about the wonderful worship, and I think she's softening."

He offered a forced smile, and I was determined to change the subject. "Ima introduced me to several of the younger noblewomen after your first month away, and we've become good friends." His genuine surprise urged me on. "Penina was the first nobleman's wife to invite me to her home. A group of almost twenty soldiers' wives began meeting weekly. We've become quite close."

He drew his finger from my shoulder to my wrist. "I'm proud of you. You seem stronger. Happier. More settled in our home."

"I am. It just took me a while to adapt."

The day sped by too quickly. A few of Hezi's advisors visited and welcomed him home. The physician came to change his bandage twice. Before I was ready for the day to end, my exhausted husband fell into a sound sleep without any help from poppy-seed tea. He woke this morning seeming refreshed. The doctor insisted on another bandage change before the king left for court. Hezi's leg was tender after having the wound cleaned again, but the infection had lost its rancid smell and appeared to be healing well.

Now, sitting on the balcony with Yaira, I watched as she dipped a stylus into the henna pot, working more detail into the intricate design on my right foot. She stuck out her tongue while drawing an especially delicate part, perfectly matching the lovely swirls and florals on my left foot. "How did you learn to do this, Yaira?"

"The harem maids taught me. Some of them served royalty in Egypt, so they know all sorts of beauty secrets." She added a small set of dots on the side of each big toe, then sat back to inspect her work. "There. Finished."

My feet looked like a garden. I lifted my robe to my knees and danced into our chamber to Yaira's rhythmic clapping.

"Hezi will love it," I called out to her. "I hope he doesn't have too many disputes in court today so he can—"

A man's shouting stole our attention. Directly outside the palace, under my balcony. Yaira and I exchanged a puzzled glance and both hurried to investigate. We leaned over to see the street below. Yaira saw him first, squeaked, and backed away. Her cheeks bloomed like roses.

"What?" I leaned over again, searching the street for what she'd seen. "Oh!" I backed away and covered my eyes. But some things can't be unseen. Sliding to the marble tiles, I covered my face in shame. What was Abba doing?

His voice echoed off the palace walls. "Why make a treaty with Egypt to save us from Assyria? Are not the Egyptians mere mortals? Their horses flesh and not spirit? When the Lord stretches out

His hand, those who help will stumble, those who are helped will fall, and all will perish together."

Egypt? Who told him Hezi sent Shebna to Egypt? And why, oh why, was he naked? Had he truly lost his mind as Hezi feared?

"Hephzibah!" Hezi's angry voice called from our chamber. "Hephzibah!"

I felt like a boulder had landed in my stomach. Pushing myself to my feet, I made it to the archway of the balcony. Hezi came storming through the chamber and nearly knocked me over.

He held a carved Asherah in one hand and shook a scrap of parchment in the other. "Do you know what this says?"

That was an odd question. "How could I know?"

He shoved it into my hand. "Read it."

I'd never seen him so angry. The small parchment read: *Ask your wife about her friend.* The note was written in Rizpah's hand.

"Who wrote this?" he asked. "And why are there still idols in my palace? Who would dare accuse my wife of condoning—"

Hezi was interrupted by the deep voice from below our balcony repeating the words, "Why make a treaty with Egypt to save us from Assyria? Are not the Egyptians mere mortals? Their horses flesh . . ."

Hezi stepped around me to look over the

edge of our balcony. The Asherah in his hand forgotten, he turned to face me, trembling with rage. "Explain, if you dare, why your abba is naked in the street, telling the whole city about a treaty with Egypt that not even my private council knows about yet."

His last words came in a roar, and I stood shaking in the wake of his fury. "I don't know why he's naked, and I didn't tell him about sending Shebna to Egypt."

"No one else knew, Zibah!" He threw the idol, and it shattered on the floor, revealing a gold ring among the shards. I didn't dare move, but Hezi picked up the ring and read the engraving. "To my rock, Selah." His eyes narrowed, and through gritted teeth he said, "Yaira, leave us."

She drew me into her arms. "I'm sorry, my king, but I won't. Not until you've calmed down and I'm sure Zibah is safe."

He marched past us through the archway and into the chamber. "Naam!" he shouted. The chamber guard entered immediately. Hezi pointed to where we stood, still on the balcony. "Remove Yaira and her belongings from my chamber immediately. She can return later to collect the queen's personal items. Both women will move to the harem as their permanent residence."

I felt Yaira tense as Naam drew nearer. "Go, Yaira. I'll be all right."

She screamed as Naam pulled her from me and

fought as he dragged her out the door. I covered my ears and closed my eyes but saw only an image of flapping stonechats in my mind. Hezi and I would wound each other deeply if I stayed any longer. Why had I imagined I could find a peaceful nest?

When I heard the chamber door slam, I opened my eyes and saw hatred consume my husband's expression. He was a man I didn't know. "I can't trust you, Zibah." His words were clipped. Spoken through lips drawn tight in a scowl. "If you were a man in my regiment, you would be arrested for treason."

"Without even a fair hearing?" Tears threatened, so I turned away to hide my weakness.

"Look at me, Hephzibah." His voice, quieter now, was still as hard as granite. With a deep breath, I faced him, and he continued, "There will be a full investigation of the harem. Any woman found with idols or pagan engravings of any kind will be stoned."

"As the Law dictates, and as you have warned. It is a fair and just ruling, King Hezekiah." I bowed.

"Now you mock me?"

I squeezed my eyes closed and swallowed a caustic reply. "I was not mocking." Opening my eyes, I met his gaze. "I'm telling you I don't condone idolatry, and I believe you're right to deal with it quickly and harshly." Stubborn tears betrayed me, but I dared not turn away again.

A moment of sadness invaded his anger. "I never thought you and your abba would conspire against me, Zibah. I guess no one is completely trustworthy."

"I hope someday you realize how wrong you are."

He glared at me, and I had to turn away, unable to bear the disdain any longer. I scanned the chamber I'd lived in for two years. The tapestries, the carpets, the fine furniture. It was more fragile than a dove's nest. As easily destroyed as random twigs and garbage gathered hurriedly by wild birds. None of it brought peace. My henna-covered feet poked out from beneath my silk robe to mock me. How ridiculous they looked. Lifting my gaze to the angry king before me, I remembered the boy I first met on the litter. Lifeless and empty. Then tender and delightful. He'd given me life. He'd given me words. He'd given me love.

"I will miss you, Hezi." I started for the door, stepping over the shattered Asherah.

"Stop, Hephzibah. We're not finished talking."

"We didn't talk, Hezi. You passed judgment, and I was condemned."

I walked by him, but he grabbed my arm. "You tell Isaiah to put on a robe or I'll throw him in the dungeon to rot."

I looked down at his fingers digging into my

arm and then into his blazing anger. "I haven't talked to Abba in three weeks. Perhaps you should tell him."

He released me, and I left the chamber to the tune of his angry cry. "Then how does Isaiah know about Egypt?"

41

"How can we know when a message has not been spoken by the LORD?"

If what a prophet proclaims in the name of the LORD does not take place . . . , that is a message the LORD has not spoken.

—Deuteronomy 18:21–22

Isaiah bore his humiliation with courage while proclaiming God's message in the street, but when Judean soldiers covered him with a blanket and marched him into the palace, he thought he might die of shame. Whispers and sneers ushered him down the long hallways as two of the king's guards escorted Isaiah into Hezekiah's private chamber.

Eliakim waited in the audience chamber, somber and silent, but Hezekiah met Yahweh's prophet at the doorway. "Who told you I sent Shebna to Egypt?"

Startled, Isaiah had expected to answer for his nakedness and hesitated.

The king bristled. "Don't lie to save your daughter. I've already banished her to the harem."

Isaiah shifted from angry prophet to irate parent. "Then you've wounded your innocent wife, and you're more of a fool than I imagined."

"Careful, prophet. I'm your king, not your student, and I will only abide messages directly from Yahweh." Hezekiah moved closer, grinding out the words. "Who told you about Shebna?"

"Yahweh." With Isaiah's single word, all color drained from Hezekiah's face. Isaiah almost felt sorry for the young king. Almost. "Why, Hezekiah? Why would you send *anyone* to Egypt for help against Assyria rather than trusting Yahweh for our protection? How many times did we study Yahweh's prophecy to King Ahaz, when the Lord promised to protect us from Israel and Aram if your abba would simply trust God fully? But what did he do? King Ahaz stripped the Temple and sent gifts to Assyria, begging them for protection. Now we find ourselves indebted to Assyria under imminent threat."

Hezekiah's face turned crimson. "I am not my abba."

The simple yet venomous words were true, but his need to say them revealed his own doubts. "No, son. You're not your abba. Neither are you the anointed King of my prophecies."

The young king staggered back, mouth gaping. Sound escaped but no words. Finally, gathering his wits, the king's eyes grew pleading. "Would Yahweh have me sit on my hands and do nothing to protect the people of Judah? Should I wait for Him to rain down gold from the heavens to fill our treasury? What is the responsibility of a king if not to forge peaceful alliances with the nations around him?"

"Then why not send me, Hez?" Eliakim moved closer. "Shebna has as much tact as a mad dog in a sheepfold."

Hezekiah turned on him. "I've already told you—we need you here to construct a tunnel, to bring water from the Gihon spring into Jerusalem."

"No!" Isaiah's heart nearly failed him. "You can't alter the Gihon. It's the holy place where Judah's righteous kings have been crowned for centuries."

Hezekiah pulled at his hair and shouted, "Is that another word from the Lord, Isaiah? Did Yahweh tell you we shouldn't bring water into the city through a tunnel in case of an Assyrian siege? Or did you just speak another *opinion?*" The king fell silent, measuring the length of Isaiah, wrapped in his woolen blanket. "Please tell me you aren't walking around naked to get people's attention because they've stopped listening to your prophecies."

Isaiah's neck and cheeks flamed. "How dare you! I'm risking my home, my reputation, my wife's shame to obey the word of the Lord."

"You didn't answer my question." Hezekiah glared, challenging. "Is your warning about the tunnel a mere opinion or a message from Yahweh?"

Isaiah ground his teeth. "Must I be mute in your presence unless speaking God's words?"

Hezekiah dropped his gaze and shook his head. "So condemning the tunnel was your opinion—as was your belief all these years that I was the anointed King." He returned sad eyes to his teacher. "You know my heart, Isaiah. Why can't you trust that Yahweh is working through me to make these decisions?"

"Why can't you trust that Yahweh is working through me to speak to His people?" Isaiah dropped his blanket, exposing his nakedness.

"Cover yourself!" Hezekiah's face flamed, and Eliakim rushed to wrap Isaiah in the blanket.

Isaiah bowed his head, wishing for Aya's arms. "Trust is not so simple when human decisions are required."

Hezekiah took a deep breath and blew it out. Then with a gentle voice he asked, "Why are you walking around naked, Isaiah?"

"Because Yahweh commanded it—yes, a direct command." Isaiah held the king's gaze. "And it was a direct command to rebuke you for seeking a treaty with Egypt."

Hezekiah studied him for a long while. "You have sent scroll after scroll of so-called words from the Lord, none of which have come to pass, Isaiah. What am I to believe? You're the one who pressed the words of the Torah into my heart and mind, 'If what a prophet proclaims in the name of the LORD does not take place or come true, that is a message the LORD has not spoken. . . . Do not be alarmed.' How can I take any of your words seriously when none of these recent prophecies have come true? When you offer both Yahweh's words and your own opinions with equal zeal?"

Isaiah felt a slight prick of conscience but dared not agree lest the young king disregard all he'd said and written. "I also taught you that prophecy may have many fulfillments. Some in the present—in contexts both personal and corporate—while other fulfilments occur well into the future. Some even so distant that none of us will see them fulfilled. I cannot control God's ways or His timing, but I must speak when He gives me words, Hezekiah."

The king exchanged a dubious look with Eliakim and whispered something Isaiah couldn't hear. Eliakim hurried out of the chamber, and Hezekiah suddenly changed into the gracious host.

"Come, Isaiah. Let's sit down and have a cup of sweet wine." He rang a bell for the servants and invited Isaiah to his audience chamber, making an awkward attempt at small talk. Isaiah played along, uncertain if he was waiting on soldiers or Aya to take him away, but it was obvious the king had called for reinforcements.

When the knock sounded, Hezekiah called out, "Come!" and two sets of sandals slapped the floor. Eliakim was surely one, but who else?

Curiosity gained the upper hand, and Isaiah glanced over his shoulder. *Hephzibah.*

Face tear stained and eyes swollen, she fell to her knees behind him and pressed her cheek against his blanket-covered back. "Abba, are you all right? Tell me what this is about."

Tortured beyond humiliation, Isaiah felt as if his heart was torn from his chest. *Yahweh, will my obedience cost Hephzibah her marriage?* He couldn't face her. "I must obey Yahweh's command to walk stripped and barefoot for three years as a sign and portend against Egypt and their Cushite rulers—who will be marched, buttocks bared, by the Assyrians into captivity." He met Hezekiah's stunned features. "You will soon receive word that Assyria's King Sargon has conquered Ashdod, which gives him a clear path to Egypt."

"You've lost your mind, Isaiah." Hezekiah finally spoke the words his expression had screamed since Isaiah arrived in his chamber. "Assyria may very well conquer Ashdod, but their supply lines will never reach far enough west to support their army's total invasion of Egypt—let alone farther south to Cush." He stepped around Isaiah and lifted Hephzibah to her feet. "Reason with him, Zibah. I can't allow him to walk around Jerusalem naked."

"Really, King Hezekiah?" There was fire in her

voice. "Will you attempt to silence all Yahweh's prophets as King Ahaz did, or just my abba?"

Isaiah bowed his head, pride and fear welling up in the strained silence.

"I will clothe him and return him to your ima, where she will surely keep him at home."

Standing, Isaiah pulled the blanket tighter around him and aimed his question at Judah's king. "Do you question the prophecy itself or simply the fact that I must be naked to deliver it?"

Hezekiah answered with a question of his own. "Tell me now, in your daughter's hearing, have you changed your *opinion?* Am I the anointed King of your prophecies?"

Isaiah glanced at Zibah's hope-filled eyes, but he couldn't lie. "You are not the chosen Root of Jesse, Hezekiah."

Zibah covered a whimper, and Eliakim studied his sandals. Only the king held his gaze. "Isaiah, it seems we've lost faith in each other, but no matter what you think, I haven't lost faith in Yahweh."

The declaration was healing balm to Isaiah's soul. "That's what matters most, son."

"Indeed. Of next greatest importance is the nation of Judah and our city of Jerusalem, both of which I must protect against your wild accusations and fear-filled projections. You are relieved of all royal duties, Isaiah, and confined to house arrest until you abandon this madness."

"Hezi, no!" Hephzibah ran to her husband, but he brushed her aside.

"Eliakim, summon two guards to escort Isaiah home." Eliakim bowed curtly and offered Isaiah an apologetic glance before obeying his king and friend.

Hephzibah hugged Isaiah, weeping. "I believe you, Abba. I know you speak for Yahweh. I know it."

Hezekiah stood aloof, alone.

Eliakim returned with two guards to escort Isaiah, but Hephzibah hugged him tighter, refusing to let go. The king gently tugged at her arm, but she shoved him away.

Provoked, Hezekiah pulled her forcefully from Isaiah. "You can visit him later."

She yanked her arm from his grasp. "Leave me alone."

Hezekiah set his jaw and stepped away, the chasm between them growing wider before Isaiah's eyes.

His heart ached for the children of his heart. Two souls Yahweh had knit together, now torn apart. Had he caused their rift? Could he somehow make it right? Aya would know. As the guards led him from the chamber, Isaiah called over his shoulder, "I'll send your ima to check on you, Zibah. Hezekiah, you vowed to care for my daughter!"

42

He must not take many wives, or his heart will be led astray. He must not accumulate large amounts of silver and gold.

—Deuteronomy 17:17

Hezi stood at the chamber door, a camel's length from me. Abba's good-bye cut me like a battle-ax, *"Hezekiah, you vowed to care for my daughter!"* Hezi had cared for me well—until today. I rushed toward the door, needing to escape before more tears stole what dignity I had left.

Hezi snagged me in his arms and wrapped me tight. I could barely breathe. Was it because he held me too tight or from the ache inside me? "Please, Hezi. Let me go."

Eliakim walked past us. "We'll talk more about the tunnel later, Hez." I'd forgotten he was in the room. The door closed behind him.

I was alone with the man who had crushed my heart to dust. I'd rather be anywhere else. I'd rather be nowhere else.

He rubbed my back and rested his cheek on my head. "I'm sorry, Zibah. I accused you and didn't give you a chance to explain. Your abba said Yahweh, not you, told him I sent Shebna to Egypt."

Silence was my only friend. Words would only swell my rage, expose the rawness, and open my heart to more pain.

Finally, he released me and tipped my chin. "Has one disagreement killed your love for me?"

"Disagreement?" I choked on the word. "You said you'd lost your trust in me, Hezi. That's more than a disagreement."

"I was angry."

"That's true, but you believed I'd *conspired* with Abba against you." Pausing to rein in my emotions, I breathed deeply and spoke again. "You had guards take away Yaira as if she were a prisoner. You banished me from your chamber. And you've placed under house arrest one of Yahweh's most faithful prophets."

I wrapped my arms around my waist, fear and anger battling inside. "All this after you returned from your first battle as king. It sounds terrifyingly similar to the story your ima tells of King Ahaz's transformation from loving husband to . . ." My words were strangled by my emotion, but I dared not drown in tears. I fought them like a soldier, holding his gaze, awaiting his reply.

Jaw tight, Hezi took a deep breath before speaking. "Let's not talk about your abba or mine. Can we concentrate on us?"

"I think our abbas are part of what drives us apart. How can I ignore King Ahaz when I see you repeat some of his same behaviors?"

His eyes sparked with anger. "How can we repair our relationship if you continually defend your abba and criticize me?"

We stared at each other, locked in silence. As I stood there, in the chamber of Judah's king, very harsh and true realizations dawned. King Hezekiah owed a wife no explanation for his actions. In fact, as Rizpah had pointed out when she saw the guards moving my belongings into the harem, Hezi could reject me altogether and take another wife at any time. My little "nest" was very fragile indeed. And I had no idea how to make it stronger.

"I should go." I started toward the door again, but Hezi stepped in front of me.

"All right. Let's talk." He pressed his lips against my ear. "I'm not my abba."

My defenses began crumbling. "But you're different after leading your troops as king. Impatient. Suspicious. How do I know you won't become someone I don't recognize?" I saw Abijah's battered face in my mind. Hezi would never . . .

He tenderly gripped my arms and looked into my eyes. "I won't be like Abba because my focus is on Yahweh and my family—you, Zibah. *You* are my family now. Not Ima, Isaiah, or Mistress Aya." He raised his eyebrows and grinned. "You and whatever children Yahweh gives us."

My heart flip-flopped, the fear of barrenness a

constant hum in the corners of my mind. "What if I never conceive, Hezi? The line of David must continue on Judah's throne. You must take another wife if—"

He pressed his finger against my lips. "I will never take another wife. You will conceive, and Yahweh will continue the line of David through us." He lifted that silly left brow. "You should move back into my chamber so we can work on it."

I ached with love for him, but I was still angry he'd cast me out of our chamber and terrified to trust again so soon. "No, Hezi, not yet." The light in his eyes dimmed. "Let me stay in the harem with your abba's widows and spend more time with Selah. If I discover she worships Asherah, I'll tell you. She is my friend, but I am your wife. My loyalty is to you above all."

He stood silent, and I wondered if he would argue—or maybe command me to return to his chamber. Instead, he offered his hand. "May I walk with you to the harem, then?"

I stared at his hand for a long while. My decision to live in the harem sounded so brave moments ago. Now, I wanted nothing more than to fall into his arms and never leave.

"Ishma."

His voice caught my attention and drew my eyes to his.

"Please, Hephzibah—delight of the Lord.

Forgive me for hurting you today." His hand still waited, coaxing. I held my breath and reached for him. He gathered me close, this time tenderly. "I treasure you, Zibah, my delight." His kiss was like a butterfly's wings brushing my lips, teasing, tempting. With a groan, I surrendered to his embrace, finding freedom in my first small steps of forgiveness. I would remain in the harem until my heart mended, but I knew Hezi's arms were my true home.

43

You have set our iniquities before you,
our secret sins in the light of your presence.
　　　　　　　　　　　　　—Psalm 90:8

Hezi wiped his sweaty palms on his linen robe, smoothed his beard, and drank another sip of wine. He nearly knocked over the goblet when he set it back on the table. Food trays full of spilled wine—that would have been a lovely start to his first meal with Zibah in seven days. Why was he so nervous? Tonight was just a meal. With his wife. Who had chosen not to see him for a week. "Ugh." He rolled his eyes and fell back on the pillow behind him. Had she forgiven him yet for ordering her out of his chamber?

One knock on the door, and Samuel opened it. "Queen Zibah, my king."

Hezi stood as his wife crossed the threshold, timid but smiling. Her guard, Amram, stood like a twin pillar beside Samuel. "I'll wait outside, my queen."

She nodded and waited until the door clicked. When she looked up, lamplight reflected in her sandy-brown eyes. "Good evening, Hezi."

His name on her lips made his throat suddenly dry. He wanted to pull her into his arms and beg her forgiveness. Instead, he smiled and offered his arm to usher her to the table. "Our meal has been prepared."

Zibah lowered herself onto her favorite red cushion, and he moved to his customary spot across the table—but paused. No. Tonight, they would be Hezi and Zibah, not king and queen. "Come," he said. "You carry the cushions and the wine. I'll get the food and plates. Let's eat on the balcony."

Surprise lit her features, and they escaped to their private sanctuary as if they were children avoiding chores. They ate. They laughed. They remembered their days in Isaiah's classroom with Eliakim, Shebna, Mattaniah, and a host of other children who now surrounded them in the palace each day.

When their laughter faded and memories were spent, Hezi asked the question that had burned on his heart for days. "Have you seen your abba?"

She reached for a candied date. Took a bite. Nodded. "I saw him today for the first time since . . ." Avoiding mention of their last painful encounter, she set aside the date and wiped her hands on a cloth. "I hope to see Abba each week. He's doing well. He said he's overwhelmed at the consistent flow of words from Yahweh since his obedience to this calling." She chuckled and looked up. "That was actually why I went today. He ran out of parchment, and the chief scribe provided more to Jashub, his prized employee, to give to his abba,"—her cheeks flushed—"the naked prophet."

Hezi reached for her hand, but she drew away. An awkward silence fell between them. "I'm sorry, Zibah. I can't imagine what this has done to your abba's reputation. To your ima."

"I thought the same thing," she said, "until I went to visit today." She stared into the night sky. "He was sitting in his study, his back to the doorway, and we talked for most of the afternoon. About my life here at the palace. About my brothers."

"He wasn't concerned what others said about his nakedness?"

Zibah stared at Hezi, her eyes growing moist. "He was most concerned that his obedience might have damaged our marriage."

Speechless, Hezi was humbled by Isaiah's selfless love.

"I should go." Zibah fairly leapt to her feet, seeming embarrassed by his silence.

"No wait. Please!" He reached for her arm, and she hesitantly returned to her cushion, eyes downcast. Hezi gently stroked the arm he held captive. "You can assure your abba that it was not his obedience that hurt my wife. It was my brutish behavior." He lifted her hand to his lips. "And I am rebuilding my wife's trust."

Zibah gently drew her hand away but offered

a halting smile. "Thank you, Hezi. I'll tell him. There are two things you could do that might return me to your chamber more quickly—if you're willing."

Anything! he wanted to shout, but he nodded respectfully instead. "Tell me, and it is done."

"First, I need your counsel on the harem wives. Most of the widows are beginning to talk to me, but Rizpah seems to despise me for no discernable reason. I don't know the women's relationships well enough yet to know why she would lie about Selah."

"Rizpah hates everyone. She's an unhappy, bitter woman."

"Rizpah speaks very kindly to Selah." She twisted her mouth in an adorable quirk. "Well, kinder to Selah than to anyone else."

Hezi pondered his memories of Abba's wives. He didn't know Selah. She was the youngest of the women, and he'd met her only a few times, but he'd known Rizpah his whole life. "What are Ima's thoughts about Rizpah and Selah's relationship?"

"Your ima hates me more than Rizpah does."

"Zibah," Hezi scolded. "Ima doesn't hate you, and she's known Rizpah the longest. They have sort of a . . ." How could he describe the relationship of a king's first and second wives? "They have a mutual respect and disdain for each other."

Zibah laughed, the sound winding a cord around Hezi's heart. He didn't want her to leave. "You mentioned two things I could do to speed your return to my chamber. My counsel regarding the first is to talk to Ima about the women's relationships. What's the second?"

Mischief brightened her eyes. "Keep feeding me candied dates." She snatched the date off Hezi's plate and leapt from her cushion, running toward the audience chamber to escape his playful wrath.

He caught her in two strides and pulled her into his arms. A moment of indecision, and then he lowered his lips to hers. The taste of his wife was sweeter than any candied date.

Hezi lay in bed, alone on this Sabbath morning, aching for his wife. He dreaded the coming day. No court. No scheduled meetings. *Forgive me, Yahweh.* Worship in the Temple was his only pleasure, but even there Zibah was separated from him. Hezi would stand under the king's canopy, where only he and his officials were admitted, and watch his queen laugh and smile with Abba's widows. When he become jealous of other women?

Zibah had lived in the harem for four months—four *torturous* months. And it had been nearly two weeks since she'd visited his bed. Not that he was counting. Yes, he was counting. All men counted.

He could summon her; she'd come willingly before. Was she angry? No, if she was angry, she'd tell him. Zibah had never been one for games.

Or had the harem changed her? Did she now prefer the company of her friends to the presence of her husband? Niggling fear ate at his gut. *Yahweh, don't let Abba's wives change her.* Harem life had changed Ima. He remembered cowering in a corner as Ima screamed. No, Abba had changed Ima, not the harem.

"This is madness!" Hezi bolted out of bed and looked around his empty chamber. "Now I'm talking to myself." Grabbing the gold bell off his table, he rang it with purpose. He would summon Zibah this morning, before the sacrifice, and request she come to him after dark when Sabbath was over.

"Yes, my king?" His chamber servant arrived at the same time a knock sounded on the chamber door. "Would you like me to answer that?"

"No. I'll answer." Hezi walked toward the door, shouting his instructions. "Send a message to Queen Zibah. Tell her I'd like to see her." He opened the door—and there she was. Stunned into silence, he must have looked like a fish out of water.

She giggled. "You wanted to see me?"

She'd barely stepped across the threshold before he pulled her inside, shut the door, and trapped her against it. "I'm never letting you out of my sight again." He kissed her with two weeks of pent-up passion. Her hands caressed his back, leaving fire in their wake. "I've missed you," he said, aching.

"I've missed you too." She pressed her forehead against his chest. "I need to tell you something." Her voice quaked, and he felt as if his whole world shifted.

He backed away, fear wrestling with dread, and he realized . . . "Where's Amram?"

She grabbed his hand and pulled him toward a couch. "Everything is fine, Hezi. Come sit with me."

He followed because of her smile, but he still wanted an answer. "Where is Amram, Zibah? He's supposed to be with you at all times."

"He's outside with your guards. You would have seen him if you hadn't accosted me when you opened the door." She laughed and shoved his shoulder.

Feeling a little foolish now, he fell onto the couch and pulled her beside him. "Don't scare me like that." He brought her close and kissed her forehead. "What do you need to tell me?"

She reached for his hand and placed it on her stomach. "I'm with child, Hezi. The midwife confirmed it two weeks ago. She said no 'activity' between us for two weeks, and then I was free to tell you."

He found himself playing the gaping fish again. Joy. Fear. Disbelief. How could he describe what he felt?

Zibah's expression fell. "Aren't you pleased?"

"I've never heard anything more amazing." He stared at his hand on her stomach. "You and me in one tiny person. God did that!"

She laughed through tears, and Hezi joined her. He lay back on the couch and pulled her on top of him, but she hesitated. "Hezi, no. It's Sabbath, and the midwife said we shouldn't for at least—"

He chuckled at his prim wife. "I just want you close. Lie down on me." Her cheeks pinked, and she relaxed into the bend of his form, perfectly molded to his shape. He stroked her hair. "So, this is why you haven't come to visit me."

"Yes. I've been avoiding you. Could you tell?"

"I hated it. I was afraid you were angry with me."

Her head popped up, and she rested her chin on his chest. "You would know if I was angry, King Hezekiah."

She laid her head down again, and he closed his eyes. *Thank You, Yahweh, for my wife—and our child.* A desire to protect her overwhelmed him. "I think you should move out of the harem."

Silence. She made little circles on his chest while his concern deepened. "I can't, Hezi. I believe I know who is worshiping Asherah, and

447

I must confront the sin while I live among them."

He lifted her to her feet in one fluid motion and stood beside her, anger rising. "Who is it?"

She held his gaze. "I believe if I confront her with the other widows, we'll be able to discern if she's the only one or if there are others."

The plan seemed logical. "Have you shared your suspicions with anyone else? Have you told Amram?"

"No, because he would react the way you have and arrest her before we get further information." She crossed her arms, waiting for him to disagree. He couldn't.

"At least tell me how you discovered the truth and when you plan to confront her."

She remained maddeningly silent.

"How did you realize which widow it is?"

"She's the widow who has most to gain and least to lose."

Hezi studied her. "That makes no sense. Every widow leads a similar life. One may have a little larger chamber than the other, but they eat the same food, walk the same gardens, share the same lotions and paints. Is it their children that made the difference?"

"No, my love. When you discover the reason, it may not seem logical to you, but what drove this woman to Asherah is as real in her heart and mind as the scrolls you read each day." She kissed him gently. "I've come to love these women, and they have taught me so much in the past months. I pray they will teach me more as we raise our child. Thus, it's as important to me to root out the idolaters as it is to you."

44

Their malice may be concealed by
deception, but their wickedness will be
exposed in the assembly.
Whoever digs a pit will fall into it; if
someone rolls a stone, it will roll back
on them.
—Proverbs 26:26–27

Nearly three weeks had passed since I'd refused
to confide the idolater's identity to Hezi. He
asked every day if I'd confronted her, and every
day my answer was the same: "I must wait until
I'm sure." Would I ever be sure enough to hand
her over to the guards for execution?

King Ahaz's widows and their maids had
become second family to Yaira and me. We joined
in daily activities—carding, spinning, weaving.
We laughed and told tales of past and present.
Abijah was the best among us at embroidery.
The other five of King Ahaz's wives pretended
not to envy her. All but Rizpah. She seemed
least capable of deception. Perhaps that was her
greatest ruse.

Topics of our conversations ranged from henna
art to dirty laundry. Occasionally, we spoke of
deeper things. Life. Death. Yahweh. On those

days, the widows now asked probing, honest questions. Today was *not* one of those days. Instead, things had gotten rather silly.

"I didn't drink four full wineskins at my wedding," Selah said, looking quite serious. "My maid drank one goblet out of them." She laughed at her own joke, gaining belly laughs from the others. I exchanged a grin with Yaira, trying to join the fun, but feeling more pity than joy that Selah needed to get drunk on her wedding day. She tossed a ball of yarn at me. "What about you, Zibah? Have you ever overindulged?"

Just as I was about to answer, my stomach clenched—and then tightened like a fist. I doubled over, knocking my sewing to the floor. The cramping stole my breath and fear stole my voice. *Yahweh, please!* I remembered Yaira's miscarriage and looked up to see horror written on her face.

"Come, my queen," Yaira said, lifting me off my stool, "back to our chamber." She called over her shoulder, "Selah, get the midwife. Now!"

Rizpah was the first to my side, and Abijah supported me from behind. The other wives surrounded me like buzzing bees, tending their queen.

When we entered the hallway, Amram tried to break through. "What's happening?" he shouted at Yaira.

"Call for the king. The midwife is on her way."

I began to weep, but the buzzing bees shushed me, soothing and cooing. "It's all right, dear."

"Stay calm," one said.

Another, "Fear won't help."

"Relax and breathe deeply."

We arrived in my chamber, and Yaira removed my robe.

"Off with your tunic as well." Rizpah placed her hands on her hips. "You didn't get that baby with your tunic on. Off with it." Another contraction seized me, and Rizpah hugged me tight, smoothing my hair, rubbing my back. "There, there, little one. I know it hurts." When the contraction eased, she stripped off my tunic before I could protest.

The women fairly lifted me onto my mattress, shoving pillows under my knees and hips, covering me with a blanket. Abijah held my hand. "Relax your shoulders."

Yaira placed a cold cloth on my forehead about the time another contraction shook me. I curled into a ball and bit my lip to keep from crying out. Yaira whispered against my ear, "There will be other babies, my sweet girl." Her tears wet my cheeks, mingling with my own.

"Zibah?" Hezi's voice shattered the cloud of pain.

I couldn't bear to look at him and turned my head toward the window.

"Where's the midwife?" he shouted.

"Selah went to fetch her, Hezi." Abijah hovered at my side, still holding my hand. "Calm yourself, Son. She needs your strength."

They exchanged a glance; he nodded. Resting beside me, he pulled me into his arms. "Zibah."

My name on his lips broke me. "I'm sorry, Hezi. I'm losing our baby."

"I'm sorry you must endure it, my love."

"Ahhh!" Another contraction robbed my dignity, and Hezi cradled me as I squeezed his strong arms. My rock. My anchor. "Don't leave me," I said as the pain ebbed.

"I'm right here," he whispered.

"Excuse me, my king, but I must ask you to go." The midwife stood behind my husband. A short, rotund woman whose gray sprigs of hair stuck out from her headpiece like an uncut acacia. "Men are generally too queasy for the world of women." She stepped back and swept her hand toward the door—in case he'd forgotten where it was.

"I'm staying." Hezi brushed stray hairs off my forehead.

"I suppose I can't argue with the king, but right now, in this room, you're second in command." She kissed my forehead and patted my cheek. "I need to check your condition, my queen. It's up to you if your husband stays or leaves."

I looked at Hezi, torn, and he offered a reassuring smile. He knelt at my head, and we gazed into each other's eyes. Another contraction made the midwife's exam excruciating but confirmed what Yaira and Rizpah suspected. Our baby needed to leave my body.

Hezi rested his forehead against my shoulder. We wept together to the sound of the midwife barking orders. "Abijah, more cushions under her hips. Rizpah, more clean rags. Yaira, my basket of herbs. Selah, boil water for the queen's tea."

"Are you giving her tea for the pain?" Hezi asked, but I stole his attention when another contraction gripped me.

He held me until it passed, and the midwife was waiting with her answer. "You see, King Hezekiah, that's why I prefer women only in the room during these events. Men ask too many questions and slow down the process. I'm giving your wife giant-fennel tea. The tea lessens the chances of infection. Unfortunately, it also increases the contractions." She stroked my cheek and offered a kindhearted smile. "By sunset, the worst should be over, and then I can give you something to help you sleep."

By sunset, I'd endured the worst pain of my life. Whipping wounds couldn't match the physical pain and emotional reality of losing a child. It was the first moment in life that I'd begged for death. *Yahweh, Holy One of Israel, may I never experience such torture again.*

Hezi witnessed it all. Somehow, though he'd

lost a child too, he still tried to comfort me with a tenderness beyond my ability to receive. My pain reached so deep, I was numb.

The buzzing bees were as exhausted as I. Rizpah leaned down to kiss my forehead before shooing the rest of the women out the door. "We must give the king and queen time alone." Even Abijah left without a fight. Hezi looked at me with tears in his eyes. "I see now why you love them."

Using the last of my strength, I cradled his cheek in my hand and closed my eyes.

"I was sure I packed poppy seeds in my basket." The midwife's voice sounded far away, like a dream. "It won't take me long to go home and get them. I'll be back in two shakes of a lamb's tail."

"I'll be here." Hezi sounded tired.

I drifted through occasional cramping but nothing compared to what I'd been through. Distant voices on the edges of my consciousness . . .

". . . midwife sent me . . . this tea . . . help Zibah sleep." Selah's voice.

". . . doesn't need . . . fine . . . later." Hezi caressed my arm, soothing.

"She must drink it now!"

Startled awake by Selah's insistence, I tried to sit up but grabbed my belly, groaning in pain.

Hezi cradled me, lowering me back against two large pillows. "Shh. Rest, my love." He glared at Selah, his breathing ragged. "My wife was perfectly fine until you woke her."

"I'm sorry, really. I'm just trying to help." Selah rushed to the other side of my bed and lowered the cup so I could take a sip of the tea. "Here, Zibah. Drink. It will take away your pain."

"I can't sit up, Selah. You'll have to—"

Hezi reached for the cup to help. "No!" she said, drawing it back. Her lips quivered with a tense smile. "Rest, my king. You've tended to your wife admirably all day."

Tension sparked between them. My mind was too murky to understand why.

"Give me the cup, Selah." Hezi held out his hand.

She tilted her head and smiled. "You're tired, my king. Let me care for her now."

He extended his hand farther. "The cup. Now."

Warily, she passed the tea to him. "I was just trying to help."

"How did you make the poppy-seed tea so quickly? The midwife said she had to go back to her house for the seeds." He smelled it and lifted the cup to his lips.

"Wait! No!" Selah lunged for the cup.

Hezi stepped back, easily out of her reach. "I wasn't going to drink it, Selah. I've had poppy-seed tea with my leg wound, and it doesn't smell like this. What sort of tea are you giving the queen of Judah?"

The young widow straightened her shoulders

and lifted her chin, glancing first at me and then back at Hezi. Silent.

"Must my guards question you in chains?"

His calm chased away my haze. Selah was the widow I'd suspected of worshiping Asherah. Rizpah had sent Hezi the idol not to threaten but to caution us both. I knew Selah was calculating, but I hadn't suspected her capable of anything this sinister.

Backing away from my bed, Selah's lips began to quake. "I would never hurt you, Hezi. Never you."

My husband's eyes narrowed. "I am King Hezekiah to you, woman."

"But my abba promised you'd be mine!" She buried her face in her hands, weeping.

"Selah," Hezi said, "I never even met you or your abba until the day of your marriage to King Ahaz."

Her crying stilled, and she lifted her eyes to my husband, pleading. "At my birth, Abba made a contract with King Ahaz that I would marry Crown Prince Bocheru. After Bocheru died, I was promised to the next crown prince. When King Ahaz chose my firstborn brother for one of the New Moon sacrifices, Abba panicked and offered me as a bride to King Ahaz instead if he would spare my brother from Molek's fire."

Selah turned hate-filled eyes on me. "You have the life I should have, Zibah, the love I should have." Her lips curved into a sinister smile. "Now, Lady Asherah has taken your baby as I asked her to do."

Hezi threw the cup of tea at the wall. "Amram, get in here!"

Selah stood with the solemn boldness of an impassioned traitor. All pretense was gone, and I regretted the dangerous compassion that had restrained me for months.

Amram entered, sword clanging against his brass-studded armor. "Yes, my lord?"

"Take Selah to the dungeon," Hezi said with terrifying calm.

Selah's eyes were so full of hate, I hardly recognized her. "We don't worship alone," she spat. "Your honorable guards were delighted to join in the pleasures of Asherah. I've been winning guards to worship since King Ahaz first taught me the rites."

Battle fury shook my husband. "Amram, take Asherah's high priestess away. She'll be stoned at dawn for inciting guards to idolatry." Face crimson, fists clenched, he turned toward me after they left, his rage slowly dying. "Samuel will replace the guards on this wing and question all the maids to find out which guards have been drawn in."

My emotions raw, I could barely whisper the words. "I'm sure Selah's maid also worships with them, Hezi." I closed my eyes, pushing through the exhaustion. "The other widows and their maids are faithful to Yahweh. You can trust their testimonies—and Amram's."

Hezi laid his head against my arm and then fell to his knees at my side, weeping. "What if I hadn't been here to protect you, Zibah? What if . . ."

My strength spent, I felt a tear escape the corner of my eye. I had no words to console.

He lifted his head and then sat on the bed beside me. Leaning over, he brushed my lips with a kiss. "I need you with me—in my chamber. Yaira can care for you there while you recover."

I lifted my hand to his cheek with the last of my strength. "Yes, my love, I want you to take me home now."

45

May the favor of the Lord our God rest on us; establish the work of our hands for us—yes, establish the work of our hands.
—Psalm 90:17

I lay on a new mattress next to the balcony in the king's chamber; it was brought in especially for my recovery. Hezi was forbidden to touch me during my bleeding, nor could he touch anything I'd touched. We ate together. He talked, sang, dreamed. "We'll have other children," he said, thinking his words would fill my emptiness.

"I can never hold my first child in my arms. He—or she—is just gone, Hezi. As if a baby never existed." I laid my hand over my stomach, a womb now empty. "But *I* know there was life there, a child I'll never know."

He sat on his hands. I knew he wanted to hold me. I also knew he could not. The king of Judah, like a high priest, dare not purposely make himself unclean. "I love you," he said.

"I know." It was all I could give.

The double doors swung open and in walked Abijah and Rizpah. I groaned and turned on my side to face the balcony, away from the women who had tormented me until the miscarriage.

Hezi met them before they reached me. "Zibah is not accepting visitors today. She needs rest."

"She needs to walk and regain her strength." I heard the swish of Abijah's robe draw near. "Yaira, we need you!" she shouted.

"Ima!" Hezi followed her.

I turned, seeing Rizpah marching alongside the Gevirah. "Your wife needs the care of women, Hezekiah. If you will not leave her in the harem, the harem will come to her."

Yaira opened her door and scanned the crowded room, then looked at me. I didn't need to speak. I held out my hand, and she hurried to my side.

Abijah nudged my husband toward the door, whispering as they walked away. I could make out only a few words. "Your wife . . . pain . . . support . . . go . . . court." Hezi cast a lingering glance over his shoulder and left the chamber.

"Well done," Rizpah said as Abijah returned.

The Gevirah released a sigh. "That may have been the hardest thing we do today."

Rizpah pulled a stool close to my mattress. Abijah did the same. Both were . . . pleasant, almost smiling.

I was flanked by the two women who hated me most, and they looked as if they would enjoy slaughtering me like a lamb. I held tightly to Yaira's hand, fear shoving aside my grief. "Why are you here?"

Abijah stared at me as if I were a fool. "I said

we'd come to tend you, dear. Didn't you hear?"

"Why?" I'd pondered their kindness from yesterday and reasoned it to be sheer instinct. In a crisis, people simply react. Perhaps for Abijah, it was a sense of urgency because I carried Hezi's child, her grandchild. Perhaps Rizpah responded out of duty when she saw the king arrive.

Rizpah lifted my left hand, drawing my attention. "Do you know the worst part of living in the harem, Hephzibah?"

I stared, speechless. She'd never spoken my name.

"The lack of purpose." She nodded at Abijah. "Do you think Abijah likes embroidery?"

The Gevirah grinned. "I have stacks of it in baskets that I'm sure you'll throw away when I die."

"I hate embroidery," Rizpah said. "I've tried weaving. I'm terrible at it. Your dovecote looked like an interesting pastime, but I'm put off by all the bird droppings. I know you use it to fertilize our garden—"

"The flowers have never been more beautiful," Abijah added.

"Agreed," Rizpah said, and then looked at me. "I haven't yet found an activity that captures my attention, so I sit in my chamber alone—and think. It's the worst thing a woman can do in a harem."

Abijah nudged Yaira's hand out of mine and

took it herself. "Tending to someone else fills a woman's deepest longing. You came into our world utterly capable. You needed nothing from us."

"So we had no need for you," Rizpah concluded. "Let us care for you now. It will give two old women someone to tend."

Abijah sneered at her. "Speak for yourself, *old* woman."

Rizpah answered with a grunt. "Yaira, get more rags. We'll get her on her feet. She needs—"

I squeezed Rizpah's hand. "Yaira is not my servant. She's my friend. If you tend me, you must treat her as you would your own friend."

The woman raised her brows and looked at Abijah. "All right, then. You get the rags."

The Gevirah laughed and asked Yaira where she kept the supplies. The chamber was suddenly a hive of activity, my busy bees caring in ways only they could. Though my womb and arms remained empty, my heart overflowed under the nurture of women who needed me as much as I needed them.

46

In that day I will summon my servant, Eliakim son of Hilkiah. . . . He will be a father to those who live in Jerusalem and to the people of Judah.

—Isaiah 22:20–21

Hezi exchanged a knowing grin with Zibah, who sat beside him on the historic throne of Queen Bathsheba. During the past three years of pregnancies, miscarriages, and dashed hopes, his wife needed purpose in her life, so she occasionally joined him for court sessions. And she had proved his best advisor. Today, Zibah had joined him for a most joyous occasion. His wife was with child again, and her three clucking hens—Yaira, Rizpah, and Ima—felt after three missed moon cycles, it was safe to share the news. They would wait until foreign business ended to share with Judean petitioners.

Hezi signaled Shebna to announce the morning's first petitioner.

Shebna gave a quick nod in return, and then announced to the gathered crowd, "King Hezekiah welcomes to his court the ambassador from Egypt." Their long-ago classmate had resumed his position as palace administrator after returning from Egypt with a signed treaty. Shebna bent to whisper to the king. "I worked closely with this man in Egypt, my king, and trust his judgment. Please, accept his gift."

Zibah heard the exchange and glared at Shebna. This wasn't the first time he'd coached the king on a response. Hezi held his tongue but would reprimand his palace administrator at midday break.

The Egyptian ambassador was Cushite like their king—a tall, dark-skinned man with well-muscled arms contrasting his white linen robe. He knelt before the throne, and Hezekiah nodded, signaling the man to rise. "Welcome, Ambassador."

"I bring greetings from the good god, mighty in power, son of the sun god Amun-Re, Pharaoh So, who wishes to inform you of his great successes."

The Egyptian droned on, but Hezi's patience ran short, eager to announce Zibah's pregnancy. "Please convey my best regards to King So, the great king of Egypt's Two Lands. What brings you to Judah today, my friend?"

The ambassador bowed humbly and then snapped his fingers at his attendant, who offered up an ornate box. "May I approach?"

Samuel moved between the man and his king. Hezi noted the ambassador's cheek quiver with a nervous tick. Trying to make light of Samuel's caution, he chuckled. "My personal guard seems as anxious to see my gift as I am." The ambassador was less than amused.

After inspecting the contents, Samuel placed the ebony-and-ivory-inlaid box in Hezi's lap and bowed. "It appears Egypt has offered Judah's king a new seal." He resumed his place at Hezi's right shoulder.

Inside the fanciful box were a dozen royal seals, small baked pieces of clay with the insignia of a winged sun. Hezi offered the ambassador a puzzled look. "Whose royal seals are these?"

"Yours, King Hezekiah."

Confusion quickly changed to anger when Hezi remembered Shebna's coaxing. The king tugged on the leather string around his neck and produced the dung-beetle seal for Shebna to see. "Have you forgotten what my seal looks like, Shebna?"

"No, my king. I—"

"Why would I allow a foreign king to determine my royal seal?"

Without waiting for his answer, Hezi turned to Egypt's ambassador. "Perhaps King So has forgotten. The dung beetle on my seal holds great meaning—and has since the first day of my reign."

Tension silenced the audience and drew every eye to the ambassador. "In Egypt, the dung beetle is common and earthbound—"

Shebna lifted his hand, and the ambassador fell

silent. Again overstepping, he whispered to Hezi, "King So feels the dung beetle is inappropriate for a king who must stand firm against Assyria and . . ." His whisper died when Hezi stared at him with enough venom to kill a cobra. Shebna wisely resumed his stance.

"Please thank your king," Hezi said, stepping off the dais to return the gift, "but the king of Judah chooses his own seal."

The ambassador fell to his knees and stretched out his hands. "King So implores King Hezekiah to trust the power of Amun-Re, the winged sun on these seals. With each use, these seals prove your allegiance to the great god, who will strengthen your army and block Assyria's advance into Egypt."

Fury seized Hezi, but he took a breath and controlled his voice. "Rise, Ambassador." He waited until the man looked at him. "Because King So has been my longtime friend, and because I understand his concern about Assyrian aggression, I take no offense at his gesture. However, the dung beetle remains my seal. Yahweh will strengthen Judah. And Judah will never again trust in any god but Yahweh."

A cheer rose from the audience as the ambassador dusted off his robe, offered a curt bow, and hurried his servant toward the exit.

Hezi returned to his throne and pinned Shebna with a stare. "Announce the next petitioner."

Before Shebna drew a breath, another voice rang out. "The Lord has called me to prophesy in the hearing of His people."

Zibah's face grew pale. "Abba?"

Hezi searched the crowd, wondering how the naked prophet had escaped from house arrest. He saw Zibah's reaction before he spotted Isaiah.

Her eyes filled with relief. "Hezi, he's dressed."

Tenderness flooded the king's soul when he saw God's prophet in his royal robes, hair oiled, and feet shod. Hezi wanted to call him forward, but was it safe? Could he be trusted here, in the presence of foreign dignitaries and the leading officials of Judah?

"Speak, Isaiah, but remember you have permission to speak God's words alone."

Zibah reached for Hezi's hand, squeezing as her abba drew nearer.

Isaiah's eyes were locked on the king. When the prophet reached the edge of the crimson carpet, he leaned forward, keeping his voice low. "You handled the Egyptian ambassador admirably."

Before Hezi could thank him, Isaiah turned and pointed a bony finger at Shebna. "This is what the Lord, the LORD Almighty, says: 'Who gave you permission to cut out a grave for yourself on the heights? Beware, you mighty little man, the LORD is about to take firm hold of you and hurl you away. He will roll you up like a ball and throw you into a large country. You will die there, and the chariots you're so proud of will become a disgrace to Hezekiah's house. You will no longer serve as palace administrator. I will summon my servant, Eliakim son of Hilkiah, to replace you. I will clothe him with your robe and fasten your sash around him and hand your authority over to him. He will be a father to those who live in Jerusalem and to the people of Judah."

Isaiah turned his attention to Eliakim, who sat gawking in the advisors' gallery. "Yahweh declares, 'I will give Eliakim the key to the house of David. What he opens no one can shut, and what he shuts no one can open. I will drive him like a peg into a firm place. He will become a seat of honor for his abba's house, and the glory of his family will radiate through his offspring—great and small. But there will come a day,' declares the LORD Almighty, 'when the peg driven into the firm place will give way, and the load hanging on it will be destroyed.' "

When the echo of Isaiah's voice died, silence reigned. The prophet turned next to Hezekiah. "The LORD has spoken. Do with it as wisdom dictates." Isaiah walked toward the double doors, without further comment or explanation, to the sound of the crowd's murmured wonder.

"Isaiah, wait!" Hezi stood, confused and overwhelmed. "Samuel, escort Yahweh's prophet to my private chamber. Court is adjourned for today."

He offered Zibah his hand, but Shebna turned

Hezi to face him. "Let me explain, my lord. I prepared my tomb on the Mount of Olives in the Egyptian style because—"

Hezekiah lifted his arm from Shebna's grasp and silenced him with a glare. "I made you my palace administrator because you work hard and are an intelligent man, but Yahweh sees the heart. If I determine that Isaiah has indeed heard from the Lord, I will obey without question." Hezi placed his hand at the small of Zibah's back and left Shebna gaping.

Hezi wondered on his short walk to his chamber how he would know if Isaiah's prophecy was born of God or was blatant favoritism. Shebna's personality had grated on Isaiah since their days in class, and Eliakim was the son of Hilkiah, Isaiah's dear friend. *Yahweh, give me wisdom to discern Isaiah's motives.* He stole a glance at his wife and saw her lips moving in silent prayer.

Isaiah followed Hezi and Zibah into their chamber; Samuel came as rear guard. As the king and queen took their places on a couch, Isaiah sat facing them. His daughter was first to speak. "I'm glad to see you dressed, Abba."

Isaiah ducked his head with a slight grin. "No one is happier than I. Yahweh released me this morning."

Hezi relaxed a bit. It was a good beginning. "Is that when you received the word about Shebna and Eliakim?"

"Yes."

Hezi waited but received no further explanation. "I wasn't aware of Shebna's fanciful grave and chariot obsession. Since you've been under house arrest for three years, I'm curious to know how you discovered the information."

"Really, Hezekiah?" Isaiah looked at him from beneath wiry gray brows. "Do I need to explain how a prophet hears from Yahweh?"

Fire rose in Hezi's belly. "Do I need to explain why I must ask if your prophecy is opinion or divine revelation?"

"Stop it!" Zibah said. "Both of you. Can we agree that you're both called by Yahweh to serve His people and begin to build trust on that?"

Isaiah took a deep breath and bowed his head. After a momentary pause, he lifted his eyes to meet Hezi's. "I'm sorry. You asked how I knew of Shebna's activities. Yahweh informed me this morning."

Hezi measured his teacher. The man's eyes were clear and free of challenge. In all the years he'd known Isaiah, he'd never lied. Maybe Yahweh had truly commanded him to walk around barefoot and naked. Hard to believe, but not impossible.

"Are you telling me to replace Shebna and make Eliakim my palace administrator instead?"

"It's not my request." Isaiah held his gaze, revealing no venom and seemingly no agenda.

"I'm not giving you back your job." Hezi grinned but he wasn't kidding.

Zibah touched her abba's arm. "Hezi named Magen ben Joshua as foreign minister, Abba."

"I don't want to be foreign minister."

"What do you want?" Hezi asked.

A slight smile. "I want a grandson. Do you have news?"

Hezi laughed, but Zibah grumbled. "Did Yahweh tell you before we had the chance?"

The prophet came off the couch and hugged his daughter. "No. But I had my suspicions when I saw your glowing countenance in court today." Hezi stood too and opened his arms to the man he'd once loved like an abba.

Awkward, but tender, Isaiah patted his shoulder and released him. "I should return home to tell Aya. She'll be so pleased."

"Let me walk you out." Hezi accompanied his teacher out the door, through the Middle Court, and out to the palace steps. They talked about the weather, the coming harvest, and Zibah's brave perseverance in waiting for this child.

Hezi paused on the platform outside the palace entrance and scuffed his sandal on the limestone. "I think this is the longest we've talked without arguing since I became king." He tried to laugh, but he noted Isaiah's intense gaze.

"I wish it weren't so, Hezekiah. I hope that can change."

"As do I." Hezi offered his hand, and Isaiah grabbed his wrist, locking their commitment with a pledge. They pulled each other into a hug and parted ways, leaving Hezi's heart lighter.

When the king returned to his chamber, Yaira had served their lunch on the balcony, and Zibah was waiting for him. "We're having your favorite. Lamb stew with lentils, melon, and . . ." She pressed her stomach and paused.

Hezi's heart skipped a beat.

She looked up and must have noted his concern. "It's fine. I think it's a little indigestion from this morning's olives. Come, my love. Sit down. Let's eat."

"Are you sure you're all right?"

"I'm fine, really." She scooped a generous portion of stew into his bowl and offered him a piece of bread. Zibah ate very little. He assumed her stomach was still unsettled.

When they'd eaten their fill, Hezi offered his hand to his wife. She rose with grace—but winced as she straightened. "What is it?"

Zibah waved it away and tried to smile. "I'm sure it will be fine, but perhaps I'll lie down for a while."

Bile rose in his throat. *Please, Yahweh. Not again.* "Of course. Let me help you." He supported her arm as they moved to the chamber.

Before they reached the bed, Zibah clutched at her belly and doubled over.

"Yaira!" Hezi shouted.

The sound that erupted from his wife voiced pain beyond physical suffering. Her spirit was shattering.

Yaira rushed in, her face as white as Egyptian linen. Nudging Hezi aside, she guided the queen toward her side chamber. "Call for the midwife, King Hezekiah. Hurry." Her voice broke as she escorted Hezi's wife into the bedchamber and closed the door.

Hezi turned to leave, but Samuel stood in the doorway. "I heard the queen's scream." He approached and placed his hand on Hezi's shoulder. "I've already sent Naam for the midwife."

"Thank you, Samuel." Hezi stared at Yaira's chamber door. He should go in, be with his wife again. Support her. Console. But his feet wouldn't move. He'd faced Philistines in battle and never been this frightened. *Yahweh, we can't do this again.* He examined his hands and watched helplessly as they trembled. How could he support his wife when he couldn't control his emotions? He could command generals and kings but couldn't command his child to live. *Only You, Lord. Only You give life and breath. Breathe life into our baby.*

The midwife burst through the door without knocking. "Is Yaira with her?"

Hezi stared blankly, nodding.

The midwife rushed toward Yaira's chamber, and without further thought, Hezi followed. When the midwife reached the door, she whirled and stopped him. "Not this time, my king. You need not endure it again."

The king of Judah stood like a statue while the midwife slammed the door in his face. Guilt overwhelmed him at the relief he felt. "I'm sure Zibah doesn't want to endure it again either," he said to no one.

"We must pray." Samuel led him back to the couches. He'd forgotten his friend was in the chamber.

Looking into those deep-set eyes, hooded by bushy black brows, Hezi was at a loss. "Pray, Samuel. I don't know what to say to my God."

The big man didn't hesitate. "God of our fathers, Giver of life and breath, You are our Rock, our Fortress, and our Deliverer in times of trouble. It is in You that we take refuge when the cares of this life grow too heavy to bear. You are our Shield in every battle, our Stronghold when we must rest, and the Strength of our salvation. We entrust Queen Zibah into Your care. She is ours, but she is Yours first and foremost. Save her. Keep her. Protect her. Let it be so." He squeezed Hezi's shoulder. "Trust Him, my king."

Peace flooded Hezekiah's soul, and he wrapped his guard in a ferocious hug. "You should have been a Levite! That prayer was anointed, my friend."

He slapped Hezi's back and released him. "*You* are the anointed one, my king. Remember that. Yahweh will give you a son, someday. Don't despair."

47

And the LORD was with [Hezekiah]; he was successful in whatever he undertook. He rebelled against the king of Assyria and did not serve him.

—2 Kings 18:7

Hezi paused before entering the private door to the Throne Hall and cradled my hands in his. "Are you sure you're all right to return to your advising role? You don't seem quite yourself."

"Not myself?" Until a little over a month ago, I was more than myself. I was growing another person inside me. Not anymore. "I'm fine. Really."

"It's understandable if you need more time to rest—"

"I've *rested* for forty days, Hezi, as the Law requires for a woman's uncleanness. If I have to spend another day in our chamber with Rizpah and your ima, I may be brought to trial for murder." After my seventh miscarriage in eight years, I'd had enough nurturing from the traveling harem.

"All right, my love." He kissed my cheek and then led me through the doorway.

The courtroom was empty except for the

gallery of advisors. All fifteen men were engaged in intense discussion until nudges and whispers forced the council into uncomfortable silence. Every eye was on the queen who couldn't produce an heir. My last miscarriage had been my worst experience—in many ways. It commenced here, in this courtroom, in front of these men, and it began after my stomach had rounded, announcing to the whole world my progress—and then my defeat.

Hezi and I climbed the six steps to our thrones, and he held my hand as I lowered myself to the place of honor beside him. He turned to his council but didn't yet take his seat. "Please welcome Queen Hephzibah back to our midst. She is one of the bravest people I know."

The council members applauded; some stood. I bowed in recognition, wishing Hezi would simply move on with whatever was on today's agenda.

As the applause died, Hezi nodded to Eliakim, the palace administrator, who searched through a pile of scrolls to find our first item of business for the day. Our childhood friend wasn't as organized as Shebna, but Eliakim had made Hezekiah's palace an edifice of hospitality, where the petitioners from Judah felt heard and foreign delegates were welcomed.

Finally, finding the scroll he sought, Eliakim delivered it to Hezi's hand. "We received it from one of our Assyrian spies, who arrived at the Horse Gate just before dawn."

Hezi broke the seal and began reading, his brows drawn down in severe lines. He set it aside without letting me read it. I tried to tamp down my annoyance—without success. Again, my husband stood to speak, and I found myself staring at his back. "Assyria's King Sargon is dead." Rumblings fluttered through the council as Hezi continued. "The report says he was murdered in his palace, but as yet the assassin is unknown."

"Hail to the assassin!" shouted Commander Jokim.

"Yes!" Hezi led the council in celebration, but what was there to celebrate?

"Will there be a struggle for power," I asked, "or will his son, General Sennacherib, be king?" Only Hezi heard my question amid the rejoicing.

"Come now, Zibah." He offered me his hand. "We must rejoice over even one dead Assyrian."

I ignored his proffered hand. "You're being ridiculous." My words broke into the joy like a dissonant chord in a Levitical psalm. The room fell silent again.

Hezi chuckled in the awkward moment, returning his attention to the council instead of discussing my concerns. "The scroll says Assyrian messengers were sent to inform General Sennacherib, who was fighting on the frontier.

He'll assume Assyria's throne in Nineveh, which means his early reign will be consumed with putting down another rebellion in Babylon—and, of course, retribution for his abba's death." Hezi stepped off the dais and approached the gallery of advisors, leaving me alone on the platform. "Now is the time, men. While Sennacherib is distracted, we join Egypt to assert independence and discontinue tribute payments to Assyria."

"No!" I shouted, my heart in my throat. "Sennacherib has a reputation more ruthless than any general before him. He's a military genius and will look to expand Assyria's borders." I descended the dais to join my husband at the advisors' gallery. "If you give Sennacherib a reason to march against Egypt, he'll gladly destroy Judah as his army marches through!" My voice broke. "Please, Hezi, don't do this. Please!" I began to tremble.

Hezi's neck and face bloomed crimson, and I thought he'd shout at me. Then I saw that he avoided the silent advisors' stares. My husband wasn't angry. He was embarrassed.

Humiliated, I covered my face. Backing toward the dais, I stumbled on the steps. Hezi tried to steady me, but I pushed him away. "You can't stop paying them. Assyria will come. They'll come . . ." I finally sagged into his embrace, giving myself over to the emotions I couldn't control. "I'll never give you a son if Assyria takes you from me. We'll never have a son, Hezi. Never."

My husband lifted me like a child into his arms, and I buried my face against his shoulder. I couldn't stop trembling. What was wrong with me?

I heard Hezi address our guards as we passed from the hall to our chamber. Hezi lowered me to our bed and knelt beside me. Waiting. He let my tears ebb before trying to speak. "I love you, Zibah, with all my heart, but you will not attend another council meeting until I can trust you to control your emotions."

The rebuke stung. "My emotions did not cloud my judgment of Assyrian reprisal. If you stop tribute payments, Sennacherib will punish Judah."

"That may be your opinion," he said, anger rising, "but it's only one opinion among many advisors. You cannot dissolve into hysterics in my courtroom!"

His shouting rattled me. I shut my eyes and squeezed my hands together, trying to stop their shaking. "Please, Hezi. I can't bear your shouting."

"Zibah . . ." He sighed and joined me on the bed, taking me into his arms. "I know you don't want to hear this, but I think you need more rest."

I was quiet. Thinking. The midwife said my body was tired. The physician said another pregnancy could kill me. Perhaps I needed to get out of the palace and breathe fresh air. "I want to see Abba and Ima." I hadn't seen them since the miscarriage, and my heart ached for someone familiar yet outside my daily existence.

Hezi kissed my forehead. "All right, but don't stay too long, and please rest when you return."

I watched him leave our chamber and felt relieved. I was tired of disappointing him. Sometimes, I wished to be alone without another soul to take care of or to care for me.

Yaira was with the harem maids this morning, so I called for Amram to escort me. Before midday, we arrived at my parents' home and found the courtyard deserted. Odd. By now Dinah and Leah should be preparing the table. Abba was normally reading outside, and Ima weaving or spinning.

Amram nudged me aside. "Let me go in first." He walked slowly, hand on his sword, and I followed. He turned and motioned for me to wait in the courtyard. He entered the house, and I watched him walk past Abba's study and down the hall toward the kitchen, my heart pounding. He straightened, relaxed, and began talking quietly with someone I couldn't see. He motioned me inside.

I heard only men's voices and entered the kitchen, where Abba and my brother Jashub sat on cushions beside the table. Neither looked like they'd slept for days. "What's wrong? Where's Ima?"

Jashub's eyes were red and swollen. "She and the others are tending to Hallel." He buried his face in his hands, and Abba looked up to explain.

"Hallel has been laboring nearly three days with their fourth child." He shook his head, silently saying what every woman knew. No one survived three days of labor.

I wanted to run. What was this duty called *birth* with which every woman had been cursed by Eve's sin? Why must we bear a child like a grunting beast in the field? Or release our babies' souls before their bodies were formed? I pressed my fists to my eyes, staunching tears that came too often.

Abba's arms enfolded me, and I leaned into his embrace. "Go back to the palace, Daughter. You need not be here. Jashub's children are well cared for, and we'll send word when . . ." He hugged me tighter. "We'll send word. Go home."

I couldn't speak. I could only nod and push him away. Then I fled, running as I'd done when Ima scolded me as a child. Amram kept pace. He didn't scold but merely jogged alongside, sheltering me from curious stares. Up the palace stairs, through the courts, and down the king's hall I ran. The chamber guards opened the doors as I approached, and I fell into Hezi's arms, sobbing, panting, pleading.

"No more, Hezi. No more."

He stroked my hair gently, but he was angry with my guard. "Amram, what happened?"

"I'm sorry, my lord, but the queen wished to visit her parents. When we arrived, we found that Jashub's wife . . ." He hesitated.

"Hallel's dying, Hezi." Speaking the words burned the truth into my spirit. I stilled in my husband's arms.

"Thank you, Amram. You may go." He held me without moving, barely breathing. "What do you mean, 'Hallel's dying'?"

I wiped my face with my head covering and looked into his eyes. "Hallel has been laboring three days with their fourth child. Neither mother nor child live after three days of labor, Hezi."

His expression softened. "You don't know that for certain, Zibah."

"What?" I choked out a humorless laugh. "So, I know nothing about Assyria *or* pregnant women?" I pushed him away. "Just say it, Hezi. I'm a burden to you, worthless."

"You are Hephzibah, delight of the Lord, and Zibah, my del—"

"No! Don't call me Hephzibah." I began trembling. "My name is Ishma. I am desolation, Hezi. I am desolation."

He slid onto the couch and held his head in his hands. "I don't know what to do to help you, Hephzibah."

I didn't know what to do either. I stood staring at a good man, who I continued to hurt. Where could I go to escape—for both our sakes? I couldn't go back to Abba's, and I didn't want to call for Yaira. Feeling like a bird without a nest, I walked to the balcony. Perhaps there I could breathe.

The scent of almond blossoms met me on the breeze. Spring. A time for war. What was this war inside me? Everyone said "rest," but my body had recovered. It was my heart and mind that felt exhausted. How does one rest a mind or strengthen the heart? My doves would be returning soon, but I felt little interest even in them.

I peered over the edge of our balcony at the people milling about in the streets. They were blissfully unaware of my brother's dying wife and the terrifying new king of Assyria. Would my life have been better had I been raised in Bethlehem? Yaira said my life would have purpose. Queen of Judah—what was my purpose if I couldn't produce an heir?

"Zibah, come away from the edge." Hezi stood at the archway, hand outstretched. "Come to me, my love. Please." His face twisted in grief, a sorrow I'd never seen mar that handsome face.

I stepped closer to him, proving my intention to live and not die. "You must take another wife, Hezi." He tried to protest, but I pressed

485

two fingers against his lips. "No, my love. It's time. Rizpah and I have been talking about it for months." I tried to sound brave. "She always knew your abba loved Abijah most. I'll always be your Abijah, but my womb is incapable of carrying a child. The midwife told us two pregnancies ago, but we refused to believe it." I shook my head, unable to stem the tears. "How many more children must precede us into paradise before we listen?"

He wiped my cheeks with the belt of his robe and then kissed me tenderly. "We'll take precautions for a while. We'll use the midwife's herbs and won't let you conceive again until you're stronger."

"No, Hezi. No." I straightened my shoulders. "Jashub's wife carried her child to term, and today, he'll lose them both. Even if I were to reach birthing, my age makes a first delivery very dangerous." Fear raced through me at the thought. I'd never voiced it before, but now I was even more convinced. "You're thirty-five, Hezi. Still young enough to build a household of children. You must consider the line of succession. King David's promise."

"It is Yahweh who will keep His promise to David, Zibah. My focus is to love my wife and build a strong nation—which I'm doing." He stepped toward the balcony's edge and swept his hand across the landscape. "Judah is prospering as it did in the days of Solomon. Yahweh has blessed every decision so far, Zibah. We must keep trusting Him."

"Judah is prospering, Hezi, but not me. Can't you see? I'm not prospering."

Hezi looked at me, really looked at me, for the first time in months. His features changed, and he drew me into his arms, silent.

Fear coiled around my heart, certain he was working out the details of a second wedding. What girl would he choose? Someone I knew? She would most likely be half my age. Kings chose women as young as fourteen for subsequent wives. I squeezed my eyes shut. *Yahweh, give me strength. Wisdom.*

Hezi laid his cheek on my head. "You will move back to the harem."

I felt the blood drain from my face. I mustn't cry, mustn't cry. "When will you take your new wife?"

He nudged me away and braced my shoulders, his features stern. "Enough. No more talk about a new wife. I've given my word that I will take only one wife as did Uzziah and Jotham. I want you to move back to the harem for a time of rest." He held my gaze. "You must rediscover your name, *Hephzibah*. I believe only Yahweh can heal your inner wounds." He pulled me back into his arms and held me. "You'll know when it's time to return to our chamber."

. . .

For nearly a year, I sequestered myself in a quiet chamber at the farthest corner of the palace's second floor. My spirit revived in the stillness, while the midwife's herbs and Yaira's aloe rubs strengthened my body. Yaira slept in an adjoining chamber but often delivered my meals and left. Even Abijah and Rizpah limited their visits to once a day, and Hezi shooed them out when he arrived for our evening visits.

Today, Yaira had gone with the widows and their maids to walk in the gardens. They had invited me to join their ranks—as they always did—but I had gracefully declined. As I often did. I sat at my writing table with the balcony doors open, a gentle breeze carrying the tune of a mourning dove. Another spring had come to bring new life, and I felt its refreshing to the core of my being. *Thank You, Yahweh, for the changing of the seasons.*

Facing the open balcony, I read the last of Abba's scrolls. I'd begun reading them as a distraction, but they quickly became my life and breath. I scoured every prophecy and copied each one. Then I tried to give the prophecies some semblance of order, not necessarily chronologically according to the time they were received or delivered, but in an order that presented the picture of Yahweh's faithfulness amid His people's rebellion, for that was Israel's story. Judah's story. My story.

Though I had not openly rebelled with pagan worship, I had set up my own unseen idols, allowing my pursuit of a home and peace to steal my attention from the One Source who could truly give me both. Abba's words—Yahweh's words—had refocused my heart and mind on the eternal. I'd learned that the absolute peace I yearned for could only be found in my eternal home, but as I immersed myself in Yahweh's words, the tender peace of His presence made this life bearable.

I didn't just copy Abba's words; I found a rhythm and arranged them by context, according to history and setting. Abba's calling in Yahweh's great throne room added depth to his prophecies and provided a foundation for his obedience when he was called to obey impossible commands. Next came the woes and blessings for many nations on earth, including Israel and Judah. Somehow, they didn't seem so frightening when the light of eternity brightened their meaning.

Most intriguing to me, of course, was the captive remnant and the anointed Son of David. I saw now that Yaira and I and the other captives with us were not the faithful remnant returned to a New Jerusalem, and Hezi—as Abba said—was not the anointed King. But couldn't we each be a foreshadowing? Couldn't the promises meant for the future be accessible in the present when we served the Eternal?

As I looked at all the scrolls, I felt a gaping hole. The question of Assyria's future lingered like the verse of a song yet unsung. They would invade Judah, but when? God would destroy them for harming His people, but what army could stop Assyria's ever-growing power?

"Mmm," my husband whispered, nuzzling the back of my neck.

My arms prickly with gooseflesh, I turned into his embrace. "You finished with court early today."

"It's too lovely a day to be separated from my wife." He glanced at the scrolls sprawled on my table. "Almost done?"

"I'm on the last one." I picked up the scroll to show him my latest copying. "I know it seems that all you hear is prophecies of gloom from Abba, but there is also blessing in store in the New Jerusalem, Hezi. Listen, 'Never again will there be in it an infant who lives but a few days, or an old man who does not live out his years.'" My voice broke, but my smile remained.

He tucked a stray hair behind my ear. "Do you know when the New Jerusalem will come?"

I chuckled. "No idea." We laughed together. It felt good to laugh.

My husband took the scroll from my hand and placed it on the table. He cradled my hands, kissed them, and then held them between us. "Your eyes are clear, Hephzibah—delight of the

Lord. Has Yahweh healed you inside and out?"

My heart skipped a beat. "I don't know if Yahweh will give us a child in this life, Hezi."

"That's not what I asked." His smile never faded. "Are you ready to come back to me?" Hope glistened in his eyes.

I'd been considering the question for days. "To your chamber, yes, but do you want me in your courtroom?"

He kissed my hand again. "Let's talk about that." He led me to the balcony, allowing my question to drift on the breeze. "I want you to fulfill Yahweh's purpose for you, Zibah, but I cannot let you repeat what happened on your last day in court."

I focused on the courtyard below us, feeling the sting of his rebuke. If I was to reenter his world, I must toughen my hide and sharpen my mind. "I was emotional in the way I expressed my opinion that day. And for that I'm deeply sorry." I turned to face him. "However, my dissent with your decision was correct, Hezi. I still believe stopping tribute payments to Assyria is wrong. For that, I won't apologize." I felt no imminent tears. No quivering inside. *Thank You, Yahweh.*

Hezi pressed a finger to his lips, deep in thought, and then turned a pointed gaze at me. "Can you offer your opinions in court without emotion, the way you've done just now?"

I lifted an eyebrow and smiled. "Can you?"

He threw back his head and laughed. "You're ready for court, but are my advisors ready for you?"

PART 4

After all that Hezekiah had so faithfully done, Sennacherib king of Assyria came and invaded Judah. He laid siege to the fortified cities, thinking to conquer them for himself.

—2 Chronicles 32:1

48

In the fourteenth year of King Hezekiah's reign, Sennacherib king of Assyria attacked all the fortified cities of Judah and captured them.

—2 Kings 18:13

Since Zibah had returned from her harem retreat three years ago, she'd insisted on tending to Hezi's morning ministrations. Normally chattering like a bird, she asked about the upcoming day in court and if there was to be a council meeting and then told him about her friends and the widows' antics. While chatting, she combed his hair, trimmed his beard, and oftentimes chose his robe for court.

Not so, this morning. She stood silently behind him, yanking an ivory comb through a tangled curl. Hezi squeezed his eyes shut, bearing the pain. Would he have any hair left to hold up his crown? "Are you feeling all right, my love?" he asked.

"Yes, and you?" Her tone was clipped, voice high. Continuing to fuss with his tangled curls, his wife fell silent again.

She couldn't be pregnant. Her time of uncleanness had just ended. Was she upset about that? He could stand it no longer. He turned on his stool and drew her close. "Tell me, Zibah."

With unnerving calm, she stared into his eyes. "Why didn't you tell me?"

He laid his head against her chest. She knew Assyria was coming. "I didn't want to frighten you." He heard her heart quicken and felt her body tense.

"You thought I'd be less frightened if I heard from Yaira that Assyria was advancing toward Judah?"

He released her and met her gaze. "How did Yaira know?"

"I'm afraid the movement of the largest army in the world is not something you can keep secret until you're ready to discuss it, King Hezekiah. Merchants bring news. Panic spreads. Servants are often the first to hear. You must be prepared to face frightened people in court this morning."

"I was going to tell you before I left. I didn't want to say anything until I was certain the Assyrians had crossed Judah's borders."

She laid her hand on his cheek, eyes penetrating. "How long have you known Assyria was coming?"

He dared not tell her he'd feared it six months ago, when Sennacherib advanced against the rebellious Phoenicians who had discontinued their tribute. "I didn't *know* they were coming until they crossed our border, Zibah." The argument was flimsy.

She shook her head, seeming more disappointed now than angry. It laid his heart bare.

Hezi had told himself he was protecting his wife, but was it her he was protecting or himself? Maybe it was the same thing. He felt like he'd almost lost her when she miscarried four years ago—not to death but to despair. He couldn't risk her spiraling into hysteria again at news of Assyria's invasion. The harem respite had restored his wife, and they'd guarded her peace by keeping a balanced schedule—visits to the harem or her family in the mornings and court business limited to afternoons. Zibah was informed but not immersed in the cares of the kingdom.

But Assyria's advance would soon consume everyone's mind. With a resigned sigh, he left his stool and led his wife by the hand to their favorite couch. She followed willingly, her expression open—but tinged with fear.

"I'm sorry I didn't tell you earlier about Assyria's advance toward Judah. Perhaps it was my fear more than yours that kept me from it." Her brow formed the adorable V that showed her confusion, and he smoothed it with his thumb. "I can't lose you again, Zibah. If Assyria invades, I need you to be my grounding, my anchor in the storm." It sounded selfish when he said it aloud.

"I am not your grounding, Hezekiah—son of David, king of Judah." His wife snuggled into his chest. "You are Yahweh's servant chosen to lead

His nation at this moment in history. I can be a wick in the lamp, but Yahweh must be the fuel and the fire."

"I adore you, Hephzibah bat Isaiah." He hesitated, considering how the morning might be different now that word had leaked out. "Do you want to know the full Assyrian situation before I brief my advisors?"

She was quiet. No quick answer. Good. "No. I'll wait until you tell them, but let me say something first."

He tilted his head, intrigued. "Go on."

"Abba's prophecies predict two things about Assyria that are yet to be fulfilled: they will invade Judah as part of God's judgment, and because of Assyria's brutality against His people, God will destroy them."

"I know, Zibah, but Isaiah never answered my questions of when or how—"

"Please, Hezi. Just listen."

He sighed and crossed his arms.

"When Abba's prophecy condemned you for forming an alliance with Egypt, you said the treaty could help fulfill the prophecy of Assyria's destruction, that you could be the anointed King who ushers in the New Jerusalem."

Her eyes dimmed. "Hezi, after studying the prophecies, I don't believe you're the anointed King, and we may not live to see the New Jerusalem."

Her words hit him like a stoning, landing hard and heavy on his mind and heart. "So you agree with your abba?"

She brushed his cheek. "Not completely. I don't believe Yahweh removed the anointing from you because you let unconsecrated people eat the Passover meal or because you altered the Gihon spring or even because you made a treaty with Egypt. I don't believe you were ever Yahweh's anointed Son of David." She pulled him close, speaking close to his ear. "You are a whisper, Hezekiah. The Root of Jesse will be a shout."

Hezi swallowed hard, processing all his wife had said and hungry for her thoughts on Assyria. "I don't know whether I'm relieved or more confused. Should we interpret Assyria's invasion as God's judgment for our sins, or that Yahweh will use our treaty with Egypt to finally destroy them?"

"I don't know, Hezi." She began fidgeting. "I'm either too dull to see it, or it's not there. I feel Yahweh has given clear insight on many things, but the parts on Assyria He's left completely hidden."

Seeing his wife's angst, he gathered her into his arms and let their teacher's words console. "Your abba told us, 'Prophecy—even when we don't fully understand it—is given so we can watch God's sovereignty and power unfold.' We must be watchful, Zibah. Assyria is coming, and we must trust Yahweh's power will unfold for our good." He sounded so brave, but the tension increasing in his wife's arms matched the knots in his gut.

They sat in silence, and he knew Zibah wouldn't enjoy her visit with family or friends today. She would think of nothing but political strategy. Kissing her head, Hezi nudged her off the couch and toward the dressing area. "Yaira, we need you!" he shouted.

Surprised, his wife stood like a statue. "What? Why?"

"Hurry and get dressed. You should be in court with me this morning to help address the people's fear. They trust you, Zibah. They trust us. We must show them how to trust Yahweh." He smiled at the irony. "Perhaps I'll let you speak to that point." He picked out her robe as Yaira applied the necessary lotions.

They rushed out the door and made the short walk to the hidden courtroom entrance, where Samuel waited to escort them. Stepping inside the Throne Hall, Hezi felt as if they'd entered a tomb. His normally bustling courtroom was deserted except for the advisors who sat somberly in their elevated gallery.

Eliakim cradled his head in his hands. Shebna, now a royal secretary, stood by himself and was scribbling on parchment. Hilkiah looked as if he'd been awake for a week, with bags under the bags under his eyes.

Shebna was first to notice Hezi's arrival. "My king! Any word from—"

"Be seated, Shebna." Hezi led Zibah to her throne and perched on his. "Eliakim, where are my morning petitioners?"

"We canceled this morning's sessions, my king. All had questions about Assyria, and since we advisors hadn't yet been briefed, we felt it important to have a closed session."

"A wise decision, Eliakim. Thank you." Hezi felt the weight of his delay. He should have called a special meeting last night when the spies reported to him privately. "I'll tell you what I know and then hear your reports—and the rumors. Then we'll make a plan, my friends, to withstand Assyrian aggression." His first attempt at encouragement yielded a few raised brows, but his counselors sat a little straighter and were at least listening.

Joah, the recorder, prepared his reeds and pigment for the official record. Hezi ran his hands over the lion-headed armrests on Solomon's throne. *Yahweh, give me wisdom.*

There was no easy way to begin. "Our spies have reported that Assyrian troops have crossed our northern border and will attack even our southernmost fortified cities within three days. I've decided to pay King Sennacherib the total tribute we owe from the years we've skipped, hoping to forestall his wrath." The expected murmuring ensued.

Jalon, the director of forced labor, raised the concern that likely plagued them all. "How can we gather such an exorbitant amount of gold and silver?"

It was a question that had kept Hezi counting stars late into the night. "Judah's treasure sits in two locations—Jerusalem and Lachish—but we can't risk moving it from Lachish to combine it. Our spies assured us Assyria doesn't know Lachish is a treasury city yet, but their scouts are roaming our hills. Hilkiah's made a thorough accounting of what we have in the palace treasury alone." Hezi paused, gathering his nerve. "It is insufficient for the debt to Assyria."

The advisors exchanged uneasy glances, but no suggestions arose. Hezi swallowed hard, nearly choking on his pride. "At this point, I see no other solution. We'll add to the tribute all silver from the Temple treasuries and strip off the gold from the doors and doorposts of the Lord's Temple." Objections erupted like a boiling pot of stew. Repeating the deed of King Ahaz was not how Hezi wanted his reign to be recorded in the annals of Judah's kings, but he could think of no other way.

Hezi lifted his scepter for immediate silence. "Our chief priest, Azariah, offered his account of the Temple treasury, and Hilkiah has calculated the full amount of tribute." Hezi nodded to

Eliakim's abba, who stood to read from his report. The room fell silent except for the scratching of Joah's reed on parchment.

Hilkiah's hands trembled as he cleared his throat. "A total of three hundred talents of silver and thirty talents of gold will be sent to King Sennacherib of Assyria." He sat down to the groans of his peers.

"What if the Assyrians keep the tribute and invade Judah regardless?" The high priest's tone betrayed his lingering anger.

Before Hezi could respond, Zibah reached for his hand and spoke calmly. "Does anyone have a better idea?"

Silence answered.

Hezi squeezed her hand, grateful again for the gift of her support. "Eliakim, how is the tunnel coming along?" he asked. "We need it now, my friend."

Eliakim shook his head and stared at his sandals. "I'm sorry, my king. I can't tell you when the men will connect the two shafts underground. They are working below ground without stop." He looked up. "A tunnel isn't like building a watchtower or a wall, Hez."

Feeling his anger rise, Hezi tried to steady his voice. "I told you ten years ago we needed this tunnel, Eliakim. I would think we could have dug to Lachish by now."

Eliakim's spine stiffened like a rod. "I took

the prophet Isaiah's rebuke seriously and spent the first three years seeking the Lord before defiling the sacred spring. I spent the next three years inspecting the natural faults and fissures in Mount Zion. We've been digging since—*my king.*"

Hezi squeezed the bridge of his nose, forcing calm. "I'm grateful for your integrity, Eli. I am. But Assyria doesn't care about natural faults and fissures. When will we have a water source inside Jerusalem's gates?"

"The natural fault lines are a guide as we dig through a mountain from both sides. We hope to connect in the middle."

"Hope, Eliakim? You hope to connect?" Hezi's voice rose with each word.

Eliakim held the king's gaze. "You asked me to do the impossible, Hez. The truth is, unless Yahweh intervenes, my men could dig for years and never find each other."

His counselors' hopeless, frightened faces reminded him of his frailty. He'd let his frustration and fear stretch his nerves too tight again. They needed a leader focused on Yahweh and, like Zibah said, empowered by Him.

Zibah leaned close. "Perhaps if Assyria had no water sources outside our walls, they couldn't threaten those of us without water inside our walls."

He smiled, grateful again for his wife, and

offered her suggestion to his council. "How many wells and springs lie within a half day's walk *outside* Jerusalem's walls?"

They discussed among themselves and finally, Hilkiah said, "Dozens. A half day's walk covers a lot of villages. Each one has at least one well with several springs nearby."

Hezi rubbed his chin. Dozens would be too many to block.

Commander Jokim broke into his thoughts. "I believe I know what you're thinking, my king, and it's a wise strategy." The other advisors still looked puzzled, but Jokim's eyes brightened. "We should shrink the perimeter to include wells and springs within a *short walk* around Jerusalem. My soldiers are already spread too thin guarding and fortifying the walls, so we must employ citizens for the task."

Jalon, the forced labor director, furrowed his brow. "I don't understand. Why are we blocking our own water supplies?"

Hezi explained his military thinking for the civilians in the room. "If the Assyrians attack Jerusalem, the water outside our gates will become their water supply. If we block it now—after giving our citizens time to draw and store their own supply—the Assyrians are considerably crippled if they have no water for their troops."

Seeming appeased, Jalon rubbed his chin. "Consider our forced labor at your disposal, my king.

Hundreds are already working on the tunnel, but we can—"

"No, Jalon. Thank you, but no." Hezi sighed. "The tunnel is our first priority, but the general is right. We need citizens to work together if we're to stand firm against Assyria. The coming days will test us all—our character, our strength, and our faith."

He looked at Eliakim, and Isaiah's prophecy came to mind: *"He will be a father to those who live in Jerusalem and to the people of Judah."* "Eliakim, my friend, you must speak peace to the people of Jerusalem. Give them a sense of security by dividing the city into sections and appointing military officers over each segment. Train them to work together, drawing sufficient water and then blocking the wells and springs. They'll feel cared for, and we'll be ready if Assyria knocks on our gates."

49

From now on I will tell you of new things,
of hidden things unknown to you.

—Isaiah 48:6

I returned to our chamber after this morning's closed council meeting fighting an ever-growing sense of dread. Hezi asked if I'd like to accompany him and Eliakim to inspect the work on the tunnel. I declined, thinking time alone on my balcony sounded better.

"Zibah?" Yaira peeked out of her chamber when she heard Hezi leave ours. "What did you learn in the closed session? Can you tell me?"

I opened my arms, and she ran into them, hugging me fiercely. "Hezi is taking action to avert Assyria's wrath," I said. "If it doesn't work, the Assyrians will attack Judean cities within three days." The tears I'd held in check all morning began to flow. "Pray for the villagers, Yaira. Pray for the children."

We held each other, memories stirred, hearts pounding. Would the Assyrians take captives as Israelite soldiers had done in Bethlehem more than thirty years ago? No. Worse. The Assyrians' barbarous acts of war were infamous.

Yaira began to tremble but held me tighter.

"Will they lay siege to Jerusalem?" she whispered.

My every instinct said they would, but with every shred of faith, I prayed they wouldn't. "I don't know."

Finally, she released me and wiped her eyes. "The palace servants have been buzzing about it all morning. Can you tell me the truth so I can combat rumor?"

I led her to our couches, rubbing her back. "I can tell you facts but not strategy, of course."

She nodded. "I don't care about strategy, Zibah. I just want to feel safe. Jashub would want to hear strategy though—" Yaira's breath caught, and she pressed her lips together. Cheeks pink, she hurriedly refocused. "You said three days, and Assyria will invade from the north?" Her hands fidgeted with her belt as she awaited my reply.

"Yes, three days." I was intrigued by her mention of my brother. "When do you see Jashub?"

Eyes focused on her belt, she spoke barely above a whisper. "For about a year now, I've returned to your parents' house in the afternoon to watch Jashub's youngest child while your ima and the twins deliver food baskets."

"You watch Ellah?" I tried to hide my hurt. Why hadn't Yaira told me? Why hadn't Ima or anyone else told me, for that matter. "That's very kind of you to care for my niece."

Yaira discarded the belt in her hands and met

my gaze, challenge sparking from her eyes. "I didn't tell you because I knew you would make more of it than need be. Jashub's older children can care for themselves, but five-year-old Ellah needs a little extra care. Jashub and I are friends, Zibah. That's all!" Her cheeks were redder now than before.

"All right."

"All right," she huffed.

"That's all," I repeated.

"Yes, that's all."

"If that's all, Yaira, why are we talking about Jashub instead of the Assyrian invasion?"

Her facade began to crumble, and she returned to fidgeting with her belt. "I've tried to stop loving him, Zibah. He is assistant to the chief scribe. I'm only a—"

"You're a friend of noblewomen, best friend of Judah's queen, Yaira. Why must you see yourself as a servant—no, a slave?"

"I'm not a slave." Her head shot up, indignation lacing her tone. "I serve by choice. No one forces me."

"Perhaps a captive, then?" I asked gently. "We were freed in Samaria, my friend, but your heart still lives in chains." Pausing, I watched her carefully to be sure I hadn't offended. She lowered her eyes. I could tell she was thinking. "The excuses of the past have been answered by Yahweh's faithfulness, Yaira. Jashub has three beautiful children, and you are a respected woman in the Upper City. Your presumed barrenness will not rob him of being an abba—or you of being an ima."

I waited in the silence, sure I'd said enough. Finally, she spoke. "I can't let my heart love him now, Zibah. Not with Assyria at our gates." She looked up then. "When I heard they were coming, the warnings felt like those we received in the days before Bethlehem was attacked. Some wanted to leave. Others were certain Yahweh would save us. But they came, Zibah. The soldiers came, and we were helpless." Her voice broke, and she rubbed the work-hardened calluses on her hands. "I hope you don't remember."

We'd never talked about it. As children, we were swept from captivity into Isaiah's household and had little time to dwell on feelings. "Yes, Yaira, I do remember. And I'm afraid. I'm afraid of Assyria's approach, but I also fear for you." She looked at me, eyes brimming with tears. "For as long as I can remember, Yahweh has given me the gift of your love and friendship. But I fear you'll hold too tightly to me or to your painful memories and miss the better things Yahweh would give." I pulled her into my arms. "People will fail us. Armies can't always save us. But Yahweh is faithful forever."

"I know you're right, Zibah. It's just hard to trust in the moment."

I nodded, releasing her to look into her eyes. "My words sound brave, but you've seen me at my best and my worst. No one trusts all the time."

"Zibah, you have become stronger since you spent time copying the prophecies."

I smiled a little. "We must keep our eyes on eternity, my friend, for today is sometimes more than we can bear."

The waiting was excruciating. Jerusalem's gates had been closed for two days, and our carrier pigeons brought no word of Assyrian movement from outlying villages. Yaira and I had visited the harem yesterday morning, trying to allay fears and answer questions. Abijah told me of the underground tunnels where she and Hezi hid during Israel's siege on Jerusalem many years ago. I pretended surprise. Would she be amused or offended if I told her Isaiah and Aya—her best friend—had hidden the prophets in those same tunnels? The Abijah I knew now would likely laugh with me.

Today, Yaira and I hurried along the cobblestone street to Abba and Ima's house accompanied by Amram and three additional guards. Hezi said he'd rather I stay in the palace, but I needed to see my parents. Sentimentality, yes, but I also needed to speak with Abba. Perhaps Yahweh had spoken to clarify something I could share with Judah's king.

When we entered the courtyard gate, Abba was

waiting with an unsealed scroll. As he extended the scroll to me, Yaira hurried into the house. Abba's expression revealed nothing. "Deliver this to Hezekiah. It is the word of the Lord without my personal opinion."

His faint grin hoisted the weight from my shoulders. I took the scroll from him, hope rising within. "Is it good news?"

He could hide his smile no longer. "Read it for yourself, Daughter. I'm sure Hezekiah will share it with you."

I unrolled the parchment with trembling hands and began reading my abba's familiar scrawl. "The Holy One of Israel says, 'Look around you. Will you admit now that I am God? I told you long ago that these things would happen so you could not say, "My idols brought them to pass." From now on I will tell you new things, hidden things, you've never heard before. For my own name's sake, I will delay my wrath. For the sake of my praise I hold it back from you, so as not to destroy you completely. See, I have refined you and tested you in the furnace of affliction because I will not yield my glory to another.' "

I released the breath I was holding. "Did Yahweh just promise He wouldn't destroy Jerusalem?"

Abba's brows rose. "Yes, He did."

I threw my arms around his neck and wet his shoulder with my tears. "Thank you, Abba."

"I'm only the mouthpiece, my girl. It's Yahweh we must thank. It is His mercy that saved us. But His judgment may yet test our northern villages."

I sobered, dropping my arms. "Did He reveal that Assyria will attack them?"

He looked briefly at his sandals. "No. It is only my *opinion,* which is why it's not written in the scroll. I've given much thought to Hezekiah's complaints of my opinion versus prophecy, and I believe I still have a right to express my opinion as long as I clearly distinguish it from Yahweh's words." He lifted both eyebrows. "Assyria will still invade our northern villages, Zibah. *That* is the opinion of a man who served as foreign minister for three kings."

I heard the rebuke in his voice and looked at the scroll in my hand. "Why didn't you deliver this scroll to Hezi yourself? He's the one who needs to hear what you've just explained about distinguishing prophecy from opinion."

The lines in Abba's face suddenly seemed deeper, the rings under his eyes darker. "I can't engage in a word battle with Hezi right now. And that's what most of our discussions become." He dragged his hand down the length of his face, releasing a weary sigh. "Yahweh said He would *delay* His wrath, Zibah, which means the rod of His judgment still depends on the decisions of our king and the people of Judah."

"What do you mean?" My anger flashed quick

and hot. "What more can Hezi do to please Yahweh?"

Abba stood silent, eyes closed, lips pressed firmly together. I would get no answer from Yahweh's prophet.

I rolled the scroll in my hand and recited the first of the Ten Commandments before responding. "I'll point out the word *delay* to our king. I'm sure he'll remain vigilant—as he has from the first day of his reign until now." I looked at Abba again.

He seemed as weary as every advisor in the palace, but this time his eyes held compassion for his daughter. "Like my prophecies in which doom often overshadows promises, Hezekiah hears my criticism more than my praise. Even in this, I must obey Yahweh first, Zibah, rather than curry the favor of a king I love like my son." He kissed my cheek and turned toward the house.

I watched him walk away. A little slower. A little more stooped. And my heart ached. I shouldn't have responded in anger. "I love you, Abba."

He stopped and turned to look at me. "And I you, Daughter—delight of the Lord."

50

In the fourteenth year of King Hezekiah's reign, Sennacherib king of Assyria attacked all the fortified cities of Judah and captured them. Then the king of Assyria sent his field commander [Rabshakeh] with a large army from Lachish to King Hezekiah at Jerusalem. When the [Rabshakeh] stopped at the aqueduct of the Upper Pool, on the road to the Launderer's Field, Eliakim son of Hilkiah the palace administrator, Shebna the secretary, and Joah son of Asaph the recorder went out to him.

—Isaiah 36:1–3

Hezi sat on his throne in an empty courtroom clasping a tiny parchment in his hand. The terrible news had arrived on a carrier pigeon, the band on its leg bearing the colors of Judah's fortified city of Sokoh. The parchment read, "Assyrian attack. City falling."

King Sennacherib had kept the tribute and attacked anyway. The report from the Judean spies had also proven exact. Three days. Assyria had officially invaded Judah—and Yahweh had not intervened. After two days of no pigeon communication, today's birds had flown in from all directions, reporting major devastation. Faithful Judeans were dying torturous deaths, staked on poles as high as their fortified walls once were. No miraculous victories.

"Is it true?" Her voice was small, vulnerable, like the first time he'd heard it.

Hezi lifted his eyes to his beautiful wife, approaching like a lost lamb. "Reports are still coming in, but we know Assyrian troops have taken Sokoh. Their walls had been fortified because it was a military depot, so the weaker cities nearby have likely already been destroyed."

Zibah took a deep breath and straightened her shoulders. No tears. "Will the Assyrians take prisoners?" She was trying so hard to be brave.

"A few will serve the soldiers in camp." Hezi left his throne and pulled her into his arms. "Assyrian troops wait until the end of a campaign to relocate captives." *Relocate.* It sounded so neat and tidy, but it meant a nation lost its identity when most of its citizens were forever removed from their homes and family.

She looked up at him, trembling now. "Is there anything we can do to help the villagers?"

"We sent extra troops in hopes they could hold the cities under siege, but even the fortified walls fell quickly against the Assyrians' new war machines." Hezi squeezed her tighter. "Jerusalem's citizens have worked night and day to block nearby springs and wells. Assyrian spies almost certainly reported back to King Sennacherib by now, so he'll likely come here last." *"Almost certainly . . . likely."* Could she tell he was terrified too?

They stood in the cavernous courtroom in silence for a long time. Waiting. Praying. "Hezi?"

"Hmm?"

"What do we do now?"

He searched the windows of her soul. There was fear, of course, but also strength in those depths. "I've asked Eliakim to assemble the whole city at this evening's sacrifice. We must prepare our hearts to stay faithful when Assyria comes. Will you stand with me?"

She looked away. "I won't break God's Law and stand under the king's canopy, Hezi."

He tipped her chin, drawing her to look at him. "I wouldn't ask you to break the Law. I'll stand among the people—with you."

Her breath caught. "That's a wonderful idea."

"They must know that I am with them. If Jerusalem falls, I fall with it." He nearly choked on the hard truth. The whole line of David was at stake, God's eternal promise. *Yahweh, You must hear and answer!*

Zibah hugged him as if he were a lifeline. He couldn't let her sense his fear. Nor could he show it to the thousands of citizens who would gather at tonight's sacrifice. *Can fear and faith dwell together in one heart, Lord?* It must be so. Because in this moment, Hezi believed Yahweh could deliver Jerusalem. But would He?

Hezi folded his arms across his chest and exchanged a wry glance with Zibah. She looked weary, but relief brightened her features. Yesterday he'd delivered the news of Judah's fallen cities and seen despair darken her lovely eyes. Last night's sacrifice and worship had been healing balm and kept them at the Temple until the moon reached its zenith. But it was Eliakim's predawn shouting at their door that infused his wife's face with hope this morning.

The royal advisors whispered and pointed at Eliakim's empty chair.

"I called this special meeting," Hezi said, "because our palace administrator—and chief engineer—woke me before dawn with the news." He paused, relishing the anticipation on their faces. "The tunnel connected! We have water inside Jerusalem!"

The gallery of advisors erupted in applause, the response Hezi had hoped for. They needed something to celebrate after having closed Jerusalem's gates three days ago.

After sharing their joy, Hezi called the group to order. "Let's hear the rest of your reports."

As conscientious as ever, Shebna was first to stand. In his role as palace secretary, he'd garnered every statistic in the land. "We closed our gates three days ago, so we have no income from merchant taxation. Twenty-seven new babies since yesterday's report and seven deaths." He glanced at Hezi. "No deaths in Jerusalem were war related."

How many had died outside Jerusalem's walls? Shebna was thinking it, and the same grief shone from every advisor's eyes as Hezi scanned the gallery. Each of them had friends or family in outlying villages. "Thank you, Shebna," Hezi said. "Any other reports?" Averted glances and shaking heads told him to move on. "Commander Jokim, yours is the report we're all waiting to hear—the war-related deaths in Judah."

The general's booming voice echoed off the near-empty courtroom walls. "Of the five military depot cities, we've received messages by carrier pigeon from Sokoh, Hebron, and Ziph. They've suffered total destruction. Signal flags tell us Lachish is currently under heavy siege." Hezi's heart skipped a beat. His brother Mattaniah had been governor in Lachish for ten years now. He hadn't visited Jerusalem in that time. Ima said he was simply too busy to attend Yahweh's feasts and festivals. Hezi feared Lachish, where pagan worship had been strongest under Ahaz, might have resumed pagan worship. Abba's early influence on Mattaniah may have proven too strong for his little brother to overcome.

The report on Jerusalem regained Hezi's attention. "We're the only military stronghold untouched by the Assyrians. We expect King Sennacherib to split his army after a concerted push against Lachish and then send a significant force against us soon thereafter."

Hezi saw his advisors whispering concerns and voiced his own. "How long can Lachish stand against such an assault, Commander?"

"Lachish, like Jerusalem, has favorable positioning atop a plateau." He turned to the council with a reassuring lift of his brows. "And its walls and gates were fortified by the sweat of our own king's brow."

"What about Egypt?" one of the advisors shouted. "Weren't they supposed to help us?"

Jokim stood, taking a commanding position over the other men. "An Egyptian force is currently moving northerly to provide aid and protection for our coastal cities along the Great Sea. They'll move east into the coastal plain when General Tirhakah joins the regular troops with his elite guard."

"Thank you, Commander." Hezi noticed an uneasy rumble among his advisors. "Our Egyptian friends are honoring our treaty." A few nodded their agreement. Others still looked as if the sky might fall tomorrow.

Zibah leaned close. "Perhaps now is a good time to remind your counsel of Yahweh's prophecy that Jerusalem will not be destroyed." She straightened on Bathsheba's throne, graceful and gentle, with the heart of a lion and the strength of an army. She had no idea how beautiful she was.

A commotion in the back of the courtroom stole Hezi's attention. Eliakim flung open the door and ran up the aisle. Still covered in mud from the digging and celebration, he stopped at the foot of the dais, hands on his knees, breathless. "King Sennacherib sent his officials, Hez. And they brought thousands of their friends."

Hezi swallowed the boulder in his throat. "Have they made demands?"

The advisors stilled, and Eliakim's voice filled the room. "Assyria's top three soldiers—the Tartan, Rabsaris, and Rabshakeh—came from Lachish. They will meet only with King Hezekiah."

Zibah grabbed Hezi's hand. "You can't meet with them. No matter what they say or promise, you can't trust them."

When Hezi turned for advice from his counselors, they looked as if he'd already been skewered on an Assyrian stake. "I've heard from my best advisor. What do the rest of you say?"

All spoke at once, but every one of them agreed with the queen.

Hezi returned his attention to Eliakim, who shrugged and said, "I'm going, Hez. Who will you send with me?"

Hezi's throat tightened. Eliakim had always

been his protector. *Yahweh, protect him now.* He scanned the gallery of advisors. If he asked for volunteers, Commander Jokim would be first to stand and would single-handedly ignite King Sennacherib's fury.

He must send someone familiar with the Assyrian language in case they attempted to veil their communication during the face-to-face negotiations. "Shebna, are you willing to accompany Eliakim?"

Shebna stood too quickly. "I am at your service, my king."

Hezi's heart ached a little at the next appointment. "Joah?"

The young recorder lifted his reed from the parchment and looked up, seeming oblivious to what was about to be asked of him.

"There must be a record of the conversation between the Assyrian officials and the leaders of Judah." He waited until his meaning dawned on the man's features. "Are you willing to serve?"

His gulp echoed in the room. "I am willing, my king." He quickly wrote down their conversation—perhaps so the recorder himself couldn't change his mind.

"It's settled then." Hezekiah stood, and his counsel stood with him. "We will wait and pray while our three friends conduct business with our enemies. We'll reconvene after the midday respite."

51

Then Eliakim . . . Shebna . . . and Joah
. . . went to Hezekiah, with their clothes
torn, and told him what the [Rabshakeh]
had said.

—2 Kings 18:37

The council filed out of the courtroom, and
Samuel escorted Hezi and me to our chamber
for more waiting. I had memorized Abba's most
recent prophecy and recited it silently, trusting
Yahweh to delay His wrath on Jerusalem as He
promised—even though thousands of Assyrians
now waited outside Jerusalem's gates. Could
Abba have heard wrong? *No. Yahweh spoke. He
will prove faithful.*

After Samuel deposited us in our chamber and
closed the door, Hezi searched my face. "What
are you thinking?"

How could I describe my deceptive heart? "It's
as if my emotions are a dark cloth that covers my
eyes and distorts what I know to be true."

His brows knit together, considering my
description, and then he offered his hand. "Let's
sit in the sunshine while we wait and pray."
Seven lamps lit the room with only a sliver of
sunlight peeking through the curtains.

523

I followed Hezi toward the balcony. "It looks like a beautiful day," he said. "I wonder why Yaira left the curtains closed."

He yanked them open, and I gasped, wishing he'd left them closed. Below in the Kidron Valley, like a sea of black and crimson, thousands of Assyrian soldiers camped. Seeing them was worse than hearing about them.

Hezi walked out and leaned over the railing, straining to see farther south. "Zibah, come look."

My feet felt rooted to the limestone balcony. I couldn't move, couldn't speak. Shaking from head to toe, I stared at the sea of soldiers and could think of nothing but death. The horrific death that awaited city leaders who refused to open their gates to Assyrian oppressors. Wives and children tortured while their husbands watched. Hezi would see me die. But death wasn't the worst of their tortures. *Yahweh, take me now before they destroy my humanity.*

"Zibah, come away. I'm sorry I asked you to look." Hezi's strong arms whisked me off my feet and into our chamber. I buried my face against his chest, trying to hide from the tormenting pictures in my mind.

"Zibah, look at me. Talk to me."

I looked into his eyes and saw fear as great as mine.

Tears streamed down his cheeks. He rocked

me back and forth, back and forth, repeating, "Yahweh will keep in perfect peace those whose minds are steadfast, because we trust in Him. We will trust You, Lord, for You are the Rock eternal. Yahweh will keep in perfect peace those whose minds are steadfast, because we trust in Him. We will trust You, Lord . . ."

The words of Abba's prophecy nudged aside the fearsome images, and I joined the rhythm of his repeated promise. "Yahweh will keep in perfect peace . . ." It became a chant, a song, our prayer. And Yahweh answered.

"Look at me Zibah. Let me see your eyes."

I gazed into the face of one who had returned my words as a child and so often restored my shattered emotions. I saw love—only love. "Yahweh is our grounding," I whispered.

"And you are my delight." He brushed his lips across mine like a gentle breeze.

I heard a faint singing and went still, tilting my head toward the sound. Hezi heard it too and did the same. The sound grew louder, and we realized it wasn't singing—it was wailing. It spread from the southern city, rising on the wind like a storm, brewing and then swirling into the palace.

We sheltered in our chamber together, huddled on our favorite couch, whispering the now requisite section of Abba's prophecy, claiming peace when our world had none. The chamber door swung open, without a knock or announcement, and in walked the three brave men who had faced the Assyrian officials. Shebna speechless, Eliakim shaking, and Joah weeping.

Eliakim seemed the only one able to communicate. "The Rabshakeh is a skilled negotiator, my king."

Hezi stood and directed them to the couch across from us. "Tell us what happened."

Eliakim breathed out a long sigh and began the recounting. "The Rabshakeh spoke faultless Hebrew. When we asked that he speak Aramaic, so our citizens couldn't hear our negotiation, he spoke louder and clearer Hebrew, saying the people had a right to hear. He looked up at our watchmen on the wall and shouted, 'If you don't surrender now, you'll eat your own filth and drink your own urine by the end of this siege.'"

I shuddered. Hezi cast a concerned glance my direction. "Can you bear this?"

Stiffening my spine, I said, "Yes, and I'll rejoice when Yahweh annihilates them as He's promised."

Eliakim closed his eyes. "It's easier to believe in Yahweh's deliverance when I'm sitting here than when I was standing out there."

"All three of you were very courageous." I was ashamed to tell them of my despair at seeing the army from the safety of my balcony. *Yahweh, strengthen our faith to overcome what our senses can't deny.*

"What else did they say?" Hezi focused on his best friend.

Eliakim dropped his head in his hands, and Shebna took over the reporting, his fear turned to sudden fury. "The Rabshakeh said our army and military strategies are inferior, our God is too small, and our king is a liar. He'll give us two thousand horses if we can put riders on them—which we can't." His hands shook as he stared at Eliakim. "Does that about cover it?"

Joah added, "You forgot that he promised if we surrendered now, every person would 'eat from his own vine and fig tree and drink water from his own cistern.' That is, until they move us to another land that's just like ours—except in the new land, the Assyrians won't destroy us."

Hezi clutched his hair with both hands. "The Rabshakeh reminds me of King Tiglath-Pileser. When I visited Damascus with Abba, Pileser could reduce a man to tears with just a few words." His knee bounced with nervous energy, his eyes focused on the ceiling. "What do we do, men? What would Yahweh have us do?"

Eliakim scrubbed his face as if scouring away the memory. "Let's focus on what we know. The Assyrians are getting their information from someone inside Judah who knows of Yahweh and Isaiah's prophecies. They knew you'd ordered the high places destroyed—even the ones where Yahweh was worshiped—and he said this attack was God's retribution, that the Assyrian army is 'the weapon in Yahweh's hands.'"

My husband's dwindling peace shattered. "The weapon in Yahweh's hands?" He looked at me, panicked. "Has your abba done this? Has he sent messengers to the Assyrians?"

"Hezi, no! How could you even think it?"

"Hez, I'm sure they've planted spies." Eliakim spoke gently. "It's what we've done to our enemies." He waited until Hezi met his gaze. "Somehow, the Rabshakeh also knew about the prophecies that predicted this invasion."

Hezi began to tremble, and Eliakim fell silent. Every eye was on the king, and now, even I wasn't sure what he might be thinking. My husband cried out, grabbed his collar, and rent his garment. "Yaira!" He launched himself off the couch. "Get our sackcloth robes. The queen and I will wear them until Assyria is defeated." Yaira appeared at her door, nodded, and disappeared again without a word.

At least my husband wasn't completely despairing if the robes were to be worn until Assyria's defeat—or was he putting on a brave face for his advisors? "The three of you will also change into sackcloth and go to Isaiah, demanding an answer: Will Yahweh deliver us or not?" He pinned Eliakim with a pleading stare. "Tell him if this invasion is because of my sin, let God's wrath fall on me, not my people."

"Your sin?" I said. "Hezi, only the Egyptian prophecy condemned *your* sin, and the prophecy Abba spoke since then was one of redemption. Yahweh promised not to destroy Jerusalem."

"But Zibah, what if your abba has been right all this time? What if Yahweh is punishing all of Judah because I allowed unconsecrated people to eat at Passover? Built a tunnel. Involved Egypt. What if the Rabshakeh is right and tearing down the high places was offensive to our God?"

I left the couch and framed my husband's face between my hands. "Hezekiah, Yahweh's judgment is on the *nation* of Judah. If God had chosen to discipline you, His child, He would have given you clear instruction on what you've done wrong, not left you guessing."

My husband pulled away and began pacing. "Isaiah will tell us if this is my fault and if I can fix it. Perhaps I should have listened to his opinions. Maybe they weren't opinions."

Shebna began pacing with Hezi, his face as red as our enemy's flag. "Are we to make decisions for Judah based on the whims of an old prophet? Do you think Assyria cares about your sins, King Hezekiah?"

Hezi stopped pacing. "Samuel!" The mere name on his lips doused Shebna's insolence.

Hezi took a single step toward the palace secretary. "Shebna, you will wear sackcloth with

Eliakim and Joah to Isaiah's home, or you can grow old counting rats in my dungeon."

Samuel entered the chamber. "How may I serve you, my king?"

Hezi lifted one eyebrow, and Shebna answered the big guard. "King Hezekiah would like you to escort Eliakim, Joah, and me to Master Isaiah's home after we change into sackcloth."

The four men exited our chamber quickly and left my husband to resume his pacing. "What if this invasion is judgment for my sins? Did Yahweh really speak to the Rabshakeh? The Lord has spoken to pagan leaders before—like Abimelech in the days of Abraham or Balaam on his donkey. But why would He tell Isaiah one thing and the Rabshakeh another?"

"Hezi."

He looked up, startled, as if he'd forgotten I was in the room.

"The dark cloth is distorting your view. Trust Yahweh, and trust Abba. They both love you very much."

52

When King Hezekiah's officials came to Isaiah, Isaiah said to them, "Tell your master, 'This is what the LORD says: Do not be afraid of what you have heard—those words with which the underlings of the king of Assyria have blasphemed me. Listen! When he hears a certain report, I will make him want to return to his own country.' "

—2 Kings 19:5–7

Hezi woke to the sound of thundering hooves outside his balcony, and he shot out of bed. Grabbing his belt, he strapped on his sword over his tunic and flung open the balcony tapestries. Dawn had just touched the eastern sky, but clouds of dust dimmed its glow. He rubbed his eyes to clear his vision. Was this a dream?

Thousands of Assyrians, riding under the Rabshakeh's black and red standard, sped away from Jerusalem on horseback. Dust filtered up to his balcony; he coughed and waved it away. He didn't cough in dreams.

"It's happening, just like Yahweh promised." Zibah stood beside him, wrapped in her robe. She turned and appraised Hezi's condition,

531

a mischievous grin appearing. "Or perhaps they were terrified when they saw you in your undergarment with your sword girded about your waist."

Hezi was not amused. "The scroll your abba sent said the Assyrians would hear a report that made them return to their own country." He pointed west, the direction the horses went. "Assyria is in the opposite direction, Zibah. They've either forgotten how to get home, or this is not the fulfillment of your abba's prophecy."

She hurried inside and returned with the scroll from his bedside table, pointing out the wording. "It says when he hears a certain report, Yahweh will make him *want* to return to his own country. Perhaps whatever report he's heard is sending him in another direction." She looked up, hope lighting her features. "I don't care where they're going, Hezi. They're leaving Jerusalem."

"Not all of them are leaving. Look." He pointed to the northern half of the Assyrian camp. "None of their tents have been moved, and the supply animals—camels and donkeys—are still tethered on the far side of the camp. At least some of the Assyrians are staying."

Joy drained from his wife's face. He wished she would argue. Think of some explanation for the lingering Assyrians. But her silence confirmed his fears. They'd waited a week since the Rabshakeh's threats to see how Yahweh would fulfill the promise on Isaiah's newest scroll. Hezi could wait no longer. He needed to visit Zibah's abba.

He hugged his wife close to his side. "I'm going to Isaiah's house today. Would you like to come?"

She was quiet for several heartbeats. "Do you want me to come?"

It was a good question. Would she take Isaiah's side on every argument? Hezi's confidence was already shaken. He questioned his decisions, God's promises, even Isaiah's loyalty. "Yes, I want you to come." There was no one else he trusted more than his wife.

Hezi and Zibah invited Yaira to join them on their visit to Isaiah's household. Yaira seemed as eager to see the family as Zibah—perhaps even more so. Samuel relieved Amram of his overnight guard duty at their chamber to escort the royal couple himself. Late-summer birdsong made the stroll through Jerusalem's bustling streets all the more pleasant. The exodus of half the Assyrian troops had rolled back the city's shroud of fear, and Yaira even whistled as they walked.

The sound reminded Hezi of Zibah's doves. "Do you still tend your dovecote in the royal courtyard?" he asked. "Or do I keep you too busy with court business for you to enjoy your beautiful birds?"

She reached for his hand and hid it between their robes as they walked in public. "I sit in the courtyard and feed them occasionally, but they don't know me like they used to. They don't come to me for comfort anymore." She looked up at him with a smile. "Nor do I rely on them for my peace since Yahweh provides it."

He wanted to kiss her, but it would be a scandalous breech of decorum. "Maybe if I kissed you, here in Jerusalem's market, we'd give our citizens something other than Assyria to talk about."

She laughed, the sound mingling with the chatter in the market. Hezi inhaled deeply and let the sun bathe his face. It was good to escape the palace. Why hadn't he done that more?

"Shalom, Jashub!" Zibah waved to her brother as they approached Isaiah's courtyard gate.

He waved back, but his smile bloomed for Yaira. "I'm glad I lingered after the midday meal." He opened the gate and swept his hand toward the courtyard. "Ellah and I have been waiting for you."

Hezi was smitten by the little girl with inky-black curls, who ran directly into Yaira's arms. The woman beamed. "This is five-year-old Ellah, Jashub's youngest," she said. "Ellah, this is King Hezekiah. You must bow in respect when you see the king." The little one nodded and then shyly hid her face against Yaira's shoulder.

Jashub bowed also, his expression kind. "Welcome, my king. It's been a long time since you've visited. We were excited to receive the message that you were coming. The women in our house have been preparing a 'snack' for you." He directed them toward the family table, where Isaiah and Aya waited. Then bowed again and placed his hand gently at the small of Yaira's back, directing her into the house.

Hezi raised his brows and looked at Zibah, who chuckled and shushed him until her brother and his guest were out of sight.

Isaiah grinned. "I think it won't be long until we have a wedding."

The cheerfulness felt good as they sat down to a table strewn with grapes and figs, dates, almonds, and pistachio nuts. Isaiah pointed to the bounty. "I told Aya we'd just eaten our midday meal, but"—he held Hezi's gaze—"what brings the king of Judah to my courtyard after he's stayed away for more than ten years?"

Setting aside his defenses, Hezi reached for a grape, maintaining a serious expression. "An Assyrian army outside my balcony provides significant motivation to visit Yahweh's prophet." He popped the grape in his mouth and winked at Isaiah.

The old man grinned. Zibah and Aya laughed out loud, reaching across the table to embrace each other's hands. Surely, their two wives had suffered most while tension kept the men at odds.

Letting his true concern rise to the surface, Hezi held his teacher's gaze. "I need to know what your latest prophecy meant, Isaiah." He pointed toward the eastern Valley of Kidron. "Have you peeked over the wall to see what the Assyrians are doing?"

"I didn't need to see them," he said. "Aya and I felt the ground shaking when they left at dawn."

Aya reached for Isaiah's hand, smile fading. "Dinah, Leah, and I heard talk in the market. They say only half of the troops are gone."

"That's right, Mistress Aya. That's why we've come." Hezi turned again to Isaiah. "The Assyrians rode west, not north toward Assyria. Where are they going?"

Isaiah's brows shot up. "That seems a question better suited for Commander Jokim, Hezekiah, not God's prophet." He didn't seem angry or defensive.

"You never answered Hezi's original question, Abba." Zibah's words sparked with tension. "He sent Eliakim, Shebna, and Joah to ask if the invasion was Yahweh's judgment on Hezi's personal sins. The scroll offered the good news of Yahweh's deliverance but no answer on Hezi's personal standing."

The prophet lingered only a heartbeat on his daughter before turning toward the king.

"Perhaps I can best answer the question of your sin and God's judgment by addressing your accusations that I prophesied my opinions."

Hezi started to moderate the word *accusations,* but Isaiah lifted his hand to halt his protest. "Please. Let me explain, and you can argue with me afterward." Hezi grinned, trying to ease the tension again, and let him continue. "When I hear Yahweh's voice echo in my spirit, I write on a scroll exactly what I hear, or I repeat it word for word to whomever God specifies. Interpreting prophecy is an entirely different matter. Our understanding is still God directed but is, unfortunately, subject to human fallibility. Opinion—as you, Hezekiah, have so frequently pointed out—comes completely from my own intellect."

Hezi prodded his teacher, "So, has Yahweh told you *directly* that this invasion is because of my sin?"

One side of Isaiah's lips curved up in a grin. "Good question. No. He has not."

"Have any of your prophecies been a direct correction of my sin?"

Isaiah paused a moment and then studied his hands. "I believe the only prophecy that specifically condemned your actions was in regard to the treaty with Egypt. That, Hezekiah, was not pleasing to the Lord." He held Hezi's gaze but offered no commentary, no fiery judgment, and for the first time, Hezi felt remorse for that decision.

"What can I do about it now?" he said.

"You must do what Yahweh expects of us all. Only the blood of a lamb can cover our sins."

Hezi stared at him for a long while, thinking, praying, pleading. "How can I know I'm forgiven?"

Isaiah laid his arms across the table and opened his hands, waiting for Hezi to place his hands in them. The king did, and the prophet held them tight. "You must go *directly* to Yahweh with your questions, Hezekiah. I was your teacher for a while. I'm the prophet God has chosen for this time. But Yahweh is your God for eternity. It's best to strengthen that relationship now."

53

Your word is a lamp for my feet, a light on my path.

—Psalm 119:105

Each morning at dawn, Hezi split the tapestries and peered into the Kidron Valley. Each morning there were new stakes with writhing Judeans to number his failures as king. Commander Jokim said the victims had lived in surrounding villages, taken captive for this very purpose—to weaken the king's resolve, to get him to open the gate. Hezi would never open the gate. He'd seen what Assyrians did to royal officials and their wives.

This morning, he slipped out of bed, leaving Zibah undisturbed. He slid through the heavy curtains, leaving the room dark so Zibah could sleep since they'd both tossed and turned into the wee hours. Morning dew on the balcony wet his bare feet as he moved toward the edge. He stared out over the valley that now had exposed spaces barren of tents. They'd received no information yesterday on where half the Assyrians had gone. Was there anyone left outside Jerusalem's gates who would dare give Judah information on Assyria? His spies were likely in hiding. Their fortified cities could no longer send pigeons with messages or use flags for signaling. Jerusalem was cut off from the world with half an Assyrian army still camped outside its gates.

His wife's embrace both startled and pleased him. "I tried to let you sleep."

"I'd sleep better without Assyrians sleeping next to us." She peeked around him to see the valley. "The Rabshakeh's troops are still gone. That's good."

"Mm-hmm, but are they coming back?" he said over his shoulder.

She remained silent and held him tighter.

"I've called a council meeting this morning. We'll find out if Commander Jokim has heard any new developments."

She kissed his back. Still no words. She'd been especially quiet since they returned from her parents' home yesterday afternoon.

He turned into her embrace and tipped up her chin. "I love you, Hephzibah bat Isaiah. Are you going to tell me what's weighing so heavily on your heart?" He grinned. "I mean besides the Assyrians outside our gates."

She rewarded him with a grin of her own. "I love you too, Hezekiah, son of David, king of Judah." She laid her head on his chest. "I want to say something, but I don't want it to sound prideful or judgmental."

This from the girl who—when they were children—taunted him each time she won a game, race, or debate. "Say it, my love. I know your heart."

"My year of studying Abba's prophecies while in the seclusion of the harem gave me the strength I've needed to hold tightly to Yahweh." She looked up then. "I know you were frustrated when Abba told you to take your questions about his prophecies directly to Yahweh. But, Hezi, when I spent time copying Abba's scrolls—really studying them—I understood God's words in a new way."

He began shaking his head before she finished. "I don't have a year to hide away in the harem, Zibah."

"I know, my love. I'm simply saying perhaps we could spend more time in the evenings, reading and studying the sacred writings—the Law, David's psalms, Solomon's wisdom and poetry, and all the prophets. You'll become familiar with how Yahweh's voice echoed in the hearts of others, and perhaps that same echo will become discernable in your own."

A ram's horn sounded from every parapet on palace grounds, announcing the morning's council meeting. Zibah started to walk away, but Hezi caught her hand and pulled her back. "Thank you," he said, cupping her cheeks. "Your suggestion is a wise one. I'll begin reading the texts tonight after our evening meal." He kissed her forehead and then lingered at her lips.

She pulled away, grinning. "We must have no more of that, or we'll miss our meeting."

Both Hezi and Zibah dressed quickly, forgoing their normal morning routine. Samuel escorted them through the private entry into the courtroom, where counselors trudged into their seats in the gallery. They looked as rumpled as Hezi felt.

Without fanfare or even Shebna's statistics, Hezi addressed the sole reason for the meeting. "Commander, have we any information on the Rabshakeh's retreat?"

The big man stood, holding a bloody sackcloth bag. "We have very little information because of this." He emptied six dead carrier pigeons on the pristine tiled floor. Zibah covered a gasp and turned away.

"Get those pigeons out of here!" Hezi shouted. Two guards rushed from the back of the room to gather the dead birds.

The commander glanced from the king to the unsettled queen, his face a mask of confusion. "I'm sorry. I don't . . . I didn't know . . . They're just birds."

Hezi leaned over, touching Zibah's shoulder and whispering, "Are you all right? Do you need to return to the chamber?"

She shook her head. Samuel stepped from beside Hezi's right shoulder and offered Zibah a clean cloth from his belt. "Here, my queen. Wipe your eyes. The birds are gone now."

Zibah thanked him with a forced smile and took the scrap of fabric. After wiping her eyes, she sat straighter on her throne and addressed the commander. "Forgive me, Jokim. I have a tender spot for doves, and pigeons look far too similar." Her chin quivered, and she paused to rein in her emotions. "I know you meant no harm. Please continue with your report."

The commander's gruff exterior softened. "Again, my queen, I apologize." He bowed and then turned his attention to Hezi. "The only city left to send messenger pigeons would be Lachish. Assyrian archers shoot them down, steal the messages, and then hoist the dead birds onto our wall. More of their mind games—and it's working. We must discover our enemy's plan, my king. Without information, we can't prepare a battle strategy."

"What if we had a spy?" Hezi leaned forward. "Someone who could slip out of Jerusalem undetected, cross the western mountains, and report on the Rabshakeh's troops."

Judah's top soldier offered a cynical grin. "While we're asking for the impossible, I'd like a week to enjoy the springs of En Gedi." His smile died. "No one can evade the Assyrians. It would be suicide to ask one of my men—"

"I won't ask one of your men." Hezi's boldness silenced the room and startled Zibah.

She clenched the tear-soaked cloth in her fist. "Who then?"

Hezi turned slowly to meet her gaze. "You and two other men evaded Abba Ahaz's soldiers while hiding the prophets for many years. I would require only your brother's service."

"No, Hezi." Zibah had begun shaking her head before he finished. "Not Jashub."

"Jashub ben Isaiah?" Jokim seemed as doubtful as Zibah. "He's a scribe, my king."

"I'm aware." Hezekiah took a calming breath. "Years ago, when my regiment was camped at Ziph, Isaiah's eldest son snuck into my camp and out again—past my best sentries—completely undetected. He may be the only man in Jerusalem who can do this. If any of you have a better idea . . ." He shifted his stare to his wife.

Zibah pressed her lips together, and the general resumed his place among his peers.

"It's settled then." Hezi spoke over his shoulder to Samuel. "Send two of your men to summon Jashub to the palace." He leaned close to his wife. "I'll give him the choice to serve Judah or not. I won't force him."

"That's not a choice, Hezi. You know he won't refuse. He loves you, he loves Judah, and he'll trust Yahweh to protect him."

He raised one eyebrow. "Isn't that why we all serve, my love?"

54

When the field commander heard that
the king of Assyria had left Lachish, he
withdrew and found the king fighting
against Libnah.

—2 Kings 19:8

Four days had passed since Jashub left Jerusalem.
Yaira had gone to Isaiah's house to say good-bye
and was the last one to see Jashub's face as he
lowered himself into the tunnels through the wine
cellar. He would continue through the tunnels
to the caves in the western hills of the Judean
wilderness and from there follow the very obvious
path left by thousands of Assyrian horses.

Hezi knew the dangers of the Judean Mountains. He'd crossed them numerous times on
his campaigns against the Philistines. Jashub
would face wild animals, the terrain itself, and,
of course, the Assyrians. But Hezi faced danger
at home that increased each day Jashub was
gone—Yaira was angrier than he'd ever seen her.
She served their meals, transferred Zibah's to
the table, but left Hezi's on the tray and exited
the room. "Is it safe to eat?" he asked Zibah this
morning. "Is she angry enough to poison me?"
Zibah rolled her eyes as if he were kidding.

"I saw them together at your parents' house, but I didn't realize Yaira would be so upset by Jashub's absence." He shrugged and popped a grape in his mouth. "How serious can their relationship be if there's no betrothal?"

Zibah looked at him as if he were a two-headed cow. "How can you be wise in so many things and so . . ." She let Hezi fill in the rest. "Jashub asked to marry Yaira when they were very young. She refused, believing herself beneath his station in Judean society."

"Did she love him?"

Zibah nodded. "And he loved her, but because she wouldn't have him, he married Hallel and was faithful to her. In the end Jashub loved both women but built his life with Hallel."

Hezi remembered the day Hallel died in childbirth. "How old are Jashub's children?" He felt a measure of guilt that he hadn't paid closer attention to Zibah's family.

"Jashub's oldest daughter, Michal, was married four years ago and now has a child of her own. My brother's son, Jacob, is in military training." Zibah offered a piece of bread smeared with date paste. "Ellah, the girl we met when we visited Abba and Ima last week, was born in Hallel's later years. Hallel died only a year after Ellah was born, trying to deliver their fourth child, who never opened his eyes in this world."

Zibah's gaze grew distant, and her finger idly

drew circles on the table. Hezi set aside his plate, scooted closer to his wife, and reclined her against his chest. "Do you have any idea how much I love you?" he whispered.

Samuel burst through the chamber door. "He's back!" Taking note of their intimate pose, he halted and bowed. "Forgive me. Jashub has returned and is waiting in court with his report."

Shofars blew, punctuating Samuel's announcement, calling the advisors to the palace.

Hezi rose to his feet and helped Zibah do the same. "Thank you, Samuel. We'll meet you in the hall." Before leaving, Zibah knocked on Yaira's door and whispered the news. A subdued squeal made Hezi's heart lighter—and made more sense now that he knew of Yaira and Jashub's history.

The king and queen arrived in the courtroom as the advisors filed in. Jashub sat on the bottom step of the dais, covered in days of travel dust. He rose and bowed when he saw Hezi and Zibah.

She hugged him like a little sister would and then inspected his arms and legs to confirm he was unharmed. "Are you all right? Have you seen Abba yet? He was worried. He sent a messenger every day asking if I'd heard from you."

Jashub chuckled and hugged her again. "I'm fine, and no I haven't seen Abba and Ima yet. I'll go first to see Michal. She's kept Jacob while I've been gone. Then I'll visit Ima to take Ellah

547

home." He stared at Hezi over Zibah's head. "Unless the king needs further service from me."

Zibah released him and cast a pleading glance at her husband. "I'm sure the king will let you return to your duties as the assistant chief scribe."

Hezi's crown weighed heavier on some days than others. Today it felt like a boulder. "I must hear Jashub's report before we'll know if his service is ended."

His wife's brows furrowed, but Jashub bowed humbly. "As you wish, my king. I'm honored to serve."

Zibah hurried to her throne, and advisors from all over the Upper City began arriving to take their places in the gallery. Shebna was the last of the fifteen men to arrive, and Hezi called the meeting to order.

"Jashub, we're anxious to hear your report," Hezi coaxed. "Please, speak freely."

Isaiah's eldest glanced at the royal advisors and expelled a shaky sigh. He was a scribe, not a public speaker. "I suspect the Rabshakeh is the most honored of King Sennacherib's three generals because his was the only regiment the king summoned for reinforcements. I followed the Rabshakeh's forces to Libnah three days ago, where the Egyptians and King Sennacherib's troops were already engaged in heavy fighting. I remained hidden in the mountains to assess the overall battle in the coastal plain."

Commander Jokim stood. "But King Sennacherib's troops are besieging Lachish."

Jashub bowed respectfully. "I beg your pardon, Commander, not anymore. It would seem Egypt has drawn the Assyrian king away from Lachish. And King Sennacherib summoned the Rabshakeh away from Jerusalem." He turned to the king and bowed. "Egypt appears to be honoring their treaty with Judah, my king. May Yahweh be praised for your wisdom."

The courtroom erupted into applause, and Hezi felt his cheeks flame. Yahweh had not held Hezi's sin against him, and He had honored the intention of Hezi's heart above his stupid mistakes. *Thank You, Yahweh! Thank You!* While the room celebrated, Jashub lifted a tentative hand, requesting permission to continue speaking.

"Quiet! Quiet!" Hezi shouted. "Jashub, you have more to report?"

"I do. It's a strange happening that I fear you may struggle to believe—as I did, even though I saw it with my own eyes." He glanced at his sister. "Zibah, have you ever known me to lie?"

It was an odd question and a strange time to ask it. "No, Jashub," Zibah replied. "You wouldn't be the king's second scribe if you were prone to dishonesty."

Jashub turned to the council. "From my mountain perch, I witnessed Assyria soundly defeated both yesterday and the day before—but not by Egyptians. Upon my honor . . . they were defeated by rats."

The room fell silent. Jashub scratched his brow and seemed hesitant to explain. "I've never seen anything like it. On both mornings, Assyrian soldiers flooded from their tents shouting and cursing as furry creatures scurried between their feet. The Assyrians held chewed breastplates, bows, and shields. Every leather weapon was fodder for the rats. The Egyptians attacked soon after, forcing the Assyrians to fight with stones and sticks. Egypt drove them back, and now they're retreating to Lachish."

"Lachish?" The commander glanced at Hezi. "Their disciplined troops can make the hike to Lachish within three days. And if they were defeated as Jashub has described, they'll return to that city with fury."

Hezi felt the knot in his stomach draw tighter. "Is the Rabshakeh headed back to Jerusalem?"

Jashub shrugged. "I'm sorry, my king, but I don't know. It appeared that all the Assyrians were moving toward Lachish, but I didn't get close enough to hear the Rabshakeh's commands. I'm sorry if I failed you."

The advisors began voicing their concerns and questions in a jumble of panic, but Hezi left his throne, eyes focused on Jashub alone. Placing both hands on Jashub's shoulders, he said, "You gave us much-needed information. We know that Yahweh worked for us in Libnah—without weapons or loss of Judean lives. He's using the Egyptians as well as rats to defeat our enemy." The advisors fell silent. "If you'd drawn closer to hear the Rabshakeh, you might have been captured, and we would never have known this information. You are relieved of duty, Jashub, not because you've failed but because you've done well. Thank you."

Eliakim stood and bowed to Jashub as he took his first step toward home. Others followed suit as he made his way up the center aisle. Hezi turned to wink at Zibah and was rewarded when she mouthed, *Thank you.* Her tears were proof he'd sufficiently honored her brave brother.

As Jashub exited court, the double doors opened wide, and two royal guards appeared with an Assyrian messenger between them.

"This vermin brings a message from his king." One of the guards shoved the courier down the aisle. The man fell to his knees and struggled back to his feet.

Walking between the guards, the Assyrian looked almost feeble, hunched and shivering with dark circles under his eyes. The man lifted a leather-bound scroll and Hezi approached him to receive it. "King Sennacherib would rather fight your God than the Egyptian gods that send rats to eat our weapons."

Hezi grabbed the scroll. "Egyptian gods

are wood and stone. Our God is the Maker of heaven and earth." Suddenly aware of something crawling up his arm, Hezi looked down at the scroll and saw a half-dozen fleas. He inspected the messenger and found him infested. "Get him out of here!"

The guards lifted the Assyrian and shoved him toward the exit with their spear shafts, now keeping their distance.

A shiver worked up Hezi's spine. It felt as though bugs were crawling all over him. He felt the first bite on his wrist, then his leg. Growling, he caught one of the insects between his fingers and squeezed. He began to panic when it survived the squishing. "How do you kill these things?"

Shebna stood in the council gallery. "In Egypt, they wash their clothes in a solution of natron and water, and if the infestation spreads to their homes, they sprinkle the natron solution around the house as well." He reached up and scratched his cheek. "As I'm sure the king is aware—natron is only found in Egypt."

"Do we have any remaining natron from Egyptian gifts?" Hezi said, and then slapped at another flea.

Hilkiah jumped to his feet. "I'll check the treasury records." He rushed out the side entry, and the whole council looked as if they wanted to follow.

Still holding the offending scroll, Hezi dropped

it to the floor and unrolled it with his toe. He saw another flea and crushed it between the sole of his sandal and the tiled floor. He crushed another one between two fingernails, feeling some vindication, and then knelt to read the scroll aloud.

"Thus says the great Sennacherib, mighty king of the world, to King Hezekiah of Jerusalem: Do not let your God deceive you by promising that Jerusalem will be saved from Assyria's hands. You have heard what the kings of Assyria have done to other nations, completely destroying them. How can your God deliver when all other gods failed?" He read the rest silently, his fear rising. Assyria was coming back to destroy Jerusalem.

He rolled the scroll and stood, staring into the increasingly pale faces of his wife and counselors. "The rest of the message is filled with more blasphemy and slander against the Lord our God. I'm going to the Temple to pray. I would encourage the rest of you to remain faithful in your offerings to the Lord. Yahweh promised to deliver us, and He will be true to His word."

Hezi hurried out the private entrance without waiting for Samuel or Zibah. Breaking into a run, he raced through palace courts, Isaiah's admonition replaying in his mind: *You must go directly to Yahweh with your questions.* Scroll in hand, he ran down the palace stairs and toward the Temple, panic rising. Finally, he crossed the threshold of the Guard's Gate and entered the inner court, where only priests, Levites, and the king were allowed. Amid the wondering stares and concerned glances, King Hezekiah fell on his knees before the brazen altar and spread out the Assyrian scroll before the Lord.

In a loud voice, he cried, "O LORD, God of Israel, enthroned above the cherubim, You are the only True God. Do You hear and see how the king of Assyria mocks the Creator of heaven and earth? Yes, he has laid waste every nation and land and cast their gods into the fire—but they were not gods. You alone are God. So now, save us from his hand so that all the earth will know that You alone are God."

55

In those days Hezekiah became ill and was at the point of death.

—2 Kings 20:1

Yaira and I had been cooped up in my chamber for two days, peering out between the balcony tapestries to watch the Rabshakeh's troops returning. Their disciplined arrival arranged their camp into the same perfect lines they'd formed outside Jerusalem's gates nearly two weeks ago.

My initial terror had given way to doom as Hezi spent long hours with his advisors and the commander, creating a plan to stave off a siege that would inevitably come. But the Assyrians had done nothing more than loiter outside the gates. *Nothing.* The Rabshakeh and his troops barely left their tents, and the rest of the army milled around like ants on a hill.

My sense of doom was then swallowed up by anger. I was tired of living in a state of indecision—so I made a decision.

I stopped Yaira's busy hands from clearing our morning dishes and gently pulled her down to sit on a cushion beside me. "You and Jashub should marry." She looked at me as if I'd asked her to milk a camel.

"Perhaps, Zibah, but I refuse to discuss this when thousands of Assyrians are waiting to torture and kill us." She tried to stand, but I tugged at her sleeve.

"Now is exactly the time to discuss it. If you were married to Jashub, you could be cleaning up the dishes from his table, a meal you prepared for him, Jacob, and Ellah."

The longing on Yaira's face was palpable. "Perhaps someday, but my place is here with you right now."

There it was. Just as I'd suspected. "I've talked with Hezi, and we feel it's time for you to live your own—"

"What did you tell the king?" Her cheeks flamed.

"He asked why you were so upset by Jashub's absence, so I told him a bit about yours and Jashub's history."

"We do have a history." Jashub's voice held a hint of merriment, startling Yaira from her anger—or rather redirecting it.

"Why are you here, Jashub?" She stood, fussing with her light blue robe, refusing to look at him.

I cast an *I'm sorry* glance at my brother. I was supposed to have prepared my friend for his arrival, but he didn't seem disturbed. He walked directly to the woman he'd loved his whole adult life and cradled Yaira's hand. "Tell me why you're upset, my friend."

"Why are you here?" she repeated more gently this time.

"Zibah asked me to come. She had hoped we could decide on a date for our wedding."

I cringed at his honesty. Couldn't he have softened the truth just a little?

Yaira dropped her eyes, avoiding us both, but Jashub tipped up her chin. "Are you upset because I'm here or is something else troubling you?"

Yaira's chin began to quiver, threatening her armor of control. I had done this. I'd placed her in this impossible position. "Jashub, I'm sorry," I said, walking toward them. "Perhaps you should go."

"No." He turned to me, voice firm. "You should go, little sister."

Stunned, I halted three steps from them and exchanged a glance with Yaira. She appeared as surprised as I—and then a little grin appeared. My heart leapt. "Of course, Jashub. I'll wait in Yaira's chamber to give you some privacy."

An awkward silence filled the room until I disappeared into the adjoining chamber. I left the door ajar so I could hear, refusing to forgo the conversation I'd waited almost thirty years to witness.

Jashub's voice was low and intimate, but I could make out a few words. ". . . simple man . . . love you . . . my children . . . marry me now."

". . . Assyrians outside . . . take away . . . must wait . . . can't lose . . . break my heart."

Yaira's words were clear enough to be heartrending.

A lingering silence made me ache to peek out the door, but I waited. Jashub's voice was softer and husky. Then I heard Yaira say, "All right, Jashub. Yes."

Really? I wanted to squeal, but I cleared my throat, coughed, and knocked before reentering, hoping to cut short a prebetrothal kiss before anyone was embarrassed.

"Well, I hope you've made a decision we can celebrate." My timing and tone undoubtedly betrayed my eavesdropping.

The couple stood side by side, Jashub's arm possessively around his bride-to-be. "She's agreed to be my wife, Zibah. Thank you."

Tamping down that stubborn squeal, I tried to act as queenly as possible. "Will you wait the prescribed betrothal period?" If they said *yes,* I'd have Hezi arrest them both immediately and witness their wedding in the dungeon.

Yaira's cheeks pinked like the dawn. "Why wait? We've waited long enough."

"I think today is the perfect time for a wedding," Jashub added. "There's been very little activity in the soldiers' camp, and our family needs to celebrate something!"

The familiar red-hot iron of fear poked through

my belly. "Hezi says the Assyrians could be weak and wounded, or resting and planning their attack."

Jashub's playful spark dimmed, concern knitting his brow. "I could sneak into their camp to gain that information."

"No!" Yaira and I shouted in unison. "Sending you to follow the Rabshakeh was another sin on the list Abba Isaiah is keeping against Hezi. I'd hate to hear his rant if Hezi sent you into their camp."

Jashub's features softened. "Abba loves Hezi. It's tearing him apart to—"

The chamber doors banged open. Samuel and another guard appeared, Hezi's limp form draped between them. "Get him into the bed." Samuel made no attempt at formalities, which terrified me.

"What happened?" I shouted, following them. Hezi shook violently between them.

"He collapsed during the council meeting." Samuel and the other guard placed him on the bed.

I knelt before my husband, his eyes dark ringed, shoulders slumped and shaking. "You left this morning with a headache. What happened, my love?"

"It c-c-came on s-s-so quickly." He toppled onto his side, aiming his face at the lamb's wool headpiece and pulling his knees to his chest. "B-b-blankets. I n-n-need blankets."

I looked over my shoulder to find Yaira already waiting with an armload of woolen warmth. When I reached for them, she squeezed my hand, infusing me with her strength. I shook out the first blanket and let it fall over my trembling husband. Heat radiated from his body as if a fire burned from within.

"Call the physician, Samuel." I could barely croak the command.

"Already done, my queen."

We waited moments that seemed like days. Finally, the physician ran into the chamber. Glancing around the crowded room, he raised a crooked finger toward the door. "Out. Everyone out." I ignored him as did Samuel. The other guard escorted Jashub and Yaira from the chamber.

Gently placing his hand on my shoulder, the physician whispered, "My queen, I must examine King Hezekiah. If his ailment is as I fear, you will not wish to be present."

My head snapped to attention, and I met his eyes for the first time. "What ailment?"

"I've observed and recorded the activity— or should I say *lack* of activity—in the Assyrian troops. After returning two days ago, few have left their tents. This morning, those under the Rabshakeh's red standard began digging a large ditch behind their camp." He paused, raising one eyebrow as if I should understand what that meant.

"What does that have to do with Hezi?"

Frustration sharpened my words. I took a calming breath.

Hezi groaned. "Zibah, you should go."

"No, tell me what that means." I pinned the physician with a stare.

"They're preparing for mass deaths." Samuel's voice was barely audible, his eyes kind. "Since the Rabshakeh's troops have been confined to their tents, it's likely they're ill."

"Is it a plague?" The words escaped my lips on a whisper. Yahweh had used plagues to destroy the wicked in many stories I'd taught my students. I understood judgment on the Assyrians, but . . . I looked at my husband's quaking body and then back at the physician. "King Hezekiah can't have the same illness." My husband had done nothing to be judged by a plague from God.

"As I said, my queen, perhaps you should step out of the room."

Samuel cupped my elbow, gently lifting me to my feet. "I'll stay with him. Come, my queen. I'm sure Yaira is just outsi—"

"No! I'm staying." I yanked my arm from his grasp and addressed the doctor. "Tell me how to help."

"We must undress him."

Hezi's shivering increased as we removed his blankets and outer robe, leaving him in his tunic alone. His arms and legs were covered with small blisters.

"Flea bites," the doctor said. "Now, for the tunic."

My cheeks warmed at the thought of exposing my husband's nakedness in the presence of two men, but I couldn't leave now. When we removed his tunic, a hideous boil on the left groin area stared back like a festering black eye. I turned away before Hezi could see my revulsion, my fear.

"What is it?" Hezi's voice trembled still, but I heard fear now, not just the chill.

"Let's put these blankets back on." The doctor unmistakably avoided the hard question.

With my back still turned, I assumed the shuffling behind me meant Samuel and the doctor were dressing their king. My hands trembled wildly, and I suddenly realized my cheeks were wet with tears. This must be a nightmare. Surely, I would wake and find comfort in Hezi's arms—my strong, brave, *healthy* husband's arms.

"I saw this in Egypt during my studies," the physician began.

"Saw what?" I asked.

The physician ignored me. "When did you begin feeling poorly, my king?"

"This morning."

The sound of Hezi's timid voice pierced my heart and beckoned me to his side. I couldn't let him face the hard truth alone. "He woke with a headache," I said, sitting on the bed beside him again. I took his hand and smiled into his terrified eyes. "He complained of general fatigue and body soreness, but we've both slept poorly because . . ." Bitterness choked off the words I really wanted to say. *Because of the filthy Assyrians outside our balcony.*

Hezi squeezed my hand. He seemed calmer now. "The sickness that you saw in Egypt—was it contagious?" He paused. "Fatal?"

Choking on a sob, I pulled his hand to my lips and closed my eyes, bracing for the answer my heart already knew.

"We called it Black Death. I saw only one person survive it—out of hundreds."

Four heartbeats passed in silence. "Leave us," Hezi said. "Both of you."

The physician and Samuel protested, each listing their reasons and rights to remain, but my sweet husband knew we needed the nourishment of each other in that moment—the darkest valley of our lives.

The door clicked shut, and we were finally alone. I crawled into bed beside him, and we released the torrent of emotion held in check while others were present. "I can't lose you." The words erupted from the depths of my soul. "You are my light, my breath, my words."

He kissed the tears from my cheeks; deep, racking sobs shaking him at the same time.

I don't know how long we wept, but my next realization was of waking in his arms. The sky outside our balcony was dark. For just a moment, hope flitted across my clouded mind that this had all been a bad dream, but heat from my husband's trembling body reminded me of our ugly reality.

I kissed Hezi's cheek, and he turned sad eyes in my direction. "I'm sorry, Zibah."

I stared at him, puzzled and heartbroken. "What could you be sorry about, my love?"

"I'm sorry that I'll die without giving you a son of David." He raised his hand to touch my face, and I screamed for the physician. My husband's fingers had turned black.

56

Isaiah son of Amoz went to [King Hezekiah] and said, "This is what the LORD says: Put your house in order, because you are going to die; you will not recover."

—2 Kings 20:1

Jashub snatched Isaiah's walking stick from the corner of the kitchen as if stealing it could keep Yahweh's prophet from delivering the message. "Please, Abba. I heard you and Ima talking. Surely, you misunderstood Yahweh's words."

How Isaiah wished he hadn't heard Yahweh clearly. As he did during the days he'd been called to prophesy naked and barefoot, Isaiah had begged God to send someone else. "I'll go without the stick if I must, Jashub. Yahweh was clear. I'm to pronounce judgment on Judah's king at dawn."

His eldest son stood his ground, rebellion screaming in his silence. Aya walked into the room, glanced at her two men, and marched over to their son. "Give me that walking stick right now." He obeyed, and she brushed his cheek with the gentleness of a dove's wing. "Your abba is heartbroken. Don't make it worse."

She placed the stick in Isaiah's hands and nudged him toward the door. "Go. The sun is peeking over the hills." He turned and kissed her before hurrying out the door.

What would he do without Aya? What will Zibah do without Hezekiah? They'd loved each other since they were children. *Yahweh, I know the boy has sinned, but . . . .* He shook his head, trying to dislodge the faithless thought. He'd been taught by the great prophets at Tekoa—Jonah, Amos, and Hosea—a prophet must deliver God's message without question. "And sometimes without understanding," he whispered to himself. *I trust You, Yahweh, but sometimes it's easier than others to trust You wholeheartedly.*

Too soon, he arrived at the palace, and curious eyes followed him down the king's hallway. Not a single guard tried to stop him even though he hadn't visited the palace in years. As he approached the king's chamber, he recognized Samuel at the door.

The big guard looked as if he hadn't slept in days, but he perked immediately when he spotted Isaiah. "Your presence is either extremely good news or extremely bad."

Isaiah's silence was answer enough.

Samuel planted his feet and crossed his arms over his chest. "I will not allow you to enter this chamber and cause more suffering, Prophet."

Relief surged through Isaiah. "I would rather

you cut me down with your sword than deliver this message to our king." Tears robbed his dignity, and he pressed his fingers against his eyes. Breathing deeply, he regained control. "If I don't speak, the Lord will raise up another to deliver His message to Hezekiah." Samuel's eyes registered understanding, and he stepped back, opening the door for Isaiah.

The room smelled of putrid flesh. Tapestries were drawn across the balcony and over every window. Only two lamps lit the physician's table in the audience chamber. The rest of the room was utter darkness.

"Abba?" Zibah emerged from the darkened area, disheveled and dismayed. "Why have you come?" Fear marred her lovely features. She knew.

"I must speak the word of the Lord to King Hezekiah."

Tears gathered on her lashes. "Do you want to see him first? Talk with him?"

Emotion strangled Isaiah and opened the floodgates. Zibah clung to him, and they wept, hearts broken over the boy, the man, the king they loved. "I can't, Zibah. I'm afraid if I talk with Hezekiah, if I see his suffering, I won't be faithful to God's command. I must be faithful, Zibah. I must."

She shoved him away, her eyes accusing. "Why, Abba? Why be faithful to a God who speaks in mysteries we can't understand and then tortures us by *almost* giving us our dreams?"

"Hephzibah . . ."

"No!" she shouted. "I am Ishma! Desolate and barren."

Yaira appeared from the shadows and cradled Hephzibah in her arms. "Go, Master Isaiah. Do what you must."

Isaiah met the physician's disdain and borrowed one of the lamps from his table. A slow march to the king's bed didn't prepare him for the sight. Hezekiah's nose had turned black, his hands as well. Two large lumps had risen under his right armpit with black veins reaching like a spider's web in all directions. The strong and handsome second-born of King Ahaz was quickly wasting away.

Hezekiah lifted his hand to shield his eyes. "Get that light out of here."

Weeping, Isaiah blew out the small flame, hoping the young man he loved wouldn't recognize the prophet speaking judgment. "Hear the word of the Lord, Hezekiah ben Ahaz: Put your house in order for you are going to die. You will not recover."

Isaiah turned to go, but a weak voice stopped him. "Is that all? No imagery or list of woes? Surely, you won't waste the last lesson Yahweh is teaching your prized student."

The words cut like a dagger into Isaiah's belly.

He didn't understand the lesson himself. How could he explain it? Yet he turned and found his way back to speak his last words to Judah's king. "I have only one lesson left to teach you, Hezekiah. Pride is a man's worst enemy. You were right when you said I offered too many opinions to accompany God's revealed word. That, Hezekiah, was my prideful heart." He paused, but Judah's king had no quick reply. "We have both made mistakes while leading God's people, my son. It breaks my heart that you bear the wrath in your body."

Isaiah rose, kissed Hezekiah's forehead, and left the room to the sound of the king's weeping. He rushed down the hall and toward the Middle Court, aching for Aya's comforting arms.

57

Hezekiah turned his face to the wall and prayed to the LORD, "Remember, LORD, how I have walked before you faithfully." . . . And Hezekiah wept bitterly.
—2 Kings 20:2–3

Hezi watched the man who had been his friend and teacher walk away. He wasn't sure which hurt worse—the confusion of Yahweh's judgment or leaving Zibah childless. Hezi had believed Yahweh would empower him to rule Judah with honor and that Zibah would give birth to another in the line of David's descendants. How had he sinned so grievously, bearing now the judgment of sin in his body, and not known it? With a low groan, he turned his face toward the wall.

"Your majesty, are you in pain?" The physician hovered like a vulture.

"Leave me alone."

Zibah appeared and sat on the edge of his bed. "Please prepare some poppy-seed tea for the king." She leaned over his shoulder and whispered, "Perhaps this was Abba's opinion, Hezi. We've seen Yahweh bless the good work you've done."

"His opinion, Zibah?" He turned slightly to

look at her and choked out a cynical laugh. "I will die, Zibah. Death is judgment, not opinion."

She had no reply, only eyes full of tears and pain.

"Leave me." He turned to face the wall again. She tried to lay her head on his shoulder, but he shrugged her off. "I said leave me."

Eyes closed, he heard her retreating footsteps, and in that moment Hezekiah ben Ahaz felt utterly bereft. Weeping bitterly, his words were heard only by the One who formed him. "Please, Yahweh, remember me. Remember that I have walked faithfully before You with my whole heart. I've done everything I thought was right in Your eyes. Everything."

How could God leave him? His whole life had been focused on doing right. When Abba had done evil, when Ima had schemed, Hezi had followed God's Law and meditated on His Word. When Zibah had remained childless, Hezi had remained steadfast, certain Yahweh would give them an heir.

Was he a fool? Was Yahweh a figment of his imagination like the idols of wood and stone? No. Yahweh was real. He must be real. What about all the prophecies that had come to pass?

What about those that hadn't? Would Assyria march through Jerusalem's gates?

He reached for his hair but couldn't tear it out because his hands were rotting away. "Yahweh, why?" he sobbed. Everything within him believed there was a God listening to his questions, sharing his sorrow, and deciding Judah's future. Why had He suddenly grown distant?

Weary to the bone, Hezi closed his eyes, his breathing shallow. Few spoke of death's mysteries. How long before the mystery became his reality? How long before he met Abraham in paradise? Would he see Saba Jotham and Great-Saba Uzziah there? "Perhaps even King David," he whispered, a tentative smile working at the corners of his mouth. The pain would end. The shivering would stop. If he could have provided an heir to his throne—a son to care for Zibah—perhaps he could even look forward to paradise.

A commotion in the hallway interrupted his brooding. He didn't dare open his eyes for fear of pain at the slightest light.

"No, Abba. You can't see him again." Zibah's voice, panicked.

"But . . . see him . . . another word . . . Lord."

Hezi groaned again. Was it part of a prophet's training to be relentless? Heartless?

"Hezekiah!" Isaiah's booming voice startled him. He was laughing, almost giddy. "This is what the LORD, the God of your forefather David, says: I have heard your prayer; I have seen your tears; and I will heal you. On the third day you will be clean of your disease and go up to the Temple to worship; and I will add fifteen years to your life. I will deliver you and this city from the king of Assyria, and I will defend this city for My own sake and for My servant David's sake."

Hezi opened his eyes barely a slit, just enough to see the crazy old prophet. "You never change a prophecy."

Isaiah's eyes sparkled with unshed tears. "I've never known God to change a prophecy either, but I'm glad He did." He looked at Zibah. "I'd barely made it out of the Middle Court when I felt the hand of the Lord press me to the ground with the new message."

Hezi could feel his strength ebbing. "Please, Isaiah. I need a sign that I'll go to the Temple in three days."

Isaiah stood silent and staring for several heartbeats, and Hezi wondered if he'd offended the old man again. As it turned out, the prophet was listening. "Here is your sign, Hezekiah, that you, yourself will choose. Will the shadow on your sundial go forward ten degrees or backward ten degrees?"

Hezi opened his eyes wider, anticipation growing, and noticed a crowd had gathered in his chamber. Zibah and the physician, of course. Ima and Rizpah had come down from the harem. Yaira and Samuel were also there. Jashub and several guards must have followed the excited prophet into the chamber.

"It's an easy thing for the shadow to lengthen," Hezi said. "Let the God of Creation make the shadow drop back instead."

Isaiah hurried to the balcony and threw back the tapestries, inviting the blinding light of a new day into Hezi's dark world. The king growled and buried his face in his lamb's wool. "My apologies, King Hezekiah." Isaiah's tone betrayed a smile. "Will you brave the light to see God's miracle?"

Hezi squinted at the man who'd been more of an abba than his own. "I'm ready for a miracle, Isaiah."

"As am I, Hezekiah."

All eyes shifted to the Babylonian sundial on the king's balcony—the piece Hezi and Zibah had carefully inspected and approved when all of Judah was cleansed before the first Passover. Too weak to stand, Hezi was grateful when Zibah and Ima rushed to his bed and helped him sit up to see the towering sundial. Waiting was excruciating. In the silence, Hezi wondered repeatedly if his eyes were playing tricks or if he was really seeing the shadow descend on the stepped-stone markers of the dial.

Zibah gasped. Ima too. "It's happening!" Ima whispered.

Hezi, unable to look at the sun, could only shield his eyes and watch the shadow on the dial. Just as Isaiah said—just as Yahweh promised—the shadow slowly moved back ten degrees.

Hezi's fever still raged. His fingers were still painful and blackened. But his healing had begun—inside and out.

Isaiah walked toward the door but spoke to the physician on his way. "Lay a fig poultice on the boil, and he'll recover."

"Wait!" The king's shout garnered everyone's attention. "Isaiah, did you suggest my physician should actively 'help' Yahweh's healing process? Should we not trust the Lord completely instead of trying to help—as I did with a tunnel and a treaty?"

His father-in-law paused, glancing at the anxious faces around the room. Finally, he looked back to Hezi. "The LORD has this to say concerning the king of Assyria: 'Sennacherib will not enter our gates. He will not shoot an arrow here or lift a shield or build a siege mound against us. He will return to Assyria the same way he came. For I, the LORD will defend this city and save it for My own sake and for the sake of My servant David.' " Isaiah bowed and hurried from the room, leaving a wake of holy anticipation.

The royal physician turned toward the king, brows raised and waiting.

"The man said to use a fig poultice." Hezi grinned and broke the tension. Still shivering, he could hardly believe in three days he'd be healed, but the moving shadow was hard to ignore. *Thank You, Yahweh, for a sign I can't explain away— and a prophet who is faithful to Your voice.*

58

Surely, he took up our pain and bore our
suffering,
yet we considered him punished by God,
stricken by him, and afflicted. . . .
The punishment that brought us peace
was on him, and by his wounds we are
healed.

—Isaiah 53:4–5

I'd been awake most of the night. Staring at my
husband in the light of a single lamp as he slept.
That big nose I teased him about was still as
black as the night sky.

At least he slept. His chest rose and fell. *Thank
You, Yahweh.*

Amram sat across from me, awake for the night
watch, while Samuel slept on a goatskin rug on
the floor. Samuel hadn't left Hezi's side. He was
a good friend. They were both good friends. How
could we repay their kindness?

We. Hezi and I had always been *we.* There was
no me. No Ishma or Hephzibah. "I am yours,
Hezekiah, son of David, king of Judah." Even
my whisper sounded like an echo in the darkened
chamber. "Don't leave. I cannot be *we* without
you."

I heard the rumble of horses' hooves outside our balcony. Samuel stirred and was on his feet, racing to the balcony with sword drawn, before I could stand. "What's happening?"

At the same time, Amram bolted to answer the pounding of a spear on our chamber door. Dagger at the ready, he opened the door only a slit and then admitted one of the guards. "My queen," the guard said, breathless, "the commander needs to speak with King Hezekiah immediately."

I looked to Samuel before answering. He returned from the balcony, brows furrowed. "The moon is full, so I was able to see about a thousand horsemen riding due east." He shook his head. "I don't understand it, my queen."

Hezi rose on one elbow, his voice still weak. "Isaiah's prophecy said they would return to Assyria without shooting an arrow or lifting a shield. Maybe they'll leave a thousand at a time." He fell back onto the bed. "Send in Commander Jokim."

Amram guided the commander to Hezi's bed. The towering man staggered back at the sight of his king. "I . . . I . . . My king, I . . ."

"Don't be alarmed," Hezi said. "Isaiah said Yahweh will heal me. Now, what have you to report, Commander?"

Spine stiffening, the man pulled a small piece of parchment from his belt. "Our first message from Lachish arrived on a carrier pigeon a few moments ago. It says, 'Plague rampant. Judeans and Assyrians dying.' " He let his hand fall to his side, speechless.

Hezi stared at the ceiling. "Mattaniah," he whispered. "No word on my brother, the governor?"

I wondered if Mattaniah was lying on a bed with a black nose and hands. *Or have You spared his life, Yahweh?* I refused to consider he'd followed King Ahaz into Sheol.

Samuel stepped forward. "One thousand Assyrians just abandoned the Jerusalem encampment. If a carrier pigeon got through, it means their archers are sick, gone—or dead."

The realization was like a breeze of hope blowing through the room. Hezi turned his head toward me slowly. "We'll need someone to slip out of the city undetected and get close to the Assyrian camp—maybe even sneak into the tents."

I knew he was suggesting Jashub. Yaira would strangle us both if we sent Jashub into harm's way again. "I'm sure the commander has a soldier trained for such work."

"Zibah." Hezi's frustration matched his weariness.

I refused to argue with my weakened husband. Turning to the commander, I vented my frustration. "Don't you have other men who could slip into the camp?"

Yaira stepped into the lamplight and placed her hand on my shoulder. "Jashub would never forgive himself if he could have served but was passed over because of our fear." She looked down at Hezi, hands on her hips. "I'll allow you to send my bridegroom into the Assyrian camp if you promise to serve as Friend of the Bridegroom at our wedding."

Lips trembling, Hezi nodded. "I promise. Thank you, Yaira."

The commander bowed. "I'll send a contingent of guards to Jashub's home."

"No. I'll go," I said. "I'm sure he's at our parents' home. Jashub has been living there with the children since responsibilities here at the palace have kept him late most evenings." I turned to Yaira. "Do you want to come with me?"

Shaking her head, her eyes filled with tears. "I'll see Jashub when he returns safely."

Hezi reached for my hand as I stepped away but drew back before touching me with his blackened hand. "Tell Isaiah I'll see him at the Temple in two days." A tear slipped from the corner of his eye. "And tell Jashub I would be honored to serve as Friend of the Bridegroom—if he'll have me."

I leaned over to kiss my husband's cheek. "I'll tell them both and then come back to break my fast with you. I'm sure by then you'll feel better." Oh, how I wanted to believe it, but the stench of the fetid flesh on his nose nearly made me retch. The Law required complete healing of all skin lesions before a man could be pronounced clean, and Yahweh's priests—by Hezi's own decree—would follow the Law to the letter. How could Yahweh make him fully clean in two days? "Come, Amram." I fairly ran from the room to hide my tears, the big guard jogging behind me.

The sun barely peeked over the eastern hills. Why did God seem to work best at dawn? Perhaps I only noticed because dawn's quiet made me more aware. Birdsong buoyed my spirit, reminding me that although Hezi's sores and swelling remained, he seemed stronger. A thousand Assyrians had ridden away, and Yaira and Jashub would soon be married. It was a good start to the day.

Amram followed close behind, his shadow hovering over me like a giant shield. Perhaps I would speak with Jashub alone. If Abba and Ima heard me ask my perfectly healthy brother to investigate the possibly plague-ridden Assyrian camp, they might disown me. The squeaky gate was only steps away. I squared my shoulders, pushed it open, and found Abba waiting in the courtyard.

"Good morning, Daughter." His face fairly glowed. "I've been waiting for you to arrive. Is Hezekiah's healing complete yet?"

He looked so hopeful, I didn't want to disappoint him. "No, Abba, but we're eagerly awaiting Yahweh's restoration."

"No matter. It will come. Please," he said,

pointing to two stools, "sit down. I have much to tell you."

Amram questioned me with his eyes, and I nodded for him to sit. "Perhaps you and Amram could talk. I must see Jashub. Commander Jokim needs someone—"

"The Assyrians are dead, Zibah. Sit down." His matter-of-fact tone directed both Amram and me to our stools. "Yahweh woke me in the night when the angel of the Lord struck down the soldiers in their camp. You'll find 185,000 dead Assyrians when Hezekiah opens the gates."

Amram shifted uncomfortably on the small stool. "We can't open the gates until we're sure they're dead, Isaiah. Surely, you understand."

"Abba, are you saying that God sent a plague to kill all 185,000 Assyrians?"

He looked at me as if I was his slowest student. "Only half the Assyrians went to Libnah, Zibah. Only half the camp was infected, but the whole camp has been destroyed—minus the few needed to spread the word about the miracle."

Amram glanced at me and back at Abba. "You're telling us the Assyrians Samuel saw riding away on their horses this morning were spared by God to testify that only half of their comrades who died were killed by plague?"

"That's right. The other half of the Assyrian army was perfectly healthy when they went to sleep last night."

Amram looked as stunned as I felt. The immensity of such a miracle slapped me with its practicality. "What will we do with the dead?"

Ima rushed out of the house, tying her robe. "Zibah! You're here early." Then, seeing our expressions, her eyes brightened. "Has Hezi been healed?"

Another reality to bring me back to my purpose. "Not yet, Ima. I really must speak with Jashub."

I started to rise, but Abba grabbed my arm. "There's no hurry, Daughter. The Assyrians in that valley aren't going anywhere."

To my surprise, he wasn't angry or trying to stop me from involving his eldest son. "I believe you, Abba, but we must still use caution. Even one Assyrian still living could put Jashub at risk."

Jashub appeared at the door, hair disheveled as if straight out of bed. "I'll go wherever the king sends me."

Abba waved both him and Ima over, mild frustration tightening his brow. "Please, shalom everyone—peace. It matters not who checks the Assyrian camp or when. No one in Jerusalem will contract this plague."

His indifference was wearing on my patience. "We received a message this morning from Lachish. Many Judeans have already died and are dying, Abba. We must use caution."

"Those in Lachish died because of God's wrath on the city where Judah's idolatry began."

"You heard that from Yahweh?" I needed to be sure before reporting it to Hezi.

"Yes, Daughter." Taking a deep breath, he focused on me intently. "Listen to me, Zibah. Yahweh's wrath on all of Jerusalem was spent on the body of *one man*."

Gooseflesh lifted the hairs on my arms. "What are you saying, Abba?"

He bowed his head and began speaking as if reading an invisible scroll. "This is what the Holy One of Israel says: 'He grew like a tender shoot, and like a root out of dry ground. He had no beauty or majesty to attract us to him, nothing in his appearance that we should desire him. He was despised and rejected, a man of suffering, and familiar with pain. Like one from whom people hide their faces he was despised, and we held him in low esteem. Surely, he took up our pain and bore our suffering, yet we considered him punished by God, stricken by him, and afflicted."

I stared at him, nausea rising. "Hezi? You said he's not the chosen King."

"Listen, Zibah. Listen to the rest of the prophecy." He closed his eyes again, sending a stream of tears down his cheeks. "He was pierced for our transgressions, he was crushed for our iniquities; the punishment that brought us peace was on him, and by his wounds we are healed. We all, like sheep, have gone astray, each of us has turned to our own way; and the LORD has laid on him the iniquity of us all."

I placed my hand on his arm, and he opened his eyes. "Abba, Hezi wasn't pierced or crushed."

"Don't you see, Zibah?" he said, intense and certain. "Hezekiah isn't the chosen King, but he is a foreshadowing of the King that will come one day. The anointed Son of David will be a suffering King. Perhaps, like Hezekiah, he'll grow up with a difficult childhood. Maybe suffer for his strong faith. Hezekiah stepped between Jerusalem and God's wrath for our sins, saving us from a fate like Lachish, but the anointed King will take on the sins of all Israel—maybe all nations."

In my spirit, I knew this prophecy and its interpretation were the verses to our song that had been so long unsung. I'd known for years that Hezi's righteousness was but a foretaste of the anointed One's perfection. Now, with bittersweet understanding, I knew his suffering was also a sign of the coming King.

Abba framed my cheeks. "There's more, Daughter: 'Though it was Yahweh's will to crush him and cause him to suffer, and though he has become a sin offering, Yahweh will give him offspring and prolong his days.'" He searched my eyes. "Yahweh gave Hezekiah fifteen more years so you could bear a son, Zibah, an heir to King David's throne."

I stood, knocking over the stool, and turned away. I didn't want Abba to see the doubt streaming down my cheeks. I could believe many things—but not this.

Abba's hands rested on my shoulders. "May I tell you the rest?" Unable to speak, I nodded and squeezed my eyes shut. "After he has suffered, he will see the light of life and be satisfied."

Sobs broke loose, and Abba turned me into his arms. "Shh, my girl. You have waited years to bear a son. Yahweh has now promised one and given your husband fifteen years to enjoy him."

I wanted to believe, but a son seemed more impossible than dead Assyrians or Hezi's healing. I was approaching the change of women. I was at peace with the God I'd found in the harem—in His words, in His presence. I had truly become Hephzibah in so many ways, yet my womb was still Desolation.

"You are Hephzibah," Abba said, as if reading my thoughts. "Delight of the Lord, and He has promised."

59

Go and tell Hezekiah, "This is what the
LORD, the God of your father David, says:
I have heard your prayer and seen your
tears; I will add fifteen years to your life."
                                            —Isaiah 38:5

Amram followed at a distance as Jashub and I
took our time walking back to the palace. Jashub
took my hand, perhaps sensing my churning
thoughts. The tender gesture tightened my throat,
but I hoped distraction would staunch my tears.
"I forgot to give Abba the message that Hezi
would see him at the Temple in two days."

Jashub's brows rose. "Has Hezi improved since
last night?"

I shook my head, stubborn tears betraying
lingering doubt. Perhaps I'd try a happier topic.
"Hezi sent a message for you too. He'll be
honored to be Friend of the Bridegroom. Yaira
made him agree before she would allow you to
spy on the Assyrians—that was before Abba said
they were dead Assyrians."

He chuckled and squeezed my hand. "I would
be honored to have Hezekiah as my Friend."

I heard a dove's coo and closed my eyes for a
moment, blocking out everything else. The sound

drew me. I would visit the dovecote today. Pray. Ask Yahweh why we suffer in this life. Then refocus on eternity—for the hundredth time. Jashub pulled me to his side, and I saw a stray stone that I'd almost stumbled over.

"You should pray with your eyes open, little sister." I nudged him with my shoulder, reveling in our ease. We walked the rest of the way in silence. Jashub, likely dreaming of his wedding. Me, pondering the impossible promises of a miracle-working God.

When we arrived at my chamber door, the guards exchanged nervous glances. I looked over my shoulder to see if Amram had noticed.

He had. "Naam, what's going on?"

The guard threw open the double doors. "See for yourselves."

I saw Abijah first—beaming—and then my husband sitting up in our bed, clothed in a loose-fitting robe and eating broth. Holding his spoon in strong, flesh-colored hands.

I ran to the side of the bed, staring. I wanted to jump into his lap and hug him, but I was afraid I'd spill his broth. He looked absolutely normal except for those silly flea bites on his chest. Even the putrefied skin had been replaced with his beautiful tanned skin tone. "Your nose!"

He paused his slurping. "I've been told it's a little big for my face, but it appears to be attached for the foreseeable future."

"Oooh! Yaira, take this broth!" I grabbed the tray, handed it to my friend, and prepared to assault my husband with a thousand kisses—when a thought occurred to me. I peeked under the covers to see if the terrible boil had been leached out by the fig poultice.

"Zibah! Stop that!" The king of Judah blushed the color of ripe grapes, and the whole room erupted in laughter. I caught a glimpse of the fig poultice still in place. He chuckled. "Not everything is completely healed, my love, but I expect to worship in Yahweh's Temple in two days."

"Oh, Hezi. I'm sorry. I forgot to tell Abba your message." Then I remembered Abba's report and glanced at Amram. "Would one of you like to tell him about the Assyrians, or should I?"

Both men bowed, offering me the honor. "The Assyrians are dead, Hezi."

He glanced at Jashub. "Have you already checked the camp?"

"No, but Abba was waiting for Zibah when she arrived early this morning. Yahweh had already told him about the Assyrians, and"—his brows rose as he saw the warning in my glare—"we'll still need to check of course," he said. Was he about to tell Hezi that Abba had prophesied an heir?

Hoping to distract Hezi from Jashub's ill-spoken words, I turned to my husband's guard.

"Samuel, could you summon the commander and work with him to supervise the plunder and burial of the Assyrians?"

While Amram gave more detail to the king, Jashub took my arm and pulled me close, keeping his voice low. "Hezi deserves to know the full prophecy, Zibah. By bearing this illness, he saved the whole city. Yahweh will reward Hezekiah with a son and fifteen years to enjoy him. Tell him, Zibah. Rejoice in God's promise and watch it unfold."

Watch it unfold. Wasn't that what Abba always told us when we didn't understand a prophecy—watch it unfold and then praise Yahweh for His sovereign power? I turned to my husband. He finished the briefing with Amram and held out his hand to me. Beckoning. Jashub was right. He deserved the truth.

"Please, everyone, clear the chamber." I raised my voice, startling even myself. "I'd like a few moments alone with my husband." Bowing my head, I couldn't look at him. I stood rooted to the floor until the door clicked and we were alone.

"Come," he said. "Sit with me."

I obeyed, my head still bowed.

"Tell me. Your abba must have said something else. It's the only thing that could have upset you this much." He reached for my hand, but I pulled away.

My emotions raw, I needed to say it without his compassion. "The fifteen years you were given . . ."

I paused, and he asked, "Have they been taken away?"

"No. No!" I looked up and saw his relief. "It's just that . . ."

"Zibah, tell me. It can't be worse than what we've already endured."

I laughed, frustration and fear warring within. "I thought I was finished *enduring* the struggle for this promise. Now, I must war with my faith again."

"Faith is a battle we fight every day, my love." He opened his arms. "Come, tell me the promise so I can pick up my sword and battle with you."

I surrendered to the familiar curve of his arms. "The first part of the prophecy explains your illness." I recounted how Hezi foreshadowed the coming King and His redemption. We wept together at both the honor and burden placed on my husband.

"Is that why you're upset?" he asked.

"No." I rested my head on his chest, unable to look at him. "These were Abba's final words of prophecy: 'Though he has become a sin offering, Yahweh will give him offspring and prolong his days.'"

Hezi was silent, but I heard his heart pound faster.

"Abba believes it means you and I will have a son during these last years of your life." I paused, waiting for him to respond.

Silence.

I didn't dare look up. My heart was too fragile. "Maybe it refers to the anointed King rather than—"

My husband's body shook with sobs. I cradled his face and drew near. "What? What is it? I'm sorry. What did I say?"

"Yahweh has answered my prayer."

Which prayer? Confused, I affirmed what I thought he meant. "Yes, He is so good to heal you and extend your life."

"No, no," he said. "When I was dying, I told Him that I could look forward to paradise if only we had a son who could take care of you when I was gone." He wrapped me in his arms and wept grateful tears.

I wept too, but my heart was torn. Would I have the son I'd longed for—only to lose the husband I'd loved so long? Why was life so fragile and faith so hard? Why not trust, believe, and be done with it? *Yahweh, give me the will to trust when my faith fails so I can lean into You till the answer comes.*

60

When the people got up the next morning—there were all the dead bodies! So Sennacherib king of Assyria broke camp and withdrew. He returned to Nineveh and stayed there.

—2 Kings 19:35–36

Three days ago, Hezi was a dead man. This evening, he stood with his wife and family on the eastern portico of the Temple. The priests had inspected him from head to toe. He was clean. Every skin lesion gone. Not even a lingering flea bite. Now the meticulous Law keepers were busy with this evening's offerings. The lamb, the grain, the drink. According to Isaiah, Hezi himself had been made a sin offering—and he'd never felt more blessed in his life.

Surrounded by Judeans from as far away as Ziph and Timnah, Hezi lifted his voice in praise with the faithful who had been freed from Assyria's iron grasp. His brother Mattaniah had sent a message early this morning that Sennacherib broke camp in Lachish and drove his troops northeast as if the spirits of Sheol were chasing them. Hezi prayed the Assyrians were caught and tormented as they'd so inhumanly tortured others.

Mattaniah had quarantined himself in the Lachish palace and was one of the few who had escaped the plague. Perhaps someday he would return to Jerusalem—and to Yahweh.

Zibah slipped her hand into Hezi's, veiling the sign of affection between the folds of their robes. He wanted nothing more than to hide in their chamber for the next week, but it was Jashub and Yaira's turn. They were long overdue for marital delight.

Hezi whispered against his wife's head covering. "Are tonight's wedding plans finished?"

She nodded, keeping her voice low amidst the singing. "After the private ceremony, they'll stay in one of the harem chambers—at the far end, away from Rizpah's helpful intrusions. One serving girl will attend them, and Samuel assigned two chamber guards. Everything's ready."

Satisfied, Hezi rejoined the praise, looking over the sea of faces. Behind him, around him, and in the streets beyond, people worshiped even though they couldn't see the sacrifice. Yahweh's presence had overflowed the walls of His Temple and was shining from every Judean's face. Only the Passover crowd at the beginning of his reign had been larger, but the worship had never been sweeter.

Hezi noticed the stolen glances between Yaira and Jashub, their long wait nearly over. What better way to crescendo Yahweh's praise than to unite these precious friends in marriage. When the sacrifices at the Temple ended, the high priest met family and friends in the royal courtyard at the moon's zenith. Yaira had planned for a wedding under the stars—appropriate for a couple in their twilight years. She was forty-three yet as giddy as a maiden and Jashub much the same.

After the ceremony, Hezi quieted the celebrating guests. "As a token of my gratitude, I appoint Jashub to my royal council and"—he produced a scroll from his pocket—"you now own a private estate in Jerusalem's western hills."

The newlyweds exchanged an awkward glance, and Yaira inspected her sandals. Jashub bowed. "We're grateful, my king." But his tone sounded like Hezi had just handed them rotten dates.

The king looked from one to the other. "Why the long faces?"

Yaira's cheeks pinked. "Your gifts are more than generous, King Hezekiah, but we enjoy our lives and would rather stay close to our family."

Hezi was grateful for her honesty. "Then you shall have your pick of chambers in the palace."

Zibah laced her arm in his. "With the exception of Hezi's and mine."

Yaira's laughter was like the patter of rain on pottery. Soft. Gentle. Cleansing.

Jashub couldn't take his eyes from her. "Can

we choose the chamber after the wedding week?" The anxious groom then whisked his bride away amid cheers and well wishes.

Hezi leaned heavily on his bride. "I'm exhausted. How about you?" She nodded, and they began their short walk to their chamber.

His wife had been joyful and pleasant during the wedding, but he sensed an underlying sorrow. He suspected Isaiah's prophecy still weighed heavily on her heart. She'd been pensive and withdrawn since hearing it. Hezi wasn't offended. He trusted Yahweh now more than ever. And he trusted his wife's commitment to find Yahweh amid her pain.

He kissed the top of her head as they neared their chamber.

She looked up. "What was that for?"

"Because you were the most beautiful woman at the wedding." She smiled, but the joy didn't reach her eyes. His heart ached for her. *Yahweh, please bless us with a child soon.*

Guards opened the double doors of their chamber, welcoming them into the low-lit peace of their private world. Yaira had chosen a new chamber maid, who had done her job well. Hezi walked straight to the bed, sat down, and began removing his sandals.

Zibah had stopped halfway across the room. "I'll still be all right if I don't have a baby, Hezi. Yahweh has given me family to care for me after you're gone." She rushed to him, kneeling at his feet. "I want our last years to be happy ones, not waiting on a pregnancy that may never come. Can't we go on living as if Abba never spoke the prophecy?"

Weariness crushed his bones, but the burden his wife carried seemed even heavier. He kicked his sandals aside and drew her into his lap. "When one of God's prophecies doesn't come to pass, it's not because He failed; it's because we misunderstood it." Her features softened, giving him permission to continue. "Your abba believes you and I will have a child—perhaps several children. But remember what he said about interpretation? It's God directed but susceptible to his—and our—human fallibility. If Yahweh's intention is different than Isaiah's interpretation, we'll praise God for the miraculous ways He's already blessed us, and we'll watch for His alternative fulfillment."

She blew out a deep breath and looked at the ceiling, blinking back tears. Tricks she'd learned through the years to control her emotions.

Hezi drew a single finger from her cheek down the length of her neck and kissed where it landed. He'd regained her attention. "Zibah, we're married. That's a miracle. Judah worships Yahweh. That's a miracle. I'm alive. That's a miracle."

She wrapped her arms around his neck and held

him tight. "You and abba talked the whole night without arguing. Now *that's* a miracle."

He laughed. "You see? Yahweh does great and marvelous things." Their teasing ebbed to silence, and he pulled her arms from his neck and looked into her eyes. "It's hard to trust God when reality drains our hope, but God must be our hope for a new reality."

61

Hezekiah had very great wealth and honor, and he made treasuries for his silver and gold and for his precious stones, spices, shields and all kinds of valuables. He also made buildings to store the harvest of grain, new wine and olive oil; and he made stalls for various kinds of cattle, and pens for the flocks. He built villages and acquired great numbers of flocks and herds, for God had given him very great riches.

—2 Chronicles 32:27–29

Yaira braided my hair into an intricate weave, wrapping strings of gems around the ever-encroaching gray streaks in my dark curly locks. Two-year-old Kenaz toddled around, finding every forbidden trinket in Auntie Zibah's chamber. He was the joy of my life. Ellah, now eight, considered herself his second ima, and he was the reason his wet nurse always looked exhausted.

"Yaira," I said, "let me tend Ellah and Kenaz this morning and give you and his maid a little respite."

I studied her reflection in my bronze mirror,

a habit I'd established when we ourselves were still girls.

She whispered like a conspirator. "Why don't the children and I stay for the morning? I need no respite from God's miracles. I'm not sure Kenaz's maid feels that way. I'll feed him yogurt and give her a break."

Yaira's perfect work on my braids complete, my maid held up the new robe Hezi had given me last week, made with silk from Persia. I slipped my arms into the sleeves and shivered at the softness.

Yaira whistled through her teeth. "That's the most beautiful robe I've ever seen."

I smiled, inspecting the sleeves and the design. "Do you ever remember our first days in Jerusalem and then consider where we are now and wonder, Why me, Yahweh? Why have You blessed me so?"

Yaira snagged little Kenaz as he ran past her. "I think it nearly every day, my friend." She tickled her son's tummy to hear him giggle. "Why are you dressing so regal today? Are more foreign guests coming to pay honor to the miracle king of Judah?"

I struggled to cinch my belt and motioned for my maid to help. "Yes, I believe he said something about more Cushite ambassadors from Egypt this week. I've lost track. Hilkiah says Judah's treasury hasn't been so full since the days of Solomon."

The maid kept pulling and pulling to get my robe together, but either I'd grown larger or the keeper of the wardrobe had made serious miscalculations. "Yaira, look how small they've made this robe."

"Zibah, your tummy!"

My cheeks warmed. I knew I'd put on weight around my middle, which Ima said happened with women as they approach forty. "I've tried to cut down on fruit."

Yaira covered a grin. "How long since your last moon cycle?"

I couldn't remember. My cycles had become so sporadic over the past year, I'd stopped keeping track.

My maid offered her best guess. "I think it's been five months, my queen." Her eyes sparkled. "Do you think . . . ?"

Abba's prophecy rang in my ears. *Yahweh will give him offspring and prolong his days.* I stared into Yaira's expectant eyes and refused to hope. "Those first months after Hezi's healing were excruciating. Each moon cycle brought renewed disappointment. When my body began changing, we started counting each day as both ecstasy and sorrow because every sunset pushed us closer to the end of Hezi's fifteen-year gift of life." Fighting a rush of swirling emotions, I fell into my friend's arms, fear and grief colliding. "I can't lose another baby and Hezi too."

Yaira held me, her words gentle and firm. "I know you've lost others, but this child will live, Zibah. This one was ordained by Yahweh."

I released her, eyes wide as she placed her hand on my belly. I laid my hand over hers and squeezed my eyes shut. *Please, Yahweh, let it be so.*

It had been a week since the bittersweet realization of my pregnancy. Fear made me wait to tell Hezi, but hope grew as my body embraced this baby as it hadn't the others. Little things I'd overlooked in past weeks were suddenly evident. My breasts had grown larger. I was tired all day. And the heartburn! Only yogurt could calm that burning at the back of my throat.

I wanted to talk with Ima about what I was experiencing. Abijah and Rizpah would be a wealth of information and would rejoice with me as Yaira did. But I couldn't tell anyone until Hezi knew.

"Zibah, where did you put my jeweled leather belt?" My husband was leaning over a basket, tossing out the contents one by one. "I thought it was with my embroidered collars."

"Hezi, I need to speak with you."

He kept rummaging through the basket. "I was sure I put it in this basket." He stood, hands on his hips, and glared at me. "The Tyrian ambassador arrives today to discuss an increase in our trade agreement."

"And a jeweled leather belt will prove we have more grain?" I couldn't help it. He looked so silly standing in the basket carnage.

He cocked his head and lifted an eyebrow. "I'm serious, Zibah. We need to make a good impression. An increased trade agreement with Tyre means shipping, which expands Judah's market beyond the borders of Solomon's trade."

"I'm pregnant, Hezi."

He looked straight at my belly. Expressionless, he said, "Even more reason to find my jeweled leather belt."

I stomped my foot. *"Ooh!"*

Before I could find something to throw at him, he swept me into his arms, laughing and twirling in circles. "Is this more like the reaction you expected?"

"Put me down, King Hezekiah!" I hugged him tight and buried my face in his neck.

Gently, he set my feet on the floor and looked into my eyes. "How long have you known?"

My cheeks grew warm. Would he be angry I'd waited so long? "Yaira told me last week."

He chuckled. "Of course. Yaira would notice before anyone else." Sobering, he brushed my cheek with the back of his hand. "You were afraid to tell me sooner?"

I nodded, ashamed.

"This child will live, Zibah. He is God's promise to us in these last years of my life."

The reminder struck both fear and solace into my heart. "I believe it."

He kissed the tip of my nose. "We'll announce our son at the end of today's court proceedings."

"Our son?" I smiled at his presumption. "Are you so sure this child is a boy?"

He cradled my face tenderly, all levity gone. "He will be a son of David, called by Yahweh to sit on Judah's throne, to fulfill both covenant and prophecy."

Our child wasn't even born, and he—or she—already bore such heavy responsibility.

My husband assaulted me with a quick hug. "Come, we must find that jeweled belt and get you dressed for court too. What splendid timing! We'll announce my successor on the same day the Tyrian ambassador arrives."

"Push, Zibah. Push!" Yaira shouted and supported my back on the birthing stool. "Your son is almost here."

"One more big push, my queen." The midwife held the blanket as if this child would shoot out like a stone from a sling.

"Aaaaahhhh!" I pushed with all my strength and felt the release of new life from my body.

"Welcome to the world, little prince." The midwife caught the slippery fellow in her blanket and began rubbing him with salt and wine—much to his displeasure. His cries tugged at my heart, the most pitiful yet wondrous sound in the world.

Yaira and I laughed and cried together while Ima rejoiced at my side with Abijah and Rizpah. Finally, at age forty, I had joined the sisterhood of imas.

"He is a handsome boy." Ima bent to kiss my forehead. "Have you chosen a name to bestow when he's circumcised?"

Of course, I had dreamed of naming a child since I was a child myself. The names changed from a little girl's whims to a woman's careful deliberation, but one had grown dearer with each challenge I faced. "His name will be *Manasseh*."

The midwife swaddled my son and laid him in my arms. "I think it's the perfect name. *The Lord has caused me to forget* will challenge the young prince to keep moving forward through life. Never lingering in regret."

"That's a wonderful thought, but my reason for choosing it was far more selfish." I twirled his fine, curly black hair around my finger. "The Lord will cause *me* to forget my sorrow as I raise this child to be a man. His abba and I will enjoy every day we are together, and Manasseh and I will remember his abba every day after he's gone."

I studied every part of him. He had my nose—praise Yahweh—and rosebud lips. Ten little fingers and ten long, narrow toes. Finally, a child I could call my own. I kissed his downy soft cheek and was drawn to a familiar sound at the window. There, sitting on the ledge, was a dove carrying a budding twig from an olive tree. "Yaira, look what Yahweh has sent me."

"I see." Yaira joined the other women, marveling at the creature. "Is it one of your doves from the dovecote?"

Mimicking the dove's coo, I trilled at the bird to call it. She turned, looking at me with one bright eye, no doubt wondering how such a strange-looking creature could coo like her mate. Without another sound, she winged away with her olive twig to fortify her nest.

Manasseh cooed in my arms, an entirely different sound, but one more precious than all the doves in the world. My nest was being built with sturdier stuff than olive branches. After each of life's storms, it seemed Yahweh had strengthened my peace—and my nest—with more faith. Manasseh's little hand wrapped around my finger, and I whispered so only he could hear, "Yahweh must be your peace, my son, when you rule on Judah's throne."

EPILOGUE

Hezekiah rested with his ancestors. And Manasseh his son succeeded him as king.

Manasseh was twelve years old when he became king, and he reigned in Jerusalem fifty-five years. His mother's name was Hephzibah. He did evil in the eyes of the LORD . . . He rebuilt the high places his father Hezekiah had destroyed; he also . . . bowed down to all the starry hosts and worshiped them.

—2 Kings 20:21–21:3

AUTHOR'S NOTE

Long ago, Hephzibah became my favorite woman in Scripture because I loved the meaning of her name: *God's delight is in her.* I wanted that to be true of me. I became even more intrigued when study revealed she was the wife of Hezekiah, Judah's most righteous king, and mother of Manasseh, Judah's wickedest ruler. My heart for Hephzibah sent me to the library to research six years before a publisher contracted this book.

Immediately, the research uncovered difficulties with ages and dates of succession for Uzziah, Jotham, Ahaz, and Hezekiah. In the book, I've followed the biblical record and formed a storyline that, though foreign to our modern thinking, could have been quite realistic in the ancient Middle-Eastern monarchy.

Scripture clearly names two of Isaiah's sons (Isaiah 7:3; 8:3) and calls his wife a prophetess (also Isaiah 8:3—though it gives her no name). In my previous book, *Love in a Broken Vessel*, I had given Isaiah two sons early in his marriage and named his wife Aya. So when this story begins, Isaiah's sons are older when he receives the prophecy of an additional son to mark the time of Israel's and Syria's demise. The third son becomes the second named son in Scripture, meaning one of the older boys required a fictitious name (Kadmiel).

Commentators are divided regarding Assyria's attack on Judah and threat on Jerusalem. Some say 2 Kings 18:13–19:37 occurred in 701 BCE during a single invasion. Others hold that after King Hezekiah paid tribute in 701 BCE, Sennacherib returned to Assyria, addressing rebellion in Babylon until a second Judean invasion in 688 BCE. I chose a single invasion during the year 701 BCE that incorporated the legend of the mice/rats' infestation of the Assyrian camp mentioned in the ancient writings of the historian Herodotus.

The timing and type of Hezekiah's illness is also heavily debated. The idea for his fulfillment of the suffering Savior prophecy in Isaiah 53 stemmed from a scholarly article by Margaret Barker titled, "Hezekiah's Boil" [*Journal for the Study of the Old Testament* 95 (2001): 31–42].

Which brings me to the most difficult and perhaps the most rewarding part of writing this book: the prophetic interpretations. The Bible's prophetic books are beautiful literature, but they're so much more. I believe they are divinely inspired words from the One True God spoken by the Hebrew prophets. I don't believe, however, that these godly men necessarily understood what their words meant, nor how they would be fulfilled—in their days or in days to come.

Because God's Holy Scriptures are His *living* Word, they have been fulfilled in many ways in many generations and will be fulfilled in ways yet to come. My interpretation of Hephzibah's story is a *fictional* scenario of an ancient queen who rose from men's desolation to God's delight. She learned to dwell on this earth in God's peace while remaining focused on eternity. May you and I, dear one, build our nests with the same focus.

READERS GUIDE

1. In chapter 1, little Ishma says, "Sometimes my prayers worked. Sometimes they didn't. Mostly they didn't." Have you ever felt that way? Do you think of God as more like: a) a genie in a bottle, b) a righteous Judge, or c) a wise Father? By the end of the book, how do you think Zibah viewed God and prayer?

2. In chapter 5, Isaiah struggles to hear God's direction but listens to the wise counsel of his godly wife. Later in chapter 14, Queen Abijah turns to her father—the former high priest—for support but succumbs to King Ahaz's bullying rather than holding fast to Yahweh. What is the difference in Isaiah's and Abijah's choice of counselor? Why might Abijah have chosen her abba rather than Aya when seeking advice?

3. In chapter 8, Eliakim explains Isaiah's prophecy of Immanuel's coming and Assyria's attack with the lesson his abba taught him about discipline, "Abba swats me, and it hurts. But he hugs me after." Can you relate a story from Scripture or a time from your own life when the Lord has sent "His presence to comfort at a time when His discipline [was] most severe"?

4. Chapter 12 describes Hezekiah's final day in Samaria after the six-month visit to meet the Assyrian king. In what ways did this journey mold Hezekiah into the king he became? How did it shape his understanding of his father, Ahaz? His perception of a righteous king? His aspirations to make Judah a godly kingdom?

5. In chapter 16, Hezekiah and Ishma raise the same question many Bible readers have asked for generations: "What benefit is prophecy when we can't understand it?" Isaiah answers, "Prophecy—even when we don't fully understand it—is given so we can watch God's sovereignty and power unfold." What parts of Isaiah's explanation satisfy you, and which parts leave you wanting better understanding? Are there any of Isaiah's prophecies that you understand better after reading this book?

6. In chapter 17, Isaiah challenged Ishma with these words, "I know change is hard for you, my girl, but we can't fulfill God's plan and purpose for our lives without changing." Have you found this to be true in your life? How do you cope when Yahweh exchanges your comfortable for new and improved?

7. In chapter 21, Yaira comforts Hephzibah by reminding her of the purpose of pain. "I experience joy more deeply because I've

known sadness. And I treasure the bonds of family because I've been lonely. The caves taught me to embrace the darkness so I could fully appreciate the light." In what ways did Hezi and Zibah's pain hone them for their roles in God's plan? In what ways have you seen the same happen in your own life?

8. In chapter 25, Hezekiah explains to Zibah why he has honored the wishes of his dishonorable father to leave Jerusalem and stay away until Ahaz's death. "It is a choice I made to obey Yahweh, not because my abba is honorable, but because I am." How did you feel about Hezi's choice? Was there another option that still honored Old Testament Law?

9. When Hezekiah begins his reign, he asks the impossible of Yahweh's priests and Levites but encourages them with these words, "We must attempt more than is humanly possible to witness what only God can do." How did the various characters attempt the impossible and see God's power at work? Isaiah? Hezekiah? Hephzibah? Eliakim? Have you ever attempted something that seemed impossible and seen God make it succeed?

10. In chapter 35, Zibah realizes Hezi is pounded by other people's words all day long, so she works to make their chamber a place of respite for him. In what ways can you make

your home a place of peace and refreshing for your family and friends?

11. When Isaiah tells Aya that God has called him to prophesy naked and barefoot for three years, Aya's response is, "You said from the beginning that God called you to proclaim His message to a people ever hearing but never understanding, ever seeing but never perceiving. As long as you're obedient to Yahweh, my love, there is no shame." How does Aya's commitment to Isaiah mirror Isaiah's commitment to Yahweh? Is there anything in life to which you're *this* committed? Why or why not?

12. In chapter 47, King Hezekiah, blinded by the duties of the throne, overlooks the warning signs of his wife's emotional pain. Zibah tries to hide the depth of her pain but publicly explodes, proving to them both that only God's intervention can heal her inner wounds. During Zibah's year of seclusion in the harem, what was the key to her newfound peace? Can we find similar focus and peace—without a year of seclusion?

13. In chapter 58, Isaiah explains Hezekiah's illness—and subsequent three-day healing. "Hezekiah isn't the chosen King, but he is a foreshadowing of the King that will come one day." The prophecy he quotes in this chapter is from Isaiah 53, Isaiah's

prophecy of the Suffering Savior, that is most often quoted to describe Jesus Christ. In what ways was Hezekiah's illness similar to Christ's suffering? How did Hezekiah's three-day illness foreshadow Christ's death and resurrection?

| Books are produced in the United States using U.S.-based materials | Books are printed using a revolutionary new process called THINKtech™ that lowers energy usage by 70% and increases overall quality | Books are durable and flexible because of Smyth-sewing | Paper is sourced using environmentally responsible foresting methods and the paper is acid-free |

Center Point Large Print
600 Brooks Road / PO Box 1
Thorndike, ME 04986-0001 USA

(207) 568-3717

US & Canada:
1 800 929-9108
www.centerpointlargeprint.com